BONE MACHINE

About the author

Born and brought up in Newcastle upon Tyne, Martyn Waites was an actor before becoming a writer. He has written six novels as well as short stories and non-fiction. He has held two writing residences, one at Huntercombe Young Offenders Institution and, most recently, HMP Chelmsford. He currently runs arts-based workshops for socially excluded teenagers.

BONE MACHINE

Martyn Waites

PEGASUS BOOKS
NEW YORK

BONE MACHINE

Pegasus Books LLC
45 Wall Street, Suite 1021
New York, NY 10005

Library of Congress Cataloging-in-Publication Data is available.

ISBN: 978-1-933648-35-4

Printed in the United States of America

For Linda

Acknowledgements

People: Detective Inspector Paul Bentley; Ali Karim; Councillor Nick Kemp; Deb Kemp; Chris Myhill, Area Manager, Gateshead Libraries; Jane Shaw, Information Specialist, City Campus Library, Northumbria University; Penny Sumner; Kerry Ward, Marketing Services Manager, Port of Tyne; Kate Lyall Grant, Digby Halsby and Tara Wigley at Simon and Schuster; Jane Gregory, Claire Morris, Emma Dunford, Jemma McDonagh and Terry Bland at Gregory and Company; Linda Waites.

Books: *Mapping Murder*, David Canter; *The Shadow of the Gallows*, Barry Redfern; *Beyond the Grave: Newcastle's Burial Grounds*, Alan Morgan; *Somebody's Husband, Somebody's Son* and *Happy Like Murderers*, Gordon Burn.

Music: *Calenture*, The Triffids; *I Am A Bird Now*, Antony and the Johnstons; *The Dirty South*, Drive By Truckers; *Winnemucca, Post To Wire, The Fitzgerald*, Richmond Fontaine.

1

She could no longer tell whether her eyes were open or closed. All was darkness.

She couldn't open her mouth to scream. Or speak.

Couldn't move.

She had to escape, had to run. She tried to pull her arms up. Move her legs. No good. He had tied them too tight. She moved around, pushing, wriggling against whatever it was she was tied to. Rough and cold. Sharp. It hurt when she moved.

She lay back, breathing heavily. Forcing air through her closed lips. Her mum. Her dad. Her sister Catherine. Even her dog, Barney. She had never wanted them so much in her life.

Her life. It seemed a thousand years away, something she had only dreamed.

She could have cried. But she was beyond tears. Remembered the pain the last time she had tried to force her mouth open. Sighed a jagged sigh.

If only.

If only . . .

Before this, she would have thought herself too young for regrets. Wrong. She played that moment over and over again in her head, each time with a different outcome. She wished she had ignored him. Wished she had never stopped to help. Not expecting him to . . . Not someone like that . . .

They'd shown films at uni, first year, given them lectures. About rape. Strangers. Not making herself vulnerable, not walking home alone at night. She had attended, taken every-thing in. Not been worried. That wouldn't happen to her. She was clever, sensible. Those kinds of things always happened to someone else. Not to her.

Never her.

Another wave of emotion built again within her, waiting to crash. Wave after wave of emotions had come smashing into her. Like a crumbling sea wall in an El Niño storm, she hadn't been able to withstand them. Self-pity. Panic. Regret.

Fear. She hadn't really known what real fear was until she had found herself here. Then it had smashed into her like a runaway bus, leaving her screaming in pain, lying shattered, helpless. Anger.

If only . . .

She tried to scream again. Felt the pain in her face.

Tried to pull her body upright. Felt only the restraints digging into her.

And then, with a change in the air, a movement, a different smell – he was there. Speaking. His voice, how she hated it. Pouring over her like thick, rancid oil. Telling her things were all right. That they would soon be better. Telling her she was going on the most exciting journey of her life.

She had tried to talk to him at first, like they told her at uni. Reason. Make herself out to be a person. Get him interested in her, see she was another human being, worth something. She had tried. Her immobile mouth was his response.

She tried to speak, shout at him, plead. That pain again.

She felt him climb on top of her. Heard a ripping sound. Felt something cold, sharp, against her skin. Her clothes. He was cutting off her clothes.

A fresh wave of panic ran through her. She pulled, pushed. Struggled. Couldn't move. His voice, excited now, building up in pitch. Pouring over her, drowning her.

His hands on her.

She tried to scream. Couldn't.

She felt every sensation a body could feel; simultaneously, she felt nothing.

Another attempted sigh.

If only . . .

2

The night was cold, the winter wind carrying the threat of ice, the hardened slush on the ground showing the dirty reality.

Katya was glad she was indoors. As much as she could be glad about anything. She wasn't yet used to the northern climate. She wasn't yet used to this life.

She looked around: an anonymous bedroom, sparsely and poorly furnished. A single bulb with a dust-magnet shade threw weak, soul-sapping light over the bed and bedside table. The bed cover a cheap floral design, regularly turned and rotated to disguise any stains, the carpet old and nylon, a swirling vortex of threadbare blue, the curtains thin and unlined.

The house was on a nondescript road in the west end of Newcastle. A street of poor families and slumming students. The kind of place that, if you didn't live there, you needed a good reason for coming to. Men, she thought, must want sex badly to come here. Or not really want it at all.

Katya adjusted her plastic miniskirt, pulled up her stockings. The bra was pinching under her arms. Her garments were cheap, nasty. She was told to wear them but hated them, tried to think of them as armour, something to put between her and the men. But that didn't work. She often didn't have them on long enough.

She sat on the bed, sighed. Waited. The night shift. The worst of the lot once the pubs closed. Then out came the drunks, the losers. Slouching towards her room. Those with nowhere else to go or somewhere they couldn't face going. The haters and hurters. Those who wanted to vent their failures and frustrations on her. It was beginning to make her hate in return. She hated this world. She hated herself in it. She hoped she would never accept herself in it.

She listened. There was a new girl in the next room. Or at least a different girl. She had tried to engage Katya in conversation on the way in, all girls together. Blonde hair pulled back into a ponytail, make-up garish and crude, like an Asian theatre mask. To hide the natural features and be seen from a distance. Must have just stopped working on the street, Katya thought, then chastised herself for that. She was starting to get used to it, think like one of them. The thought depressed her.

The girl had kept talking, chattering about how cold the weather was, even digressing to mention the missing student who had been in all the newspapers for the last week or so. Katya just nodded, pretended she didn't understand English. In fact, she thought she had a pretty good understanding of English. But that was before she had ended up in Newcastle. She found the locals, with their speedy, singsong dialect, harder to understand. She understood enough to know what they were calling her. Asylum seeker scum. Fuck off back to your own country. She didn't need a great grasp of the language or the dialect to understand that.

Katya had nodded, ignored the girl, just waited for the previous tenant to finish off her client, vacate the room. She didn't want to talk, didn't want to feel like one of them. It just reminded her how far she had fallen. So she had entered, the girl taking the room next to her. Katya listened. No sound came through the wall. Unusual, she thought. The other girl's door had opened and closed a few times; she had heard it. Punters weren't usually so silent. She shrugged, stood up. Not her concern.

She missed her home. Her old country. The way it used to be, before the bombs started dropping, the soldiers started arriving. Before her neighbours used the war to legitimize long-pent-up hatreds for anyone they decided they could no longer tolerate. Before most of her family was killed, her home destroyed. She tried not to think of the past too much. It was another time. Another place.

She sighed. Two. Only two punters so far for the night. The first bad enough, the second even worse. Sweaty, ugly, nondescript men. She had given them the talk, remembered the script, but they hadn't been interested. Just unloaded their lust, paid and left. And with every punter she serviced, a little more of her died. Soon, she thought, she would be able to stick a knife through her hand and feel nothing. Her heart, even. Maybe she should; take a blade to her arms, cut. Just to see if she can still feel. Still hurt.

She shook her head, stood up. Not wanting her thoughts to go down that route. She walked around the room, aware she was pacing like a caged animal at the zoo. A depressingly appropriate analogy, she thought.

She pulled the curtains aside, looked out of the window. The black Peugeot 406 was still parked across the street where she knew it would be. She could just make out the two burly silhouettes in the front seats. Making sure she worked, didn't run. Protecting their investment. Making sure she handed over every penny she made.

Katya could feel them watching her. She shivered from more than the cold. She would have to go with a punter soon, repellent as that was to her. Because if she didn't, the treatment she would receive later would be even worse.

She looked up the street. A lone boy, a light-skinned black teenager, was practising stunts on his BMX. It was late for him to be out, and he seemed underdressed for the time of year, but then she doubted this was an area where they

cared too much about things like that. Further down the
street towards the city centre, a drunk was making his com-
ically tortuous way up the road, his lack of progress
heightened by the icy pavement. Her heart sank. He could
be her next punter.

As she was thinking this, a car pulled up in front of the
house. She tried to identify the make and model. It was
dark, a soft top; she could see that much. Maybe a Saab, or
a Mercedes even. As she watched, a man got out of the
driver's side, locked the door and made his way to the house.
Tall, his hair perhaps slightly longer than was fashionable,
wearing a brown-leather jacket, jeans and boots. He was
quite attractive, she thought. For a fraction of a second she
found herself hoping he would come to visit her.

She heard him knock on the door. Heard the door open,
Lenny the landlord talk to the punter. She listened closely,
imagined she heard Lenny, his snivelling little voice, his oily
skin, pocketing the money, directing the punter upstairs.
He was a creep. She had seen him peering around the door
when she was working, getting his thrills from watching.
She had been told about him, warned. Found the warnings
accurate.

The knock at the bedroom door made thoughts of Lenny
dissipate.

Her stomach lurched. Even if he was attractive, she
didn't want to have sex with him. That should be her
decision.

Katya felt bile rise from her stomach to her throat, swallowed it down again. She breathed deeply, tried to compose
her features. She had no choice. Slowly, like an invalid who
had just regained the power of movement, she made her way
towards the door. Inwardly screaming, crying tears of rage,
pain and loss, outwardly her face displaying all the emotions
of a prison wall. She reached the door, opened it.

He had kind eyes, she thought. A shy smile. He couldn't keep eye contact with her. She stood aside, let him in. He walked slowly into the room, looked around. The first one to do that, she thought. He didn't seem to like what he saw. He sat down on the bed. Katya stood, looking at him. He still hadn't looked properly at her yet. He said nothing.

Katya began to get nervous. Perhaps this man was a psychopath, a killer. Perhaps he was the one who had taken this student they were all talking about. Or, worse, perhaps he was police, immigration, ready to deport her, stick her on the next plane back.

She swallowed hard. Tried to talk. 'What's your name?' she asked.

'Joe,' he said after much deliberation.

She nodded. 'Good. So . . . Joe . . . what can I do for you?' The words sounded hollow and false, like a serial adulterer's promise.

'Depends,' Joe said eventually.

He turned, looked at her. His eyes were kind – she was right – but there was something more in them. A sense of loss, a glimpse of darkness even.

Katya looked at him, tried to smile. 'On . . . what . . . ?' she asked haltingly.

The man sighed, shook his head. 'Sorry,' he said. 'I can't do this.' He put his hand into his inside jacket pocket.

Katya felt her heart skip a beat. This was it, she thought. He was going to produce his warrant card. Or his knife.

He looked at the door before speaking, checking no one was listening. 'Is your name Katya?' he asked, his voice low.

Katya couldn't get her breath. 'No,' she said quickly, 'it's not. My name is Mandy. Mandy.'

'Look,' said Joe, a sense of urgency creeping into his

voice, 'I'm not police, I'm not immigration. I'm not here to harm you. Honestly. Now please. Is your name Katya?'

She found herself nodding. It was as if he had read her mind.

'Good,' he said. 'I've got something for you. From Dario.'

'Dario?' She started to stand, almost shouted.

Joe quietened her down, putting his hands on her shoulders. Guiding her back to a sitting position on the edge of the bed.

'Don't shout,' he said, removing his hands once he knew she wouldn't shout again. 'Yes. Dario. But you have to come with me.'

'When?'

'Now.'

She almost laughed at the absurdity of the suggestion. 'I can't. No. Impossible.'

'It's not impossible. You just have to come with me.' Joe's voice was calm, trustworthy even. 'Just come downstairs with me. Get into the car and we'll drive away.'

'You make it sound so easy.'

'It is.'

Panic crept into her voice. 'They're watching, they won't let you go. They will do terrible things to you.'

Joe smiled. 'You don't think I came here on my own, do you?'

Katya frowned. Joe stood up, looked again around the room.

'D'you need to get anything?'

Katya shook her head. She felt like she had stumbled into a dream.

Joe leaned across to a chair in the corner, lifted Katya's plastic coat, handed it to her. 'I think you'll need this.'

Numbly she nodded, put it on over her working clothes. Belted it tight.

'Good,' he said. 'Come on, then.'

He opened the bedroom door, held it open for Katya to exit first. She smiled at him as she passed. It felt like the first act of kindness anyone had done for her in a long time. If her heart hadn't been beating so fast, she might have shed a tear.

Joe walked to the next bedroom, knocked on the door. Katya frowned at him. He just smiled.

'Are you decent?' he said as he opened it.

'Very funny,' came the reply from inside. It was the girl who had tried to talk to her earlier. She sounded different. Not such a thick accent. She came to the door, closed it behind her.

'Ready?' said Joe.

She nodded.

'Peta – Katya, Katya – Peta,' he said, gesturing quickly with crossed arms to the two women. 'Time for proper introductions later. Come on.'

He walked briskly down the stairs. At the bottom, Lenny, the weasel-faced landlord, appeared. His eyes widened as he saw the three of them coming towards him.

'What the fuck d'you think you're doing?' he said, twisting his already rodent-like features into a more feral look. 'Get back upstairs. Now.'

Joe walked right up to him, using his height against him, face impassive. Lenny flinched, stepped back.

'We're leaving. All of us. Problem?' Joe's tone of voice left no doubt that he hoped there would be.

Lenny tried to laugh. It sounded more like the cry of a sick horse. 'Try it. Step outside. See what you get.'

'OK.'

Joe brushed Lenny aside, opened the door. As he stepped through, Lenny made a grab for Peta, the last in line.

'Where d'you think you're going?' he said, his sweaty hand clamped to her wrist.

Peta turned. She twisted her arm, shrugged off Lenny's grasp and forced his arm behind his back so quickly that Katya barely registered that she had done it. There was no mistaking the snapping sound, though.

Lenny gave out a shrill howl. Peta took her hand away, allowing him to crumple to the floor.

'Pick on someone your own size next time,' she said.

And then they were in the street, the door closed behind them, Katya staring at the other woman in admiration and amazement. Joe pointed his keys at the Saab, walked briskly around to the passenger door.

'You be careful,' said Peta, standing aside. 'That car's my pride and joy. Harm that and you'll get the same treatment as our friend back there.'

Joe smiled. 'I don't doubt it.' He looked up at Katya, then across the road, then opened her door before walking around to the driver's side. 'I think you'd better get in. Before the party gets gate-crashed.'

Katya followed his gaze. Her two minders were out of the Peugeot, angrily slamming the doors behind them, setting off across the street.

Panic welled inside her. Touching the door handle, Katya froze.

'Come on,' said Joe from inside the car. 'We'd better get going.'

'But—'

'Don't worry about them, just get in.'

Katya snapped out of her trance, did as she was told as Joe locked the doors. She looked at her two minders while Joe found the key.

They were unable to cross the street. The boy on the BMX had chosen the moment of their crossing to practise his stunts in front of them. They were dodging about trying to get around him. She heard the threats, recognized them from her own language. The boy wouldn't move; whichever way they went, he went. Their voices rose, the threats intensified.

Another voice joined the fray. The minders, in trying to dodge the boy, had bumped into the drunk man making his way up the street. The man, angry at having his progress impeded, was letting them know what he thought of them. One of the minders threw a punch at the drunk. Katya, having felt the power behind that punch on many occasions, feared the worse for the man. However, what happened next surprised her. The drunk stood his ground, slipped out of the path of the punch with almost nonchalant ease, twisted his body so that he fell against her minder, taking the man's legs out from under him and leaving him on the pavement. The BMX boy was still zigzagging interference in front of the other one.

Joe started the engine. Katya looked around, side to side, frantically.

'Please, hurry . . .'

'Don't worry.' The car started. Joe sped away. Katya looked behind her as she went. The BMX boy had turned and was pedalling away, the drunk man, who she now realized was Asian, had floored one of her minders and looked ready to take on the other one. He no longer looked unsteady on his feet. Peta, she noticed, had crossed the road to join him.

'Oh, by the way,' said Joe as the car sped along, 'I'm Joe Donovan.' He awkwardly extended his hand. She shook it.

'Katya Tokic.' She smiled. 'You gave me your real name.'

'I didn't think telling you lies was a good way to earn your trust.'

Katya thought, nodded. 'Where are we going?'

'Not far,' he said. 'But far enough away from them.'

They drove around, Katya unfamiliar with the streets, the area, to know where they were going. She looked out of the window, became aware of change in the environment. Red-brick and stone houses gave way to greenery. Donovan drove down towards the river, past a pub and restaurant, its lights sending out a warm glow over the surrounding trees and bushes, then further on towards the water, coming to a stop in a secluded, gravelled car park.

Katya looked at him, a seed of apprehension taking root. 'What now?'

'We wait. But not for long, hopefully.' He sat back, sighed. 'Well. That was exciting, wasn't it?'

Katya smiled. The apprehension died within her.

'Oh, by the way,' said Donovan, digging into his inside pocket, 'this is for you.'

He took out an envelope, handed it to her, looked away, giving her what privacy he could in the confined space of the car.

She opened it, read the letter. Before she reached the end, tears were streaming down her cheeks. Everything tumbled out of her: her life in the old country before the soldiers, her new one with the horrible men, and everything in between. The hopelessness. The hope. Falling out in huge, racking sobs.

When the other car came, a nondescript saloon sidling up alongside, she barely registered it. She had read the letter four times, tried to memorize the words. She looked up. Donovan was standing by the side of the car, opening the door.

'You OK?'

She rubbed the tears from her cheeks with the back of her hand, folded the letter and returned it to the envelope. She nodded.

'Good. Come and meet the gang.'

He held open the door for her, helped her out. Standing in the car park, illuminated by the headlights of the two cars, stood the three people she had seen earlier, the cold turning their breath to smoking vapour.

'Peta you know,' he said, pointing to the blonde woman who smiled in return.

'What you did to Lenny . . .' Katya began.

Peta shrugged. She had managed to scrape off most of the make-up and throw a padded jacket over her clothes. Without her high-heeled shoes she looked much smaller. Wiry and taut. 'All in a day's work,' she said.

'This is Amar,' said Donovan. The Asian man nodded. He was young, she noticed, about medium height. His designer parka was open, displaying a chest-hugging T-shirt that showed off his well-defined muscles. He was also flexing fingers that looked bruised and swollen.

'Are you hurt?' asked Katya.

Amar smiled. 'Only my pride.' His voice, when he spoke, was quite light. 'I must be out of practice.'

Peta laughed. 'He needed a girl to help him out. Doesn't want to admit it.'

Katya smiled. Adrenalin was still coming off them in palpable waves.

'And,' Donovan said, pointing to the young light-skinned black boy in the street clothes, 'the BMX bandit here is Jamal.'

Jamal, now wearing a hooded sweatshirt, extended his hand, the formal gesture belying the teenager's urban appearance. She shook it.

'Well,' said Donovan, 'that's the introductions made.' He looked at the others, smiled. 'Well done, team. A good night's work.'

Katya looked at the four of them, then at her surroundings. The trees shifting in the breeze, the river beyond. She breathed in deeply, took air fresh and unpolluted into her lungs. She smiled.

'Thank you,' she said. 'Thank you all . . .'

She felt the tears begin again and made no attempt to hold them back. Because right there, in that place, at that moment, she felt safe.

Safe.

3

'Jesus. Aw, Jesus . . .' The uniform turned away, vomited.

'Well done.' DI Diane Nattrass looked at him, face professionally blank. 'You waited until you were outside the tape. Well done. You'll go far.'

The young man, kneeling in the gutter, hand outstretched, grasping for something to steady himself against, looked up. Red-faced, he wiped his mouth along the back of his hand, began mumbling the prologue to an apology.

'Never mind,' Nattrass said. She put out her arm, helped him up. 'First time?'

He nodded. Once he was on his decidedly shaky feet, she looked at him. Even under the orange streetlight he looked pale. He didn't look old enough to drink, vote or fight for his country. He certainly wasn't old enough to be exposed to what lay before him. Nattrass doubted there came an age when anyone should.

'I won't say you get used to it, because I hope you never do.'

She looked ahead, past the tape: POLICE: DO NOT CROSS. She saw the outline of what had made the young man vomit. Sighed. 'Can't say I blame you, though,' she said.

Hope and fear. They went hand in hand for Diane Nattrass. She had hoped for a night out; cruise along towards five o'clock, knocking-off time, on a tide of mundane paperwork then go home, change and go out on the first date she had had for ages with a solicitor she had been introduced to by friends desperate she was going to grow old alone and childless. But, as she had feared, her date hadn't happened.

As a reactive detective inspector working out of Market Street station, in the centre of Newcastle, she had to respond to calls that came in. Murder, theft and, since she was female and trained in sexual offences, rape. She was also investigating the disappearance and possible abduction of the college student Ashley Malcolm. She would expect to be top of the list for an out-of-hours call for something like this.

She stood up, pulling her long coat tight around her, hoping it would hide her party clothes underneath as much as keep out the cold. With her long brown hair teased into something she considered stylish, her make-up expertly applied, she felt overdressed for a murder scene. She scoped around. Westgate Road cemetery was a small, disused, triangular-shaped burial ground at the corner of Elswick Road and Westgate Road in the west end of Newcastle. Once the area's main necropolis, it was now overgrown and ruined, the railings surrounding it long since stolen and melted down. Gravestones lichened and crumbling, broken, prone or resting at irregular geometric angles as tree roots nourished themselves on the composted bodies and dust-returned bones of previous inhabitants. Now it provided both a dumping ground for passing pedestrian refuse and temporary accommodation and respite from the daily grind for the local junkie and wino population. Given the area's general condition, that was a growing population.

Outside the cemetery were homes, the streets now cordoned off with blue and white police tape securing the crime scene, uniforms directing traffic away from the area. On two sides were old brick and stone tenements, untouched by the city's creeping gentrification; on the third loomed a collection of 1960s high-rises, etched tombstone-like against the night sky, the darkness hiding their decay.

Melting, wet, slushy snow covered everything, rendering the scene in stark, depressing monochrome.

But there was nothing hiding the body. Nattrass looked, trying to peer in, but couldn't see it. Just as well. Once she had attended the post-mortem and stared at the accompanying photos, she would have seen more than enough. All she could see were the SOCO team going slowly about their work, their white-paper, hooded suits making it look as if they were clearing up after a chemical attack.

Discovering and protecting the route, in and out, that the perpetrator must have made. Picking up anything, no matter how inconsequential, that may suggest a link that could tie the dumped body in with the dumper, or an accomplice, or at the very least a witness. Making the radius as wide as possible, bringing it down eventually to a small, manageable level.

Nattrass wasn't allowed in, she knew that. Didn't expect to be. She couldn't lean in close, peer at the body, prod and examine. She could destroy evidence, contaminate the scene. It wasn't like the movies. It wasn't like TV. Clues weren't left out in the open. Life, for her, wasn't like that.

'What's up, boss? Havin' a seance?'

Knowing the voice, she turned. It was her partner, DS Paul Turnbull. Awkwardly rolling on a pair of surgical gloves. Nattrass looked at his hands.

'Having trouble with the latex, Paul?'

Turnbull smiled. 'You know me, boss. Can't beat bare-backin'. Anythin' else is unnatural.'

Nattrass swallowed her retort. 'Well, you won't need them,' she said. 'He hasn't arrived yet. Forensic scientist.'

'Is he on the way? Wetherby?'

Nattrass nodded.

'I'm looking forward to the day when the Home Office can email one to us.'

'I'm looking forward to the day when we won't need one at all.'

'You're going to have a long wait.'

Nattrass sighed. 'I know.'

Nattrass looked at her younger colleague. He was still suited, collared and tied. His hair short and tidy. A straight-down-the-line copper, no grey, just black and white. She imagined he slept standing up in his clothes, just in case he should get a call like this one, just in case he was needed. For him, she thought, the job came first. Always.

Turnbull was looking at her. 'Interrupt you doing something special?' he asked with a smile. The kind of smile, she thought, that indicated he was looking at her in a new light. And not necessarily a light she would want him to regard her in.

For work, she usually dressed in as professional and sexless a manner as she could manage. Nothing that would detract from doing her job. Straight hair, straight clothes. She didn't just have to compete with her male colleagues; she had to be twice the men they were. However, after work, her time, what there was of it, was her own. And Turnbull wasn't used to seeing her, made up and dressed up.

'Yes,' she said. 'As it happens.'

'Anyone I know?' He was almost smirking, unable to contain his surprise at the revelation that his boss was also a woman.

'No,' she said. 'Now let's concentrate, shall we?'

'OK, then,' he said, businesslike again. 'Catch me up.'

Nattrass looked at him. Hid a smile, even. 'Have we been watching *CSI* again?'

Even in the dark she could see him reddening. '*NYPD Blue*,' he mumbled. 'Repeats on Sky.'

'Right. Well, here's what I know.' Nattrass swept the area with her eyes, took in the whole scene. The uniform was still hovering at her shoulder, as if unwilling to move too far from her, out of his comfort zone. 'What's your name?'

'Snell,' he said on the second attempt. 'PC Snell.'

'Right. Well, we received a 999 call just after nine thirty. Saying a body had been sighted in the cemetery. Anonymous. No name given.'

'Tracing the call?' asked Turnbull.

'Of course.' If the call came from a callbox, then the caller may have been picked up on CCTV. If it was a mobile, the caller could perhaps be traced by billing. A landline likewise. If the call came from the killer, then all bets were off. 'Never know, we might get lucky.' She looked around the towerblocks. 'We'll have a word with the community managers in the morning. Get their teams to go around, do a door to door. See how that goes. Maybe think about setting up a mobile unit if all else fails.'

Turnbull nodded. 'Better them than us. Land of the bloody blind for us around here.'

Nattrass didn't comment. 'Anyway, PC Snell here was the first on the scene. Saw the state of the body and called for the area to be cordoned off. Quick thinking.'

PC Snell took the praise with a small smile.

Turnbull turned to him. Asked him if he had seen anyone in the area. Snell shook his head. 'Just a couple at the bus stop. We've taken statements.' He swallowed, finding his voice. 'The first they knew of it was when I questioned them.' They had been dismissed, he said, a contact address taken. They weren't serious contenders for killers.

'What does the body look like?' asked Turnbull.

Snell looked as if he was about to be sick again. He held it down. Described what he could remember. 'Young, blonde. Naked.' His voice began to shake again. 'Cut . . . several wounds. I didn't count how many . . . and the eyes, the mouth . . .'

'What about them?' asked Turnbull.

Nattrass stepped in. 'Sewn shut. Not prettily, either.'

Turnbull expelled air. It seemed to leave his body in a hard mass. 'Jesus . . .' He shook his head as if to shake loose the image that was starting to take up residence there. 'Anything else? The body arranged in some kind of shape?'

Snell shook his head. 'I couldn't tell. She looked . . . all . . . contorted.' He outstretched his fingers into talons. Held them rigid. 'Like that. I didn't touch it, though.'

'Good work,' said Nattrass. She and Turnbull exchanged glances.

'A bad one,' he said.

'They all are,' she said, 'but this one is worse than most. Cadaverous spasm, it sounds like. She didn't go gently.'

Turnbull suppressed a shudder.

She sighed. 'Any more than that, we'll have to wait for the Home Office bod to get here.'

'Any ID?'

Snell shook his head. 'Not that I could see. I didn't want to—'

'I know,' said Turnbull, cutting him off. He turned to Nattrass. 'You think it's . . .' He left the name hanging.

The facts, unspoken, were embedded in both of their brains. For the last week they had taken priority over everything else.

Ashley Malcolm. Nineteen. First-year student at the University of Northumbria, studying photography. Disappeared six days ago leaving no word, no note, no clues. Like she had just vanished into thin air from a street in Fenham.

CCTV tapes had been watched and rewatched; witnesses, friends, lecturers and boyfriend had been questioned and requestioned. All with no positive outcome. For a time suspicion had fallen on her boyfriend, Michael Nell. They had found him uncooperative and obnoxious, two things that are guaranteed to make the police take a deeper than casual interest in a person. Nattrass and Turnbull had obliged, leaning on him somewhat in an effort to ascertain guilt or innocence, find his breaking point, but ultimately nothing had come of it. Despite their dislike of him, with no body there was a limit to how far they could go.

And now this.

'So what d'you reckon?' said Turnbull. 'Should we assume it's her? Or wait?'

'What is it they tell us in training courses?' said Nattrass. 'Never assume. It makes an "ass" out of "u" and "me".'

'But those wankers have never had to do this for a livin'.'

'True.' Nattrass tried to look anywhere but at the cemetery. She failed. 'Instinct tells me it *is* her. I mean, I hope it's not but in a way I suppose I hope it is too.'

Turnbull looked at her, nodded. 'I know what you mean. If it's her we can get going. If it's not . . . we've got a nutter on the loose.'

'I think it's safe to say we've got that anyway, Paul.'

Turnbull stood up. 'Hope for the best, fear the worst, eh?'

Nattrass looked around. She had to call it in. Wait for an SIO to be assigned. Contact the General Hospital, arrange for the body to be transferred to the mortuary there. Accompany the body along with the pathologist. Maintain the chain of evidence.

She sighed. What she hoped. What she feared. Rarely the same.

'Always the same, isn't it, Paul?' Nattrass said. 'Hope and fear.'

She and her team were going to be in for a very long night.

4

Katya opened her eyes. Looked around. The room was strange, unfamiliar. Seconds went by while she orientated herself, while memory caught up with waking. Then realized where she was. And smiled.

Katya stretched languidly, then curled herself up into a ball. She sighed. Pulled the duvet up over her chin, wrapped it tight around her, closed her eyes. Stayed as still as she could. Listened to the silence.

No one to tell her to get up, shout orders at her, punish her for transgressions she wasn't aware she had made, abuse her because they were bored and she was their property. No one to use her body against her will.

A proper bed. Not a stinking, lumpen mattress on a bare, cold floor. Rows of shivering, dirty bodies with snot-teared faces. Sleep virtually impossible because of the noise, the fights, the casual rapes. Cries of pain and beyond-pain, the stink of bodies and hopelessness. A house of human degradation.

From there she would be taken to the other house. Where men paid to use her body and the creepy landlord watched. The money she made snatched from her. Her loan, still repaying. Then into the car, back again. And on. And on.

She screwed her eyes up tight, tried to banish the images from her mind, make them dissipate like the fog of a nightmare. Focus on the present.

She had just woken from her best night's sleep in ages.

The best waking she had experienced for months. So rested she could have been out for days. She allowed her mind to float, unable to remember the last time she had been so relaxed. She luxuriated in her body's freedom like she would in a warm bubble bath. She snuggled down hard, not wanting the comfort to end, not wanting to face the harsh world again. Wanting to stay safe.

But she knew she would have to get up soon. If for no other reason than her bladder told her so.

Reluctantly she threw back the covers. Cold air crept over her body like a dawning reality. She got out of bed. Her pyjamas had been provided for her by the woman, Peta. They weren't a perfect fit, but, compared with what she had been used to, they felt wonderful. She crossed to the window, looked out. Saw trees, fields, hills. Heard birdsong. The sky wasn't a perfect blue, there were clouds hovering, but to Katya it seemed like fairy-tale sunlight. She couldn't help herself from smiling again.

She looked around her bedroom. The furniture was good quality but basic: a double bed, wardrobe, chest of drawers with a TV on it, bedside table. Stripped floorboards and rugs. Neutral-coloured walls and ceiling. No personal pictures or photos. It smelled recently painted and, although pleasant enough, had the ambience of a hotel room; like someone hadn't been there long enough to make their mark or were just passing through.

They had been kind to her so far, but she was still wary. She told herself not to be; the letter confirmed that she should trust them.

The letter. On the bedside table. She picked it up, read through it again. She would have read it once more, but the pressure on her bladder was increasing. She put it back down, crossed the room, quietly twisted the knob, stepped out on to the landing. There were another three doors. She tried the nearest, crept it quietly open. The light-skinned black boy from the previous night was in there fast asleep, sprawled over the bed, duvet wrestled around him. She closed it again, tried the next door. Locked. The third door was the bathroom. She quickly stepped inside.

Donovan woke under a duvet on the sofa, opened his eyes.

No dreams. At least none that followed him into waking. Good.

He shook his head, tried to clear the tiredness from it. Worked out why he wasn't in his bed. Heard the bathroom door close upstairs. Remembered.

Katya. His guest.

Yawning and stretching, he swung his legs to the floor, rubbed his face and padded into the kitchen to make coffee. He knew he would have to wait to get into the bathroom now.

Once done, he returned to the sofa, mug in hand, threw the duvet over him once more and pointed the remote at the TV.

Detective Chief Inspector Bob Fenton was giving a press conference. Face stern and set. Waiting to impart something of importance. Blinking slightly, flashbulbs popping, cutting the electric air. Donovan had heard of the man but never met him. At Fenton's side sat DI Diane Nattrass. Donovan knew her. Had been part of a previous investigation of hers.

It was what everyone had expected. The news story the whole region, perhaps the country, had been following. Fenton explained that a body had been found the previous night in Westgate Road cemetery. Fenton confirmed it was that of the missing student Ashley Malcolm. He sat back, allowed the news to sink in.

Flashbulbs popped again. The sounds of a restless, agitated

audience filled the silence. Champing at the bit, eager to ask their questions. Donovan could almost feel the adrenalin in the room. It wasn't that long ago when he would have been there himself.

Fenton, his suit pressed and careerist-smart, his shirt a crisp white, his tie unmarked and his senatorial-style hair shot through with authoritarian grey, handed over to Diane Nattrass. She, in contrast, looked as if she had been out the previous night and hadn't made it home yet. Her hair flattened, her make-up hastily reapplied, her clothes crumpled and creased. She looked weary beyond tiredness. Her eyes, when they caught the camera, were black-rimmed, as if she was staring out from a deep, dark cave, reporting on what she had found in there. Donovan could sympathize.

Nattrass confirmed details, made appeals. Gave as much information as she could without hampering the investigation. She came across, Donovan thought, despite or probably because of the tiredness, as not just a professional doing her job but as someone with a personal stake in finding Ashley's killer. The approach, whether inadvertent or not, worked. She attempted to field some questions but Fenton jumped in to answer them. Nattrass seemed relieved to have the spotlight deflected away from her.

Donovan didn't envy her the job ahead.

Then another journalist, asking if this killing was linked in any way to a girl's body found two months previously at Barras Bridge in Newcastle. Fenton looked momentarily aggrieved by the question before giving a stoic, noncommittal answer, refusing to link speculation. More flashbulbs.

Donovan remembered that girl. It had been all over the media in the run-up to Christmas. What was her name? . . . Lisa Hill. Early twenties, worked in a pub in Byker. Knifed to death. The papers made her out to be a part-time prostitute and put her death down to an angry customer. No one was ever caught or tried for the crime. Her death wasn't given a high priority. Some commentators even said she had asked for it; that was the game she was in and she knew the rules.

He heard the toilet flush, the bathroom door open and close. He looked up. Katya was standing at the top of the stairs. Pulling her pyjamas around her, she seemed unsure whether to come down, go back to bed or just stand there.

He smiled, sat up.

'Hi,' he said. 'Coffee?'

She said nothing. As if unsure what answer he wanted. She reminded Donovan of an animal, skittish, taking a treat but expecting pain.

'Or tea?' he said as cheerfully as he could manage. 'You're in luck. I've got both.'

She nodded.

'Come on down, then,' Donovan said. 'I'll put the kettle on.'

One wary step at a time, Katya made her way down the stairs, arms still tightly wrapped around herself, until she was standing by the sofa. Donovan put his coffee down, flicked off the TV, got to his feet. He was wearing his usual sleeping combination of T-shirt and boxers. He reached for his long black hooded dressing gown that was draped over the back of the sofa, began to put it on. He didn't want to scare his guest.

Katya's eyes roved all around the room, wide, fearful. Still trying to take in her surroundings, Donovan thought. Not wanting to believe her luck, wary of the catch. Understandable, considering what she had been through. He would have to treat her gently. Put her at her ease.

'The boy is still in bed.' She spoke as if she expected a sudden attack.

'Jamal,' said Donovan as unthreateningly as possible. 'His lordship won't rise for a few hours yet.' He stretched, yawned, his dressing gown hanging open.

Katya nodded. 'What is that?' she said, pointing to his chest. 'Does it mean something?'

'What?' said Donovan looking down.

'That symbol. On your chest.'

'Oh, that.' He smiled. 'Green Lantern. It's the symbol from his costume.'

She looked at him blankly.

'Superhero. Justice League.' He smiled weakly.

Another blank look.

'Comic books? Y'know, "Through brightest day, through darkest night, no evil shall escape my sight"? That kind of thing.' He found himself gesturing. Slow down, he thought. Stop trying too hard.

'American superhero? Cartoons?'

'That's him.'

'You seem a little . . . old. For that.'

Donovan blushed. 'For superheroes? Nah. I'm only thirty five. Anyway, they deal in moral absolutes. Right and wrong. Never too old for that.'

'You make it sound so simple.'

Donovan shrugged. 'If only. Now, tea or coffee?'

'I . . . do not mind.'

'Coffee it is, then.' Donovan went into the kitchen to put the kettle on.

Katya moved over to the sofa, sat down. Her eyes were still darting over every surface, around every corner, looking for dangers real or imagined, clues that her rescuers were not what they seemed. Looking ready to run.

Donovan couldn't blame her. He would have felt the same in her situation. And he had nothing but hatred for Marco Kovacs.

Marco Kovacs. The name had meant nothing to Donovan until two weeks previously. Until Francis Sharkey, the solicitor Donovan and his team usually worked for, had explained it to him.

'Kovacs is trying to make inroads into this country,' Sharkey had said a fortnight earlier, legs stretched out, feet crossed at the ankles, hands clasped over his expanding waistline, enjoying, as usual, the sound of his own voice.

Donovan, sitting opposite on a leather sofa in the planning suite of Albion, his company, had watched him as he had talked. The offices were the ground floor of an Edwardian bay-fronted house in neo-gentrified Summerhill Terrace behind the motorbike shops and second-hand/fenced goods shops on Westgate Road. They hadn't been in long; the fresh paint and new wood smells reminding Donovan of his cottage in Northumberland. Three surprisingly comfortable dark-leather sofas went around the walls and into the bay. They were supposed, Peta had explained, to put people at their ease. In the centre of the room was a low-slung glass-topped table. On that was an open laptop.

Donovan felt a swell of pride rise within him. Albion. He loved the name. Sounded like some superhero team. Would have to be the X Men or the Doom Patrol, he thought wryly. A collection of extremely gifted misfits or damaged outsiders pooling their talents. He didn't dare share that thought with the others, though. He could imagine the response.

They had achieved a lot in a short time. It was over a year since Jamal, then surviving as a rent boy, had, literally, run to Donovan for help and in doing so not only brought Donovan back to life again but also introduced him to Peta and Amar. Sparked the chain of events that led to the formation of Albion.

Peta Knight sat back on the sofa, totally at ease, taking occasional pulls from a bottle of water. Ex-policewoman and private security consultant, black belt in tae kwon do. Not that anyone would know that to look at her, he thought. All they would see was an attractive, slim blonde. Something that Donovan knew she was not against using to her advantage.

Next to her sat Amar Miah. He had been working with Peta's short-lived private detective and security company when Donovan met him, using his audio-visual skills for surveillance work. More worryingly, he had also been using his camera skills to film private gay orgies for a rich client, a job that although lucrative was threatening to leave Amar with a spiralling cocaine habit and a prematurely shortened lifespan. Thankfully he had pulled around and was past that now, drug free and a keen gym partner for Peta. Donovan, despite many invitations, had never felt the urge to join them.

Jamal sat opposite, leaning forward, engrossed in whatever was happening on the screen of the laptop, face furrowed, neat cornrows resting on the rim of his Stussy hoodie. Peta had expressed concerns at putting the boy on the payroll, saying he was only fourteen and he should be at school. Donovan had argued that his previous life on the streets and at the mercy of predatory adults wouldn't make for a happy school life. Jamal was better off working with them, and they could all take a collective responsibility for his education. And since social services didn't know he was there in the first place and would only send him to a children's home if they did, Peta, with some reluctance, had agreed. Amar was fine about it. Jamal had also made friends with a boy who lived in the village that Donovan was very pleased about. He hoped it would help him regain some of his lost childhood.

He tried not to smile, the pride was so strong. It wasn't much and they all had to take turns in rotation in managing the office, but it was working. It was working.

Sharkey looked around. 'Lights, please,' he said.

'Jamal?' said Donovan. 'If you could tear yourself away from *Grand Theft Auto* for a moment, please?'

Jamal looked up, startled to find others in the room with him. He reluctantly closed the game down, stood and switched off the room lights at the wall and reconfigured the laptop, plugging it into a projector.

'Thank you,' said Sharkey, who then stood by the panel of lighted wall. He motioned to Jamal, who hit a key on the laptop. An image appeared on the wall of a balding man, suited, talking into a mobile phone. Black and white, face blurry and grainy: the image taken from a distance without the subject's knowledge.

'This is Marco Kovacs,' said Sharkey. 'Restaurateur, property developer. Runs an import and export business. Owns a couple of cafés, a Lebanese restaurant, Italian as well in town. Both upmarket. Good chefs. Entrepreneur. If there's money to be made, he's there.' Another nod, the image changed. It showed the same man shaking hands with a local footballer, giving a posed smile for the camera. Sharkey continued: 'Flamboyant. Wants everyone to know how well he's doing.'

'Legit?' asked Peta.

'Gives that impression,' said Sharkey. 'Doesn't directly manage anything, gets up-and-coming locals to do that. Giving something back to the community, blah blah. But he's toyed with the idea of taking over Newcastle United. Or at least talked about taking it over. Becoming some kind of Geordie Abramovich, I suppose.' He gave a grunt of a laugh. 'Buying off the locals. Anything to overcome their inbred fear of outsiders. You know what they're like up here. Even wary of me.'

'They're not wary,' said Donovan. 'They just don't like you.'

Peta and Amar stifled a laugh. Sharkey affected not to notice.

Sharkey had a confidence that didn't just border on arrogance but battered it into submission and tap-danced around it. A casual observer would never have believed that almost a year previously Sharkey had lost his very well-paid job, been on the verge of bankruptcy, injured by gunfire and had even been threatened with the prospect of prison. And had been physically attacked by Joe Donovan. Twice. For which Donovan was completely unrepentant. He'd even enjoyed it.

'Right, so I think I've heard of him,' said Donovan. 'Why should I be interested in him?'

'Because he's Serbian,' said Sharkey.

'And he runs Lebanese and Italian restaurants?' said Amar.

'Both countries with better cuisines than his own,' replied Sharkey. 'Not much of a market for beetroot soup.'

'So you want us to send the nasty foreigner back, is that it?' said Donovan. 'Is this job on behalf of the *Daily Mail*? Or are you working for the BNP now?'

Sharkey threw back his head and laughed. Jamal jumped, startled by the suddenness of it.

'That laugh was as false as Victoria Beckham's breasts,' said Donovan. 'When you laugh like that, it usually means you want me to do something I don't want to do.'

'Not at all, Joe,' said Sharkey, voice all emollient. 'In fact, you might like this one.' He looked around the others. 'All of you.'

Sharkey turned to address them, arms behind his back in his barrister stance. Donovan knew the pose. It meant Sharkey was about to impart information that was important.

'Kovacs' nationality is not the issue here,' said Sharkey, his face now serious. 'It's his clandestine activities that present us with the problem.'

'Don't tell me,' said Donovan. 'He's really a gangster.'

'He certainly is.'

'How original.' Donovan looked at Peta and Amar, shrugged. 'An East European gangster. Any more cultural stereotypes up your sleeve? Lazy Jamaicans? Thick Irishmen? Bomb-toting Muslims?'

Sharkey sighed. 'Mr Kovacs, we believe, deals in drugs.'

'Surprise, surprise,' said Peta.

'And, more important, people,' said Sharkey. 'Illegal immigrants. Refugees. Asylum seekers. Call them what you want. Mr Kovacs and his associates are modern-day slave traders.'

Donovan shook his head. 'Oh, here we go.'

'Will you listen to me, please? And perhaps you'll learn why this case is right up your liberal street.' Sharkey's words were edged with anger. Donovan fell silent. 'Thank you. Now cast your mind back to 1999. The Kosovan war. Milošević. Ethnic cleansing and all that. Remember?'

Donovan heard the seriousness in Sharkey's tone.

'Remember Arkan?'

Donovan thought for a moment, then nodded. 'Arkan. Ran an outfit called Arkan's Tigers, gangster, assassin, thug, secret policeman, Milošević's right-hand man. Well-feared bloke. That right?'

Sharkey raised an eyebrow, impressed.

Donovan continued. 'Ethnic cleansers r us. Responsible for supposedly hundreds of acts of genocide during the Kosovan war. Assassinated at the end of it by an Albanian, I think. How am I doing so far?'

'Very well,' said Peta.

Donovan looked at her, smiled almost apologetically. 'The paper I worked for covered the war extensively.' He shrugged. 'Naturally, we opposed it. And the West's attitude to it. And won awards for doing so.'

'Naturally,' said Sharkey. 'Well, from what we can gather, Arkan had an associate. A second in charge, just as bad as he was. No one knew his real name. Only his codename. Zmija. The snake. But when Arkan was killed and Milošević was indicted for war crimes, he—'

'Slithered away?' offered Jamal.

Donovan laughed. Sharkey smiled indulgently. 'Very good. There were rumours he had gone under ground. Across Europe. Into racketeering, drugs, prostitution, protection rackets. Arms. But nothing substantiated. Then reports stopped appearing. And he was forgotten, presumed killed by a business associate. But then, Marco Kovacs, businessman, pops up in Newcastle.'

'Do they look alike?' asked Amar.

'The Snake was never photographed; no one could give a description of him.'

'So why do you think it's this Marco Kovacs?' asked Peta.

Sharkey smiled, enjoying the drama. 'Because we have a witness.'

'Who?' said Donovan.

Sharkey nodded to Jamal, who hit another key. The image on the screen changed. A head-and-shoulder shot of a young man appeared. The photo was in colour and official-looking: an ID card or passport photo. Or a mug shot. The man was dark-haired and hollow-eyed. He looked tired, hungry.

'This is Dario Tokic,' said Sharkey. 'A former slave of Mr Kovacs. He was brought over here. Promised a new life and put to work on an industrial-sized farm, somewhere in the north-west, we think. Owned, indirectly, by Kovacs. Mr Tokic managed to escape, came to Newcastle. He says he has evidence for us.'

'What kind?' asked Peta.

Sharkey paused. Knew he was about to impart something of importance. 'The farm received a visit from its owner one day.'

'Kovacs?'

Sharkey nodded. 'Mr Tokic remembered him from the old country. With Arkan's Tigers. Massacring a village. His village.'

'And he's identified Kovacs?' asked Donovan.

Sharkey nodded to Jamal. The slide changed. A grinning, dinner-jacketed Kovacs was flanked by a burly bald bodyguard.

'Broke down in tears when he saw this,' said Sharkey. 'Seemed genuine enough. Couldn't look at it any more, apparently.'

Donovan looked suitably impressed. 'And he's going to testify?'

'He is. But with certain strings attached.'

'Such as?'

'He entered this country illegally; he wants to stay here legally.'

'Shouldn't be a problem to you,' said Donovan.

'It isn't. But there's something else.'

'What?' asked Amar.

Sharkey nodded at Jamal again. The image changed to that of a young woman. Pretty and smiling. Blonde and well dressed, she looked as if she didn't have a care in the world.

'This is his sister, Katya. The picture was taken a couple of years ago when she had just started at Priština university. European literature, I believe.'

'And where is she now?' asked Donovan.

'Somewhere in this city. A slave. Of a more sexual nature.'

'And this is down-to Kovacs?' asked Peta.

'Indirectly, we think,' said Sharkey, nodding to Jamal who pressed a key. The image on the screen changed. A young man, mid-twenties, appeared. Sunglasses, dark spiky hair, leather jacket. Cigarette in the corner of his mouth, mobile clamped to his ear. 'This is Derek Ainsley. More colloquially known as Decca. Local gangster wannabe.'

'Form?' asked Peta.

'Minor but escalating,' replied Sharkey. 'Cars, drugs, protection, that kind of thing. Marked down as one for the future. At least everyone thought so.'

'And what now?' asked Amar.

'Had a Damascus road conversion,' said Sharkey, unable to keep the disbelief from his voice. 'Went straight. Runs a coffee bar in the city centre. Among other things.'

'This coffee bar. Owned by Kovacs?' asked Donovan.

Sharkey smiled. 'Very good. And in addition to that, Mr Ainsley has started making frequent trips back and forward to Eastern Europe. He claims it's where he finds staff. We think that's just a front. A sop to respectability. We think it's where he finds young girls to bring back and force into sexual slavery.'

'And this girl's one of them?' asked Peta.

Sharkey nodded. 'We believe so.'

Donovan nodded. 'And how do we find her?'

Sharkey smiled. 'That's where you and your team come in, my boy.'

Donovan looked at him. 'Thought it might be.'

'Can I just ask,' said Peta, 'why aren't the police doing this? Immigration Services?'

'Compromised,' said Sharkey. 'Now I'm not suggesting for one minute that our boys in blue are anything but honest, hard-working sons of toil, but Mr Kovacs is, as we know, a very wealthy man, and the promise of a share of that could turn even the most resolute of heads.'

'Nicely put,' said Donovan.

'Plus,' continued Sharkey, 'there was a recent joint attempt by police and Immigration Services to break a people-trafficking ring that Kovacs was suspected of being behind. Fish-gutting factory on the north-east coast. Cheap labour. That fell apart due to large sums of money going where it shouldn't have been. No convictions, just careers quietly curtailed.'

'Kovacs paid them off,' said Donovan.

'Exactly. The police do take crimes of this nature very seriously,' said Sharkey, 'but there tend not to be too many upper-level convictions. If this is planned well, it could change that.'

'So why do they think that we in the private sector are incorruptible?' asked Donovan.

'Because we're rolling in it,' replied Amar.

They all laughed. It died away.

'There's a police crackdown on people trafficking targeted mainly in and around London. All ports and points of entry are being watched. Making it tricky for them to conduct their business down there. But that business didn't disappear; it just dispersed.'

'Up to here?' asked Amar.

Sharkey nodded. 'Among other places. Kovacs runs an import–export business. With a very large warehouse at Tyne Dock, a port which has plenty of trade coming in from the Baltic. And, of course, our boy is strongly suspected of having links to organized crime in Eastern Europe.'

'So . . .' Donovan looked at Sharkey expectantly.

'So there's a new ongoing investigation against him.'

'Hopefully better put together than the last one,' said Peta.

'I think we can take that as a given,' said Sharkey. 'It's a completely new team. Rumour has it, they've managed to get one of theirs on the inside.'

'How does what we're doing tie in with that?' asked Amar.

'It doesn't,' said Sharkey. 'Apparently there's a new shipment due soon and they're on to it. We just do our bit, keep out of their way and when they need what we've got make sure we hand it over to them. And in the meantime . . .' Sharkey pulled a sheaf of papers from his briefcase, handed it to Donovan. 'This is everything Dario Tokic will tell us about his sister and how to reach her. Everything we know. It should help.' Sharkey looked Donovan straight in the eye. 'We need to find her. He won't say anything until he knows she's safe and sound.'

Donovan nodded.

'And ensure that Mr Kovacs will have the full weight of English justice brought to bear on him.'

'Who's paying us for this?' asked Peta.

Sharkey couldn't resist a smile. 'Let's just say exclusive media rights have already been signed. Think of it as a pre-nuptial agreement.'

Peta raised an eyebrow. Donovan caught it. 'We'd better get started, then,' he said.

'Best of luck.' Sharkey motioned for the lights to be turned on again; Jamal obliged. Sharkey then began moving papers around, indicating the meeting was coming to an end. As he did so he talked of contracts, money, made appreciative comments concerning the new offices.

Peta, Amar and Jamal filed out. Donovan waited behind. Sharkey looked up from his briefcase, saw him standing there. Donovan stared.

'Any other word?'

Sharkey slipped the CD from the laptop, put it in his briefcase. Avoided Donovan's eyes. He looked suddenly uncomfortable. 'Word on what?'

'You know what. The job you're supposed to be helping me with.'

Sharkey sighed, shook his head. 'No, Joe, I'm afraid not.'

'Are you looking? Properly looking?'

The room seemed too hot for Sharkey. 'Yes, yes . . . of course I'm looking. I've got, got . . . lots of people out there.' He swallowed hard. 'Looking.'

Donovan kept the stare up.

'Joe, I'm keeping my end of the bargain. I'm honestly looking as hard as I can.'

'Never trust a lawyer when he says he's being honest.'

Sharkey sighed. 'Do you think I would lie to you on this? Really?'

Donovan kept staring.

'Really?'

Donovan sighed, broke the gaze. 'No, Sharkey, I don't. I think you'd be a fool if you did.'

Sharkey's hand went involuntarily to his throat. 'You're right, I would be. I'm looking, Joe. I'll keep looking.'

Coffee made, Donovan carried it into the front room, placed the tray on his coffee table.

While preparing the cafetière, he had studied her. She was of medium height and quite thin, as if undernourished. Her hair was blonde, although her roots were beginning to show. She was young and would have been pretty had not her face been etched with worry, her eyes only partially caging the ghosts that lay behind them.

'Didn't know what you wanted to eat, so there's some biscuits. Chocolate Hobnobs.'

She looked confused but grateful. She thanked him.

He plunged the cafetière, poured the coffee, added milk and sugar in the proportions she had requested, handed it to her. She sipped. Smiled. The ghosts retreated.

'Thank you. It is good.'

'All part of the service.'

She placed her mug down on the table, picked up a biscuit, started eating. As she did so, the ghosts returned to her eyes.

'Am I . . . prisoner here?' she said through a mouthful of crumbs.

'Prisoner?' Donovan shook his head. Perhaps too enthusiastically in his effort to convince. 'No. No, definitely not. You can come and go as you please.' He smiled. 'Not that there's much around here to come and go to.'

She picked up another biscuit. 'Where am I?'

'Northumberland. Just north of Newcastle. You're safe. They won't find you here.'

She nodded, picked up her mug, took another mouthful. 'And who are you?'

'Joe Donovan. Like I said last night.'

'And who is Joe Donovan?'

Donovan took a sip. 'Good question. In a previous life I was an investigative journalist. Now I run a team called Albion. You met the other team members last night. We're information brokers. We work on assignment, from solicitors usually. We broker information, set up deals. Do investigative work.'

'You are . . . detectives?'

'No, we're not. Although one of us used to be with the police.'

Katya frowned. 'Which one?'

'Your partner in the house. Peta.'

Katya's eyes widened. 'Really? But she was . . . going with punters.'

Donovan gave a small laugh. 'She may have let them into her room. But she certainly wouldn't have done anything with them.'

Katya looked confused.

'Let's just say she can still act and sound like police when she wants to.'

A tiny smile appeared on Katya's face. 'I see.' She picked up another biscuit.

'You hungry?'

Katya paused, biscuit on the way to her lips. Her eyes took on a fearful aspect. She put the biscuit back on the plate.

'No, it's OK, keep eating. That's what they're there for. I'll make something more substantial if you like.'

She looked at him warily. Donovan scratched his head.

'Look, Katya, there's absolutely no reason why you should trust me, I know, but I'm not going to hurt you or force you to do anything against your will. Like I said, you're not a prisoner here. If you're hungry, eat. If you're thirsty, drink. If you want to go out, go out. You won't be punished for it.'

She looked into his eyes, checking for lies, wanting to believe him. Donovan didn't move while she did so. Eventually she nodded.

'Thank you,' said Donovan. 'Now help yourself to biscuits and I'll make a proper breakfast. How does bacon and eggs sound?' He saw the expression on her face, stood up, smiled. 'Bacon and eggs it is.'

Donovan went into the kitchen. Katya watched him go, a small smile playing on the corners of her lips.

They breakfasted at the dining table by the window with its view down past the dunes to the beach and beyond, the North Sea. Jamal came down to join them, the smell of bacon cooking too much of a lure. He wore his hip-hop T-shirt and baggy jeans and was on his best behaviour before Katya. She seemed to take to him, thought Donovan, smiling when the boy spoke.

Once the meal was under way, Katya had more questions for Donovan.

'When can I see Dario? When can I see my brother?'

'Soon,' said Donovan, forking egg into his mouth. 'Like it said in his letter I gave you last night, I think it might be best if you stay here for a while. If Kovacs finds out about the whole thing it might get very nasty.'

Katya sighed. 'Kovacs. Always Kovacs.'

'Hopefully it won't be too long, though.'

The meal over, Jamal surprised Donovan by volunteering to clear away.

'You feeling all right?' asked Donovan.

Jamal looked at him as if he had sprouted another head. 'Whassamatter wit' you, man? Makin' out like I never do nothin'.'

He went into the kitchen, plates balanced on his hands.

'He is a good boy,' Katya said to Donovan. 'Is he your son?'

Donovan laughed. 'No,' he said, feeling his cheeks beginning to redden. 'Just another stray that I picked up.'

'An' you be glad you did,' Jamal shouted from the kitchen. 'Katya, you shoulda seen this place when I moved in. It was mingin', man. Like a buildin' site. Not fit for human habitation.' Jamal came to the kitchen entrance, stood in the doorway. He counted his next words out on his fingers. 'I had to plaster, paint, put proper floors down, choose furniture, get the heatin' fixed, plant the garden . . .' He gave an elaborate sigh. 'Tell you, man, if I hadn'ta moved in, old Joe here would still be livin' in the Stone Age.'

'Yeah, right.'

Donovan made more coffee. Katya was beginning to relax.

'So what happens now?' she asked.

'Well, I've got to go into Newcastle today, sort some stuff

out with the solicitors, let them know you're safe and sound. I'll leave you in the capable hands of Jamal.'

Jamal nodded, gave a small wave. 'My mate Jake's comin' round later. We goin' play some serious X Box. You can join in if you like.'

'There you go,' said Donovan, smiling. 'That's your day mapped out for you.'

'Thank you,' said Katya, attempting to return the smile. 'And will I see . . . Peta? Is that her name?'

'You might later,' said Donovan. 'But she's out today. Reliving her youth.'

Katya looked confused.

'Gone back to college,' said Donovan. 'Get another degree. She might be along later, though. In the meantime you'll find some clothes in the room you slept in. I hope they fit you. So until I get back, just, y'know, chill.'

Katya smiled, placed a hand on his arm.

'Thank you, Joe Donovan. You are a good man.'

Donovan gave an involuntary but instinctive look on to the landing, his eyes resting on the locked door. He managed a smile.

'I try,' he said.

5

Slatted, weak sunlight streamed in through the white-plastic blinds, illuminating the dust motes against the blackberry-coloured walls in slow, lazy, now-you-see-me-now-you-don't swirls. The workdesks in the small room had all been arranged into a semicircle, leaving a desk in the centre of the room plus space in front of it. Pacing space, Peta thought.

She entered the room, found a space at one of the semi-circle of desks and sat down. She began taking out files, folders, books and pens from her shoulder bag. She smiled to herself. A good night's work previously, a session in the gym first thing. She was doing a job she enjoyed that paid and left her able to fulfil ambitions, expand her horizons. She hadn't felt this happy in years.

Others were coming, doing the same. Some smiled, talked to her. Most just nodded or ignored her. She smiled back, made small talk while setting up her place at the desk.

Jill sat down next to her. 'Hiya.'

'Hi,' replied Peta.

'Thought I was gonna be late,' Jill said, taking out notepads and textbooks identical to Peta's, her Lancashire accent rendering most of her words pretension-free. 'Just woke up half an hour ago at Ben's. An' he lives in Gosforth.' She sighed. 'Jesus. An' what a hangover.'

'Good night?' asked Peta.

Jill's face split into a smile. 'Crackin'. Went to see the Bravery over at Newcastle uni.'

'Were they good?'

'Brilliant.' Jill stopped talking, regarded Peta with a frown. 'Anyway, what happened to you? Thought you were comin'?'

'Oh, yeah . . .' Peta remembered she had said she might go. But that had been weeks ago. Before work got in the way. 'Sorry. Something came up at the last minute and I had to take care of it.'

Jill looked interested. 'Oh, what, family or friends, like?'

No, actually. Going undercover, pulling an East European prostitute off the streets and taking her to a safe house so that her brother can give evidence against a gangster, like.

'Yeah,' said Peta. 'I had to go out with friends.'

Jill nodded, satisfied with the explanation.

Peta sensed relief too. She knew Jill had only asked her to the gig out of politeness. Although Peta didn't look that much older than the rest, and was no stranger to jeans, trainers and combat jackets, she was, she knew, regarded as an anomaly within her year group. A mature student. And whatever she said or did, however she tried to fit in, she knew she couldn't really. Because she had been out in the world, made a living, and decided to come back to university and get a degree. So she carried with her something alien: the smell of work and mortgages, taxes and pensions. The smell of the outside world.

Jill busied herself with unloading books on the desk. Peta knew what she must have been picturing. Friends. Bottle of wine. Chatting around the kitchen table. Like her mother would do. Knowing how far that was from the truth, Peta hid a smile.

Jill leaned across, almost conspiratorially, eyes wide. 'They found her, you know. The body.'

'I know. I heard.'

Jill shook her head. 'Makes you think, doesn't it? My God.'

Peta agreed. 'And they haven't found out who did it. They're still out there,' she said. 'You take care of yourself.'

Jill smiled. 'Yes, Mum.'

Peta smiled in return. Unpacked her books.

Working with Albion satisfied Peta. On one level. But something had always nagged within her. Something about unfinished business. Her parents, both liberal, middle-class *Guardian* readers, had wanted their daughter to go to university. Study the arts. Perhaps become a lecturer like themselves. But Peta, in a spirit of youthful rebellion, had taken what she saw as the most contentious route for herself, and the one that would annoy her parents most: she had joined the police force.

Her parents were mortified. They felt they had let her down in some way. Peta, for her own part, hadn't enjoyed the reaction as much as she thought she would have. They were deeply hurt, far more so than she had imagined they would be. And that impacted on her. She tried to back out but left it too late, was too far into her training by then. So she vowed instead to make them proud of her. That didn't work either.

When, five years later, she left the force, almost physically beaten down by being patronized, relegated to demeaning tasks, seeing people she had initially had to help climbing the ranks ahead of her, the force's institutionalized sexism, plus a burgeoning problem with alcohol, her parents had insisted it wasn't too late. They would regard those last few years as a temporary blip, a gap-year project that had got out of hand. She could still find the right course, still go to university. They would help her, pay for her. Although sorely tempted by this offer, she turned it down. She still had something to prove. So, hoping to utilize skills and contacts she had made in the force, she set up her own private investigation and security business. That, eventually, folded. And then, thankfully, came Albion.

But still that nag, that sense of unfinished business. And here she was. Thirty-one years old. Studying psychology at university. Over ten years later and her liberal, *Guardian*-reading parents had been right all along.

Not that she would admit that. Nor how much she enjoyed it.

Her body got regular workouts in the dojo. Her mind very rarely. This was the perfect counterbalance. Plus the lecturer had a lot to do with it. Peta had never met anyone like him.

The door opened. As if on cue, in he came. Medium height, slim build, he walked with a slight limp, as if the bones hadn't set right from an old injury. And his right hand was covered in scar tissue, gnarled and deformed. But that wasn't the most remarkable thing about him. He was dressed, as usual, like a walking antique. His suit hailed from any time during the 1940s or 1950s and had clearly been originally intended for a much bigger man, the wide, grey, fireman's braces and thick, black-leather belt holding up his trousers bearing testament to that. On his feet were lace-up DMs, beneath his suit jacket a black T-shirt. His dark over-coat was similarly old and flowing – Peta was sure she had glimpsed a Utility label inside when he had hung it up once – with a bright red, paisley scarf thrown over the top, the swirls drawing attention like some kind of fantastical space vortex. Topping it off was a grey-felt hat that may have been a homburg or a fedora. Peta wasn't sure. He looked like a child's idea of a responsible adult.

His briefcase, an old doctor's bag stuffed with books and other ephemera, was hefted on to the desk. He took his overcoat off, draped it over the back of his chair, along with the scarf. Placed his hat on the desk. His dark hair was shot with grey and cropped close. He wore a pair of old round glasses as modelled by John Lennon in the late 1960s. Peta had tried to work out his age, given up. He was anywhere between thirty and fifty. Probably. It was hard to tell. He seemed unaware of any eccentricity, perfectly at ease with himself. This was him as he was.

Professor Graham McAllister. Usually, as he had stressed in his first seminar four months previously, just called the Prof.

'Good morning, you fine-minded people.' His voice was dark and rich, ruminative yet not without a Geordie accent. 'Now, what shall we discuss today?'

The same introduction as always. Getting any unfocused discussion out of the way before beginning properly. And it still hadn't worn thin, Peta thought. Although this was only the second term.

'What about Ashley Malcolm?' one of the students, a well-built, shaggy-haired boy, shouted.

The class almost froze. The whole university, Peta had thought on walking in, had a morning-after feel in the wake of the discovery of Ashley Malcolm's body. The students, and staff it seemed, had talked about nothing else all week. First her disappearance, then this. Warnings had been issued, escorts encouraged for all girls. A definite atmosphere hung over the university: loss and shock, certainly, but also a kind of sick electricity. A sense that amid all that horror and upset there was vicarious thrill-seeking to be had. Peta put it down to the fact that the students' personalities were incomplete and they hadn't found the appropriate reaction to tragedy yet.

The Prof stopped, stared. Not so much angry that he had been called on to deviate from his usual speech, more curious.

'Why Ashley Malcolm?' he asked.

The student shrugged. 'Thought you could, y'know, give us some insights.'

The Prof perched on the edge of his desk, leaned forward, frowning. 'Insights?'

'Yeah, y'know. You being a psychologist an' all.'

'Something which I believe you aspire to, is that not the case, Mr Carson?'

The student shrugged.

The Prof gave a slight smile. 'Then perhaps you could give us some—' he paused, verbally placing the word in inverted commas '—insight of your own.'

The student, Jack Carson, shuffled uneasily in his seat. 'Well . . . she was murdered.'

'Yes,' said the Prof. 'That much is incontestable.'

'Horribly. Although we don't know the details. The police haven't released those yet.'

The Prof nodded. 'Horribly. I wouldn't think there was an un-horrible way to be murdered. Go on.'

A few nervous titters went round the room. Jack Carson continued: 'Well, don't they always say they know their attacker?'

The Prof raised an eyebrow. 'Do they?'

'Unless it's a . . .' He tried to laugh while saying it. 'I don't know. Serial killer.'

The Prof didn't laugh. Instead he nodded, thoughtfully. 'Thank you for that, Mr Carson. You're right. Most murder victims do know their murderers. It's usually someone close to them who has something to gain from their death. By that I mean financially. But from what I've seen so far that doesn't seem to be the case here.'

'So what's your take on it, then?' asked Peta. 'If you were advising the police, how would you tell them to proceed?'

The Prof gave Peta a look of scrutiny. He seemed to be making his mind up about her in some way. Conclusion reached, he leaned back on the desk, adopted a thoughtful pose. On anyone else it would look ridiculous, thought Peta, but he managed to bring it off somehow.

'How would I tell the police to proceed . . . ? Well . . . Now, bear in mind I know as much as anyone else. I've watched the news and read the papers. Like I said, those who commit premeditated murder usually have something to gain. I'd say the same is true in this case. Although I have no way of knowing what that would be. But I doubt very much it's financial. I would advise the police to look into Ashley's background for a start, but I doubt they need me to tell them that.'

The Prof frowned, nodded to himself. 'I'd also make a detailed examination of where she was taken. A street in Fenham. Likewise where her body was found. An old, disused graveyard.' He ruminatively enunciated the words. Closed his eyes. 'Hmm. I'm just speculating here, but I don't think she was placed there by accident. No, not at all. I think there's something special about that place. Something that means a lot to the killer. It's a clue or a set of clues. A puzzle. What we have to do is solve the puzzle. It might not lead us to him, but it might make us think like him . . .'

Silence echoed around the class.

The Prof became aware of that silence and slowly opened his eyes again. He looked startled to be back, Peta thought.

'Ah, yes.' He stood up. 'Well. That's enough of that for now. Can't have you hanging around campus repeating my half-baked theories.' He looked at Peta. 'Then I would be, as you say, advising the police. Although not in the way you meant.'

A small ripple of relieved laughter went around the room.

'Anyway, enough,' the Prof said. '*Tempus fugit*, does it not? Let us move on. Take out your textbooks, turn to page 192. Internal conflicts and the compulsions that can be derived from them. Rather apt, I think.'

Peta opened her book, flicked through to the correct page. She kept her eyes on the Prof, though. Scrutinized him. When he had opened his eyes following his discourse, he had seen something disturbing, she thought. And the depth of it had unnerved her.

Her police sixth sense was still functioning. It might be nothing, she thought. But then again it might very well be something.

Whatever, it might be wise to keep an eye on the Prof, she thought.

6

DS Paul Turnbull had his victim. And because of that, his righteous anger.

He pulled the Vectra to the kerb, turned off the ignition. Looked up at the old Victorian bay-fronted semi before him. From the passenger seat, Nattrass moved to open the door. Turnbull remained still. Nattrass looked at him. Not returning her enquiring gaze, he took out the photo, its edges rounded now, thumbprinted and creased from overlooking. He held it in his hands. The image poignantly familiar, the news media having splashed it all over TV and computer screens, newspapers. He had the original. Ashley Malcolm. Alive. Smiling and laughing at a student party, toasting the camera with a can of lager. A strappy, silky top and skirt, long hair. Pretty. She would never grow old, go grey, put on weight, have a satisfying or unsatisfying career, have children, get married or get divorced. She would be for ever locked into joyous, youthful immortality. Freeze-framed by the click of the shutter.

His victim.

From Westgate Road cemetery he, along with Nattrass and DS Deborah Howe, the SOCO Senior Manager, had gone with the Home Office pathologist and body to the mortuary at the General Hospital, staying to witness the post-mortem.

The pathologist, Dr Nicholas Kemp, was clearly in his element in the sterile room surrounding the stainless-steel table with the ceiling-mounted mic.

Turnbull had watched, as he had done before, while Kemp went about his business, reducing Ashley Malcolm until she was just a collection of weighed and catalogued inner organs, tissue samples. A carcass of clues. He had watched, struggled even more than usual to find the professional detachment he knew he should have had by now.

Then on to the incident room at Market Street police station in the centre of Newcastle, sitting through DCI Fenton's morning briefing along with everyone else on the case. The mood had been dark and concentrated, tense and expectant, as if a raincloud had come in through the air-conditioning and was threatening to engulf them all in freezing-cold, needle-sharp rain.

Fortified by heavily sugared coffee, aware of what he must have looked like. Pulling an all-nighter, too tired and wired to wear it like a badge of honour. He and Nattrass had looked at each other.

'D'you want to go home?' she had said. 'I don't mind. You've got a family. I understand if you do.'

Turnbull had thought of home, of what was there for him. Or what wasn't. He thought of Ashley. Felt something burn hard and bright within.

'I'll stay.'

Nattrass had made any contributions on his behalf. His eyes had followed the board's tortuous trail. It looked to him, as always, not like a chart but more a game whose ending was rigged. A snakes and ladders of horror. Roll the dice and up the ladder. Ashley alive, smiling. Roll the dice and move along. Ashley gone. In her place photos of her friends, her boyfriend. Maps of her last known whereabouts, descriptions of her clothes. Conjecture. Supposition. Roll the dice and down a snake. Ashley dead. The wilfully destroyed and mangled bodily components bearing no resemblance to the earlier photo. No life or joy left there.

Roll the dice and down further. Ashley reduced to gory red, butcher's backshop close-up. Ashley anatomized. Down again. And still down.

Turnbull had his righteous anger. Controlled. Fuelling his day.

Preliminary results showed a positive match, Fenton had informed them. The body was that of Ashley Malcolm. Toxicology and DNA within twenty-four hours.

They had known what that implied. Ashley's murder had been allocated a high grade. Which meant money and manpower. Twenty-four hours. The more they paid, the quicker the results.

Fenton had gone on, the politician from the press conference of an hour ago now in the descendent, the hard-nosed DCI in the ascendant. He read from reports, talked from memory. Always with authority. Ashley's parents in Runcorn had been informed and were on their way to Newcastle along with her sister, all broken-hearted.

The body had been mutilated both pre- and post-mortem. Eyes and mouth sewn shut. Stab wounds; no final figure yet, probably between ten and fifteen. Signs of sexual activity. And a couple of strange bruises on the back of her neck that they were still looking into. It was, he said unnecessarily, a bad one.

He had asked about leads. The door to door hadn't shown up anything positive yet. Shadowy figures tended to come and go in the cemetery. They were paid as little attention as possible. No sign of a vehicle as yet.

The same as her abduction, Turnbull had thought. Like she vanished into thin air and reappeared again.

A comment about a Tardis.

Someone put forward the name Lisa Hill, asked if there might be a connection.

Lisa Hill. A part-time prostitute and crack aficionado

with convictions for dealing and aggravated assault, whose body had been discovered the week before Christmas. She had been badly beaten, sexually assaulted, murdered. Stabbed repeatedly, frenziedly. Her body dumped at Barras Bridge by the Haymarket.

Conscious of any accusations of bias or lack of sensitivity to what might be perceived in certain sections of the media as an unsympathetic victim, they had investigated her death thoroughly. And come up with nothing. The consensus was a mad punter who, unless he was caught doing something similar in the future to another prostitute, would go unpunished.

With no progress after a month and other cases eating up budget and manpower, Lisa Hill was gradually forgotten. Marked 'open', left unsolved.

Fenton gave the name some thought, said he didn't think so, but at this stage they couldn't rule anything out.

A question about bringing in a profiler. Fenton making a face in reply, mentioning budget, saying they would see how they went.

Then on to possible suspects.

Nattrass had talked about Michael Nell, Ashley's boyfriend. Photography student. Not a nice person. Handy with his fists, especially where the ladies were concerned. Miserable and moody. Liked things rough. Previous for drunk and disorderly. Rich dad to protect him, bail him out. Untouchable, or so he thought.

Questioned twice and both times seemingly unconcerned about Ashley. Not worried. With no alibi for Ashley's disappearance. Nattrass said she had felt he was hiding something. Covering. Turnbull had nodded, corroborating.

Light had caught Fenton's eyes. Made them shine. He asked Turnbull and Nattrass to pay Nell a visit.

Then a closing speech from Fenton warning the team to guard against complacency, not to assume that Nell was the murderer and to keep working as many avenues as possible. No one had been convinced. The eyes had given him away.

In the car, Nattrass had asked him if he wanted to go home, get some sleep.

Turnbull had turned to her. Saw her tired and drawn face, imagined he was her mirror image. 'Do you?'

Nattrass hadn't answered. Turnbull had started the car. Not saying another word.

Just drove, aware of the photo of Ashley in his jacket pocket, over his heart.

'You ready?' said Nattrass, hand on the door lever.

Turnbull looked up, put the photo away, nodded.

Nattrass stayed where she was. 'Emotions are running high and neither of us has had any sleep.'

He turned to her, challenge in his eyes. 'Meaning?'

'Meaning I don't want you going maverick on me. You're a professional. You're a policeman. We do this properly. Understood?'

Turnbull, reluctantly, nodded.

Nattrass opened the door. 'Then let's go. I'll lead.'

Up the garden path. The house looked like any old building given over to multiple rental occupation. Especially by students, thought Turnbull. The first time they had been away from the embrace of their overprotective middle-class families. The first time they had had to cook, clean and look after themselves. The paintwork needed updating, the front garden relieving of its weed collection. A battered Peugeot 206 sat in front of the house.

'Takes you back,' said Nattrass.

'Not me.' Turnbull almost spat the words out.

Nattrass ignored him, tried the bell. No sound.

'They probably haven't worked out how to buy a battery,' said Turnbull. 'Or rewire it.'

Nattrass turned to him. 'Wait in the car.'

'I'm fine.'

She shook her head. Knocked on the door. Waited. No reply. She knocked again.

Eventually they heard movement from within the house. Someone making their slow, unhurried way to the door. It opened.

'Hello Michael,' said Nattrass. She reintroduced herself and Turnbull to remind him who they were, showed their warrant cards, then asked to be let in. Nell moved aside, let them into the hall.

Music, loud and indie, came from one of the downstairs rooms. It sounded to Turnbull like the stuff his older brother used to listen to in the sixth form in the early 1980s but guessed it was probably modern.

Turnbull looked at the young man. Tall and thin, his sleeveless T-shirt exposing wiry, muscled arms etched with dark, swirling tattoos, his hair shaggy and tousled, his lips falling into a pouting sneer so mannered and practised it had become natural. Turnbull looked into the boy's eyes. They stared back with mocking cruelty. Turnbull wanted to slap him on principle.

'I suppose you've heard the news?' Nattrass, her voice impassive, spoke.

Michael Nell shrugged. 'What news?'

Nattrass looked around the cramped hallway. Posters for bands covered the woodchipped walls. Arctic Monkeys. Maximo Park. 'Could we come in, please?' she said above the noise. 'Perhaps sit down.' She began moving up the stairs, towards where she remembered his room was.

'Not up there,' Michael Nell said. 'It's not convenient.'

Nattrass looked around, her eyes hard and flat. 'I think it would be best.' Her tone brooked no argument.

She went up the stairs, Michael Nell reluctantly following. Turnbull brought up the rear. They reached Nell's room. Nattrass placed her hand on the handle. Nell seemed agitated.

'Wait,' he said. 'Just a minute.'

He slipped inside the room, closed the door behind him. They heard the sound of voices, hushed yet urgent. Then frantic movement. Nattrass and Turnbull said nothing, exchanged a glance. The door opened again. A girl came out; small and dark, her hair sticking out at angles she had never intended, her clothes creased and clutched around her. She kept her eyes downcast as she made her way rapidly down the stairs and out of the front door.

'Hope we weren't disturbing you,' said Turnbull.

Nell reddened.

'Perhaps you're not interested in what we have to say.' Nattrass walked into the room, sat down on the unmade bed. Turnbull stayed standing, looked at the CD case lying beside the player. The Arctic Monkeys: 'Whatever You Say I Am That's What I'm Not'. I'll be the judge of that, mate, he thought. He scoped the room. Turnbull's idea of a typical student house. Posters and cards Blu-Tacked to the walls, cheap furniture, textbooks and discarded clothes. Shelved books. Piles of magazines. He checked the titles: *Skin Two. Bizarre. Tattoo.* Some less commercially minded but sporting similar themes.

'May I?' He picked one up, gestured to Nell, who shrugged.

'Whatever,' he said.

Turnbull began leafing through one.

Nell sat down next to Nattrass. 'This is all over the newspapers and TV by now; we thought you would have heard. We discovered a body last night. And I'm afraid it's Ashley.'

Nattrass watched, unblinking, as Nell took in the news. He looked down, nodded. Sighed. 'You sure?'

'We are.' Nattrass kept up her scrutiny.

'Aw, Jesus.'

The two of them turned, looked up at Turnbull. He was staring at a magazine, his face violently twisted with distaste. 'What the fuck's this?' he said. 'Extreme body modification? What's wrong with these people?'

Turnbull scanned, through narrowed eyes, pictures of split tongues, artfully amputated toes and fingers, tattooed and sliced penises, castrated bodies, heads with horns implanted. He had never seen anything like it. Nattrass looked again at Nell. The student had his eyes cast down but couldn't disguise the smile on his face.

'You have some interesting tastes, Mr Nell,' said Nattrass.

'I like transgression,' said Nell proudly. 'I don't belong in the boring straight world. I want a more interesting life for myself. On the extremes.'

He looked at Turnbull, enjoying seeing the distaste on his face.

'There are some photos over there.' Nell pointed to the bookshelves. 'Some of mine. Have a look. You might enjoy them.'

Turnbull's face showed what he would have enjoyed doing to Nell more than that. He turned to the shelves.

'Right,' said Nattrass, 'to continue. I'm afraid the body we found was Ashley. Do you have anything to say?'

'Like what?'

Nattrass shrugged. 'I don't know. Like, you're sorry, how did she die . . . ? Anything like that.'

'OK. How did she die?'

'She was murdered, Mr Nell. And I have to ask you: what were your whereabouts last night?'

Nell gave a noise that could have been a snort or a laugh. 'You're kiddin'.'

'I'm not,' said Nattrass. 'Where were you last night between the hours of eight o'clock and midnight?'

'Here.'

'And can anyone verify that?'

'Yeah. You saw her on the way out.'

'You don't believe in letting the grass grow, do you?' said Nattrass, unable to keep the distaste from her voice.

'Like I said, I'm different from other people.' Nell tried to sound nonchalant but just came over petulant and fearful.

'Boss.' Turnbull spoke. There was urgency in his voice that he was trying to disguise. 'Can you come and look at this a minute?'

Nattrass stood up and crossed the room. Turnbull was holding out a sheaf of ten by eights, struggling to keep his face blank. Nattrass looked at what he was pointing at. And audibly gasped.

The photo was grainy, blurry, and showed a girl, early twenties, dressed in black with what appeared to be an audience in the background, with her eyes and mouth sewn together. Blood running down her face.

Neither Nattrass nor Turnbull could speak for several seconds as they tried to process the information and decide how to proceed. Eventually Nattrass cleared her throat, plucked the photo from Turnbull's hands.

'May I?'

'Be my guest.' Turnbull sounded relieved.

Nattrass took the photo, crossed to Nell, resumed her position on the bed next to him. She showed him it.

'This one of yours?' she said.

'Yeah,' he said proudly. 'Took it in a club in Amsterdam.' He looked at Turnbull. 'Kind of club you've never been to.'

Turnbull was leafing through the other photos. They showed bondage, pain, humiliation. Some taken in the same environment as the other; some taken in anonymous rooms lit by bare bulbs. Most taken in what looked like the same studio. Women in various stages of undress. Humiliation. Turnbull stopped again. His heart skipped a beat.

Another woman, her eyes, mouth sewn shut.

'You take all of these?' Turnbull asked, holding them up, holding his voice steady.

'Every one.'

'In Amsterdam, or nearer to home?'

Nell smiled. 'Right under your noses. You'd be amazed at what goes on.'

Turnbull said nothing.

'So is this,' Nattrass said, her voice as calm as she could make it, 'part of your transgressive lifestyle? Hmm? Something you do for – what? Kicks?'

Nell looked up to her, his eyes challenging. 'So what? Yeah, it's a scene I'm into. And it's pretty extreme, yeah.' There was pride in his voice now. 'But I doubt it's something you can understand.'

Nattrass and Turnbull shared another look. An unspoken, almost telepathic form of communication they had worked up between them in the years they had been partnered together. They exchanged almost imperceptible nods.

'Oh,' said Nattrass, 'I can understand. Better than you think.'

She stood up, towering over the student. Turnbull moved to the side of him so he couldn't make for the door.

'Would you like to come down to the station?' she said. 'We'd like a little chat.'

Nell laughed, sneered. 'Don't be stupid. Fuck off.'

'Then, Michael Nell,' said Nattrass, her voice as professional and uninflected as possible, so that there could be no mistaking what she was saying, no later legal argument claiming she had behaved improperly or technically incorrect, 'I am arresting you on suspicion of the murder of Ashley Malcolm. You do not have to say anything . . .'

Turnbull tuned out. He had heard it all before.

Nell's face changed. The artfully constructed mask slipped away, to be replaced by surprise, then fear. It looked like the only true feelings he had expressed in the time they had been in his room.

'No, no . . .' Nell let out a high-pitched scream, made a dash for the door.

Turnbull was on him, arm up behind his back, wrestling him down to the floor. He wanted to lash out; get in a few well-placed kicks and punches, claim self-defence later, but managed to refrain. He would do this properly, like a professional. He, too, was mindful of legal technicalities.

'You calm yet?' Turnbull said. 'You gonna give me any more trouble? Eh?'

He gave Nell's arm another twist for good measure. Nell squealed.

'Good. Come on, then.'

Turnbull escorted him out of the room and down the stairs, ignoring his pleas, his protestations of innocence. He was breathing heavily, flushed with exhilaration.

He thought of Ashley, on whose behalf he was fighting for justice. Her picture over his heart.

He smiled. A good day's work.

7

The Historian stared deep into the mirror. He had been there so long he had lost all track of time. But time was a concept he didn't believe in anyway. No past, no present, no future. All events happened at once.

When he was younger, he would spend hours staring into the mirror. He would start off with his own features, memorize every pore, follicle and vein. Count his blink rate. Shave his face, trim his sideburns with a small pair of scissors. Then, that done, he would begin to look beyond himself, let his eyes trail around his outline, pull focus on items with differing reflected depths behind his face. Look into the distance as far back as he could. If he stared long enough, he thought, another world might be glimpsed, a reversed world where everything was the opposite of his own; where pain was pleasure, love was hate.

Like in Leazes Park as a boy, trying to gain the trust of a squirrel he wanted to feed and tame, he had stood, all stony and statuesque, expression neutral and passive, waiting for the creature to approach him. The thrill he had felt on it coming close, how trusting it had been to the promise of food, he could have done anything to that squirrel. Caught it and kept it, poisoned it, ate it. Anything. He never forgot that stillness, the power that could be derived from it. Like an American Indian hunting, hiding in plain view. So still as to be invisible.

And the longer his unthreatening pose went on, the more likely it would be that the mirror-world inhabitants would reveal themselves. He longed for the day when they would invite him in, let him step through the mirror into that other world, live there for ever.

But that world had never existed. Or if it did, he had never found it. So instead he stared at himself.

His gaze flinched, his concentration faltered; he saw behind him the shadowed protrusions that grew from the walls behind him and around the bath and felt a sudden stab of loneliness. The protrusions were all over the house. Hard plastic, porcelain and metal. Depressing in their functionality. Prosaically clinical. Representations of capture rather than release.

A sadness swept over him. She was gone. And all he had left were those hard reminders. Reminders of what he had lost, what he was conducting his experiments for. His lower lip trembled, his eyes became moist and he felt himself starting to go again. He wouldn't. He couldn't. Not now. He needed strength. He ignored them, just stared at himself. Looked inside himself. Conquered his emotions.

He smiled.

The Historian had watched the news constantly, bought all the papers, local and national. Read them until he could almost recite them. They left him feeling both elated and angry. Elated because the world was witnessing his brilliance. Angry because it had been viewed with close-minded dullness. The police had clumped all over the graveyard, talked to the camera in reductive, prosaic terms about barbaric acts of savagery, witnesses, lines of enquiry and appeals for help. The journalists were no better, with their shock-horror headlines, mock-appalled faces and clichéd reporting. All missing the point. Ignoring what was to him obvious and beautiful. And important. Historically important. He felt like an artist whose masterpiece is misunderstood and ridiculed by those who could never hope to accomplish what he had. He should have expected that reaction, but he was still upset by it. Still, it was better than the last time. But then it should be. He had got better.

But there was the unexpected compensation. The arrest.

He couldn't believe his luck. The police weren't giving out any details, but he had assumed, from newspaper speculation, that it was the girl's boyfriend.

Michael Nell. He smiled at the irony. Then felt a sudden stab of fear.

Michael Nell. He could say something. Do something. Mention the studio, mention the models . . .

He breathed deeply, tried not to let his imagination run away from himself. Tried to be calm. Shrug the thoughts off.

What could Nell say? What could he tell them? Nothing. Nothing that would lead the police to him directly. Nothing that would make them take more of an interest in him. He would be ready for them. Have a story. Play the part. Let them go away with nothing.

Nothing.

Nothing. He repeated the word over and over, stretching out the sound, letting it soothe him. Give him succour.

Nothing.

There was no pressure on him. He could plan for the next one without looking over his shoulder all the time.

And there would be a next one. Because he wasn't finished yet. The voices in the shadows wouldn't allow him to be, for one thing. Plus his work wasn't completed; he hadn't found the answer he was seeking to that one all-important question.

And, if he was honest, he had enjoyed it so much he wanted to do it again. That was the thing that had surprised him. That an experiment, a scientific exploration, had given him such a thrill.

In fact, he had never been so excited in his life.

He stared at the mirror, ignored what was behind him, saw beyond it: let the phantasmagoria of the last few days dance once again before his eyes. Felt the familiar tingling in his groin. He had to relive that moment.

Her death must have been painful: she had thrown her body around, convulsed and pulled as much as her restraints allowed. Even when the knife was sliding in and out, bringing with it more and more blood, taking away more and more of her life, she hadn't given up. The blade thrusts, initially patient and measured, sometimes even playful little nips, had given way to hard, sharp hacks and slashes in his rush to bring on her final act, his need to see it.

And that, in itself, had been thrilling.

He had sensed it about to happen, felt that change come over her, and pulled out the knife for the final time. Climbed on to her and watched with intense fascination, like a Victorian botanist studying a rare species, cataloguing. Looking for signs of evolution.

His fingers twitched, but he kept them still, pressed at either side of her head, resisting the temptation to help her along. His heart hammered fit to burst with excitement.

As the end came, he had lowered himself down, pressed his face to hers. Ignored the last desperate attempts at escape, her body's automatic flight impulse going through the motions, and felt her ragged, gasping breath in his mouth. He had grabbed her shoulders, held her firm, his thighs pressing against her hips. Skin on skin, his body wet from hers. His erection straining, begging to be let loose on her. Although it was difficult, he had resisted. Because he was a professional. He had a job to do.

Reluctantly he had climbed off her, checked the camera was working, the power light staring unblinkingly at her, an impassive red eye capturing for ever her final moments.

Watching and shooting, he had yearned to press his lips

down on hers, feel the wet flesh strain against rough thread, try to catch the last of her life in his mouth, suck it out of her.

But he didn't give in to that impulse, strong though it was. Because this was work, this was science.

When her body gave its final sigh, the air sliding and stuttering out of her for the last time, the voices in the shadows screaming for her release, the sight had given him the most intense, spontaneous orgasm he had ever experienced.

He climbed on to her then and lay, spent. He wanted the moment to enfold him for ever, stay locked in the arms of that special embrace.

Nothing else mattered to him. The noise of the city above had slipped below his senses, like a radio in a distant room that he couldn't turn off. Usually it would irritate him, annoy him to anger, but no more. He was happy to let its empty-headed clatter continue. It wouldn't touch him, couldn't reach him. He had been as unmissed down here as he was invisible when above.

And in the shadows they had been moving, their voices whispering. Squatting in their usual place at the corner of his vision. Behind his posed figures, out of the beams of the lights. The Historian had felt them, smelled them. But he had ignored them. They couldn't reach him either.

And yet . . .

Her last sigh.

And yet . . .

The most intense orgasm of his life.

And yet . . .

The answers weren't there. Only a sense of anticlimax. An absence where there should have been a resolute truth. Even after poring over the photographs, scrutinizing the tapes.

Once the initial euphoria had worn off he had become

angry with himself. It should have happened. The answers should have been there. The knowledge. But he was still in the dark. Just like all the other times. And he had thought that one would have been different. He would have to try harder. Do it again. Choose carefully and get it right next time. His studies had led him this far, his skills had become two well developed to stop now.

He looked in the mirror, saw not his face but hers. Sewn up, ready to be received. Just before the life left her.

That familiar tingling in his groin was still there.

He thought again of those final few delicious seconds. Not of the lack of answers but of the physical act itself. The control over her body. The knife sliding in and out.

Her last sigh.

Heard echoes of the voices in the shadows. The souls. Telling him what they wanted next. Guiding him.

He had to plan.

And soon. Just in case Nell said anything.

But not just yet. That familiar tingling in his groin. Her face; sewn up, ready to be received.

He smiled. Closed his eyes. Not needing to view the tape to see it again.

8

The Café Roma was on the corner of Mosley Street and Dean Street, in the heart of Newcastle's City district. A converted bank, its high-ceilinged, marble-pillared halls had been architecturally rendered modern and spacious, retaining knowing nods to its past. It was bright and cool, all blond-wood furniture and dark leather sofas, shining chrome and spotlit glass cabinets. Pale yellow and cream walls. Two brown wooden fans moved lazily overhead, their actions purely decorative.

A single coffee shop with Starbucks empire aspirations, it serviced a steady Monday-morning stream of office workers calling in for their lattes and almond croissants to take away, shaking misty rainwater from their overcoats and umbrellas as they entered, while a few commuters sat reading papers, books and magazines, eking out their pastries, swirling foam in the bottom of their mugs and looking at their watches, counting down until their time became someone else's.

In the corner sat a man. Middle-aged and balding, with his remaining hair razored short to his scalp, his clothes almost a parody of the office workers streaming in and out. His tailored suit was bright blue, with a white stripe way too wide to be pin, his shirt a vibrant, almost reflective yellow, his tie purple and floral, his shoes dark but highly polished. He sat with his Filofax and diary open before him, totting up rows of figures, making notes, stopping occasionally to sip from a small glass cup of espresso, watch the steady stream of customers coming in and out and throw appraising stares at the Eastern European girls working behind the counter. There was nothing lascivious or gratuitous in his look; his eyes spoke only of profit and loss, of commodity and expenditure. He watched not people on their way to work, but money pouring into his till. His eyes held no humanity, no warmth. They were reductive adding machines.

They were the eyes of Marco Kovacs.

He looked alone. He wasn't. Sitting on the aisle opposite him and pretending to read the *Sun* was Christopher, his personal assistant. If there was any trouble, anyone giving him unwanted attention or approaching his table with aggression in mind, Christopher would be on to that person within seconds.

Kovacs watched one of the staff in particular. Anita was in her late teens, blonde and pretty. Her uniform T-shirt and tight jeans accentuated her trim figure and pert breasts. Her smile, when she used it, combined with her lively personality, could be devastating. So devastating, hardly anyone noticed the now-faint cut lines on her arms. Her Lithuanian-accented English lent her an exoticism; most customers thought she was Russian. She was a head-turner. Kovacs knew she ensured repeat trade to the café.

But that wasn't why he was looking at her.

He watched her. He totted up figures. He sipped coffee.

Decca Ainsley pulled the soft-top BMW 5 Series noisily to the kerb, ignoring the double yellows, Roll Deep pumping on the sound system. He cut the motor, silencing the music. Gave his shoulders a couple of rotations, took a deep breath. Checked his reflection in the rear-view mirror, smiled.

Diamond. That was how he thought of himself. Diamond. Hard and sharp-edged. Commanding respect and admiration. And the right kind of girl's best friend.

He got out of the car, looked around. Saw Marco Kovacs

waiting for him through the window. He shivered, like someone had just walked over his grave. Kovacs was the big time. The real deal. He composed himself again. Quickly. Had to. He had a boss to impress.

He straightened his jacket, thought: How would Pacino do this? De Niro? Or Clint? Above all, Clint. Just the name he drew strength from. Made him feel taller. Clint had been a better father than his real father. Taught him everything he knew. Kept the doubts suppressed, the fear in check.

So Clint would be with him, guide his hand, give him the words.

Gangster self in place, attitude worn heavier than jewellery or aftershave, he walked towards the door of the café.

Someone slid into the chair opposite Kovacs. A young man dressed in casual Bigg Market best: artfully distressed jeans and long-sleeved dark shirt, open at the neck. A leather jacket thrown over it. His hair was dark and styled into elaborate spikes. He was finely featured and could have been handsome or pretty, even, had not his nose been broken too many times. He walked with a swagger, the arrogance of the supposed winner, and looked like the kind of person who would double-park his sports car outside. He clicked his fingers, gestured to the counter for a coffee, slid off his large brown shades, offered a smile. Anita smiled, broke off from her customer to prepare it. Kovacs looked up at him, nodded.

Christopher shifted in his seat behind Decca, just reminding him he was there. Decca turned, gave a cautious nod. Decca still didn't know what to make of Christopher. With his cropped head, scarred face, nose broken and reset and his body stacked and hardened from more than just gym workouts, he could have been taken at first glance for a typical thug – hired, unthinking muscle. But closer inspection of his eyes would reveal a different story. They were the most dazzling blue; they spoke of real intelligence. They looked as if they held secrets. He wasn't known for saying much, not to Decca anyway, and Decca never knew how to talk to him, always felt uncomfortable with him. His heavily accented English when he did speak showed him to be Serbian, but Decca's poor knowledge of geography and general ignorance meant he could be from just about anywhere.

Decca turned his attention back to Kovacs, always aware that Christopher was behind him.

'Got your message, chief. What's up?' His wrist jewellery clanked on the table as he put his sunglasses and mobile down.

Kovacs said nothing. His eyes narrowed: his thoughts seemed to shift and reconfigure like sliding desert sands. Eventually he spoke.

'I've been watching her.'

The young man laughed. 'Don't blame you, boss. I'd like to do more than watch.'

Kovacs continued as if clarifying rudimentary facts to a simpleton. 'I've been watching her. And it's time for her to go.'

The young man looked momentarily confused, then grasped what was being said. 'What for? She's an asset to the business, yeah?'

Kovacs closed his Filofax, leaned forward. 'Think with your brain, not your dick, Derek. I know what you have been doing with her. Don't bother to lie to me. Don't pretend.'

Derek bristled. He hated anyone using his real name. He was Decca. And Kovacs' words, plus the knowledge behind them, made his face redden.

'You've been fucking her,' continued Kovacs. 'And that's OK.' He shrugged. 'We all do it. Who wouldn't? What they're there for.' He leaned forward. 'But she has a big mouth. Good if you want her to suck your cock, yes?' He made a harsh, grating sound, like mashed gears. A laugh. It stopped as quickly as it had started. His features darkened. 'Not so good if you want her to keep secrets you tell her. And I hear things. Know what I mean?'

Decca swallowed hard. His throat was suddenly dry, his body suddenly wet with sweat. His earlier swagger rapidly diminishing. He tried to speak. Couldn't.

'She tells people that one day you will take over from me. That everything I have is to be yours. One day. And that day will be sooner rather than later. Yes?'

Kovacs stared at Decca, unblinking. As emotion-filled as a snake curled around a tree. Decca felt his heart racing faster. Hoped it didn't show.

Kovacs waited. 'Well?'

Decca managed to swallow, find his voice. It sounded higher than usual. 'She's . . . I like her, boss. Maybe she's got the wrong idea.'

Kovacs said nothing. Decca began sweating. 'OK. Maybe I tried to, you know . . . impress her.' He shrugged, aiming for nonchalance, fear making it more like a spasm.

Kovacs nodded slowly. 'Impress her.' The words were lightly spoken. Too lightly. 'Impress her.'

Decca nodded.

'She,' said Kovacs, stretching out the words so he wouldn't be misunderstood, 'is a whore. Nothing more, nothing less. And whores are for using. Not trying to impress.' He shook his head.

'I'm sorry, boss.' Decca said the words to the table.

Kovacs nodded. 'She is nothing. And she is telling everyone she is something. And she is making me look a fool. Do you think I am a fool, Derek?'

Decca shook his head. Hard. 'No, boss.'

'She is a whore. And a whore with ideas above her station is a liability. Nothing more, nothing less. Get rid of her.'

'Please, boss, let me talk to her. I'll get her to shut up, OK? Please, boss. Trust me.'

A glaze of ice froze over Kovacs' eyes. 'Trust. *You?*'

He needed to say no more. The two words carried more implicit threat than any number of descriptions of intended torture. Decca swallowed hard. Dropped his eyes.

'I'm sorry, boss,' he mumbled.

Kovacs almost smiled. 'You are a good worker, Derek. You have potential. I let you run this café and you do a good job for me. So I give you a chance. But you must decide who it is you want to impress. Some whore? Or me?'

Decca thought. Decca nodded.

Kovacs sat back. 'Good.'

Decca sighed. He looked as if he had been physically beaten up.

Anita chose that moment to approach the table bearing Decca's coffee. She gave both men a radiant smile, lingering longer for Decca.

'There you are.'

'Thanks, Anita.' She turned and began walking back towards the counter. Decca was aware of Kovacs watching him. Felt his eyes boring into him like two diamond drills. 'Anita?'

She turned.

Decca took a deep breath, sighed. 'I'd like to see you later. When it's quiet.'

She smiled. 'OK.'

'OK.' Decca nodded.

Anita turned and went back to work.

'Good,' said Kovacs. 'And I never want to hear another of your whores saying the same thing. Do we understand each other?'

'Yes, boss.'

'Good.' Kovacs leaned forward, opened his Filofax. 'Make sure you wait until the rush dies down and you have someone to replace her. I don't want to lose money.'

He nodded. 'What . . . what should I do with her?'

'What you like. Sell her to Lenny or Noddy. Put her in one of the houses. Make money from her.' Kovacs smiled. It was as cold as Antarctica. 'Or you could put her into my efficient disposal scheme.'

Decca flinched. Hoped Kovacs didn't see it. He had heard rumours of such a scheme but not much more. Only enough to know that he wanted nothing to do with it. 'No, no. That's OK. I'll deal with her.'

'Good.' Kovacs' face was stone again. 'I never want to see her again. Understand?'

'Yes, boss. I understand.'

'Then go to work.' Kovacs put his face back in his book of figures. 'And tell her to get me another coffee. This one's cold.'

Decca picked up his mobile and sunglasses, stood up. Kovacs kept looking at him. Decca tried to walk away, Kovacs called him.

'Derek?'

He turned.

'She was right. All this could be yours.'

Decca looked at him with a kind of joy rising in his heart. He didn't know what to say.

'Yes,' said Kovacs, 'it could all be yours. All you have to do is take it away from me.'

Decca felt himself reddening. He hurriedly made his way to the counter and from there to the door of his office.

Kovacs allowed himself a small, thin smile. He looked at Christopher, who returned it. Then Kovacs continued working, oblivious to all around him.

His mobile rang. Grumbling, he picked it up. Listened. Once more his eyes narrowed.

'Good,' he said. 'Good.'

He listened, thought.

'Yes, I heard. Lenny's arm is broken. Maybe. But leave it for now. This is more important.' He listened again. 'No . . . do nothing. Yet.' Kovacs looked at Decca's car parked outside, back to Christopher. 'I will put someone on to it. Find out if she was important. In the meantime do nothing. Everything goes ahead as planned.'

He hung up, sat back.

The morning rush hour was beginning to die down. Behind the counter, Anita caught his eye, smiled at him. Showed him she was making his coffee.

Kovacs didn't smile back.

9

DI Diane Nattrass sat back in her chair, kept her face impassive. On the other side of the table sat Michael Nell and his solicitor, Janine Stewart. Provided by his father. Gathering information and saying nothing: waiting for the right moment to speak. DS Paul Turnbull was talking.

'So, Michael. Ashley's dead. And we've seen your photos. Anything to add?'

Nell said nothing, stared at the desk.

'What was it, eh? A game that got out of hand?' His voice sounded calm but was threaded with dangerous undercurrents. 'You liked it rough, that it?'

Nell shrugged. Stared. Nothing but contempt and hatred in his eyes.

'For the tape, please,' said Turnbull. 'Was that gesture a yes or a no?'

Nell shrugged again. 'Yeah.'

Turnbull sat back, folded his arms, looked at Nell. The young man was sweating, terrified, but determined not to show it. Turnbull wanted to rub his eyes. He and Nattrass were tired, they stank of sweat and caffeine. He wanted to go home. Open a couple of cans. Have a bath. Sleep.

But not yet.

'Thank you.'

'He's cracking, looking confused. Trying to hide it. Go at him again, on the rough-up angle.' The voice in Turnbull's ear that of DS Shaw, the Interview Adviser from the Crime Management Team. Shaw would watch through the two-way mirrored glass, be in radio contact with Turnbull and Nattrass. They had agreed their strategy beforehand. Give him the minimum amount of information. Get him to commit himself.

'So you and Ashley, you were having a bit of a session, that it? Both like it rough? Nothing wrong with that.' He continued, his voice taking on a matey tone. 'You like violence, Mick? Am I right? Think it's – what did you call it? – transgressive?'

'Yeah.'

'Right.' Turnbull nodded, pretended to be thinking. 'Like the photos you took. They were good. Well framed. Good composition.'

Nell rolled his eyes. 'Thanks.'

'No problem. Don't know that the women in them were that pleased. Looked in pain to me.'

'They were models. Just prostitutes I picked up. They were paid to do that. To look like that.' A note of desperation was creeping into Nell's voice. Turnbull pounced on it.

'Were they? Did you ever photograph Ashley like that? Did you get her to pose for you?'

'No.'

'Did you try to? Did you want to?'

Nell was breathing heavily, nostrils flaring.

'Did you?'

Nell looked towards Janine Stewart, who opened her mouth. 'This isn't necessary.'

'Answer the question, please, Mr Nell.' Nattrass kept her eyes on Nell, unblinking, ignoring Stewart.

Nell gave a curt shake of his head.

'For the tape, Mr Nell is shaking his head,' said Turnbull. He unfolded his arms, his stare hardening. 'You like a bit of violence, eh, Michael? Specially against women, yeah?'

'Not especially. Just in general.'

'So let's see if I'm right. You went to that club. In Amsterdam. I don't know, maybe others. But it turned you on. Something in you . . . responded. Yeah?'

Nell said nothing. Turnbull continued.

'So you came back over here, on fire. Wanting to try everything you'd seen. So you had a word with Ashley. And she wasn't up for it, was she?'

Nell flinched.

'She didn't want anything to do with your plans. So you got some models.'

Turnbull produced several plastic wallets, each containing one of Nell's photographs. He spread them out on the table in front of Nell. Women, half-undressed, their faces and bodies battered and bruised. The nasty end of bondage. Turnbull flashed on the photo of Ashley he carried, lifting her drink, smiling.

'For the tape,' said Nattrass, 'DS Turnbull is showing Mr Nell photographs.'

'These are yours, yes?'

'Yeah,' said Nell.

'And they're models.'

'Yeah.'

Turnbull leaned forward, elbows on the edge of the photos. 'But you get bored with models, don't you? You have to pay them? Find ones who are willing, then pay them? I'm guessing the more you want to do to them, the more you have to pay, is that right?'

Nell said nothing.

'Is that right?'

'Yeah.' Nell's voice was shrinking.

'Booking a studio. Doing it properly. All costs money, doesn't it?'

Nell blinked, said nothing.

'So you thought you'd try something nearer to home. Someone you didn't have to pay.' Turnbull sat back. Folded his arms. 'And there she is. Ashley.'

A flicker of defiance passed through Nell's eyes, a sneer played at the corners of his lips. Turnbull noticed it, fed on it, pushed ahead.

'But she wasn't up for it, was she? Didn't like the rough stuff. And that made you angry. So whether she liked it or not, she was going to get some. Maybe you didn't mean to at first. Just a couple of slaps, soften her up. But you went too far, didn't you? Eh? Didn't you?'

Anger and fear had hardened Nell's arrogant carapace. 'I didn't do it.' He was trying to remain stolid, but a frail tone had entered Nell's voice.

Turnbull sighed, stared at him. 'So you didn't. So you say. Well, let's assume that you've admitted it. Let's look at it further down the line. When you get inside, Mick, when you're doin' life for this, they won't think you're bein' transgressive. The other cons.' Turnbull leaned forward, warming to his theme. 'No, they'll think you're a coward. Because you pick on women. In fact, you'll probably have to go on the VP wing. Know what that stands for? No? Vulnerable prisoners. The nonces. The rapists. The ones too scared to pick on other men. Only women. Or children. And they'll be your best friends. For the next twenty years. Plenty of time to tell them about bein' transgressive.'

Nell's lower lip began to waver. Tears formed at the corners of his eyes. Turnbull leaned further forward, his voice even smaller.

'Want to tell me about it, Mick? Eh? Make it easier. See what we can sort out for you.'

Nell opened his mouth, his lips twisting as he tried to form the words. Turnbull stared at him, unblinking. Next to him Nattrass sat likewise.

'I . . .' Nell steepled his fingers, twisted them together into the shape of a spired church. Tore it down again. 'I didn't do it . . .'

He began to sob.

'I didn't . . .'

Turnbull sat back, sighed. Looked at Nattrass. She gave a quick nod to Turnbull, the resignation obvious. Turnbull returned the nod.

'Interview suspended at sixteen hundred hours,' Nattrass said and stood.

Michael Nell kept his eyes on the table, didn't look up.

'You've got nothing . . . You've got to let me go.' He sighed between sobs. 'I didn't do it . . .'

'Just sit tight,' said Turnbull, joining Nattrass in rising. 'We'll be back soon.'

'Can I have a word outside?'

Nattrass and Turnbull turned. Janine Stewart had stood up also and was hastily stuffing papers into her briefcase.

'In a minute,' said Nattrass. 'I think you should have a word with your client first.' She turned and left.

The corridor smelled of cleaning solutions, stale air, the faint whiff of fried food from the canteen. The usual corridor smells of an institutional building. Compared with the tense, sweaty and fear-choked atmosphere in the interview room it was positively a lush glade in springtime.

DS Shaw came to join them. Small, intense. His wire-framed glasses catching the light. 'Good work,' he said.

'I nearly had him,' said Turnbull, holding up his thumb and forefinger. 'I was that close.'

'He's a tough one,' said Shaw.

Nattrass yawned.

'Know how you feel,' said Turnbull. 'Eighteen hours we've been on this now.'

'Then time for a rest.'

All three turned. They hadn't heard DCI Bob Fenton approach.

'I was listening,' Fenton said. 'Good work. But he won't crack.' He looked at his watch. 'Look, it's nearly half-four. Why don't you two knock off now, get some rest?'

'What about Nell?' asked Nattrass.

'I'm sure a night in the cells will do him a power of good,' Fenton said. 'You can have another crack at him tomorrow. See if we can get a confession before his twenty-four hours are up.'

The interview room door opened. Out stepped Janine Stewart. When Nell had made his phone call earlier, one of Newcastle's most high-profile and well-respected criminal solicitors had arrived. Nattrass and Turnbull had dealt with her before and they had both respected her. The respect was mutual. But they also had their jobs to do.

Turnbull unconsciously straightened his tie. Nattrass suppressed a smile. Janine Stewart, with her expensive accent, her Bristol university law degree and her unshowy way with designer labels, was way out of Paul Turnbull's league. But it was fun to watch him try.

'Ah, Janine,' said Fenton. 'Good. Just to let you know, your client won't be called on any more today. But we're holding him overnight.'

'I see. On what grounds?'

'Circumstantial evidence. We'll be applying for a search warrant. That should take place overnight.'

'I strongly object.'

'I'm sure you do. But that's that.' Fenton turned to Turnbull and Nattrass. 'If you'd like to go and break the good news?'

He pointed to the interview room. Nattrass, Turnbull and Stewart trooped back inside.

Diane Nattrass entered first, sat down opposite Mick

Nell. Paul Turnbull and Janine Stewart resumed their previous positions. Nell looked up.

'So that's it, then?' he said to Stewart. 'You've waved your wand, made your deal. I can go, yeah?'

'Not exactly,' replied Stewart, her voice demonstrating that what was about to follow wasn't her idea.

Nell looked around, fear rising in his eyes again. 'What . . . ?'

'We're holding you for another twenty-four hours,' said Nattrass, looking straight at him, 'during which time you'll be kept overnight here in the cells and we'll be applying for a search warrant and going through your flat.'

Nell stared at her. His mouth fell open.

'You can't do that.' He looked at Stewart, imploring her to do something. 'Tell them they can't do that.'

'I'm afraid they can, Michael.'

'Whose fucking side are you on?' Nell looked between the three of them. All previous poise and attitude now disappearing from his body like air from a party balloon. 'No . . .'

'Unless there's anything you'd like to tell us?' said Turnbull.

Nell shook his head, eyes downcast. 'Can't tell you anything, can I? I didn't do it.' He looked at Stewart, almost wailing like a lost child. 'Tell them I didn't do it . . .'

It seemed like a snake had wormed its way inside Nell's body. Try as he might, no matter how much he shifted, he couldn't seem to get rid of it.

Paul Turnbull watched the young man squirm and tried, unsuccessfully, to suppress a smile. He wasn't touched by his pleas. It wasn't a victory, but that would be only a matter of time. He would forestall the celebrations until then.

★

Michael Nell sat in the cell, darkness and shadows all around him.

He stared up at the window. Nothing but night and reflected streetlighting came through the glass bricks, the overhead cell lighting having been turned off. He checked his watch. Two hours ago.

Two hours. Time was dragging slower than an old cart with a broken wheel.

He sat hunched on the hard unyielding bed, pulled his legs into his body, rested his chin on his knees. Sighed.

He had tried to tough it out, shouting at the door after the uniformed officer had slammed it behind him, telling him what was going to happen when he got out, what his father would do, what he himself would do. Other inhabitants along the row, voices blurred with alcohol and implied violence, had informed him what they would do to him if he didn't shut up. That had soon quietened him down. He had paced the cell, read the graffiti on the walls, wondered who the writers were and where they were now, and, gradually, calmed down.

As the day had darkened, so had his spirits. When it finally turned to night, his thoughts and emotions became correspondingly blacker. And when the lights were eventually extinguished, he had begun to feel colder and lonelier than he had ever felt.

The tears had come then, self-pityingly squeezed from the corners of his eyes and down his cheeks, his body racked with sobs. Alone. No bravado, no longer able to hide behind the wall of sophisticated outsiderdom he had cultivated for himself. This wasn't getting locked up for a few hours for being drunk and disorderly. This wasn't being pepper-sprayed for giving a copper lip, stumbling out of a club in the early hours of a Saturday morning. This was serious. This, unless something happened quickly, could mean life.

Innocence had nothing to do with it. Those coppers had it in for him. And if they wanted to, they would get him.

He knew that.

He remembered his father's words the last time he had been in trouble:

'You're on your own next time, boy. I've had enough. About time you stood on your own two feet. Made something of yourself. You do this again, you get yourself out of it. See how you like it then.'

There then followed the usual list of Michael's shortcomings and failures. Michael had sat, around the dining table, listening, not daring to speak, knowing that age hadn't diminished his father's vicious right hand.

He had taken the latest character assassination, nodded, and kept on eating. All the while ignoring his stepmother's half-smile at his discomfort. His stepmother. How could he call her that? His father's vacuous, blonde, trophy second wife. Her real title.

But he had said nothing. Just sat there. Waiting for the handout that came at the end of the meal; the latest guilt offering from his father. Given, and taken, with extreme embarrassment.

And now here he was again. And this time he was really alone.

Mick Nell sat in the cell, darkness and shadows all around him. And cried.

Not for Ashley. For himself.

A clanging sound following by a heaving one. The cell door opened. Michael Nell opened his eyes. He jumped up when he saw who it was.

Janine Stewart, being led in by a uniformed officer.

He got up off his bunk, crossed the floor to her.

'Is that it?' he said, hope rising desperately within. 'Can I go now?'

Stewart gave him an understanding smile. 'Not yet, I'm afraid.'

Hope was extinguished within him, quicker than a candle in a force-nine gale. He physically slumped as if he had been hit.

'This is a legal visit,' she said. 'We're going to talk.'

Nell sighed, said nothing. Then: 'I've said enough.'

'Michael, look at me.' She placed her hand on his chin, turned his face to look at her. Her eyes were hard, businesslike. 'You've messed the police around, messed your father around and now you're messing me around.' She spoke as if he was a naughty child needing admonishment. 'And this won't do.'

Nell said nothing.

'Right now they're arranging for a special magistrates' court hearing for tomorrow morning. I'll apply for bail, but it's going to be turned down. After that you'll be remanded in custody while the police tear your flat and your life apart. Now if you want me to get you out of this place you have to cooperate. You have to talk. Got that?'

She waited. Nell eventually nodded.

'Good. Now this gentleman is going to close the door and leave me alone with you in here. And when I'm ready I'll knock on the door to be let out. How long I spend in here depends on you. And what you tell me. If you're not cooperating, I'm knocking on that door. Are we clear?'

Nell nodded again.

'Very well.' She nodded at the uniform, who turned and left the cell, closing the door behind him. 'Right, Michael. Start talking. And don't fuck me around.'

Nell blinked, startled to hear her swear. She returned his gaze, unblinking.

He started to talk.

10

Joe Donovan sat back in the chair, tried to look relaxed, knowledgeable, in command. With his brown-leather jacket creaking and squeaking against the leather upholstery every time he moved, it was difficult.

Janine Stewart sat behind her desk in a large glass-walled cubicle of an office in her law firm. The office, and the whole floor of the building belonging to the firm, was bright and airy, the design minimalist and geometric, corners of desks and shelves sharp enough to draw blood. Walking through, Donovan felt that the firm exuded simplicity and confidence. And money. He looked around the office. No family pictures, nothing of sentimental value. Just a few law books on the shelves, and even these seemed to have been chosen for their colour coordination rather than their relevance. The computer on the desk, like the desk itself, was slim and efficient. Like Janine Stewart, too, thought Donovan.

Stewart was reading an open file on her desk, aware that Donovan was waiting. Her blouse light turquoise, artfully crumpled and ruched silk, her skirt and jacket crushed, iridescent dark satin, she looked every inch the poster girl for the legal profession.

He knew of her by reputation. Ambitious, hard-working and quite brilliant at her job. On her way to becoming a big hitter. Out of deference, he hadn't worn his Green Lantern T-shirt.

She looked up, smiled. It was meant to contain warmth

and friendliness to dazzle the recipient, but Donovan had dealt with solicitors before. It held all the long-lasting promise of a pre-performance lapdancer asking for money.

Not to seem impolite, Donovan returned the smile.

'Sorry about that,' she said. 'Just checking where we are.' She gave him her full attention, turning up the wattage of her electric-blue eyes.

Contacts, thought Donovan. Got to be.

'What has Francis Sharkey told you?' she said. 'Has he brought you up to speed?'

'Not really,' said Donovan. 'I just got a phone call from him last night telling me I had an appointment with you today. Here I am. Bright-eyed and bushy-tailed.'

Sharkey had also told Donovan that there would be big money involved, but that was something he could only mention later. Donovan had argued that he didn't want to go; he had no time. Katya had spent her second night at his house, the case involving her not moving fast enough. Donovan also wanted professional help for the woman. Counselling, health checks. Nothing had been forthcoming as yet. But, as Sharkey had reminded him, he wasn't in a position to turn down work.

'I understand you're an—' Stewart referred to her notes '—an information broker.'

Donovan nodded.

'What does that mean, exactly?'

'I find things out. Either as part of a team or as an individual.'

Stewart nodded. 'I see. Like a private detective.'

'Not exactly,' said Donovan.

'What's the difference?'

'That conjures up images of fat, greasy, corrupt ex-coppers with heart conditions turning blind eyes to villains to pay off their CSA debts or their ex-wives.'

A look of amusement crossed Stewart's face. 'Really?'

'That's the British type.'

'Are there any others?'

'The American one. The private eye.'

'And what's that?'

'An unworkable stereotype in this country.'

'I see.' She gave a small laugh.

'So I'm an information broker.'

'Good.' Stewart leaned forward in her seat. 'Well, my usual . . . information broker, private detective, call him what you will, is indisposed at the moment.'

'Can I ask why?'

She hesitated, as if not wanting to divulge the information. The amused look played across her features once more. She carried on. 'A little problem with perjury. Not one of my cases, thankfully.'

'Must have been CSA and an ex-wife,' said Donovan, smiling wryly.

'Quite. Which brings us to you. You come very highly recommended. Impeccable references.'

Donovan nodded. 'By Sharkey,' he said.

'Yes.'

'By the way,' said Donovan, 'how d'you know Francis Sharkey? I didn't think he had many contacts up here.'

'Francis,' she said, her face taking on an expression Donovan couldn't read, 'is – shall we say? – very well connected. Especially if there's money involved. And even though he's no longer a practising solicitor in the legal sense, it's still his world. His milieu, you might say.'

You might, thought Donovan; I wouldn't bother.

'I see,' he said.

Stewart sat back in her chair. Donovan noticed that her breasts were straining against the silk material of her blouse. Donovan thought he might have been expected to notice.

'Let me tell you about this job I have in mind. See what you think.' Her eyes roved over him, taking in his leather jacket, Levi's, skate trainers. His hair longish, slightly greying, his stubble growing in likewise. Her assessment stopped at his shirt, black and unbuttoned, and his T-shirt underneath. It wasn't Green Lantern. It was the Clash: London Calling.

'Let me tell you about it, then,' she said again. 'See if you're the right man for it.'

Donovan sat back, tried to get comfortable. The leather let out sustained squeaks. Stewart affected to ignore the noise.

'Ashley Malcolm's body was found two nights ago in the old cemetery on Westgate Road.'

She paused, waiting. Donovan could have said that he knew Diane Nattrass, the detective investigating. But he, too, said nothing, waited for her to continue.

'A man has been charged. Her boyfriend, Michael Nell. They're trying to build a case against him now. They've kept him overnight and extended it to thirty-six hours. If they don't find anything then, they have to either apply to a court for an extension or let him go. Obviously I'm hoping for and working towards the latter. There's a lot of pressure on the police to make this stick. A lot. Michael Nell is my client. I think it prudent to build a counter-case. In the interests of . . . fair-mindedness, shall we say?'

Donovan frowned. 'Doesn't that usually happen nearer the trial date? Part of putting together a defence?'

Stewart sketched a smile. 'Michael Nell has not been the most . . . cooperative of clients, shall we say? And he comes from a rich family. His father is a very influential man.' Stewart toyed absently with her fountain pen. Donovan tried not to find it erotic. 'There could be a circus aspect to any trial. We think it best to get everything sorted out as quickly as possible. Forewarned is forearmed, as they say.'

Donovan nodded.

'We wouldn't want there to be any misunderstanding. At a later date.' She stroked the shaft of the pen. 'Any mistake.'

'Right.'

They looked at each other.

'So,' Donovan said eventually, 'what d'you want me to do?'

Stewart put the pen down. Picked up several sheets of paper from a file on her desk. Handed them across to him.

'This is Michael Nell's statement. It says where he was on the night of Ashley Malcolm's disappearance. And the night her body was discovered. This is his alibi.'

Donovan glanced at the paper, picked out a couple of words.

'If it can be proved,' he said.

'I'm sure it can.'

'Won't the police be doing this?'

She smiled. It contained many things, but no warmth. 'I'm sure they will. Such a high-grade case. They'll want to get their man.'

She slid a brown envelope across the table.

'What's this?'

'Also his alibi. Photographs. You don't need look at them now. It's all self-explanatory.'

Donovan put the paper and envelope on his lap, looked at her. 'So why d'you want me for this?'

Stewart sat back. Returned the look. 'I've checked you out, Mr Donovan. You used to be quite a brilliant investigative journalist, from all accounts. Incisive, courageous. Award-winning. Then there was that unfortunate incident with your son. I was sorry to hear about that.'

Donovan shrugged. 'Not your fault.'

'Nevertheless, it's not something one would want to happen to them. It must have been difficult.'

Donovan said nothing, his face impassive. Unblinking. She picked up the pen again. Not erotically; more to give her fingers something to do. When she spoke again it was with a slight hesitation.

'Francis tells me . . . you've rebuilt your life. That the company you've got now has great potential. He says you're the best at what you do.'

'What can I say?'

'I don't know. Is there any reason why he would lie to me?'

'I take it if I work for you he gets a cut out of this?'

She nodded. 'A small one.'

Donovan sat back, smiled. 'There's your reason.'

Stewart scrutinized him. Smiled in return, eventually. 'I like you, Mr Donovan. And if you would like this job, it's yours. Would you like this job?'

'You do know I have a job already? Something my team and I are working on?'

'Yes, I do. But I've been assured that it's something long term. This would be a much shorter-term job. There would be no conflict of interest that I could see.'

Donovan nodded. 'OK. I'll take it.'

'Good.' She put the pen down. 'Any questions?'

'Yeah,' said Donovan, leaning forward. 'A few. Technical ones. Who I report to, when, that sort of thing.'

'Nothing major, then. Anything else?'

He shook his head.

'Good. Then let's talk money.'

Donovan smiled. This was the part he had been looking forward to.

11

'So, in summing up, what have we got?'

The Prof looked at his whiteboard, underlined words he had written earlier in magic marker as he spoke.

'Social withdrawal. Antisocial behaviour. Inability to take criticism.' He smiled. 'That could be you, Jack Carson.'

A polite ripple of laughter went around the class. Jack Carson gave a look of mock aggrievement. The Prof continued.

'Hypochondria. Or other attention-seeking behaviour. Such as wearing outlandish or strange clothes.'

'That's you, then,' shouted Jack Carson.

Another ripple of laughter. The Prof pulled proudly on his lapels. 'You must learn to recognize style when you see it, Mr Carson. Right.' Then back to the whiteboard and the underlining. 'An abnormal relationship with the mother. A delusional mind. A general feeling of emptiness. No faith in the future . . .'

He talked on. Peta was making notes, although she knew most of what he was talking about. Years of police-force training courses had ensured that. But it was still interesting.

The deviant psychopathology of the serial killer. The title of the lecture.

The students were hungry for it. Lapping it up.

A student dead. Her boyfriend in custody. The university awash with media. Students finding an academic method of excusing the hunt for prurient detail. Staff too. This lecture had already been chosen before those events happened.

'Of course,' the Prof was saying, 'these are just general points. You could still have the majority of these things and not be a serial killer.'

'What would you be, then?' a student called out.

The Prof gave a small, sad smile. 'Just a very unhappy person.'

Another ripple of polite laughter.

The Prof put the marker down. 'Anyway, you all know where to go for further reading. I would suggest Ressler, as you know. Canter and Apsche are good too. I'll leave it to you to find them. You'll know where. Just play detective.'

He looked at his watch.

'Well,' he said, looking around the seminar room, 'I believe it's that time again. Thank you for your attention. I'll see you again on Thursday.'

Chairs were scraped, coats put on, books replaced in bags, lunch arrangements made.

'Remember,' said the Prof over the din, 'essay. Profiling a deviant mind through geographical psychology. A week today. Thank you.'

He turned, began putting his books back into his antique briefcase.

Peta watched him. She still couldn't make him out. He was so unlike all the other lecturers and tutors in the university. They seemed to fall into three categories: those whose job it was to teach and took it professionally, those who had the answers and imparted that knowledge in as overbearing and stentorian a manner as possible, and those who behaved as if they were still students themselves, keeping up with the latest trends in fashion and music, their receding hairlines and bigger beer bellies giving them away. The Prof was none of these. And while Peta liked him, or thought she did, she just couldn't make him out.

Perhaps it was her policewoman's training, she thought.

To treat people only as types. Compartmentalize. Pigeon-hole. Saved time in the long run. She could hear her old boss telling her that. She shook her head. That was what she was trying to get away from.

'You coming to the refectory?'

Peta looked up. She hadn't noticed Jill next to her. She checked her watch.

'You not meeting Ben?'

Jill made a face. 'Uh, no. Me an' Ben are over. Footloose again. So, you comin'?'

'Sorry, Jill. Got to meet someone for lunch.'

Jill gave a teasing smile. 'Oh, yeah? Handsome?'

'Hadn't really thought about it, Jill. He's just a friend. Someone I . . . someone I've worked with before.'

'Really?' Jill's eyes opened wide. 'Then why are you blushing?'

'I'm not,' said Peta. Her face felt hot. She must have been imagining it. 'He's just a friend. That's all.'

'Yeah, right,' she said. 'Well, suit yourself. See you later.' She began to walk off, turned. 'Hey, give him one for me, will you?'

Peta laughed, shook her head. Kept packing.

'Did you enjoy that?'

Peta looked up, startled. The Prof was standing right next to her, dressed in his overcoat and hat, antique paisley-patterned silk scarf around his neck. She hadn't heard him approach.

'What?'

'The seminar. Did you enjoy it?'

'I did. Yes. Very much.'

The Prof smiled, nodded, almost to himself. He sat on the edge of the desk next to her, his face ruminative. 'You used to be in the police force, am I correct?'

'You are,' she said. 'I was.'

'Suppose you find all this a bit . . . boring, then. Going over old ground.'

'Not at all,' she said. 'It's fascinating. Just what I wanted from this course.'

The Prof smiled, his eyes crinkling at the sides. It wasn't, she thought, unattractive.

He moved his hands on the desk. She looked at the damaged one, the scars no longer livid, but unmistakably there. He sensed her looking, pulled it back. She looked away, busied herself with her bag.

'I've been involved in a couple of investigations,' he said, his voice almost distant.

'Really?' she said. 'As a consultant psychologist? An expert witness?'

He smiled. 'Not really. More . . . in a journalistic capacity. The police were involved eventually. Naturally I gave as much help and support as I could. They were very good to me.' His hand twitched involuntarily. He pulled it completely away. 'Very positive experience of working with them, all things told.'

'I'm pleased.' Peta had her bag over her shoulder, was ready to walk out of the class. 'Well, I'll . . .' she said, gesturing to the door. The Prof made no attempt to move.

'I'm glad you're enjoying it,' he said again, 'the course. I was worried. About you benefiting. Fitting in. Because you're . . . I don't mean this in a disparaging way, but, older. Mature.'

Peta smiled. 'It's not disparaging. It's true. I'm officially a mature student. And very happy about it. And I'm enjoying the course.'

'Good, good.' The Prof still made no effort to move.

Peta stood there too.

'Listen,' the Prof said. It sounded as if, for once, he was

having difficulty with his words. Peta waited. 'I don't suppose you'd be interested . . . ?'

Peta said nothing. The Prof, haltingly, continued.

'Wilco.' Peta's face must have been blank. 'The American band. Jeff Tweedy. Alt country. Very good. Strong songs. They're playing the uni. The other uni. Monday night. I was wondering . . . I've got two tickets . . . I was . . .' He faded out.

Peta didn't know what to say. He looked up at her. Briefly. His eyes jumped to hers, then flitted away.

'Monday?' she said. 'Next Monday? I don't know. Honestly. I . . . work as well. As well as coming here. I don't know if I . . . I'm free on Monday.'

'OK.' The Prof nodded to himself, got up off the desk. 'OK.' His head was down, eyes on the floor.

Peta felt her face redden again. Definitely this time. 'No, seriously, I . . . it would be nice. I've just . . . work. I've got to work.'

'OK.'

The Prof was picking up his briefcase, making his way to the door. Eyes anywhere but on her.

'Maybe . . . maybe another time,' said Peta, a note of desperation in her voice. 'A drink, or something . . .'

But the Prof was gone, out of the door and away.

Peta sighed. Shook her head. She felt bad letting him down. She liked him. She just couldn't figure him out.

'And now I never will,' she said aloud.

She looked at her watch. She was going to be late for meeting Joe Donovan.

Thoughts of the Prof cast aside, she hurried out of the door.

'So tell me again,' Peta said through a mouthful of panini. Her next words were lost as she sprayed breadcrumbs and chicken over the table.

Donovan ducked, then gave her a pitying look, shaking his head. 'Hello, Mum, this is Peta. No, she can't help it. Congenital. Should see her eat pasta.'

'Piss off,' she said, laughing.

Amar just shook his head, gave a theatrical sigh. 'Children, please.'

Peta ignored him, swallowed, took a gulp of sparkling water. 'I said, tell me again. From the beginning.'

Donovan looked around. Pani's was doing its usual brisk lunchtime trade in Italian deli sandwiches, the stripped wooden floors and rough plaster walls echoing with the sounds of business conversation, clinking cutlery and hurrying, black-clad serving staff who barely had time to show off their perfect, gym-honed bodies and cod-Italian accents.

It was fast becoming one of Donovan's favourite haunts. Especially for meetings. Of the tax-deductible variety.

'Sharkey phoned last night,' he said, taking a swig from his bottle of beer. 'Told me I had a meeting today with Janine Stewart.'

Peta frowned.

'Solicitor in charge of the defence for the kid accused of Ashley Malcolm's murder.'

'Why did she want to see you?'

Donovan smiled. 'You mean apart from my natural good looks and charming personality?'

'Obviously,' said Amar, yawning loudly.

Donovan looked at him. He looked tired, drawn, his eyes red-rimmed.

'Keeping you up?' Donovan asked.

'Working late last night,' said Amar. 'Private contract. Didn't get much sleep.'

The atmosphere at the table changed, became darker.

'Private contract. Thought you'd given them up?' said Donovan, a genuine note of concern in his voice.

'I didn't say I was giving them up,' Amar said, defensiveness creeping into his voice. 'I said I was just . . . slowing down. Being more selective.' He sniffed, shook his head sharply. 'And I am.'

The other two looked at him.

'I can handle it, OK?' His voice was louder than he had intended. Several nearby diners looked over. When he spoke again he was much quieter. 'I can handle it. Now tell me what happened.'

Donovan and Peta exchanged glances. It was clear that Donovan was going to talk more, give him a lecture even, but Peta shook her head. Not the time or the place. Donovan let it go and, in a much heavier manner than he would have done a few minutes previously, told them of his meeting with Janine Stewart.

He finished, sat back.

'Another contract,' said Peta. 'Good old Sharkey.'

'Sod him,' said Donovan.

'So what's his alibi, then?' asked Peta.

'Prostitutes,' said Donovan. 'The rougher the better, from what his statement says.'

'Him to them or them to him?' asked Peta.

'Him to them, apparently. Liked to take photos too.' He patted his jacket pocket. 'Got them here if you want a look.'

'Lovely,' said Peta.

Donovan shook his head. 'Right little charmer, this one is. But he says he didn't kill Ashley Malcolm and that's what we're being paid to prove.'

Peta smiled. 'We need a strategy.'

'Any ideas?'

Donovan looked at Amar. His eyes were closed. 'Look, Amar, go home and get some sleep.'

Amar opened his eyes, jumped slightly at the sound of his name being said. 'No. 'M all right.'

Donovan looked at Peta. Her face was filled with concern. 'Go home, Amar,' he said. 'You're no use to me or Albion in this state.'

Amar looked sullen, withdrawn. His face was reddening, his eyes igniting. Donovan and Peta didn't know what he was going to do next. Amar looked between the pair of them. Sighed.

'OK.' He stood up. ''M going. Just tired, that's all.'

He grabbed his parka from the chair back, walked to the door and through it, never once looking back. At the table, Peta sighed and shook her head. Donovan looked at her, frowned.

'What's going on?'

Peta took a while before speaking. 'He promised me he'd given up his nocturnal adventures. He hasn't. That rich pervert he knows pestered him into making his private gay porn films for him again.'

'And he's said yes.'

Peta nodded.

'Is he looking after himself?'

Peta looked him in the eyes. 'Does it look like it to you?'

'So he's back on the charlie?'

'And other stuff too, probably.' She sighed, ran her fingers through her long blonde hair. 'You know him. He can't just be behind the camera. He has to join in. With everything.'

Donovan shook his head, looked away. Their table was like an island of silence amid the noisy wash of the lunchtime tide. Eventually Donovan spoke.

'Look,' he said, pointing to Michael Nell's statement, 'we've got to get this sorted out. Amar or no Amar.'

Peta reluctantly agreed. 'Strategy,' she said. 'We'll divide it up. I'll have a word around campus. Get a list of his friends, Ashley's friends even. Talk to them, see if they know anything about his proclivities, anything that can point us in the right direction.'

Donovan smiled. 'Proclivities? That university education must be doing you the world of good.'

'Piss off, patronizing college boy.'

Donovan laughed. 'Right. Well, you do that. In the meantime I'll try to work out who and where the charming Mr Nell has been paying for sex.'

'Perfect. Should be right up your street.'

'Hardly. Never paid for sex in my life and not about to start now.' Donovan sat back, hit by a sudden inspiration. 'But I know somebody who might be able to help.' He smiled to himself, shook his head in self-admiration. 'What a brilliant idea. Proud of that.'

Peta just looked at him, waiting to be let in on his inspiraton.

Donovan just looked at his plate, showing only crumbs, then at Peta's plate with its half-finished sandwich.

'So brilliant, it's made me hungry again.' He pointed at her plate. 'You want that?'

Peta made her way back to college. She walked up Northumberland Street, dodged shoppers, charity muggers and invitations to take part in a survey, ignored the stares of the bored, ASBOed teenagers hanging around the Haymarket Metro station, scowled at the surreptitious, yet evidently appreciative, glances at her breasts by a couple of hurrying, besuited, middle-aged men and turned right on to St Mary's Place.

The snow had almost gone, the streets drying and salt-streaked, the air sharp. She breathed deep into her lungs, the smell of Donovan's alcohol still in her nostrils. He had asked, as he always did, if she minded. She had said, as she always did, that she didn't. He had taken her at face value and had drunk and, as usual, she had needed her walk afterwards.

She knew where all the meetings were in the centre of Newcastle. But she didn't need one. The feeling wasn't on her that strongly, hadn't gripped her so much she needed help and support.

The walk was enough. It got it out of her system. Replaced it with fresh air. Or what passed for fresh air in the centre of Newcastle.

Along St Mary's Place, towards Sandyford Road.

She was worried about Amar. His tolerance level to cocaine was decreasing as he got older and, she suspected, his intake was increasing again. She would have to talk to him, sort him out. One addict to another. If she could. If he'd listen.

Along Sandyford Place. Past the University Gallery, stopping to look at Nico Widerberg's pillar man sculpture. Six and half metres tall, cast from bronze and fronted by a curving path of highly polished granite, the pillar man was part of Newcastle's Hidden Rivers project. It was a public art project placing a number of contemporary sculptures over the routes of hidden and forgotten rivers and burns that ran under ground through the city and out to the Tyne, linking the city's present to its past. Peta knew all this. She had been at the unveiling.

The project had, admittedly, fired up her imagination. What she knew of the city was what she could see, what she took for granted. Underneath her feet were cables, wires, train tunnels, sewers. Things she never thought about, never saw. And hidden rivers. Donovan had described it as the past being covered up and concreted over, made to take whatever direction the present wanted to impose on it.

She had expected him to come out with something like that and had taken him to task about his use of purple prose and flowery imagery that any self-respecting ex-journalist would be ashamed to attach their name to. But she had to admit, he had a point. It made her wonder what else was under there, what else from the past that she couldn't see, couldn't imagine.

Around the corner, down the side of the library and on to the main quadrangle. Out of the corner of her eye she noticed an increased security presence; extra uniformed officers walking, watching. But no sense of panic. Business just about as usual. She checked her watch. Early. She thought of popping in to the refectory, getting herself a coffee or a water, just to rinse away any imagined alcohol aftertaste, and headed towards it.

Just inside the door, however, she stopped. There, sitting at a table together, were Jill and the Prof. Jill was smiling, laughing, playing with the ends of her hair, while the Prof was talking. Animatedly, for him, leaning forward into his storytelling, and smiling too.

Something about their body language told her they wouldn't welcome any interruption. She turned around and walked back out. Leave them to it, she thought. Let them enjoy themselves.

She walked back on to the quadrangle, off to her classroom.

Wondering whether Jill would be going to see Wilco next week.

12

With a grunt, a sigh and a blasphemous scream, Decca came.

Panting, his breath subsiding, he began to loosen his grip, pull away. Beneath him, face down on the bed, Anita sighed.

'That was good for you, Decca?' she asked.

'Yeah,' said Decca, flopping on to his back, 'that was good.'

Anita turned over. She hadn't climaxed. She never expected to with Decca. If she wanted to, she could take care of herself later. But she hardly ever felt like that any more. She hadn't found pleasure in sex for a long time but Decca seemed to, so she did for him.

His bedroom was dark, the curtains closed against the late-afternoon light. It was like the rest of his flat. Untidy, functional. Male. Above the bed was the only concession towards decoration in the room: a huge movie poster of *Diamonds Are Forever*, Sean Connery looking down on proceedings with his usual sardonic smile. There were a few others dotted around the place: Schwarzenegger hunting *Predator* in the bathroom, Michael Caine in *Get Carter*, his icepick eyes above the sofa in the living room, a blood-spattered scene from *Reservoir Dogs* in the kitchen. And above all the Clint Eastwood posters. Framed. Clint's slit-eyed stare looking down from every room. Gave him a good, strong feeling inside to look at them. Decca loved his films, considered himself a real expert. Had impeccable taste in them. Classics, every one. Even bought *Empire* every month.

He looked across at Anita. Her blonde hair untied and

spread all over the pillow, her taut, tanned and perfect naked body filmed with a sheen of sweat. If he had been in the mood he would have licked it off, but he had just come. So he wasn't.

'Pass me a fag,' he said.

Anita leaned over to the side of the bed, shook a cigarette loose from the pack of Marlboro Lights that were there, put it between her lips, lit it, inhaled, coughed because she wasn't a smoker, and passed it over. Decca took it with a grunt.

'That was nice, yes?' she said.

Decca shrugged. He had already told her once that he had enjoyed it; why say it again?

He picked up the remote for the TV and DVD player at the end of the bed, switched it on. Clint Eastwood was striding up a deserted Mexican street, poncho slung to one side, hands just above his guns. Spanish faces peered at him from behind locked doors and shutters. He watched.

Anita turned on her side, propped her body on her elbow, faced him.

'You said you had something to tell me, Decca.' She smiled. Traced what chest hair he had with her index finger. 'Are you going to tell me now?'

He had said that to her in the morning. At the café after the rush hour. He had something to tell her. He had to see her later to do it.

She had smiled when he had said that. She was a romantic, a fact she had almost forgotten on the long journey over from Lithuania. It had been beaten, raped, abused out of her until she was no longer a person, only a commodity. That was when she had gone back to cutting herself, just to have something to feel. Just like before.

In Lithuania she had become tired of the lack of options. Of having to work in a bar or restaurant, pretending to like

the Western men who talked to her. Get fucked by them.
Accept presents from them that she then took home and
gave to her family to sell. She had hated it and left, spending
all her savings on the trip over, believing that in Britain she
would have a new start, a happy life of love and belonging.
But by the time she had arrived she had given up hope. And
then she had met Decca.

And she knew how lucky she was. Because Decca kept
telling her.

She knew he loved her, although he had never told her.
But she knew that if she clung on to him, didn't let him go,
showed how much she loved him, then they would stay
together for ever. She had thought all day about what he was
going to say. He must be about to propose to her. Marry her.
There would be a full white wedding, her family coming
over from Lithuania, showing how proud they were of their
daughter, Anita letting them know she had made something
of herself, become a fast-rising businessman's wife.

She looked at him now, waited for him to say it.

He took another pull on his cigarette, drawing the smoke
down deep into his lungs. Letting it go in a concentrated
grey stream, watching it dissipate over their naked bodies.

Anita waited.

Tumbleweeds blew across the street. A gunman appeared
behind the Man with No Name, who turned and shot him.
The man fell from the building, a badly overdubbed scream
accompanying him. The shot rang out and away until all was
silence again.

'Decca?'

He finished his cigarette, stubbed it out in a half-full ash-
tray at the bedside. Opened his mouth to speak.

'I didn't want to tell you this at work,' he said in what he
hoped was a sincere tone of voice, 'but it's something the
boss said.'

Anita frowned. 'The boss?' That creepy Mr Kovacs with his unblinking stare? What did he have to do with anything? 'I don't understand.'

Decca sighed, couldn't meet her eyes. 'He's . . . he doesn't want you working in the café any more. He . . . wants you to leave.'

Anita's mouth fell open. This wasn't what she had been expecting. 'What?' she said after a long while. 'Wh . . . why? Am I not a good worker? Do I not get on well with people? I . . . I don't understand.'

'He . . . he just wants you out, that's all. He's told me and I've got to tell you.'

'I hope you told him no.'

Decca risked a quick glance at her, then just as quickly away again. 'What can I do? He's the boss.'

Anita felt she was suddenly viewing life from the wrong end of the telescope. She could hear her heart beating, the blood pumping around her body.

'OK,' she said slowly. 'I get another job. It's OK . . . I stay here, still, with you?'

'It's not that simple,' he said. 'The boss doesn't just want you gone from the café, he wants you gone. For good.'

Anita shook her head. 'What? I don't . . . don't understand . . .'

Decca turned to her, face red. 'It's fuckin' simple, look, even you can understand it. He wants you gone. Out of the café, away from me. Out of here. Like you don't exist. That's that.'

Decca resumed staring ahead. The bandit leader had decided to show himself. Clint stood before him. There was some business with a musical box and a fly. It was obviously just a prelude to him being killed.

Decca was breathing heavily. He liked Anita, but it had to be done. And anger was the only way. He knew that. Anger and strength. He didn't do closeness. Or tenderness. That was unbusinesslike. Counterproductive. That was for poofs.

Anita heard more than her heart beating, the blood pounding around her body. She heard her future, her hopes and dreams, collapse.

'But . . . but where will I go? Do you know anywhere?'

Nowhere you'd want to go, he thought, then mentally admonished himself for being soft.

'No,' he said.

'But I have nowhere.'

'That can't be my problem, can it?' Anger rose within him again. 'I work for someone. I have to do what I'm told.'

'This is not work; this is your life.'

Decca got off the bed, stood over her. Anger. It had to be. 'Don't try an' be fuckin' smart. I work for Marco Kovacs. That's my life.'

Anita stood up also. 'Please, Decca, don't . . .'

He was around to her side of the bed and had hit her with such a slap to the face that it knocked her over, the bed breaking her fall.

Clint drew his revolver, shot the bandit leader. The bandit took a long time to die. Clint watched him, unblinking.

Decca looked away from Anita.

Anita wiped at her cheek. It was wet with tears. And blood. She swallowed back the pain. 'So . . . tomorrow, tomorrow I . . . leave.'

'Not tomorrow,' he said. 'Now. You'd better leave now.'

Decca reached over the side of the bed to his jeans which lay crumpled on the floor. He pulled out his wallet, took out ten twenties, tossed them at her.

'Here. Till you get sorted.'

Anita looked at the money. Saw red tears fall on to the paper.

Clint had turned and was walking away down the street.

He stopped to say something to the undertaker, tell him how many coffins he would be needing.

'Now go.'

'You always said I was one of the lucky ones.'

'You are. I'm lettin' you go. Know what would happen to you if it was up to Kovacs? Eh? Know what you'd have to do then?'

Anita said nothing. She knew.

'Go.' Anita didn't move. Decca looked at her, his eyes hard, glassy marbles. 'Now. Before it gets any worse.'

Slowly, her fingers moving as if numb, she gathered up the notes, got off the bed. Slowly dressed. It felt as if her movements belonged to someone else.

The Morricone soundtrack had started up. Clint was saddled and away.

Anita walked around the bedroom stuffing clothes and toiletries into a holdall.

'I'll go to a hotel . . .'

Decca nodded.

And she suddenly wanted to scream and shout at him, grab him, slap him, claw at him. Make him aware of what he had done, what he was doing to her. Beat him. Hurt him.

But she didn't.

She just continued packing and, when she was ready, stood before him.

Decca lit another cigarette.

'Goodbye, Decca.'

Decca looked at her. 'Bye. Sorry.'

She nodded. Walked out of the flat.

Decca waited until the front door had closed, then let out a big sigh. Another drag on his cigarette, another huge exhalation. He picked up the remote, stopped the film, reset it, started to watch it again from the beginning. Clint was good. Clint showed him how things should be done.

He took another drag, watched Clint ride into frame.

Went better than he had expected, he thought.

Painless, on the whole.

Donovan had gone back to the cottage from lunching with Peta and Amar to talk to Katya, ask her to do him a favour. He had entered the cottage, seen her sitting on the sofa watching TV. She had jumped when the door had opened, been ready to leap up and run.

'Just me.' Donovan carefully closed the door behind him.

She expelled air in a great sigh, her body visibly relaxing.

'Sorry.' He stepped into the room.

Katya nodded.

Donovan looked at her. She was wearing faded jeans and a red T-shirt, clothes supplied by Peta; slightly oversized, the differing folds and stress points clearly showing they had been worn in by someone else. She still looked thin and undernourished and the dark rings hadn't disappeared completely from under her eyes. But that was easy to take care of. Just a few more days and nights of full sleep, healthy, regular meals and exercise. Hair and make-up done, bit of pampering and relaxation. The doctor Sharkey had called in had given her a couple of vitamin shots and said as much.

But her eyes. They kept the nightmares in their fragile cages, locked but not securely; the key too close at hand, the bars too easy to snap. He had spoken to Sharkey, told him, not asked him, to get Katya some counselling, and Sharkey had promised he would, but so far nothing had happened.

'Yeah,' Donovan had said to him, 'but you're not the one who's heard her the last two nights, waking up all gasps and screams. You're not the one who has to listen to her sobbing when she thinks no one can hear her. Jamal's nightmares are bad enough without hers.'

Without his own, he could have added, but they were words he didn't want Sharkey to hear.

Sharkey would see what he could do.

Donovan asked after Jamal.

'In his room, giving himself tutorial on computer,' Katya said.

Donovan forced a smile. 'Playing *Doom 3* more like,' he said.

He looked around. The cottage was in a good state. He felt proud of what he had achieved. Stripped wooden flooring, rugs, furniture. A TV and DVD recorder combo sat in one corner. A hi-fi system at the far wall, the CDs segregated: Jamal's hip-hop, RnB and garage piled on one side, Johnny Cash, Elvis Costello, Morrissey, the Clash and the rest of Donovan's stuff at the other. And never the two should meet, he thought.

At either side of the firepace were bookshelves, rapidly filling with books again. All Donovan's old favourites: Graham Greene and Nelson Algren, Hubert Selby Jnr and Kurt Vonnegut, Raymond Chandler and Dashiell Hammett. Some graphic novels and comics. Alan Moore and Will Eisner. Just like old times. He had bought them in charity shops, second-hand bookstores, the old covers being the ones he was familiar with. He had read them again, trying to retrace his development, work out who he used to be before his world ended. Tried to get back there. It wasn't easy. The stories were different from how he remembered them, some better, some worse. He came away with new perspectives on old assumptions, felt mostly better for that.

He could never make things the way they were before, he understood that. But that shouldn't deter him from attempting to reclaim himself.

The cottage was still a work-in-progress, but it was

becoming something Donovan could take pride in. And it was a long time since he had felt like that about anything.

'What you watching?' he asked Katya.

'A film,' she replied. 'Old. Part of London decides it is a separate country.'

'Ah. *Passport to Pimlico*. Good film.'

Katya gave an expression of bafflement. 'If you had been in my country when it divide itself up, you would not think it funny.'

He went into the kitchen to put the kettle on. He made them both coffee, brought it out, handed her the mug and sat with her on the sofa.

'How you doing?' he asked her.

'Fine,' she said, not meeting his eyes.

'Good.'

'When can I see my brother?'

'Soon, I hope. I don't know where he's being held. All I know is it's somewhere safe. They want you both to stay where you are until it's a good time to move you. But soon.'

Katya nodded. 'I . . . I do not want to be ungrateful. But . . .' She sighed. 'I feel . . . unsettled here.'

Donovan smiled. 'I don't blame you.'

'The country is very beautiful and I love to walk, but I feel . . . like I am in limbo. Waiting for something to happen.'

Donovan nodded. 'If you want something to do, I could use some help.'

Her eyes lit up. She turned to him. 'With what?'

'It's work. I don't know whether you'd want to or not. It might be a bit – I don't know – unpleasant for you. Bring back some bad memories.'

A cloud passed over her features. 'Like what?'

Donovan told her about his meeting with Janine Stewart. The job he had agreed to take on, without mentioning Michael Nell's name. 'The thing is, he claims that when

Ashley was being abducted, he was out visiting prostitutes. Or a prostitute in particular.'

Her voice rose in anger. 'And you think this was me?'

'No, no, I don't. But I thought you might be able to help me. Point me in the right direction.'

Katya said nothing.

'I know it's not something you want to go back to. And I wouldn't ask if it wasn't important.'

Katya took a long time to answer. When she did, her voice was barely above a whisper. 'They might see me. Come after me. Take me back with them.'

'They won't,' Donovan said. 'You'll be with me.'

She gave a harsh laugh. 'You think that will stop them?' She shook her head, stood up, paced the room. 'You don't know what they are like, what they can do to you. They keep us in one room, give us one meal a day. Charge us to stay there. Charge us to use knives and forks. Fine us if we do not . . . humiliate ourselves with men. Fine us if the men do not find us attractive . . .'

She turned away from Donovan, composed herself again. Donovan said nothing. Katya continued, her voice small. 'They tell us we will have good jobs in hotel, in restaurant, then take our passports, tell us we owe them thousands of pounds. Make us their property. Tell us to do as they say or they will kill our families back home.' She looked straight at him. 'They can do all this, and you do not think they will find me?'

'Trust me. They won't. You won't see them. I've got photos of the woman and the street where she works from. And what she specializes in. She's not Eastern European. She's local. A home-grown girl.'

Katya relaxed. Very slightly.

'I was just wondering whether you'd come across her, that's all.'

Katya said nothing for a while. 'What does she look like?' she said eventually.

Donovan took out the envelope Janine Stewart had given him. He leafed through the photos, looking for one that wouldn't upset Katya. Or would upset her the least. He passed it across to her. Saw her flinch as she took it. It showed a woman, medium height, hair short and dark, slight build. Frail-looking. The camera was above her, looking down. She looked up, eyes wide and fearful.

'She caters to the S&M trade mainly,' said Donovan. 'A taker, rather than a giver.'

Katya gave another harsh laugh. 'All whores are takers. There to absorb men's anger.' The word was spat out like phlegm.

'Not every man,' said Donovan, feeling he had to say something. Katya shrugged. Unconvinced. Donovan continued. 'Anyway, do you know her?'

'She looks familiar.' Katya studied the photo, frowned. 'Yes . . . her name was . . . Shirley? Sharon? Something like that. We were not encouraged to mix with the other girls. We worked in shifts. I was taken to the house, dropped off, and they sat outside and waited.'

'Were you taken to just the one house? Or is there a chance you could have been to the one she was at?'

'There's a chance,' Katya said, looking at the floor. 'Describe it to me.'

He did. Katya slowly nodded. 'I think I know that one.'

'Do you know where it is?'

'Perhaps. When I see it again.'

'I imagine it's the same set-up,' said Donovan. 'The landlord rents out the rooms to the girls, takes a cut. If there's any trouble or a raid, it goes no further than him. And he's well paid for being a front, taking a rap. The big bosses who own the houses are hidden by a papertrail.'

Katya's eyes narrowed. 'You know a lot about whores.'

Donovan shrugged. 'Ex-journo. You're right, though. Her name's Sharon. Or at least that's what the client was told to call her.' He sat back. 'Look, I wouldn't ask you if there was another way. I just might need you to talk to her. She might not want to talk to me on my own.'

Katya said nothing.

'So. What's your answer?'

Katya looked at the screen. There was a barricade, civilians on one side, police on the other. Everyone was behaving with impeccable manners and cheerful good spirits.

'I will do it, Joe. I will try to help.'

Donovan smiled. 'Thank you, Katya. I know this can't be easy for you.'

Katya put her mug down, her face serious. 'But there is a condition.'

She told him.

One phone call and an argument with Sharkey later, Donovan had her agreement.

13

The rain slapped down on the west end of Newcastle, crackling and fizzing, turning the night to white noise and static, coating the roads and pavements with a greasy, oily sheen. The streets were almost deserted, people out only if they had somewhere or nowhere to go. Pedestrians hurried by, drivers got out of cars and ran into houses. In a metal-shuttered newsagent's doorway a small gaggle of hoodied youths, all nasty-looking, brutal and short, huddled desultorily in shelter.

Donovan sat at the wheel of the car, engine still idling, and scanned the street in front of him. A row of old red-brick houses, in a run-down area, their doors opening directly on to the street, no front gardens. Just as it had been described in Michael Nell's statement. Just as Donovan had described it to Katya.

'This look right to you?' he said.

She stared intensely at the house. 'Could be.'

'Why not ask those youths over there?' said Jamal from behind them, leaning his arms across the backs of the front two seats, pointing to the shop doorway.

'I hope you're joking,' said Donovan.

'Man, you're so prejudiced,' the boy said sulkily.

Donovan ignored him.

The rain showed no signs of stopping, sliding and rolling down the windscreen in jelly-like waves. Donovan refrained from putting the wipers on. Thought the sound of them in a motionless car one of the most depressing sounds there was.

Donovan checked the street for the Peugeot he had seen parked outside the house they had rescued Katya from. There was no sign of it.

'Coast looks clear,' he said. 'Are you OK about coming in with me? I think she'll talk more freely with another woman there.'

'An ex-whore, you mean?'

Donovan looked at her. He didn't know what to say.

Katya smiled. 'I am sorry. That was unkind.'

They resumed looking out of the window.

'You better take Katya, man,' said Jamal.

'Why?' asked Donovan.

"Cos, man, gettin' outta this car on his own got john written all over him, you get me?'

'Suppose you've got a point,' said Donovan.

'You know I have,' said Jamal. He looked around the interior, shook his head. 'This is one borin' car, you know that? Man, you need to do somethin'. You need to pimp this ride.'

Donovan didn't even look at him. 'Pimp.'

'Yeah, man. Pimp. Give it some style. Put a good sound system in, get that bass pumpin'. Maybe some DVD screens, fridge wi' Kristal in the back. Alloy wheels, fur trim.'

'Jamal.'

'Or purple.'

'Jamal.'

'Or purple fur.'

Donovan just looked at him.

Jamal sighed. 'You know what I mean.'

Donovan tried to hide his smile. 'This car's for work, Jamal. It's meant to look anonymous. Blend in. You know that.'

Like an adult sick of imparting unheeded wisdom, Jamal shook his head wearily. 'Job done then, bro. Job done.'

'Right,' said Donovan, 'we're going. You know what to do, J?'

'Sure, man,' Jamal said, as if affronted. 'Keep a lookout for any other cars givin' undue attention to the house you're at when you're in it.'

'And?'

Jamal sighed. Like a child repeating instructions by rote. 'Give you a call on the mobile.'

Donovan smiled. 'Well done. We'll make a junior detective out of you yet.'

They opened the car doors, stepped out into the rain. Donovan pulled the collar of his leather jacket close about his neck. Katya was wearing a suede jacket and a baseball cap, both oversized, both lent to her by Donovan. She huddled her thin frame within.

Donovan grabbed her hand and they ran across the street.

Unaware that they were being watched.

They reached the front door. There was nothing to distinguish it from any other door in the street. Donovan tried the handle. Locked. He knocked on it. They waited. Rain dripped off his face. Off the brim of Katya's baseball cap.

'I remember now,' said Katya. 'The man here, the landlord, his name is Noddy.'

Donovan looked at her. 'Noddy?'

She nodded.

'Nice.'

The door was opened.

A man's face, moon-like and greasy, poked out. Seeing Donovan, he was fine. Seeing a female shape next to him, he looked wary.

'Yeah?' he said. His oily voice matched his skin.

'My name's Joe Donovan. I'm working for Janine Stewart, a solicitor.' He produced a business card of hers, handed it over. It was reluctantly accepted by stubby, dirty fingers. 'We need to talk to one of your girls. Can we come in, please?'

Donovan began to move towards the door, opening it as he went. He felt resistance.

'I don't know what you mean,' said the moon-faced man. 'Go away. Piss off. This is a private residence.'

'Fuck off, it's a private residence,' said Donovan, almost smiling. 'Come on, Noddy, you really think I believe that?'

The man's eyes narrowed suspiciously behind his glasses. 'How d'you know my name?' Panic was creeping into his voice.

'I know lots of things, Noddy. Now don't fuck me about and I won't fuck you about. It's pouring with rain out here and we've both got jobs to do. Sooner you let me talk to your girl, sooner we'll be gone.'

Noddy thought, decided to bluff it out. 'I don't know what you're talkin' about.' His voice muffled from behind the closing door.

Donovan put his hand out to stop it, wedged his foot in the way. 'You want to fuck about? OK. We'll leave you. But we'll go straight to the law and bring them back with us. That suit you better? Up to you, Noddy.'

The man looked at the card, at Donovan, at Katya's obscured face. Reluctantly opened the door.

'Thank you,' said Donovan.

They stepped into the hall. It was blandly decorated, minimally furnished. Nothing gave away its true purpose. Nothing gave it any character. Noddy closed the door behind them. He was wearing filthy, stained tracksuit bottoms that had seen the inside of a kebab shop more times than the inside of a gym, or even a washing machine, a similarly filthy red T-shirt and a pair of old slippers. He stank of sweat and other bodily secretions Donovan wanted to draw a discreet veil over.

'What's this about, then?' Noddy said. 'You're not coppers. You don't have to threaten me with them.'

'Like I said, we're working for a solicitor. We need to speak to one of the girls who works here.'

'Why?'

'Can't tell you, I'm afraid. Client confidentiality.'

Noddy pulled himself up to his full height, puffed out his chest in what Donovan assumed was meant to be a threatening manner. He moved in close to Donovan. It wasn't a pleasant experience.

'Tell me or you'll get no further. I'm in charge here. I make the decisions. Nothin' happens in this house that I don't know about. You want somethin'—' he stuck a pudgy thumb in his equally pudgy chest '—you go through me.'

Donovan took a step backwards. Noddy took this as a sign of fear. Donovan just wanted to give his sense of smell a rest.

'Well,' said Donovan, trying not to smile, 'maybe you're the person I need to talk to. It's to do with a murder inquiry.'

Noddy flinched. Audibly gasped. 'Murder?'

Donovan nodded. 'That's right. And since you're in charge here, and nothing happens in this house that you don't know about, and since everything goes through you, you might be called on to give evidence in any trial.'

'Evidence?' The man's future seemed to race across his face. He didn't like what he saw. He started to sweat.

Oh, no, thought Donovan, taking another step back.

'What d'you mean?' said Noddy. 'There hasn't been a murder here.'

'I didn't say there had been. One of your girls' names has been mentioned in connection with a murder inquiry. We need to talk to her.'

'Which girl?'

'Sharon Healy's her real name.'

'Sharon Healy?'

'Calls herself the Queen of Misrule.'

Noddy frowned, giving the impression of thinking hard. Donovan and Katya could almost hear it happening. His brow unknit, and a look of what he believed to be sly cunning eventually appeared on his face. 'She's not one of my girls. She's freelance. Rents a room off us. That's all. Nowt to do wi' me.'

'Which room?'

'Upstairs at the back. Second one along.'

'Is she up there now? Is she working?'

Noddy shook his head.

Donovan gestured to the stairs. 'Can we?'

'Aye, aye. Up you go.'

Donovan smiled. 'Thank you.' He looked at Katya. 'After you.'

Katya went up the stairs.

'You'll have to pay, though. Time is money.'

Donovan turned to Noddy. Risked moving in close to him. 'You going to make me?'

Noddy thought about it. He shook his head.

'Good. And don't think of calling anyone while we're up there. I've got someone outside watching the house. First sign of trouble, he'll be in here like a shot.' Donovan shook his head. 'And you wouldn't want that. Believe me.'

Noddy swallowed hard. He believed him.

Donovan turned, went up the stairs.

Katya was waiting on the landing. She glanced around nervously, looked pleased to see Donovan.

'You OK?' he asked.

She nodded. 'This door,' she said, pointing, then looked across the landing. 'I was in that one.'

Donovan looked at her. He didn't know what to say.

'Here was no good. They moved me to the other house. Watch me better there.'

Donovan grabbed her hand, squeezed. She returned it, tried to smile.

'So that's Noddy, eh?' he said.

'Yes. An unpleasant man. But not worst. I have met worse.'

'I'm sure. You think he recognized you?'

'I don't think so. I kept my hat down. I could feel his eyes on me, though.'

'I don't doubt it.'

Donovan released Katya's hand. Reluctantly, she let go, giving him a brief, hesitant smile.

'This door?' he said. She nodded. 'Come on, then.'

They walked up to it, knocked. Waited. From down the hall came the sounds of reluctant bedsprings, unenthusiastic copulation. Beyond that, the rain. The door was opened.

'Sharon?' asked Donovan. 'Sharon Healy?'

The woman who had answered the door looked like the ghost of the woman in the photos. She was all monochromatic contrasts: white face, dark hair. Not tall, but round. Overweight. It gave her facial features a round, cheerful look that her eyes contrasted. Black bobbed hair. Pale skin, dark bruises. White or once-white terry dressing gown over glimpsed black underwear. She managed to summon up a look of expectation for Donovan that quickly died when she noticed Katya.

'What's goin' on?' she asked, her voice stronger than her looks would have suggested.

'My name's Joe Donovan, and this is an associate of mine. I'm working for a solicitor. It's about Michael Nell. Can we come in and talk to you?'

'Who?'

'Michael Nell. He was a client of yours. He took these.'

He handed over the photos. She took them, opened the envelope. Flicked through them.

'I remember him.' She sketched a ghost of a smile. 'I come out well, haven't I?'

Donovan had looked at the photos of Sharon Healy, naked and bound, humiliated and hurt. 'Well' wouldn't have been the word he would have used.

'Yeah,' he said. 'Really good. He's captured something there.'

'Ee, he's talented, isn't he?'

'Oh, yeah. He's talented. Can we come in, please?'

Sharon Healy looked at him. Caught what was going on behind his eyes. 'You don't like these photos, do you? Not into it. Wonder how I can do it. What I get out of it. Besides money, that is.'

Donovan could feel his cheeks reddening.

Sharon's face changed. A kind of sick power floated behind her eyes. She almost smiled. 'And you'll never know.'

She opened the door, let them in. The room was as depressing and bare as the rest of the house. S&M concessions had been made: tools of the trade hanging from B&Q picture hooks on the walls. A paddle. A whip. A restraint. On the bedside table a couple of vibrators and dildos. More for pain than pleasure. In a corner on the floor and out of place next to everything else was an electric kettle plugged into the power point with a plastic bottle of milk, a homely mug and a box of PG Tips next to it. Items sparsely spread out, juxtapositioned. Could have been an art installation.

'Shouldn't this be in a dungeon?' asked Donovan.

'Cellar got flooded,' said Sharon with a shrug. 'Burst pipe. Had to move up here.'

Donovan caught Katya shuddering. Resigned himself to being as quick as possible.

'So who is he, then, this lad?' asked Sharon, sitting on the edge of the bed. She seemed stronger, more in control. 'I thought he was a student.'

'He is,' said Donovan. 'Photography student. He's been visiting a few —'

Sharon smiled. That look of sick power in her eyes again. 'Prostitutes. Like me. You can say the word.'

Donovan, not looking at Katya, continued: 'Yeah. He's been visiting a few prostitutes in the city. Taking photos. Doing what he does. He says he was with you two weeks last Tuesday. Here, taking those photos.'

'Two weeks?'

'The seventh.'

Sharon shrugged. 'He mighta been. I'm here every night. It coulda been that one. I don't know. I don't give receipts.' She looked up from the photos, studied Donovan. 'You're not a copper.'

'No.'

Sharon pointed to Katya. 'And you're definitely not.'

Katya shook her head.

Sharon kept her eyes on Katya a beat too long, then turned back to Donovan. 'So what's he done?'

'He's being questioned in connection with a murder.'

'Murder?' Sharon dropped the photos like they were hot, threw up her arms. Her robe fell open, sleeves rode up. Donovan saw the scars on her forearms. Cuts. Some old. Some not so old. The bruises on the tops of her breasts. Small circular burns. New on old. He tried to ignore them, concentrate his words on her face.

'And you're his alibi,' he said. 'Have the police contacted you yet?'

She shook her head.

'They will.'

She sighed. 'God. Just what I need.'

'But you can't remember.'

She shook her head. 'Let's think.'

She put her head back. Donovan saw crow's feet at the corners of her eyes, a neck developing rings and turkey folds. She was older than she first appeared. Or the job had aged her.

'I think it was Tuesday, you know.' She nodded. 'Uh-huh. It was. I know because of the other punters I saw that night. Some of me regulars.' She looked at Donovan. 'Do I have to prove it? Tell you their names?'

'It may not come to that. But I do need to know that you would be willing to testify to that in court.'

Sharon almost smiled. 'You gonna pay me?'

'You know I can't.'

'Why would I do it, then?'

'Out of the goodness of your heart.'

'Prossies don't make the best witnesses.'

'They do if that's all the defence has.'

Sharon seemed to be thinking to herself.

'And they wouldn't, y'know, try to prosecute us?'

'They wouldn't.'

She smiled. 'That would be a laugh.'

'Thank you.' He turned to Katya, gave her a smile. She looked relieved not have been asked to take part. She returned the smile. 'That's all we needed to know. We'll be off.'

Sharon held up the photos. 'Can I keep these?'

'Sorry. I need them back. Evidence.'

'Can I get a copy? These are good.'

'I'll see what I can do.'

'He wanted to photograph us again, you know.'

'Really?' said Donovan.

She nodded. 'Said he had a studio in town he wanted to take me to. Fully equipped, he said.'

'Well,' said Donovan, 'I don't think he'll be doing that now.'

Donovan picked up the photos. Made arrangements about contacting her, organizing a formal statement. She gave him her mobile number. He gave her his business card. He headed for the door. He turned, about to thank Sharon for her time when his mobile rang. He answered it. Jamal.

'Joe? Two people comin' from a parked car way down the street. Movin' quickly. Headed for you.'

'We're coming.' Jamal started to say something more, but Donovan cut him off, pocketed the phone. He turned to Katya. 'We've got to go.'

Fear sprang into Katya's eyes.

'Don't worry.' He grabbed her hand. 'Come on.'

'Wait.'

Sharon put her hand on Katya's shoulder. Grabbed her. Katya spun round.

'I know you.'

Katya froze. She looked from Donovan to Sharon, not knowing what to say, what to do.

'I know you. You used to work here, didn't you?' She couldn't keep the incredulity from her voice. 'I've been rackin' my brains. I remember you. Foreign girl. What you doin' with him?'

Katya opened her mouth to speak; no sound came out.

'Come on!'

Donovan grabbed her, made for the stairs. They ran down them almost together, ran down the hall towards the front door. Noddy was standing at the bottom, trying to say something. Donovan ignored him. They reached the front door, Donovan stretched out a hand to open it. There was a knock.

Donovan stopped, looked at Katya.

Another knock.

Donovan spun around. 'Is there a back way out?'

Noddy just looked at him.

'Is there a fucking back way out?'

Noddy pointed to the back of the house.

Another knock.

'Come on.' Donovan turned, ready to go.

Another knock. And the sound of a voice.

'Donovan? Joe Donovan?'

A voice addressing him. He thought he recognized it.

Donovan snatched a look at Katya. Shook his head. She frowned at him. He sighed and, with great reluctance, opened the door.

'What d'you want?' he said.

There stood DI Diane Nattrass and DS Paul Turnbull. It was hard to tell which one looked the least happy to see him. Turnbull spoke first.

'You're fucked,' he said.

14

The Discovery Museum on Blandford Street was dedicated to the social history of the north-east. Housed in the old Co-operative Wholesale Society for the Northern Region, all Victorian red-brick, metalwork and turrets, it was the north-east's biggest free museum and told the story of Newcastle from Roman times to the present day.

Past the *Turbina*, once the fastest ship in the world, a series of atmospherically lit mazes led viewers through history. To the schoolchildren who trekked through it, the 1960s, 1970s and 1980s could have been as distant as the eighteenth century or the Middle Ages. Their guides tried to enthuse and contextualize, put the displays in relation to the children's own lives and histories and families, claim them as living history, since there were artefacts behind glass many people still had in their homes. The children looked and listened but laughed at the things their parents had thought of as cool. Like all teenagers, they believed themselves to be the first generation – the only generation – to have been born at ground zero. They wouldn't make the same mistakes as their parents. They wouldn't end up like them.

The Historian hurried past the displays. He had expected on his first visit to stand before the displays and experience the past all around him, see into it, talk with those long departed. But nothing had come. With their faux history, taped sounds and shop-window dummies miming action, for ever stuck in the same position, frozen in time, the displays held nothing for him. They were dead. Instead of bringing the past to life, they had killed it and displayed its empty husk, ignoring the ghosts of the dead that informed the present. Silencing their voice. The teenagers and the museum's creators were well suited. None of them understood the truth about history.

He hurried past them, on his way to his destination.

Through the double doors, turning left. The brightly lit, highly coloured twenty-first-century surroundings disappeared, to be replaced by a sombre reception area, resplendent in dark wooden panelling and opaque glass. He rounded the reception and walked down a long, straight corridor, again in dark wooden panelling, with doors at either side displaying various permutations of non-admittance stencilled on the half-obscured glass.

He slowed down, enjoying the cool feel of the place, the soundproofed walls, the carpet beneath his feet. This was better. This worked for him. With every step he took, he felt like he was walking back in time to some government offices from fifty or sixty years ago. He could hear the faint noises of big old typewriters working away behind each door as he passed, the rattling clatter of the keys, the ping of the bell, and the trilling of Bakelite phones. He could hear voices.

But then he could always hear voices.

Ghost meetings. Ghost conferences. Ghost planning committees.

They were still there. He could still hear them. He smiled. Drew comfort from that.

He reached his destination, a set of double doors at the end of the corridor. He pushed them open, went in.

The Public Record Offices. Smelling of age and must, the tobacco-yellowed walls sporting the odd council poster or genealogy group meeting, the staff by and large silent and unsmiling. Card indexes, boxed paper files, huge leather-bound books, microfilm readers. The past compartmentalized, filed away. The usual souls he always saw in there, working the microfilm and peering through old census files: odd folk in anoraks, sloganed sweatshirts and fleeces, both male and female, most of them past retirement age, all of them in some way driven to discover something. Desperate to dig up the past, make it, in some way, live again.

He checked his watch, looked around. He was later than usual. Would get only an hour or so of work done before they closed the place for the night.

He found his usual seat, sat down, began unloading from his old sports bag. Then sat still, head cocked to one side. Waiting.

For how long he didn't know. He focused, tuned in. And they came. Rising from the graves of the card indexes, clouding out of leather-bound, yellowed newspapers, uncurling from boxes of paper files, unspooling from rolls of microfilm. The voices. The ghosts.

He listened, smiled. Nodded. Their conduit, their medium. Their instrument.

At first he had thought they were in his head, a direct result of not taking his medication. But the more they spoke to him, the things they said and showed him, the truths they revealed to him, he knew they were more than that.

They directed him to plans, diagrams.

They gave him his room.

He had been thrilled when he had found it and set about changing it, making it his. The walls no longer bare, cold brick, the stone flags of the floor developing a covering. The decorative figurework. The lights. All his own. His workplace, but more than that: his studio, his sanctuary, his sanctum. Where he felt at home, where he belonged.

And the voices talked to him, asked him questions. The

same ones he had been asking himself, that had been haunting him, depressing him. They would help him, they said. Show him how to find those answers he so desperately craved.

The work had consumed him. Even the initial try-outs. The failures. The planning and anticipation giving almost as delicious a thrill as the act itself. Almost. Because nothing could match the consummation. Nothing ever would.

He had needed that after his mother's death. He wished, not for the first time, that she were still with him. He had to see her again. And he would see her again.

Soon.

He got up from his seat, found the maps he was looking for, spread them out on the desk before him.

The city of Newcastle, 1789.

He could get lost in them, tracing roads and rivers, mouthing the names as he went. Visualizing the city as it was, finding comfort in what had been before, the contemporary city overlaid on top. The past not gone, only hidden. There to be found. Ghosts walking, guiding him. To the past. The present. And beyond.

His mind wandered. The city's history became his history. The roads on the map taking him to one street in particular. One house. His house, now. Open the door, and there he was. A boy alone in the shadows of his childhood.

He blinked. Saw the white flashes of anger. Of pain.

Saw his father again.

The smell of alcohol on his breath, the foul words he used. Hitting his mother again and again. Her prayers and hymns ineffectual shields against her husband's cruelty. He glimpsed it again through barred fingers, curled into a terrified, foetal ball, wishing he had been stronger, stood up to the bully, feeling the guilt still gnaw.

He knew which memory would come next, flinched in

anticipation. His father turning his attention on him. A harsh attention. A violent one.

An invasive one.

His barred fingers as effective a shield as his mother's hymns.

He blinked, looked around the room, trying to dislodge the memory. Everyone was staring at him. Had he shouted out loud? Screamed? He might have done. His heart was beating fast, sweat on his face and hands. His fingers over his eyes. He felt his face reddening, looked down again. Tried to will everyone in the room to stop staring at him. Concentrated on the map before him. It was blurred. He waited to refocus. The image to change.

Another flash. Now ten years old, the young man of the house, sitting on his mother's knee. A cuddle that gripped too tight. Kisses that went on too long. Hands all over him, making him feel good. His mother telling him God wouldn't mind. Telling him about love. Him telling his mother she didn't need God. Or Jesus. He would protect her.

Then later, just the two of them. No more kissing and cuddling. God had decided it wasn't right, she had said. But he still loved her.

Even when MS struck and life changed. She couldn't run the shop any more. Couldn't sew or do her embroidery and cross-stitch that she loved so much. He had been planning to go to university. That was out of the question. The money saved had to go towards living expenses. He had to stay at home and help her cope. He looked after her. They coped. He still loved her.

The house became filled with protuberances. Beige and white and metal. Clinical. Things to help her get from one place to another and back again. Things to stop her going outside.

She still prayed. Sang hymns. God did everything for a

purpose, and she was going to a better place. With no pain and only angels.

He bottled everything inside. His needs. His hopes. His worries. His anger. With God and everyone else. And he couldn't let them out. Because his mother needed him.

But then he found the room. Heard the voices. Met the spirits. Who helped him to unbottle the things inside. Encouraged him. And life improved.

And then she died.

And he was heartbroken.

After the funeral he had retreated to his room. And listened. Sure he would hear her voice, see her face there in the shadows with the rest.

He never did. She wasn't there.

He searched and searched. Listened and listened. Couldn't find her. He began to doubt, to fear. He formulated a plan.

He looked up. The library was closing. Everyone packing up, making ready to go home. Giving him sly looks out of the corners of their eyes. He felt his face reddening again and hurried to join them, to slip away. But he wasn't going home. He was going to his room.

He had to plan.

15

The house was large, even by the standards of the other big houses that populated the exclusive Darras Hall area of Northumberland. Large enough and secluded enough to make dog walkers and neighbours stop, stare, wonder who lived there, what went on that they couldn't see. It was regarded with envy and suspicion among the locals. Envy, suspicion, and everything in between.

The house stood in its own grounds, gated and walled, entry applied for through the intercom mounted on the stone and brick gatepost, entry granted only after the scrutiny of the cameras and at the discretion of those behind the wall. Inside, the green, expensively sculpted grounds hid motion-sensor alarms and spotlights, CCTV: a private security firm had an on-site base replete with uniforms and attack dogs. It was half-palace, half-fortress.

Marco Kovacs took his security very seriously.

Decca Ainsley drove up in his cobalt black BMW 545 Sport, G Unit: 'Beg for Mercy' blaring, 50 Cent explaining how you didn't want to bang with the best because he'd have the doctor removing fragments from your chest, making Decca feel good. Windscreen wipers thrashing against the downpour. High-wattage beams against the darkness. He screeched to a standing stop by the gatepost, leaned out, pressed the intercom button. Gave his name and drove in, the gates swinging wide to admit him.

The house itself was an old Georgian mansion. Decca heard that it had once been a mental hospital. Figured.

Despite the amount of care and, more important, money that had been lavished on it to transform it into a showpiece home, he still felt a shudder when he looked at it, like the ghosts of the mad and disturbed still held claim to the place. He thought that if he turned around quickly he might still catch a glimpse of them staring down from the upstairs windows. The dead watching the living. The fact that it was evening and raining made it even worse.

He turned the engine off, silencing Tony Yayo in mid-proclamation that the shells hurt him but he would take them like a man, and got out of the car. Keeping his eyes fixed resolutely on the front door. Ignoring the two Ferraris in the drive, the Bentley and the Jeep Cherokee. Knowing Kovacs' other cars were garaged at a different location. Tamping down the rising jealousy, feeling that familiar hunger scraping inside him, gnawing away at him, forcing him on. One day, he thought. One day.

Before he could reach the door, it was opened for him by Christopher. Decca swallowed hard, tried not to let his unease show.

'Awright?' he said.

Christopher nodded. Gestured down the hall. Decca stepped inside; the doors closed behind him.

The hall looked as it was expected to look after so much cash had been lavished on it. Decca walked down the thick carpet, sculpting his damp hair back into place, checking it in mirrors, looking at the walls, wondering, not for the first time, whether the paintings, furniture and ornaments were all genuine antiques. He reckoned they were. That jealousy, that hunger for success was eating away inside him again. He wished, not for the first time, that all this was his. Not that he particularly liked any of it; he thought it looked awful, but it had class. It had style. It was the way you were expected to live when you had the money.

And as soon as he had the money, he would be doing it.

'He in the study?' asked Decca.

'Vivarium,' said Christopher, barely moving his lips.

Decca swallowed. He would be. The room he hated most.

He followed Christopher through to the rear of the house, past door after door, past the indoor swimming pool and fitness complex, up to a closed set of double doors. Christopher leaned forward, opened them. Ushered Decca in. Decca took a deep breath, stepped inside.

The room was huge and oblong. Windowless. And hot. Trees, rocks and foliage, real and fake, dotted the room. It was like an indoor rainforest. From the ceiling, blindingly bright lights threw down artificial sunlight. And around thick branches and under rocks were the things Decca hated. Snakes. Pythons. Boas. And in an indoor pool at the far end of the room, sculpted to look like a naturally occurring small lake, an anaconda. The big ones, the crushers. And along the far wall, glassed off from the rest of the room, the others. The mambas. The cobras. Cottonmouths. Corals. Diamondbacks. The venomous ones. The deadly ones.

And in the centre was Kovacs.

'Derek. You are just in time. Come in.'

Kovacs was standing before a large metal basin that he had placed on a table. He was looking down into it, dressed in suit trousers and rolled-up shirtsleeves. There was a smile playing at the sides of his mouth.

'Come closer.'

Decca reluctantly did as he was told. He slowly approached the table, feeling cold reptilian eyes chart his progress, eyes that, he thought, held primeval secrets, primeval evil. He tried not to let his unease show. He wondered what the lunatics would have made of the snakes. He reached the basin, tried hard not to look inside.

Kovacs was looking, enrapt. There was almost love in his eyes. 'This is a python.' he said, 'A small one.' His voice sounded regretful. It didn't look small to Decca. 'Dinnertime.'

Kovacs turned, reached behind him and brought forward a little cage. Decca heard the scampering of tiny, fearful feet from within. Kovacs reached in, brought out a brown rat. Holding it by the tail, he dropped it into the bucket. The rat tried to get out, run its way up the side of the ceramic, its claws sounding like miniature fingernails down blackboards. The snake seemed to ignore it at first, allowing the rat to tire. Then, without warning, it pounced. Jaws distended clamped on to the rat's head. It wriggled, tried desperately to pull away. It was only prolonging the agony. There was no escape now.

Decca closed his eyes. He had never heard a rat scream before.

'It will eat its prey head first,' said Kovacs. 'That way the legs will fold into its body. My snake will not be scratched or hurt. There will be nothing to stick in its throat. It will swallow its prey whole.'

Kovacs watched as the snake slowly gulped down the rat, the rat eventually giving up the fight.

'Look at that. Just muscle. No compassion. No conscience. No loyalty. Just the triumph of the will.'

When there was nothing more to watch, he looked up. Straight at Decca.

'The girl is gone?' he said.

Decca nodded.

'Completely? You did as I told you?'

Decca nodded.

'Where?'

Decca shrugged. 'Don't know. Just threw her out. Replaced her at the café. End of.'

Kovacs stared at him. 'Good.' Kovacs' eyes were unblinking. He gave Decca the same scrutiny one of his reptile pets would. 'Good.' He looked around, took in the artfully recreated jungle. 'Lenny had trouble the other night,' he said, addressing a yellow snake wrapped around an upper branch.

'Yeah,' said Decca, 'yeah, I heard.'

'He was taken to hospital. His arm has been broken in two places.'

'He didn't say anything,' said Decca. 'Told them he'd been mugged.'

'I don't expect him to say anything.'

'Some punter getting overattached, wasn't it? Running away with one of the girls.' Decca shrugged. Attempted a smile. 'Not to worry. Plenty more where she came from.'

'It might be worth worrying about.'

Decca frowned. 'How come?'

'Because I don't believe it was random. She was taken for a reason.'

'What reason?'

Kovacs looked at the python. The rat was now a distended lump in its body. It was unmoving, allowing its internal acids to go to work. 'That's what I want you to find out,' he said.

'What . . . what d'you want done about it?'

'I want her found. I want her brought back to me.' He pointed to a document wallet on the table. 'There is a photo of her. And where she was last staying. There is also a description of the people who took her and the car they took her in. A man and a woman. I want to know why they did. The girl I want alive. The ones who took her . . . use your judgement.'

Decca edged forward, stretched out his fingers, expecting the snake to jump out of the bowl at any minute and attack him.

Kovacs looked amused. 'It is a constrictor and it has just been fed. It is harmless.'

Decca gingerly lifted the folder from the table, jumped back as quickly as he could.

'I just don't like them,' he said. 'They've always given me the creeps.'

Kovacs smiled as if at a private joke. 'Nature is cruel. And that is its beauty.'

'Yeah. Whatever.' He looked at the folder.

'Take Christopher,' Kovacs said. 'He can help you. You can use your knowledge of the area. He can do the things—' Kovacs paused, looked down at the basin '—that you find distasteful.'

'Distasteful?' Decca had tried to keep his face blank and not speak but he couldn't help himself.

'You are good at hitting women, Derek, keeping them in line. And dealing with the men you put in place to manage the houses. But those women are weak and those men are cowards.'

Decca kept his face blank, nodded. He understood what was being said.

'You are being entrusted with a great opportunity here, Derek. Use it wisely.'

'Yes, Mr Kovacs.'

'He will be waiting for you at the front door. I suggest you waste no more time.'

Decca, realizing he had been dismissed, thanked his boss, told him he wouldn't regret it and turned to leave. The doors seemed miles away, the snakes watching him on all sides. He walked slowly towards them.

Once out of the vivarium he breathed a huge sigh of relief. Then another. After the third, he thought it time to go.

He walked down the hallway, looking again at the paint-ings and antiques. It was the way you were expected to live when you had money. As he walked, he smiled. He would do his best with this job. He would prove to Mr Kovacs that he was a good worker, that he was ripe for promotion. It would be a shame if anything happened to the girl or the two people who had taken her. But that wasn't his priority.

He had a boss to impress. He had money to make. A lifestyle to aim for.

He felt that hunger for success eating away inside him again.

Felt the spirit of Clint walking beside him.

No one, nothing, was going to stand in his way this time.

16

Donovan sat in the back of the Vauxhall Vectra, saying nothing, staring out of the window. The rain hadn't eased off. If anything, it was coming down harder. The only other sounds were breathing. His and Katya's. And, from the front, Nattrass and Turnbull's. Both twisted around, both staring at Donovan.

'So you goin' to tell us?' Turnbull asked again.

Donovan just looked at him. Said nothing.

'Well, well. Joe Donovan. My favourite gobshite do-gooder.' The words Turnbull had used when Nattrass and Turnbull had appeared at the door of the brothel. Donovan, knowing full well the history between himself and Turnbull, had mentally prided himself on not rising to the words, and instead hustled them both outside. He wanted Noddy well out of earshot of anything likely to be said. The detectives hadn't been too happy about him doing that. But then they weren't too happy about seeing him full stop.

After Turnbull's less-than-friendly greeting, Nattrass had stepped in. Businesslike, professional as usual. She had asked Donovan and Katya to walk with them to the car, get inside. Katya was clearly terrified. The fact that they weren't who she had thought they would be, but police instead, didn't make it any easier for her. She kept her hat pulled down, said nothing. Donovan, trying to deflect attention away from her, attempted levity. Failed.

'Good to see you again, Diane,' he had said with as big a smile as he could muster. 'How you keeping?'

'Just get in the car, please, Joe. It's pissing down.'

They got in the car.

Donovan noticed that Turnbull had been trying to look under Katya's cap all the way across the road. He knew whom Turnbull expected to find there. He knew he had to say something to stop him asking too many questions about her.

'This is a new associate of ours,' Donovan said, indicating Katya. 'Her name's Kate. She's working for me at the moment.'

Katya, picking up the hint, gave a little nod, supported by a small smile.

'Not Peta,' said Donovan. 'Sorry to disappoint you.'

Turnbull said nothing. Just looked like he wanted to hit Donovan.

In the car, riled now, he still wasn't letting up.

'Again,' said Turnbull. 'You want to tell us what you and your ladyfriend were doing visiting a known brothel?'

Donovan smiled. 'Ladyfriend? I don't think I've heard that phrase since England won the World Cup.'

'Funny fucker.' Turnbull's face showed he found him anything but.

Nattrass flashed him a warning look.

'I am,' said Donovan. 'Wait until you see my Tommy Cooper impression.'

Turnbull looked like overheating. Donovan expected to see steam rising from him. 'Just tell me what you were doing there.'

'I could ask you the same thing,' said Donovan. 'Why are two of Northumbria's finest going about harassing innocent members of the public for what they get up to in their own time?'

'Boys,' said Nattrass, a note of weary anger in her voice, 'I'm about to choke on the testosterone.'

The two men quietened down. Turnbull kept staring daggers at Donovan. Donovan winked at him. Nattrass sighed.

'Please,' she said. Then turned to Donovan. 'Let's not go through all that again. It's too tedious. We're investigating a murder. It's been classified high grade. I'm sure you've heard about it.'

'I have. I saw you on TV. You come across much better than Bob Fenton.'

Nattrass hid a smile. 'Don't try to flatter me, I'm working.' Then back to business. 'And the establishment you have just emerged from has come up in the course of our enquiries. And it's too much of a coincidence to find you there. So what's going on?'

Donovan smiled to himself. Good cop, bad cop. Perhaps they had started it as an act but, like wearing a mask for so long, it takes on the contours of your features until you become it and it you; it was hard to tell when the act stopped and they played it for real.

'What a double act,' he said. 'Better than Eric and Ernie in their prime.' He looked at Turnbull. 'Go on, show us your short, fat, hairy legs.'

Turnbull tried to get over the back of the seat and grab him. Nattrass stopped him. Turned to Donovan.

'Don't piss us about, Joe. We've got a job to do.'

'I know,' Donovan said. 'But it's fun. I'm working on the same case as you. For Janine Stewart.'

Distaste and disbelief fought for dominance on Turnbull's face. 'You? As what?'

'An investigator.'

Turnbull snorted. 'An investigator? You couldn't find your arse with both hands.'

Donovan smiled. 'Everything I know I learned from you. You're my hero.'

Nattrass sighed. 'For fuck's sake,' she said. 'Can't you two behave like adults?'

Donovan and Turnbull fell silent once more.

'Thank you,' said Nattrass. 'Now. Again. Why are you investigating this case?'

'Janine Stewart wants Michael Nell's alibi double-checked. Just to make sure there are no discrepancies.'

'Discrepancies?' said Nattrass.

'Yeah. You know what I mean. Michael Nell's not just an arrogant twat, but a rich arrogant twat. Janine Stewart thinks there might be a temptation to find him more guilty than he otherwise would have been.'

'What?' Nattrass' eyes flared.

'Only in an overzealous way to see justice done, of course.'

'We would investigate this case like any other,' said Nattrass. 'Why should she want you to do it too?'

'Like you said. It's been classified high grade. And since Nell senior's a rich man, some deaths are more important than others.'

Nattrass kept staring at him. Controlling her anger. 'So why do you care?'

Donovan shrugged. 'I don't know. I don't care. You know me. I just do what I'm told and pocket the cheque.'

'Right.' Nattrass gave him a look that said she believed he did anything but.

'So what did you find out?' asked Turnbull.

Donovan smiled again. 'Can't tell you. Client confidentiality and all that.'

Turnbull sighed. 'Mouthy bastard. I'm gonna smack you one of these days.'

Donovan just looked at him.

'Come on, boys,' said Nattrass. 'There's no conflict of interest. We're all on the same side here. Despite what Janine

Stewart might think. We want to either do him or exclude him.'

'Then I think you might be excluding him,' said Donovan. 'The woman he photographed says he was with her on the night Ashley disappeared.'

'Can she prove this?' asked Nattrass.

Donovan shrugged. 'Says she can. Says she'll put it in writing for me.'

'So you take the word of some whore at face value?' Turnbull sneered. 'You'll never make a proper investigator. You'll never make a copper.'

Donovan cast a glance to Katya. He saw her flinch when Turnbull said whore. Saw how upset she looked. This made him even more angry. 'And why would I want to? If they're all cunts like you.'

'Right, that's it,' said Nattrass. 'Out of the car. Go on, piss off. That's enough for one night.'

Donovan opened the car door, made to get out. Nattrass spoke again.

'If I need to talk to you again, I know where to find you. And if I do, you'd better pray that I'm in a better mood.'

Donovan said nothing, got out. Katya followed.

They walked back to the parked Mondeo, got in. Donovan no longer knew whether the rain had eased or increased. He no longer cared.

Jamal was waiting for them. 'I tried to tell you who it was, man, but you cut me off.'

'Sorry,' said Donovan. 'Thought it best to just run. But thank you for your concern.'

'Yeah, right.'

Donovan turned to Katya, who was taking off her cap, letting her hair loose. 'You OK?'

She nodded. 'OK. But not an experience I want to go through again.'

'Don't blame you. Let's go home.'

There was no argument with that. He started the car.

Unaware that the front curtain of the house he had just visited had been pulled aside, unaware that two faces were watching him go. Making notes.

And phone calls.

17

Those who don't learn from the past, the Historian had once read somewhere, are condemned to repeat it. And that was all he could see. Around him. All he could ever see. The past repeating itself.

The dead souls. He would glimpse them in alleyways, doorways. On buses, the Metro. Sitting in pubs or in a cinema. They guided him, spoke to him, gave him hope. Showed him the secret history of the city, where the past was hiding in the present. Gave him his special route, his places to visit.

Some places were more important than others. They spoke to him more clearly. Like this one.

Friday night. The old Keep.

He sat on a bench amid the ruined old walls of the city, the stone crumbling, making its own patterns, looking down at the Tyne. Just to his left was Long Stairs, a winding, twisting route down to the quayside. One of a number of a series of Georgian steps linking the higher and lower aspects of the city. The stairs were winding, in poor repair and badly lit; they provided ample camouflage for would-be muggers and rapists. They were often vomit dotted and provided good places for surreptitious late-night sex. Signs announced that hidden CCTV cameras had been added. Whether they were effective or not, the Historian didn't know. He was neither a mugger nor a rapist. He would never vomit or have sex in public. He was something different. Something special.

He looked down again. Through the old stone arch and down the stairs. And the flashback hit him, hard and fast: his father. That vicious, hated bastard.

And he could see again that violent, abusive man taking one last drunken stumble down the stairs. Could see again the ten-year-old version of himself watching him die.

His father lying there. Fear in his eyes, blood pooling beneath his skull. Asking for help. Remember picking up his father's head from the floor almost tenderly.

Dashing it back down as hard as he could.

Thinking how pleased his mother would be to know there was just the two of them now and he could never hurt them again.

He smiled at the memory. Could still feel the same warmth he had felt then.

A perfect moment.

He looked away. Loud music and flashing lights made their quayside siren calls up to those seeking drunken, drug-powered licentiousness. Those who wanted to lose themselves, to forget their present. The Historian saw that as a dereliction of their duty as human beings. He would never lose himself. He would never lose control.

He smiled, ignoring the rain. At his feet was one of his favourite parts of Newcastle's history. A hidden oubliette, built into the exposed stone flooring of the old fortifications. The council had put a new grate on it, bolted it firmly down so no drunks could throw their friends down it on the way home from the pub just for a laugh. Instead it had become a litter bin for those passing. Crisp packets, fast-food and sweet wrappers, old newspapers and soft drinks cans were all caught up in it. Strewn rubbish floated in the accu-mulated rainwater at the bottom. He would sometimes come with rubber gloves, bag up the litter and dispose of it responsibly. Bring a flask of instant coffee, a Tupperware of sandwiches. Make a day of it. Or a night of it. Like a relative tending the grave of a departed loved one.

In a way, that was what it was. The countless souls who had died down there for crimes they either did or didn't commit, or on the whim of some corrupt feudal chief. Just rotting away in a space too small to even stretch your arms out.

He heard the cries, the screams, the entreaties. The hopeless sobs, the last breaths. Coming down the centuries like echoes thrown up from a deep well.

He sighed. Thought of his experiment.

He had made notes, detailed and intricate, for that. It was almost ready to go ahead, the next stage. His plans were advanced. He even had an idea of who the next one would be. He had singled her out, watched her, recorded her movements. It would be so easy. He smiled. With all that was going on, he thought, you'd think people would be more careful. But some people never learn.

He smiled. Those who don't learn from the past are condemned to repeat it.

Or one in particular.

She would be the one. She would not just advance his theories; she would prove him right. He was sure of it. He could almost feel the satisfaction that would come from it. The peace. The release.

The euphoria.

He heard footsteps, voices. Someone coming up the stone stairs. Laughing, joking. Walking unsteadily. A man and a woman.

They hadn't seen him. He watched.

They stopped before they reached the top, the man pulling the woman into a shadowed alcove, kissing her exploring her with his hands.

The Historian watched.

The woman reciprocated in kind.

The Historian could feel himself becoming aroused. He slid his hand in his pocket, felt the handle of the knife he always carried, began to fondle it. He heard their gasps and sighs. He closed his eyes.

Then a scream.

The Historian looked up. The couple were looking directly at him; the woman fearful, the man angry.

The man was pulling himself together, crossing towards him.

'What's your game, eh? What d'you think you're doin'?'

The Historian looked at him, said nothing.

'That how you get your kicks, is it? Eh?'

The man stood over him. Even in the rain he was sweating alcohol and violence.

The Historian said nothing. Just looked at him, barely blinking.

The man kept clenching and unclenching his fists. He wanted to fight, to hit, but the Historian wasn't making it easy. He wasn't playing along.

The woman crossed to him, put her arm around him.

'Come on, Jeff. Let's go. We'll get a taxi, be home in twenty minutes. Come on.'

The man's anger was diminishing. But he wasn't moving.

'Come on,' said the woman again. 'He's just some weirdo. Come on.'

The man began to yield to her entreaties. He began to walk away. 'Next time I catch you, though, next time . . .'

Clenching and unclenching his fists.

The Historian could see the encounter had left him unfulfilled. Perhaps his woman would bear the brunt of that later, he thought.

The couple walked away. The Historian watched them go, then resumed looking over the Tyne, at the oubliette.

He sighed. He could hear the voices now. They were coming to him strong.

He smiled. No longer alone.

Anita was trying to get used to this. Her second night of it.

She sat on a stool at a bar just opposite one of the quayside's hotels, a hotel usually used by businessmen attending meetings away from home. She was trying to pretend that she belonged there. Convince others of it too. She wore a full-sleeved black dress, long enough to be modest, short enough to send out the correct signals, and sat with her black-stockinged legs crossed at the ankles, sipping a gin and tonic. She took deep breaths, practised keeping her hands from shaking. Her expression was as blank as she could make it. A stone wall she wanted no one to penetrate. Keep the screaming, tearful sad girl locked up behind it, like an imprisoned princess heroine in a castle from one of her old romantic stories.

Doing what she had to do to survive.

No longer one of the lucky ones.

She had left Decca's flat feeling more bereft than she had in a long time. She had phoned the two other girls she worked with but they had been told to have nothing to do with her. She understood. Didn't blame them. It was a fragile net that supported them in this country, the slightest rip could send them all tumbling.

She had walked around, thought of spending her last bit of money on a hotel. Before she could do that, she had stopped in a bar for a drink. She didn't know which one. She just wanted somewhere she could sit and think.

She wasn't alone for long. A man came to join her. She let him. He was middle-aged, overweight and red-faced. Wearing the obligatory business suit. She looked at him, caught glimpses of what his wife must have once found attractive about him.

He made it quite clear to her what he had in mind. She pretended to mull it over, weigh up his offer. All the while trembling inside. She thought of her options. They had shrunk, right down to the man opposite her. She had no choice. Accepted his offer. The only proviso being she had to spend the night. He couldn't believe his luck.

Back to his hotel. She had done worse things. With worse people. At least she had a bed for the night.

When she left him in the morning, she gave herself seven hours to find something else, another way of getting by. With seven hours up, she had failed. Every bar, shop and café she went into said they weren't interested. They weren't hiring. Not at first: they would look at her face. It was a yes. Then hear her voice. A no. She was foreign. Eastern European. An asylum seeker. A refugee. A tabloid hate figure. A pretty one, admittedly, but still. There were limits. They didn't tell her she was untrustworthy, perhaps even disease-ridden Inferior. They didn't have to. She saw it all in their eyes.

So, with the evening coming down cold and hard like rain, she was back in the bar. She moved her arm to her drink, the fresh cuts on her arms rubbing against the fabric of her dress. She moved her arms some more, just to feel them.

She had fended off several advances; none of them had struck her as being the right ones. Money, but no shelter. Then she was approached. Middle-aged again. Short and balding this time. Suited, playing with his wedding ring like it weighed too heavily on his finger. A salesman's smile. An anonymous man.

He sat next to her, went into the routine. Asked her if the seat was taken. She responded with her own part of the routine. He sat. Ordered drinks. They began talking. He lied. She lied. She didn't know who lied the most. She didn't care. Then the questions by him. The artfully placed answers by her. Encouraging, but subtle. Like wearing black-lace lingerie beneath a nine-to-five suit; offering only a tantalizing glimpse. A trailer of forthcoming attractions.

Then the negotiation. Her proviso offered, agreed to.

And off they went. He sweating and hot, she sweating and cold.

At the door, an unexpected piece of gallantry: holding it open for her. In return a smile like he had just bought her a huge diamond ring.

Then walking back to the hotel, arm in arm.

At the doors, a final word. 'You're lucky you met me, you know.'

Feigning interest. 'Why?'

'Because there's some right nutters out there, you know.'

She gives a nod. Agreement.

And in they went. The hotel doors closing silently behind them.

Sealing them in, like a castle drawbridge pulling up.

18

'So what d'you fancy, then?' asked Donovan.

'Surprise me,' said Katya, smiling.

It was late. They were back at the cottage in Northumberland. The remains of an Indian takeaway on the coffee table before them, opened bottles of wine and cans of beer and soft drinks at their sides. Jamal had taken himself off to bed, leaving Donovan and Katya alone in the front room. Donovan bent in front of his CD collection, looking for something to play. Something restful. Something that would take away the evening they had just experienced.

'What about some Tom Waits?' he said. 'Early stuff. Not later. Not what I want right now.'

Katya shrugged. Curled up on the sofa. 'OK.'

Donovan ran his finger down the spines of the CDs, pausing momentarily at Shawn Colvin's *A Few Small Repairs* before selecting Tom Waits' *Closing Time*. He slipped the disc into the player. The piano rolled lazily in, sweetly melancholic yet tuneful, soon to be joined by Waits' voice, which was still quite sweet, not yet affected by his Brechtian Beefheart bawl.

'This is nice.' Katya smiled.

'Doubt he's ever been called nice before,' said Donovan, settling down on the floor, his back to the sofa. Tried to relax.

They had driven back from Newcastle, suddenly hungry from the night's exertions. Donovan had stopped for takeaway food and alcohol in Denton, then driven all the way back as fast as he could. He felt there was nothing more that could have been accomplished that night. He would phone Janine Stewart in the morning, go about getting a written statement from Sharon as soon as possible.

As he drove, Jamal had started to fall asleep in the back of the car; Katya seemed to join him. Donovan didn't blame them. He felt like nodding off too.

He still had doubts about involving Jamal in his work, feeling that the boy should be in school. That, however, presented too many challenges. Legally, Jamal wasn't supposed to be there. Donovan should have informed the authorities that the boy was living with him. But he hadn't. Jamal had begged him not to, and with good reason: he hadn't had a very positive experience of those organizations whose job it was to provide for and protect children. Donovan, he felt, could do a better job. Plus, Jamal had argued, the things he had seen on the street, the things he had done just to survive, kind of disqualified him from being with kids his own age. Donovan had his doubts about that, but they had fallen into a loose arrangement. Jamal could stay until he was on his own two feet again. Until there was somewhere he wanted to be more. And in that time, he, Peta and Amar would take responsibility for schooling him. And if he wanted to be with kids his own age, there were children in the village he could hang out with. That was nearly a year ago. Jamal showed no signs of wanting to move on. Donovan, for his part, hadn't really encouraged him to. They enjoyed each other's company. Not that they would ever admit it, though. Plus, Jamal had struck up a friendship with a boy in the village. Donovan had never thought that would happen but was glad that it had.

Katya placed her empty wine glass down on the coffee table.

'Want a refill?' asked Donovan, reaching for the bottle, filling up her glass without waiting for an answer.

'You drink a lot, Joe. Why, I wonder?'

'No more than anyone else.' Donovan had drained his final can and was reaching to uncork a half-empty bottle of Black Bush. He poured a couple of fingers into a small tumbler.

'It's OK,' said Katya. 'None of my business.'

Donovan shrugged. Staring straight ahead, listening to the music. 'I drink. It's what I do.'

Katya nodded. Silence from the pair of them. She reached towards the table, picked up her glass. Drank. Tom Waits singing that he was wishing he could stay a little longer, how the feeling was getting stronger.

'May I ask a question?' Katya said, once they had drunk a little more, listened a little more.

'You can ask,' said Donovan with a smile.

Katya looked at her drink, her fingers playing with the stem, swirling the dark red liquid around as if she would find the words she wanted and the courage to say them within the glass. 'The locked door. What is behind it?'

Donovan said nothing. He raised his glass to his lips, drank the whisky, felt the usually smooth drink burn as it went down. Deciding what to say. Tom Waits singing that he was looking at a woman across a bar, hoping he wouldn't fall in love with her.

Had another drink. Made up his mind.

'I had a son,' he said tentatively. 'I have a daughter, too, but I had a son.'

He stopped. Katya waited.

'I had a son and he . . .' He took another drink. '. . . he disappeared.'

'Disappeared?'

Donovan nodded. 'Disappeared. One minute he was

there, the next—' he lifted his lightly clenched hand, opened his fingers '—boom.' The word spoken quietly. A distant explosion. An acid raincloud dispersing.

Katya said nothing.

'We were in a store, we were buying something for his mum. I turned around and . . . he was gone. Never found.'

Katya leaned forward. 'No trace? No . . . clues?'

'Nothing. Nothing at all.' Donovan sighed, took another drink.

'In my country during war this happened all the time. But not here.'

'I can give you chapter and verse. I've memorized it. Five hundred and seventy-five people go missing every day. Over a hundred thousand people aged eighteen or under go missing every year. Children missing for more than a week—' his voice cracked '—for more than a week have a forty-four per cent chance of being hurt.'

Katya looked at him, said nothing.

'I used to have more than a son. I had a wife. A family. A good job. When David went, all those things went with him.'

Katya nodded.

More silence. Tom Waits singing about midnight lullabies.

Katya began hesitantly: 'Your wife? Your daughter?'

'Went with the job. After the breakdown.' Donovan stared at the wall. Saw something that wasn't there, saw beyond it. 'Couples never stay together after something like that. Families can never survive. At least mine didn't.'

'So . . . that room. That was his room?'

Donovan nodded. 'It *is* his room. He's never been there. But it's his room. It's got his life in it. His past.' He put the glass to his lips, swallowed more than a mouthful of whisky. 'His future.'

'His future?'

'I've got people out there. Looking. Hunting. For any clue, any sighting. Sharkey has a network out there. When they find anything, they'll report to me. And I'll go to him. Whatever's happened to him.'

'Do you think that will happen?'

Tom Waits singing about days of roses, about there being no tomorrow, packing away sorrows and saving them for rainy days.

'I hope so,' he said quietly. 'I've got to hope so.'

He said nothing more, just stared at the wall.

'I am sorry for you,' she said. 'I know what is to lose a loved one, a family, and think you will never see them again.' She smiled. 'But I know I will see my brother again. I am lucky.'

He nodded. 'And I'm glad for you. Really.'

A cloud passed over Katya's face. 'I will see my brother again, yes? You promised?'

'I promised,' said Donovan. Arranging a meeting with her brother had been the condition she had made in accompanying Donovan. 'And you will.'

She smiled. 'Thank you. That makes me happy. You are good man, Joe Donovan. I wish the same happiness for you.'

Donovan smiled. It had a bittersweet edge, like crushed rock salt and lime around a tequila glass. 'Thank you.'

She put her hand on his shoulder. It felt smooth and warm to the touch. Donovan couldn't remember the last time a woman had touched him like that.

He looked up. She had put her glass down and was leaning forward, her other hand on him too. She bent down, her face before his. Her eyes closed. Hesitantly, she moved forward.

'Don't,' he said.

She stopped, opened her eyes as if from a dream. Pulled back from him. 'Why? Don't you . . . like me?'

Donovan almost smiled. 'Yes, I do, Katya. But I haven't had a very . . . I don't have a very good track record. In . . . with girlfriends. Partners. Not recently. And that's another story.'

'Perhaps not all stories have sad endings,' she said. 'Perhaps some end happy?'

She slid on to the floor next to him. Her arms went around him again. Eyes locked with his. He hadn't noticed how beautiful they were. Deep blue. Drowning pools.

'You have been good to me.'

'You don't have to—'

She put her fingers to his lips, hushed him. 'I like you. But you are lonely. I know what that feels like.' She bent further forward, her eyes closing again.

'This is wrong,' he said, fighting the growing sense of arousal in his body. 'I'm meant to be helping you. Looking after you.'

'You are,' she said, almost in a whisper. 'And I look after you.'

'You sure you want this?'

She nodded, her eyes still closed. Lips smiling.

Their lips met. Mouths opened. Arms entwined, bodies soon after that.

Tom Waits sang about little trips to heaven. About it being closing time.

Donovan turned the CD player off. He and Katya made their way upstairs to his bedroom.

Amar closed his eyes, opened them again. His vision was crashing against his head. He was swimming towards what he saw, struggling to stay focused. He shook his head. He didn't know what he'd taken.

Anything. Everything.

The camcorder shook as he moved it around. He was

aware of bodies moving, writhing before him, aware that although he was pointing the camera at them, he was missing what was going on.

He had told himself he would stop doing this. Told himself he had only done it because it was necessary. Because he needed the money. And for a time he had given it up.

It. Filming private gay orgies hosted in a rich man's house, by the rich man himself. Strictly behind the camera, he had stipulated. He was not to take part. not to be invited to take part. Whatever was on offer – sex, drugs, drink – was not to be offered to him. He didn't want any part of it. He wanted to stay focused. Rise above it. It was a job. That was how he regarded it.

For a while.

Then came the odd spliff. A glass of wine. A line of charlie. A cute young man offering himself up. Just the occasional indulgence. Not harming anyone. Getting for free what the others paid for. Getting paid for doing it too.

Then an escalation. More lines. Of charlie. Of young men. More wine. Blow. More. More.

Then came self-realization. He knew what he was doing. To himself. To his reputation as a professional. And with the self-realization, a complete stop. He turned down work, offers. Other work came in. Albion had started; it seemed to be going well. He concentrated on that. Let the drugs go. Cut down the alcohol. Got back into shape. Peta got her gym partner back again. And helped in the education of Jamal. He liked the boy. He really did. And with all that, he didn't need to go back. Didn't need the other stuff.

But it began creeping back. He felt something within him. Boredom? Lack of fulfilment? A writhing serpent coiled there in his guts, telling him what he wanted. What he needed.

And he listened.

Secretly at first, so Joe and Peta didn't find out. Then, when directly questioned, openly admitted it. Yes, he was back at the parties. And, yes, he was enjoying them. They had responded more with sadness than anger, asking him not to do it, but he had ignored them. He was fine. He could hold himself together for work. It wasn't affecting him.

Then came earlier in the day. Walking out of the café.

Fuck them. He was too old to be told what to do. He would do what he wanted to do. And if they didn't like it, fuck them. Fuck them all.

He looked around the room, tried to focus his lens, his eyes. As he did so, he stumbled, tripped. Fell to his knees, his fall broken by a naked man's body. The camera spilling to the floor. The man smiled, stopped what he was doing and to whom, put his arm around him. Amar let him. Amar yielded to him. Someone else joined them. Amar didn't know who, didn't see them. Couldn't see them.

He closed his eyes. Gave in. Stopped swimming, let the tide engulf him; bear him away on it.

The camera, his pretext for being there, was lost.

And soon he joined it.

Lost in the realm of the senses. The realm of the senseless. Lost.

Donovan lay awake, staring at the ceiling. Katya next to him, her body curled into his, sleeping. Or pretending to. She breathed deeply, a smile playing on her lips. She looked relaxed, contented. Dreaming.

The rain had ceased. Donovan, who should have fallen asleep first, had been lying there long enough to hear it stop.

Mention of David had done it. Started him thinking again.

Donovan still saw him. In the street. In his mind's eye. In dreams.

Always when he least expected it. He would be coping, getting on with his life, not thinking about his past. Walking down Northumberland Street, say, or Grainger Street, Eldon Square even. Or in a shop. A café. Starbucks. Off in his own world. Happy, or at least content, in the moment. Then he would hear a voice. Catch a glimpse of dark hair. Recognize a walk. And look up. And see him. Coming out of a shop. Chatting to his mates. Or head down, hoodied and denimed, texting.

And Donovan would turn, wait for that familiar skip of his heart. He would open his mouth, make to call out, start to run. Unable to stem the joy bubbling within. Rushing to hold him. Hug him. Make him feel safe.

But he would never get there, never call. Because the rational part of his brain would stop him. Make him look again. And he would stop. Do as instructed. Look again. Truly see the boy. His hair would be wrong. His walk. His eyes. It wasn't David.

It was never David.

And then he'd stand, like an inflatable toy that's had the air stamped out of it. Feeling worse than empty. And it would start again. The cocoon of the present would crumble. The past would press down on him again. Remind him how precarious his balance was in the world. Like a cancer sufferer reminded of their disease, a psychic intimation of sudden death.

And things would unravel again.

But not as bad as they had been, down as low as the point he had once reached. He had never contemplated picking up the gun again. The old revolver. Loading the bullet, spinning the chamber, placing it against his temple, waiting for the click.

Russian roulette. Just a game. But one with the power of life and death over himself. A way of taking away the pain. Permanently, perhaps.

He had vowed never to reach that state again. No matter what he went through.

He had thrown the gun away. Into the river, down the Tyne.

Lost.

But he still had dreams.

Sometimes David would sit at the end of the bed and talk.

He would have aged. Real time. Three years older. Nine years old. And Donovan would talk to him. Father and son. Ask him anything. Anything. And he would answer.

Except one question. The important one.

Where are you? Alive or dead? Where are you?

No answer. That would be David's cue to disappear, Donovan's time to wake up.

He would lie there, grasping at air, clinging.

To dreams.

He looked at the sleeping woman next to him. Wondered what was going through her head, what her dreams were about. What haunted her.

He put his arm around her, closed his eyes. He didn't want dreams tonight. He wanted sleep. And when it came he hoped it would be deep, restful.

Black and empty.

Jamal lay awake.

He had heard them talking, playing that fucking awful music. Then a silence. Then them both coming up to bed together. Then the noises from Donovan's bedroom. He knew what was going on. He wasn't stupid.

He lay there, trying not to listen.

It wasn't right. It shouldn't have happened. Katya seemed OK, but she shouldn't have gone to bed with Joe.

Didn't know why; it just wasn't right.

He lay there. He, too, had heard the rain stop. He turned over on his side, pulled the duvet around him, closed his eyes. Tried to sleep. Tried hard to sleep.

He didn't know why, but it just wasn't right.

19

The rain held off. The sun seemed to be considering putting in an appearance. There was wind, though. Threatening to be strong, cold even. Too early for spring, but even the illusion of spring would do.

Michael Nell didn't care what the weather was like. He could have stepped into the middle of a tornado and he would have been happy. Or happier than where he had just come from.

He stood on the steps of Market Street police station and took in Newcastle city centre, took in the world.

Buses. Cars. Pedestrians. People going somewhere, going nowhere. The mundanity of an existence he purported to despise. He never thought he would be as pleased to see that Saturday mundanity again.

They had let him go. He couldn't believe it. They had let him go.

Days of questioning, of sitting in that stinking room, the words going around and around in an ever-decreasing circle, each time with a little more knowledge, designed to wrong-foot him, force him into making a mistake, an admission of guilt, circling tighter and tighter until they eventually enclosed him, suffocated him, the only chance of air coming with a full confession.

But he hadn't given one. He hadn't cracked.

And then this. They had let him go.

He stood on the steps and looked around. The fledgling euphoria that had been building up within him disappeared.

There, sitting in a silver Vauxhall Vectra, were those two bastard coppers. Nattrass and Turnbull.

He felt himself begin to shake, swallowed hard.

Walk away. Just walk away. Don't give them the satisfaction.

He found his feet moving towards the Vectra. Crossing
Market Street, ignoring oncoming buses, walking, his path
direct like a heat-seeking missile.

He saw them look up, get out of the car. Saw Turnbull,
that hard-faced, evil fucker, smile. Crack his knuckles even.

Nell walked faster.

He reached the car. They were waiting for him.

'This it, then?' Nell said. 'The welcoming committee?'

'Have to be, won't it?' said Turnbull, squaring up for a
fight. 'Don't see your daddy here, do you? Or that high-
priced lawyer? Just us.' He gave a nod to the police station,
laughed. 'That's what you get when you come down here.
Just us.'

'I'm innocent,' Nell said, his voice breaking. 'I did nothing wrong and you can't touch me.'

Turnbull went up to him, nose to nose. His voice was
low, carrying the promise of violence. 'You're dirty. You did
it. We'll find something.'

Nell's earlier anger was being replaced by fear. He didn't
doubt what this copper was saying, didn't doubt that he
could do it if he wanted to.

The other one, Nattrass, stepped in. 'Be on your way,
please, Mr Nell. You're free to go. But please keep yourself
available, because we may need to interview you again.' She
almost smiled.

'I'll . . . I'll do you . . . This, this is harassment.'

Turnbull smiled, pointed at Market Street police station.
'Care to step over there and make a complaint? We'll be
happy to accompany you.'

Nell backed off. Turnbull gave another unpleasant smile. Nell could smell the alcohol simmering and sweating its way out of him.

Nell turned away. He couldn't bear them both looking at him.

'Keep lookin' over your shoulder, matey boy,' said Turnbull. 'One day we'll be there.'

There was nothing Nell could do. He began to walk away.

The rain had held off. The sun had put in an appearance. There was no wind, strong or otherwise.

Michael Nell didn't care what the weather was like. He wanted to scream, to shout.

He wanted to cry.

He walked away into the sunshine.

'So they've let him go?' said Donovan, looking at Janine Stewart.

'This morning. Couldn't keep him any longer. Failed to prove a case.'

Donovan nodded. He was listening to the words, but not hearing them. The power-dressed Janine Stewart was breaking up, the office around her fragmenting. In her place was Katya. They were still back in bed.

Her body: thin, lean, small-breasted, like a sinuous rope of muscle wrapped around him. Holding tight on to him. Digging in, pulling him further into her. Her eyes not closed but wide open, staring at him, into him.

It had been intense. More intense than he had imagined it would be. If he had had any expectations, they would have involved warmth, acceptance. An end to loneliness, an intimacy with another. He had wanted to go easy, gently: he thought she must have been damaged and fragile. But she wasn't having any of it.

Irrespective of which position they had been in, and there had been many, or what activity they had been engaged in at the time, Donovan felt, knew, that she had been in charge. Taking him with her, leading him on, getting him where she wanted him. He had been taken, roughly, violently. Her eyes either closed or fixed on something he couldn't see, perhaps something he didn't want to see.

Afterwards they had talked.

'Thank you,' she had said, her hands stroking his hot, still sweating skin. 'What I needed.'

'Good.'

'You enjoyed it?'

'Yeah,' he said, eyes flicking away from her. 'Course I did.'

'You seemed . . . not to let yourself go. Is this famous British reserve?' She gave a small laugh. 'Is your upper lip stiff?'

Donovan had smiled. 'Not my upper lip. No, I'm just a bit . . . out of practice, that's all.'

She kept looking at him.

'I just . . . didn't want to hurt you. You know. After all you've been through. Been forced to do, and that. Thought I should be . . . I don't know. Gentle. Respectful.'

She propped herself up, looked at him. 'I am not a flower, Joe. To be just admired. I am stronger. With needs. Like you. Like everyone.'

'I know. It's just . . .'

She smiled. 'It does not matter.'

She kissed him. Hard. He responded. Getting hard again. Hands over each other's bodies. She pulled away, looked into his eyes again.

'I will not break,' she said, then smiled. Secrets were contained in that smile. Secrets Donovan might want to take. 'But I will bend . . .'

And she had. And so had he.

'Joe? Mr Donovan?'

Donovan looked up. Janine Stewart was looking at him.

'Are you all right?'

Donovan looked around, surprised to find himself back in Stewart's office.

'Yeah. Yeah, I'm fine.'

Stewart looked at him as if she didn't agree with his words. Donovan felt he should say something.

'So have they . . . has there been any, erm, any other lines of enquiry?'

Stewart raised her eyebrows. It was, thought Donovan, what passed for a shrug from her. 'They're still trying to find eyewitnesses for Ashley's disappearance from her street in Fenham. Apparently two young men and an old man pushing an old woman in a wheelchair haven't come forward.'

'Can they trace them?'

'They're trying. Not holding out much hope, but you never know. Stranger things have happened. And they're doing the usual. Door-to-door community teams. Mobile office set up in the estate beside the graveyard Ashley was found in.'

'Anything?'

'Nothing so far. Nothing solid.'

Donovan nodded. 'Forensics?'

'Not that I've heard. Nothing that links my client in.' She sat back. 'But Michael Nell, despite the shaky and circumstantial evidence, is still their prime suspect. We haven't heard the last from them.'

'No.'

'But thank you for your work. Very well done.' She looked at the file lying on her desk. Donovan had made it as comprehensive as possible. Including his brush with Nattrass and Turnbull. Excluding the involvement of Katya. She was just obliquely referred to as a source.

'Send in your invoice and we'll pay you straight away.'

'Thank you.'

Donovan nodded, gone again. Back to earlier that morning, getting up.

Jamal had been in a strange mood. Donovan had met him, unsmiling, in the kitchen. Said hello to the boy, but received only a grunt in return.

'You OK?' Donovan had asked, putting the kettle on.

Jamal shrugged, took his toast into the front room. Sat on the sofa, turned on the TV. Stared at it. Hard.

Donovan followed him. 'What's up?'

'Nothin'.' Mumbled through a mouthful of toast and jam.

Jamal turned up the volume with the remote. A music video of a band Donovan knew Jamal didn't like.

Donovan sat on the arm of the sofa. 'You sure there's nothing wrong? You can tell me. You know that.'

'Can I?'

There was something behind the words, something Donovan couldn't place. Anger? Resentment? Disappointment? Donovan thought.

Katya.

He sighed. 'What's this about?' he said, having a fair idea. 'Do I know what this is about?'

On the TV was a New York band with skinny ties and abrasive guitars. Everything Jamal hated, yet he stared at them, enrapt, as if he was hanging on to their every word.

Donovan waited.

'It's not right,' Jamal said eventually, mumbling again.

'What's not?'

Jamal turned to him then. Donovan saw something had torn behind his eyes. 'You slept with Katya. Don't deny it, man, 'cos I heard yous.'

Donovan sighed. 'Yes, Katya and I slept together. Why do you have a problem with that?'

Jamal turned back to the TV. Shrugged again. "Cos. 'Snot right. That's all.'

Donovan looked at the boy, struggling with emotions he didn't understand. He wondered how best to explain, what the right words would be.

He wondered what he would say if it was his own son asking him the question.

'It *was* right, Jamal. It felt right. For Katya as well.'

Jamal looked at him again. When he spoke, there was genuine pain behind his words. 'You're meant to be protecting her, man. That's not protecting her. That's . . . that's . . . abuse, man. That's what, what used to happen to me . . .' His voice became smaller. He swallowed his final words.

Donovan's heart went out to the boy. When they had met, Jamal had been living one step above the street, selling his body to perverts and paedophiles. Donovan's intervention had changed all that. He thought the boy had grown, mentally and emotionally as well as physically. Perhaps not as much as he had thought.

'It's not the same,' Donovan said. 'It was Katya's idea as much as mine.' More so, he thought, but didn't say that. 'We're both consenting adults. That means we both wanted to do it. One doesn't force the other. It's not abuse when that happens. And, despite what she's been through, she has needs too. We both do.'

Jamal looked at Donovan, almost as if seeing him for the first time. He looked away. Shrugged. 'Just sayin'. Doesn't feel right, that's all.'

Donovan stood up. 'I'm sorry, Jamal. But it's happened, and that's that. Doesn't change anything else here.'

Jamal kept staring at the TV.

'Look, I've got to go into Newcastle today. You want to come with me? Ask Jake if he wants to come.' Jake was Jamal's friend from the village. Complete opposites, Donovan had first thought: he was white, middle class, privately educated. His parents weren't too happy about them mixing, but there was nothing they could do about it. The boys had strong friendship that belied their backgrounds.

Jamal shrugged.

'Go around the record shops. Whatever you two get up to.'

Jamal gave a small nod.

'Good.' He found a smile. 'Look, Katya being here doesn't change anything. Jamal, we're still best mates.'

Jamal nodded, tried to keep his face hard, his features set. Donovan knew the look. Knew what insecurities and softnesses lay behind it too.

The kettle clicked. Donovan walked back into the kitchen. Made coffee for himself and Katya.

Took it back upstairs. Thinking of Jamal's words and his own answers. Wondering which one was right.

'Is that all right, Joe? Mr Donovan?'

'Yeah.'

Donovan looked up. He was back in Stewart's office. He had no idea whether he had just agreed to sleep with all the men in Janine Stewart's company or run naked through Newcastle city centre. He hoped he hadn't agreed to forgo his fee. That would be really bad news.

Stewart, from the look on her face, seemed equally unconvinced by his response.

'Yeah,' he said again. 'That'll be fine.'

'So even though we don't need the written testimony, you'll be happy to undertake further work for us?'

That must have been it. 'Sure,' he said. 'No problem.' He blinked hard.

Stewart leaned forward. Scrutinized him. 'Are you all right, Mr Donovan?'

Donovan rubbed his face. 'Just tired. Was up late. Writing your report.'

'Very diligent.' She stood up, extended her hand. 'Well, thank you for your time. I'm sure we'll be in touch.'

Donovan thanked her and walked out into the street. He needed a coffee. Or preferably something stronger.

20

The Free Trade pub in Byker had, Decca thought, the best view in Newcastle. Situated at the top of a hill in one of the few undeveloped areas along the north bank of the Tyne, it gave drinkers the opportunity to gaze down the hill and let their eyes sweep along, taking in not only the bridges but also the Baltic Centre for Contemporary Art, the Courthouse, the Sage. The whole of the reworked and redeveloped river-front, even the Gateshead Hilton.

'Look,' he said to Christopher, sitting opposite him. Christopher looked. 'You can look down that hill, see all along the Tyne. There's the bridges, the Millennium, the Tyne, the Swing, the High Level, the, um, the other two, and then the, er, the last one. Beautiful, isn't it?'

Christopher neither nodded nor spoke, just continued to look. His continuing silence made Decca nervous. Made him talk.

'Makes you proud to be a Geordie, doesn't it? Well, I mean, you're not. I know that. I mean, it makes you proud, doesn't it? Looking along there.' He shook his head. 'City of me birth. That's the future, down there.'

Decca looked again at the waterfront. There was serious money behind the new developments. Serious money. Every time he looked at it he was riven with envy. Hungry to get a slice of it, aching to be on the inside of the deal-making. It would happen. It had to happen.

Christopher said nothing, his untouched mineral water in front of him.

'They were gonna build a towerblock, y'know. Here. Right in front of this window. Offices or expensive flats, somethin' like that. But they said no. People who drink here got it stopped. Must be pretty powerful to do that, eh?'

Christopher said nothing.

Decca took another pull from the neck of his bottle, looked around. 'Mind, if they are that powerful,' he said, 'they're hidin' it well.'

The pub was of a dying breed: bare-board floors, Formica-topped tables, mismatched chairs. Nicotine walls and dark wooden fittings. No sawdust, just spit. Standing outside, he wondered how it kept going, made a profit. But once inside he saw there was no shortage of customers, even for a Saturday afternoon. It was an old man's pub, but not just full of old men. Mostly young men, plus women too. All in jeans and T-shirts. The occasional old sweater, leather jacket. Smoking roll-ups, drinking pints. Putting songs on the jukebox he'd never heard of, reading papers he would never buy. Passing sections around, discussing things they came across. Some of the girls would look OK if they made the effort. Bit of make-up, some more flattering clothes. Heels. And ditch the roll-ups. Decca shook his head. The whole place felt alien to him. The girls especially. He couldn't understand why anyone wouldn't want to make the most of themselves.

He felt out of place. Overdressed in his butter-soft designer leather jacket and designer, artfully tinted and distressed jeans. Plus his expensively teased hair. He felt like a breed apart. And Christopher was no better. Wearing a leather jacket so out of fashion it was threatening to make a comeback. Not that Decca planned on telling him.

Decca looked at his watch. Past three o'clock.

'He's late,' he said, not expecting a response.

'People of his sort are always late,' said Christopher.

Decca looked up. Almost did a comic double take. 'What?'

'They are small. Then given tiny power. More than they ever had before. Think it allows them to behave as they wish.' He shook his head slowly, his eyes and features impassive. A slightly mobile Easter Island statue. 'They all learn eventually.'

Decca said nothing. The tone of Christopher's voice scared him even more than the words. It was monotonous, dead. He preferred it when he didn't speak.

'Right,' he said. 'Right.'

They waited in silence. Some unendurable rock racket on the jukebox. Decca wished for his RnB CDs. Wished he was working alone. Or on a different job altogether.

The front door opened. Decca turned. Almost sighed in relief. Lenny, his arm encased in rigid plastic and strapped down to his body, looked around. He saw them, made his way over.

'Everyone all right for a drink?' he said.

Decca pointed to his bottle. 'Same again.'

Lenny attempted a smile, went to the bar.

Christopher leaned over. Fixed Decca with his dead man's eyes. 'This is not social. This is work.'

Decca swallowed hard. 'I know.' He shrugged. 'Just . . . being polite.'

Christopher said nothing more, leaned back. Resumed staring out of the window. Decca kept his eyes on Lenny.

Lenny returned, placed a bottle of lager down for Decca, a gin and tonic for himself. He took the first mouthful, lips pulling back over his slightly prominent teeth in his rodent-like little face as he did so.

'What's that?' asked Decca.

'Gin an' tonic. What I always drink.'

Decca remembered Christopher's earlier words about the granting of power to small men. 'Tryin' to be posh, Lenny?'

Lenny shrugged. 'Don't like beer.' He took another rat-faced slurp. 'Like this, though.'

Decca leaned forward, tried to make his face as expressionless as Christopher's. 'Hear you had some trouble the other night, Lenny.'

Lenny gestured with his arm, winced from the pain. 'Aye. An' if I catch the bitch that did this, I'll fuckin' 'ave 'er. She won't know what's hit 'er.'

'Who was she?'

Lenny shrugged. 'Dunno. A freelancer, I thought. Just got dropped off there. Said the usual girl wasn't comin'. She would be takin' 'er place.'

'Have you spoken to the usual girl?'

Lenny nodded.

'And?'

'Said someone turned up. Told her to steer clear. Said the place had been raided.'

'Did you get the car numberplate?'

Lenny shook his head.

'Did you recognize who took her?'

Another shake.

'Police?'

'Nah, we'da heard about it. We make our payments.' Lenny looked between Decca and Christopher. 'Why's she so important, anyway? Some tart? They sent another one along. She's doin' better than this one you're lookin' for. Less of an attitude.'

Decca ignored him. 'So no one's heard anythin' from her?'

'Well . . .'

'Well what?'

Lenny leaned forward. 'This is good stuff,' he said, eyes alight with rat glee. 'Might be worth a little bit extra. Y'knaworramean?'

He rubbed his greasy, filthy fingers against his equally unappealing thumb.

'You want payin' for this? That what you're tellin' me?'

Lenny grinned and nodded.

Decca stared at him. 'Lenny, if you've got somethin' to tell me, you tell me.'

'Let's make a deal,' said Lenny.

'Let's not.'

They both looked up. Christopher had detached his gaze from the window and was now focusing on Lenny, giving him his dead-eyed, Easter Island, unblinking stare.

'You have information. You give us information.' Christopher's voice matched his eyes.

Lenny weighed up his options, decided on another pitch 'Look, it's got to be worth something, I—'

Christopher's hand shot out with a speed that took even Decca by surprise. He grabbed Lenny's bad arm, located the points that were giving him the most pain and pressed down. Hard. Lenny's mouth twisted in almost medieval agony, revealing dirty, decaying teeth, unhindered by any regular dental hygiene regime.

'Don't scream, Lenny,' said Christopher, pulling Lenny towards him across the table, making sure his victim's body was blocking the rest of the pub's view of what was happening, 'That would disappoint me.'

Decca almost smiled. It was the first time he had enjoyed having Christopher with him. A tingle of power ran through him. He folded his arms, sat back. Stopped himself from smiling.

'You heard the man, Lenny. Give it up.'

Lenny's breath was coming in small, ragged gasps. He could barely articulate his thoughts, let alone speak.

Christopher eased off the pressure slightly. 'Tell me,' he said. 'Everything.'

'I got a call from Noddy,' gasped Lenny. 'He had a visit from . . . the law the other night.'

Decca frowned. 'Why?'

More gasps from Lenny. 'I'm ganna be sick . . .'

'I said, why?'

'Nothin' to do with the nine to five. Murder. Oh God, I'm gonna be sick . . .'

'Not over me, you're not,' said Decca, made brave by Christopher's actions. Christopher said nothing, just kept up the pressure. Another gasp from Lenny. 'What d'you mean, murder?'

'That lass. The student . . .'

'They charged the boyfriend, didn't they?'

'Let him go this mornin'. He was with one o' Noddy's birds . . . Jesus . . . That was his alibi. That was what they were checkin'.'

Decca nodded, frowned. 'So what does that have to do with what happened at your place the other night?'

'Please, please, I'll tell you, just . . .'

Christopher relaxed his grip but kept his hand in place, ready to go again.

Lenny, panting, looked about to faint. 'The coppers, they weren't the first to come around.'

'What d'you mean? Not the first?'

'That lad's brief sent someone to check up.'

'So?'

Lenny attempted to regain his dignity. His voice took on a dramatic quality. 'He had someone with 'im.'

Decca sighed. 'This is becomin' tedious, Lenny. D'you want Christopher to magically open your mouth again?'

Lenny shook his head so vigorously he was in danger of dislodging something. 'Her. That tart from the other night. The one who got snatched.'

Christopher leaned forward. Lenny flinched, rushed to tell the rest of his story. 'That's who was with him. The whore these two came to talk to, she recognized her.'

'How?'

'Used to work there with her. Remembered her 'cos she had a bit of an attitude. Had minders to watch her all the time, make sure she worked. That's why they moved her to my place. Easier to do that from mine.'

'And Noddy?'

'When the coppers turned up, he thought he'd better tell someone.'

'And that was you?'

'Naw, that was Gyppy. Gyppy mentioned it to Weird Beard. Weird Beard mentioned it to Chainsaw. An' Chainsaw mentioned it to me. Chain of command, y'know. An' then you called.'

'Right. Did Noddy say who this bloke was?'

Lenny reached into his jacket pocket, wincing from pain, produced a grubby piece of paper. Squinted hard at it. 'Donovan. Aye, that's what it says. That's what he gave his name as. Joe Donovan.'

'Is this Joe Donovan a solicitor?' asked Christopher. 'Police? What?'

'Dunno.' His voice pleading, desperate to be believed.

'Will he be making a call to see Noddy's prostitute again?'

'Dunno. You need to talk to Noddy.'

'And what was the girl doing with him?'

'Dunno.' Lenny was shaking.

'And where can we find Noddy?'

'Usual place.'

Christopher nodded, turned his attention back to the window. Decca looked at Lenny.

'Next time something like this happens, you don't go to Gyppy or anybody else. You come to me. Straight to me. Right?'

Lenny, nodding, cast a nervous glance at Christopher. 'Can I go now?'

Decca nodded.

'Next time we call you, make sure you're on time.' Christopher didn't even bother to turn from the window this time. Lenny stood up and left, leaving his drink half-finished. The door slammed shut as he exited. Decca turned to Christopher, smiled.

'We make a pretty good team, don't we?'

Christopher didn't reply. Just stood up, walked towards the door. Decca swiftly downed his beer, took a deep breath, followed him.

Donovan was sitting on a stool in the Intermezzo cafe, stirring his cappuccino and looking out of the window while something smooth and Latin played over the sound system. He watched shoppers hurrying by, people making the most of the sunshine and meeting friends at the outside tables, lives being lived.

He sipped his coffee. Smooth, like the music, but with an edge of bitterness.

Katya had gone shopping with Peta. Partly to make Katya more untraceable and partly to help her feel better. Disguised in Peta's old baseball cap and clothes, they were hitting the city centre together. Donovan, before meeting Janine Stewart, had briefed Katya, informed her that Sharkey was footing the bill and tried to push her in the direction of expensive designer stores. Jamal was off with his friend Jake. So Donovan was alone.

But not for long.

He saw Peta walking along High Friar Lane towards the Intermezzo and blinked: he couldn't believe the other person was Katya. Her clothes had changed. The dowdy jeans and sweatshirt combination he had seen her in since he met her was gone. A new skirt, top, jacket and boots replaced them. Her make-up had been expertly applied and, most striking of all, her long, straight, badly dyed blonde hair was gone, replaced by a shorter, spikier, more layered look consisting of various shades of red. Peta, alongside her, had also treated herself to a total makeover.

They entered the Intermezzo, shopping bags bulging, spotted Donovan and made their way over to him. They stood before him, smiling.

'Wow,' he said. 'You look stunning. Both of you.'

'Thank you,' said Katya. She dipped towards him as if meaning to kiss him, but stopped. Donovan was aware that Peta picked up on that movement.

'Peta, you too.'

Peta smiled. 'Thank you. First time you've seen me in a skirt, I think,' she said.

'You were dressed in one the other night.'

Peta gave him a withering look. 'That was work.'

'Right.'

He looked at the carrier bags. Oasis and New Look, Warehouse and Monsoon.

'Thought you were going for designer stuff?' said Donovan.

'I did try,' said Peta.

'I don't need to,' said Katya. 'These stores are good.'

'Oh, well. Sharkey's money.'

The leather-upholstered booth behind them became vacant. Donovan moved his coffee to the table, the girls dropped their bags, Peta headed off to the counter. Katya sat next to Donovan. Silence fell like a heavy curtain.

'You OK?' Donovan said eventually.

Katya smiled. 'I am good.'

She leaned into him, wrapped her hand around his arm, gave it a squeeze. 'I am happy.'

'Good.'

She made as if to kiss him again. From the corner of his eye, Donovan saw Peta approaching with their drinks. He pulled away from Katya; she did likewise. Peta sat down, busied herself taking drinks and pastries from the tray.

'You had a good time, then?' Donovan asked.

'Yeah,' said Peta, then looked up at him, eyes to eyes. 'Did you?'

She knew. About him and Katya.

Donovan looked away. 'Yeah, fine.' He looked around. 'Seen Jamal on your travels?'

Peta shook her head.

'Have to give him a ring. We should have this, then head back.'

Peta said nothing, just stirred her coffee. Katya excused herself to go to the toilet. Peta kept stirring.

'She's very friendly with you,' she said without looking up.

'She is.'

'Anything I should know about?'

Defensiveness leaped into Donovan's voice. 'Like what?'

Peta looked at him, straight in the eyes. 'I just hope you know what you're doing.'

'I think so,' he replied.

'Think so? That's not enough. You better know so. Especially after what you had to say to Amar yesterday.'

Donovan sighed. 'Look—'

'I don't want to know,' she said, clanking her spoon down in the saucer with perhaps more force than she intended. 'It's nothing to do with me. It's your business. Just make sure that when it's time to be professional, you can be.'

'I can be.'

'And I hope you're taking precautions.'

Donovan looked at her, his mouth falling open.

'What d'you mean?'

'You know what I mean. Think, Joe.'

Katya returned, sat down between them. She smiled at them both.

'Thank you,' she said. 'For everything you have done for me.'

'All part of the . . .' Donovan couldn't finish the sentence. Peta was staring at him. 'No problem,' he said lamely.

Katya smiled again.

The Latin music in the background played on. Peta and Donovan sipped their coffee. It didn't seem so smooth to him any more.

It was all bitterness.

21

DI Diane Nattrass opened the double doors of the Bacchus on High Bridge and walked into the bar. She squinted, dragging an afterimage of the brittle evening sunlight in with her, making the hard wood and subdued lighting of the interior even darker than it actually was. She looked around, saw him in a black-leather corner booth, drink before him. She ignored the waiting bar staff, crossed straight to him. Stood before the table.

'State of you,' she said.

'You got my message, then.' Turnbull looked up. His speech was slurred, his body slumped. He looked like the punch-drunk loser in an old carnival boxing tent.

Nattrass sat down next to him. 'You're drunk.'

Turnbull shrugged.

'Why aren't you at home? Why have you dragged me out on a Sunday night? You said it was urgent.'

''Tis.'

Nattrass looked at her watch. 'You've got five minutes.'

'Have a drink.'

'I'm not thirsty.'

'Then get me one.'

'Get your own.'

Turnbull gave her what he imagined was an intimidatingly level stare but just managed to look like a drunk searching for focus. He got up, staggered to the bar, bought himself another beer with a large whisky chaser, returned to the booth, knocked back the whisky in one.

'Four minutes now,' said Nattrass.

'Michael Nell,' slurred Turnbull.

'What about him.'

''M gonna watch him.'

Nattrass sighed. 'We've got teams watching him.'

'Yeah, but . . . you know what that means. They won't be there every single second.'

'And you will?'

Turnbull nodded.

'Why?'

'You know why.' Turnbull took a swig of beer. 'Other avenues of enquiry. Leave no stone unturned. Bollocks. Fuckin' bollocks. Fenton expect us to believe that? Fuckin' media doesn't, why should we?'

Nattrass stood, watching, waiting.

'He's guilty as fuck,' said Turnbull, his voice raising slightly, attracting glances from other drinkers. He pointed a finger at Nattrass. 'You know it. I know it. Guilty as fuck.'

Another swig.

'So if he is,' said Nattrass in what she hoped was a calm and reasonable tone, 'then he'll make a mistake. And we'll have him.'

'Make a mistake . . . He'll make a fuckin' mistake, all right.'

Something in Turnbull's tone, a hardness, made Nattrass uneasy.

'What are you talking about, Paul?'

Turnbull smiled. The dim lighting, the amount of alcohol in his body, turned the smile into a twisted, darkly glittering thing. 'I'm gonna watch him. Off the clock. In my own time. An' when he makes a mistake, when he fucks up, I'm ganna have him. Have the cunt.' He looked up at her. 'An' you're gonna help.'

Nattrass looked into Turnbull's bloodshot, pinwheeling eyes. She shook her head.

'You're a good copper, Paul. You're my partner. Don't do this. You get results, but you get obsessed by things. Now, I know you've got problems, trouble at home—'

Turnbull snorted, picked up his drink. Nattrass stared at him.

'Go home, Paul,' she said. 'Get some sleep. Spend some time with your family. Get perspective.' She stood up. 'I'm going home now. I think it's best you do too.'

Turnbull fumbled in his pocket, brought out the now-tattered picture he carried.

'Ashley . . . What he did . . . What he did to Ashley . . .'

'Go home, Paul.' Nattrass shook her head.

Turnbull held out the photo, eyes imploring.

'I'll see you in the morning.'

Nattrass turned and left the bar.

Turnbull sat, looking at the photo. Someone put a song on the jukebox. He didn't recognize it, something with a beat, something about honest mistakes. He sat, thinking hard, breathing heavily. The rhythm of the song like a quickening heart rate, driving him along. He reached a decision.

With one last look at Ashley, he pocketed the photo, drained his glass to the bottom and stood up.

Once on his feet he nodded to himself, straightened his jacket and headed for the door.

Peta sat in the Forth, staring at the double gin and tonic on the table before her. People moved all around her, chatting, drinking and eating. Crowding her into the corner, taking chairs from around her small table to help seat even more around theirs. As their conviviality increased, so, too, did her sense of loneliness.

She tried to ignore it, block it all out. Concentrate on the alcohol in front of her. Her test of strength, she called it. A way of coping when she felt she was losing control of events in her life.

Something she had picked up from reading Aleister Crowley in her youth. Whenever he was feeling weak, Crowley would sit in a room surrounded by his worst vices and temptations – in his case cocaine and heroin – in order to strengthen and demonstrate the superiority of his will over his emotions. The fact that he had died a chronic drug addict Peta always ignored.

For her it was alcohol, not drugs. And she was stronger than him. Because every time she had tried this it had worked and she had walked away actually feeling stronger.

But this time she wasn't so sure. And she didn't know why. Nothing particularly bad had happened. No great upheaval to trigger this. Just a sense that somehow she was losing her grip on things. Despite her work, her studies, she felt there was something missing from her life.

Donovan's involvement with Katya wasn't helping. Not because it was Joe Donovan, she told herself, but because it was unprofessional. She had just lost one business and she wasn't about to let Albion go down the pan also.

She had tried upping her rate of tae kwon do classes but that hadn't helped. Just left her more tired.

And college. She had thought that getting a degree would be the answer to lots of things that had been building up inside her. Somehow she didn't think that was proving to be the case. She didn't enjoy the atmosphere there at present, found it non-conducive to studying. And then there was the Prof. She still couldn't make him out. She liked him but felt there was something he was hiding. The way he covered up his deformed hand made her think it was a physical mani-festation of something deeper he didn't want seen. And then there was the Wilco gig. Had she really been too busy to go? Could she have made time if she had wanted to?

She looked down at the table again. The gin and tonic was beckoning to her. Bubbles making their slow way up the centre, bursting on the ice, under the slice of lime. She believed she could hear its inviting effervescence above the roar of the drinkers, the thump of the jukebox. She could almost taste it: the cold sharpness exploding in her mouth, the icy aftereffect slipping down her throat, cooling her system, the mild buzz tickling her forehead like a pleasurable head massage, the hint of juniper berries and aromatics tantalizingly just out of reach of her taste buds, all urging her to take another mouthful, do it again. And again.

But she wouldn't. Because she was stronger than that.

Stronger.

And yet. It looked so inviting, the bubbles, the condensation on the glass . . .

'Hello.'

She felt a hand on her shoulder, turned suddenly, looked up, startled out of her reverie.

Jill Tennant was standing before her, pint in hand, smiling down.

'Didn't think I'd find you here. Didn't think it would be your sort of place.'

Peta looked around, noticing for the first time that the majority of the people in there were students. She shrugged, not knowing what to say.

'Are you waiting for someone?'

Peta shook her head. 'No, just . . . nothing. Sitting here.'

Jill glanced around to where her friends were looking for seats. 'Come and join us.'

Peta looked at them. Some she recognized from her course, some she had seen around campus. All of them younger than her, all seemingly without the cares she was carrying.

'I couldn't. You're with your friends.'

'Don't be stupid. You're my friend as well. Come on.'

Jill held out her hand. Peta looked at her drink, then back to Jill. The girl's eyes were so honest, no hidden agenda. She liked Peta, wanted to be her friend.

Peta smiled. 'OK.' She stood up, picked up her bag.

'Don't forget your drink,' said Jill.

'I'll get something else,' said Peta. 'I didn't fancy it really.'

Peta went to join Jill and her friends. The gin and tonic left alone slowly lost its sparkle, turned into flat, tasteless liquid.

Michael Nell had had enough.

He knew they were watching him, shadowing his every move. Turning around quickly when he was walking, glancing too fast into doorways and windows. All the way home from the police station, all last night in the pub. People looking away too quickly, pretending to look somewhere else. He could feel them doing it. Even when he couldn't see them. From behind, at the side. All around.

Every eye like an insect. An ant or cockroach crawling across his body. Tickling. Itching. Unnerving. Making him want to scratch, pull the skin red raw, cleanse it.

He didn't know who they were, but he had a good idea. Police. Press. Even other students. All wanting to see him for themselves.

The pervert.

The murderer.

Wanting to know where he is at all times, what he's doing. To make sure he doesn't do it again. Or if he does, be there to stop him. Or just to capture the moment. Or to make sure it doesn't happen to them.

One day, one night. He couldn't take it much longer. All the eyes on him.

His father wanted nothing to do with him, told him he

was scum, that he'd always known something like this would happen to him. Nell had wanted to tell him the apple does-n't fall far from the tree, but he hadn't dared. He knew what would have happened to him if he had.

So he had said nothing. Took it.

And now the eyes. All on him. His skin crawling with insect feet.

Even Emma, his new girlfriend, who was always up for a bit of fun, recoiled from his touch. It was one thing to enjoy deviant sex, another to be pawed by a murderer. She had given him the good to see you stuff, the stand by you, I knew you were innocent, never doubted it stuff. Taken him to the pub where his friends had joined in. But he had seen them, looking at him when they thought he wasn't aware of it. Scrutinizing his actions: how he holds a bottle, how he smokes a fag. His smile, his body language. Gauging for themselves his innocence, his guilt.

He had wanted to scream at them, shout. But he hadn't. He had thanked them for sticking by him. Told them he really appreciated it. What their friendship meant to him.

Cunts.

And now there was Emma, sat on the edge of the bed. Looking vulnerable, alone. Looking at him with ill-disguised fear in her eyes. Wondering whether he was going to touch her.

Kill her.

Set to run if he did.

He wanted to grab her. Make her listen. Tell her the truth, tell her everything.

But he didn't. His head was pounding. He wanted to rip his own skin off, scour away the insect looks, claw at his face until nothing remained on the surface, no one was left underneath. Lose his identity, be reborn in blood. Take the crawling, maddening pain away.

He gave a resigned sigh.

''M goin' out.'

'Where?' She could barely keep the relief from her voice.

He shrugged. 'Dunno. Just out.'

'D'you want me to go home?' The first time he had heard hope in her voice all night.

'No, you can stay here. Do what you like.'

He saw the hope turn to fear by the time he reached the door.

'Where are you going?' An edge of hysteria in her voice.

You mean, who are you going to hurt? Who are you going to kill? He almost spat the words at her. But he didn't have the energy. All he had was pain. And a weariness beyond sleep.

'Out.'

He slammed the door behind him.

Walked away.

Peta threw her head back and laughed. It felt like the first time she had done that for ages, a real roar of pure pleasure.

The students had been talking about their lecturers and peers with a mixture of both warmth and wit in a way that only those with their futures ahead of them could. Some had tried to affect worldly airs but Peta wasn't fooled. She knew they were just shields thrown up to hide their fears of being away from home for the first time. Then one of Jill's mates, Josh, had made a statement about a mutual colleague that had topped everyone else's. The only response had been to laugh. Despite, or perhaps because of, the events on campus, they had laughed. Long and hard. It was the most life-affirming thing Peta had done in months.

They were getting drunk, she noticed, while she stayed with Diet Coke. She didn't mind. Just the energy, the good humour, of the group was rubbing off on her. They made her feel welcome. Didn't mention her age, didn't exclude her from the conversation because she wasn't as fast as them on some of the cultural references, because she didn't watch *The OC* or *Hollyoaks*. And Peta for her part made no attempt to seem younger or hipper than she was. It worked; it was a good accommodation. She felt relaxed. She felt happy.

Peta noticed Jill looking at her. She turned, smiled.

'Can I ask you something?' said Jill.

'Fire away.'

'Why do you not drink?'

All the good humour of the previous two hours evaporated as Peta felt like she had moved back to square one. Her imaginary good time dissipated, reality slapping her around the face like a hangover. She opened her mouth to give what she thought was her usual defensive answer, saw Jill's face and stopped.

Jill was looking at her with such openness, such trust, that she couldn't say what she had been about to say. The question had been asked with no malice, no judgement. Just a genuine enquiry. Peta felt she had to give an honest answer.

'I'm only asking,' Jill went on, seemingly worried in case she had offended Peta, 'because my sister doesn't drink either.'

'How old's your sister?' asked Peta.

'Twenty-nine. Rachel. She's my older sister.' Jill giggled. 'Well, obviously.'

'Why doesn't she drink?'

Jill looked serious. 'She developed a problem with it. At uni. Thought it best to stop. Went to AA meetings and everything.'

'How is she now?'

Jill smiled. 'Oh, fine. She's over it. Rachel's good. I just asked because when I came in I saw you looking at that drink on the table. And you didn't pick it up. And you've sat here watching everyone else drinking and stayed with Coke. She used to do the same things. Have that same look. Thought I recognized it.'

Peta smiled. 'I'm the same as your sister. I got into a bit of trouble with it a few years ago. Had to make a decision, like her. Had to make lots of decisions, actually. Found I was better off without it.'

Jill nodded, took a sip of her beer. The rest of the table was continuing with group conversation but Jill seemed happier to talk to Peta. That was fine with Peta.

'You remind me of her, you know.'

'Rachel?' asked Peta.

Jill nodded. 'Yeah. The way I could ask her all sorts of things and know I'd be getting an honest answer. I bet you would do the same.'

'Where is she now?'

'Working in New York for a merchant bank. Done really well for herself.'

'D'you miss her?'

'Loads. And Mum and Dad.' She looked around. 'But it's good here, Newcastle. And the uni.' Another roar went up from the rest of the table. 'And I've got some good mates.' She leaned in close. Peta could smell the alcohol on her breath. 'And I've got my new big sister.'

Peta gave a small laugh. 'You're drunk.'

'Only a little bit. Just enough to feel relaxed. To tell the truth.' She smiled again. 'I knew I was going to be friends with you. Right from the first day. Reminded me of Rachel, I suppose.' She drew back. 'You don't mind me saying this, do you?'

Peta smiled. 'Not at all.'

And she didn't. It felt good to have a friend who wasn't connected with work, who wouldn't expect anything from her but friendship in return. She smiled. Yeah. It felt good.

Jill looked around again, leaned forward. 'Can I tell you something? I feel I can 'cos it's, you know, you.'

Peta leaned in also. 'Sure.'

'I've got a date tomorrow night.' She smiled as she said it.

'With Ben?'

Jill shook her head. 'Ben doesn't know about it.'

'Who with, then?' As soon as Peta said the words she knew the answer. Jill confirmed it for her.

'The Prof. He's taking me to see Wilco.'

'Oh. Right.'

Jill looked at Peta's face, frowned. 'What? You don't think I should go? 'Cos he's older than me? 'Cos I've already got a boyfriend? Well, sort of.'

'No, no, it's not that. Just . . . just a shock, that's all. No, you go. Enjoy yourself. You'll have a great time.'

Jill smiled, reassured, as if this was the answer she wanted to hear.

'Thanks,' she said. 'Anyway, there's nothing serious in it. Just a laugh. I won't get tied down; there's too much I want to do with my life. Anyway, I knew I could tell you. Knew you'd understand.'

'Right. But just be careful. That's all.'

Jill grinned. 'I will. Sis.'

Peta looked at her and, despite what she was thinking, smiled also. She couldn't deny how good it felt when Jill called her that.

For just that moment, Peta felt like there was somewhere she belonged. That she was in control of her life once more. Perhaps that was all it had needed. Not alcohol, not more work. Something much more simple.

A friend.

Darkness fell hard, bringing with it the threat of encroaching winter.

Turnbull sat behind the steering wheel of the Vectra, rubbing his hands together. The remains of an Indian takeaway on the passenger seat next to him, an old two-litre Evian plastic bottle filled with piss between his legs, his vision still blurred and doubled from the alcohol. Everything seemed so far away; like he was staring out from the back of a dark, echoing cave.

The house was just as he had last seen it: run down, giving the slumming, middle-class students a vicariously thrilling glimpse of poverty.

Michael Nell was in there. Turnbull knew he was. He had watched him enter, with that new girlfriend of his. A light, faint and diffuse, was on in his bedroom.

And Ashley not even buried yet.

He yawned, stretched. The alcohol was still in his system, but the buzz was beginning to wear down. He dug into his pocket, brought out some pills liberated from a dealer he had given a warning to, chewed, dry-swallowed them. They should keep him going for a while.

He had told the teams to go home. Pulled rank, made it seem like a favour. They had taken some persuading, but had gone.

He had phoned home. God alone knew why he'd bothered to do that. Working all night, he told the wife. Overtime. May as well have been talking to himself for all the response he got. Not even arguing, just beyond caring. Fuck her. What did she know? That was that. Her loss. He sighed. He would sit here all night if necessary, as long as it took.

He watched. He waited.

And then Michael Nell emerged. Alone. Scratching his head, his back, like he had fleas.

Turnbull leaned forward, ready to switch on the engine, paused. Perhaps Nell was going somewhere on foot.

The off-licence. His dealer.

To beat up another prostitute. To find another victim.

Anger rose within him, anger fed by alcohol and speed. Bastard. He was off again, to hurt, to kill. And there was no one, nothing, to stop him.

'But me,' he said aloud.

Turnbull was breathing heavily. Shaking.

He got out of the car. Locked it. Stood in the street, took two deep breaths. Making up his mind.

He patted his jacket pocket, checked that the photo of Ashley was still over his heart.

Began to follow Michael Nell on foot.

22

Donovan parked the Mondeo in his usual place, locked the door.

Katya emerged from the passenger side. He looked at her. Outwardly she was looking fitter and healthier than any time since she had forcibly arrived at his house. But inwardly, in her eyes, glimpsed shadows and ghosts showed the damage that had been left. They would be hard to shift, Donovan thought. He knew that from experience.

Newcastle, on a mid-February morning, not yet eight o'clock. Commuter traffic was streaming into the city up St James Boulevard, pedestrians walking to work. The grey clouds overhead created more than an absence of light; they seemed the physical embodiment of reluctant resignation that Monday morning brought for most people.

But not for Donovan and Katya. They stood there watching, letting life go on around them, belonging to something altogether different.

'You ready?' Donovan asked.

Katya took a deep breath, nodded.

'Then let's go.'

Donovan started walking, Katya next to him. He felt her hand in his, her arm around his own. He looked at her, startled.

'Do you mind?' she asked, eyes wide, looking up at him.

'No,' he said.

'Good. I am just feeling . . .' She sighed.

'I know.'

They walked arm in arm up to the Albion offices.

On to meet her brother.

The previous two nights they had ended up in bed together. Again.

The sex had been good, less aggressive, fulfilling a need for intimacy in both of them, but Donovan was beginning to feel uneasy. Perhaps Jamal had been right, he thought. Perhaps he was doing Katya more harm than good.

She had offered and he had responded. Jamal had gone around to see his friend Jake. Before he had gone, though, he had wanted to talk to Donovan.

'I can't bear it in here now, man,' he had said to Donovan when the two of them had been alone in Jamal's room. 'It's like there's somethin' hangin' there, you know what I mean?'

'Oh, come on,' said Donovan. 'We had a good night last night, didn't we? All three of us?'

Coming back from Newcastle on the Saturday night, Donovan had opened some wine and beer and Katya had insisted on treating him and Jamal to a fashion show. Jamal had laughed, joined in even, giving her suggestions of how to wear things, before he checked himself, realized what he was doing was uncool and found an excuse to retreat into his room. But Donovan had watched as Katya tried on different skirt, top and jeans combinations, flicking her hair around, taking a girlish and frivolous thrill in the whole thing that almost bordered on the childlike. Donovan couldn't blame her. Fun was something that had long been denied her and was too important to go without for any length of time.

Jamal shrugged. Didn't answer.

Donovan sat on the bed, looked at the boy. He was clearly unhappy.

'Look, Jamal,' Donovan began.

'Don't go givin' me that needs thing again, man,' Jamal said. 'I know you both got needs. An', yeah, maybe you should be takin' carea them. But there's a thin line, man.'

'I know. And I'm not going to cross it.'

'Make sure you don't. Thassall I'm sayin'.' Jamal looked jumpy, on edge. Like he had more to say but was unsure how to say it. 'Well, it ain't just that.'

Donovan frowned. 'What d'you mean?'

Jamal looked around, checking to make sure he wasn't being overheard. He leaned forward, kept his voice low. 'I don't trust her, man.'

'What d'you mean, you don't trust her?'

'Katya. I don't trust her. Somethin' shifty. Not all right about her, y'get me?'

'In what way?'

Jamal sat back, shaking his head. 'I dunno, man, just is. Like, I catch her lookin' at me sometimes. Or you. When she thinks we ain't payin' attention to her. An' there's a look on her face. Like somethin' there. Somethin' I don't like.'

'What?'

'I dunno, man. You're the guy who knows stuff.'

'She's probably reliving all the stuff she's been through, all the horror that's happened to her. You know what it's like. You think you're doing fine, but when you least expect it something like that just creeps up on you. Changes your whole mood. That's what she's going through.'

Jamal nodded but remained looking unconvinced. 'I'm just sayin', Joe. Be careful is all.'

Donovan had told him he would be.

And later that Sunday evening, with Jamal at Jake's house, Katya had asked to sleep with Donovan, to share his bed again. He had thought of Jamal's words and looked at her. All he saw was a young, attractive woman, haunted and traumatized, trying to live a normal life again. And he liked her. Enjoyed her company. Enjoyed the sex they had together.

Jamal, he thought, was imagining things.

They had gone to bed. The sex, if anything, was even better this time.

Afterwards, they had lain there, neither speaking.

'What was it like,' said Donovan eventually, his voice small and light, 'in Kosovo during the war?'

He felt Katya's body go rigid beside him, then relax slightly as a sigh escaped her.

'A war,' she said. 'There are no good wars. My family were from Albania. Lived in Kosovo for generations. Serbs and Albanians together. But not get on. We were treated like Jews in Germany before the Second World War. Tried to kill us in little ways.'

'Are you Muslim?' asked Donovan.

Katya shook her head. 'No. My family, some used to be. But they don't see difference. Our government collapsed. Kosovan Liberation Army happened. Fighting for us. All of us, they said. Serbs sent in police, army.' She turned over, her face hidden in shadow. 'This was a call.'

'To do what?'

'To kill. To cleanse us from the land. Ethnically.'

'Why?'

Another sigh. 'Because they could. They were given permission. My family lived in a village called Racak. You will not know it.'

'I do.' He tried to remember why he knew it, since his paper had comprehensively covered the conflict at the time. 'Racak . . . wasn't there a massacre there?'

'Milošević sent in Serb police and Yugoslav army. Nearly fifty people killed.' Her voice was cracking with emotion. 'Oh, they said they were killed in fighting. But not true. Not true. That is how my brother and I lost our family . . .'

Her voice trailed away, her eyes on something beyond the confines of the room. 'His face . . . I can still see his face . . .'

Donovan didn't know what to do. He held her tighter. She let him.

'All I wanted was go to Priština university, study European literature. Get good job. Have happy life. But now my family gone. My home gone. My brother and I, to have any kind of life, have to leave country, start somewhere else.'

'So how did you end up here?'

'We not allowed in anywhere. They say our lives not in danger. We pay gangsters with last of our money to smuggle us in. You cannot imagine what is like in container. On lorry, then ship. Hidden in back behind secret door, thirty of us, all breathing same stinking air through same tube, shitting and pissing in same bucket. Trying not to breathe whenever we stopped moving in case they heard us.'

Donovan pulled her closer to him.

'And then we get here, the lies we are told. They said we owe them. In money, in everything. They took our passports. What we are forced to do . . .'

He felt her body become rigid again. She was trying not to cry. He held her all the more tightly.

'You're safe now,' he said.

She nodded. 'I am safe.'

They lay like that, unmoving, for a long time. Donovan heard Jamal come in, get ready for bed. He thought Katya had fallen asleep. But she hadn't.

'Fuck me again,' she said, her voice jagged in the darkness. 'Fuck me again, Joe.'

'Katya,' said Donovan, 'I don't think that's a good idea.'

'Why not?' She was faced into him, her hands running all over his body.

'After what you've just told me, after everything you've

been through . . . I wouldn't be helping you. I would be just like them.'

She ran her hand down between his legs, felt his erection. She smiled. He saw the edges of her mouth curl up, her teeth glint against the darkness. 'This says you want to.' Her hand moving up and down. 'I say I want you to.'

She kept going. Soon, he was beyond saying no to her. He gave in.

Later, while she slept, he lay awake.

Trying to work out what he was doing. And why.

He closed his eyes. Waited for sleep to claim him.

Waited a long time.

Donovan and Katya rounded the corner, started up Westgate Road. Amar stood on the other side, leaning against a wall, reading a tabloid and glancing at his watch, looking like his lift to work was late. He saw them, gave an imperceptible nod: it was safe to approach. They kept walking, approached the turn-off to Summerhill Terrace. Jamal, standing on the corner, talking to an imaginary friend on his mobile, gave a similar nod to Amar's. Donovan and Katya walked all the way to the offices, went inside.

The meeting had been arranged the previous week at Katya's request. The logistics were complex but not insurmountable. Katya's brother had to be brought from his safe house. Donovan didn't know where it was; he hadn't been told. They had to ensure he wasn't being watched or followed. Katya would then have to be brought in from Northumberland. Again, the same precautions applied. They had needed the meeting to take place in an environment they could control. The Albion offices were the obvious choice.

'Where is he?' asked Katya once inside the door. She was

trembling, hanging on to Donovan so hard he felt her nails digging in through his leather jacket.

'Let's go in here.'

He led her into the main reception area that they used for meetings and sat her down on one of the chocolate-coloured leather sofas. He walked to the windows, began closing the blinds.

'He'll be here in a minute. Try to relax.'

Katya attempted a smile. 'Relax . . . What is that?'

Donovan returned the smile. 'Something I'm sure you'll get used to. Once this is all over, you've got the rest of your life to find out.'

She nodded, less than convinced.

They waited.

Not even a ticking clock to pass the time.

Then, nearly fifteen minutes later, there was a sound at the back door. Peta walked in first, two people behind her. Katya stood up. Behind Peta and before Sharkey was her brother, Dario Tokic.

She ran towards him, throwing her arms around his neck. He responded. They hugged, kissed. Held each other so tight it seemed they would burst the other.

Donovan, Peta and Sharkey looked at each other.

'Let's give them a few minutes alone,' said Donovan.

They walked into the back office.

Donovan could feel Peta's eyes on him. He tried not to look at her. He looked instead at Sharkey.

'Any problems?'

Sharkey shook his head. 'Couldn't wait to see her. Spent ages getting himself ready.'

'Must be the effect she has on men,' said Peta.

Donovan still didn't look at her.

'All he's talked about is his sister,' said Sharkey, unaware of the atmosphere between the other two. 'How much he misses her, wants to see her. Although since he's been a virtual prisoner, getting out for *any* reason sounds good.'

The door opened. Amar and Jamal entered.

'Any problems?' Donovan asked them.

They both shook their heads. Donovan looked at Amar. He was no longer high. He seemed to have come down. Heavily.

'You OK?'

'Yeah.' Amar nodded. 'Back on the team.'

'Good.'

Donovan smiled. Amar returned it. Donovan didn't believe him but knew it wasn't the time to say anything.

They stood there in silence, waiting. Eventually Sharkey spoke.

'D'you think they've had long enough? Or should we all go out for breakfast?'

'Come on, then.' Donovan knocked on the door. Opened it. Entered.

Katya and Dario were sitting on one of the chocolate-brown leather sofas, holding hands, tears streaming down both their faces.

Donovan looked at them. Dario Tokic looked better than he had in his photo. Impassive, like he carried an inner strength. Dark-haired and still thin, but he had filled out, slept more regularly, bathed more often. His clothes looked new, his hair cut well. He was being looked after. But there was something there, something that betrayed him: his hands, nervous and fidgeting, a glance freeing the ghosts behind his eyes. His expression of inner strength looked as if it could be easily wiped away. Like Katya. Like thousands of others.

Katya looked up. Smiled at Donovan. 'This is my brother.' She looked around the room. 'Thank you. Thank you for doing this . . .' Another well of tears overflowed.

Donovan and his team waited until the two had calmed down, then sat next to them. Jamal and Amar had been elected to make coffees and teas. They left for the kitchen.

Sharkey spoke first, saying how pleased he was that they could be reunited; it was what made his work so rewarding. Donovan and Peta exchanged glances. Sharkey then went on to explain what would be happening next.

'When you both leave here, you'll be going back to your respective safe houses. We just wanted to get you together to demonstrate good faith. It shouldn't be long now. There's a legal team working on building the case against Marco Kovacs. The police have a man inside. Intelligence suggests there's a new shipment coming in to Tyne Dock soon. Days rather than weeks. Then once Marco Kovacs is in custody we bring you in, you identify him for war crimes, he gets put away for life and we all live happily ever after.'

'Where is he?' asked Dario. His voice was dry, like old, trampled leaves left on a forest floor. 'Kovacs? Where does he live?'

'Northumberland,' said Sharkey. 'Well, just outside the city. Darras Hall.'

'A big house?'

'It is, yes.'

Dario curled his lip. 'Built on the blood of others. The lives of innocents. Built by fear.'

Sharkey applied his legal smile. 'Well, that'll all be changing soon. Thanks to your testimony. And then you and your charming sister can get on with your lives.'

Dario nodded. Donovan and Peta exchanged another glance.

Tea and coffee arrived, they talked. Nothing of great importance, keeping it small, light.

'Well,' said Sharkey, looking at his watch, 'I'm afraid it's time for Mr Tokic to go.' He stood up. 'We'll give you a moment alone together to say your goodbyes.'

He rose and left the room. The others did likewise.

'Touching scene,' Sharkey said.

'As if you give a toss,' said Donovan.

Sharkey looked hurt. 'You constantly underestimate me, Joe. Those scenes are what makes our jobs worthwhile.'

Donovan's retort was halted by the ringing of his mobile. He flipped it open, checked the display. Not a number he recognized. Put it to his ear, listened.

He turned, taking in the words, and saw Sharkey's face looking at him. This wasn't for his ears. He walked away from the lawyer, opened the front door, went outside. Crossed the cobbled road, listening all the while, nodding. He stood by the railings of the overgrown Victorian recreation ground. Looked back at the Albion offices. Listening to the voice in his ear all the while.

His legs getting weaker with each word. Trying to process what he had heard already.

The Missing Persons Hotline.

They had found a body.

A boy's body.

23

'Where?'

Donovan found his voice. Waited for the reply.

'In Wales,' said the voice on the other end of the line. A woman. Alison, she had given her name as. Professionally soothing. Concern and compassion in her tones. 'Local police are still trying to establish the boy's identity. They've reached out to us.'

'And you think . . . ?' Donovan's voice cold, croaking, like it had rusted over. 'You think it might be my son?'

'To be honest with you, Mr Donovan, it doesn't look likely,' said Alison as sensitively as she could. 'But in cases like this, with an unidentified body, we ask everyone on our list of possible matches to give a DNA sample to—'

'OK.'

'I was going to say,' she continued smoothly, as if being interrupted was all part of the job, 'to their local police, who'll then get it transported down to Wales.'

Donovan looked around, surprised to see the world still where it had been. Houses, offices, grass and railings. The street. The pavement. Air and clouds. Behind him, the stark children's play area in among the overgrown grass. Deserted. Looked like no child had touched it for a while.

Everything as it was. Donovan's precarious tightrope act of walking through the real world still holding up.

Just.

'I'll go,' said Donovan. 'I'll go down.'

Alison sighed. 'There's really no need. Look, tests aren't

completed yet. We're not even sure if the predictive computer ageing will come up with a positive match for your
son. The DNA sample can be taken locally. You don't need
to upset yourself any further.'

Upset yourself any further. He thought of the years he had
spent not accepting his son's disappearance, willing him to
reappear, then looking for him, obsessively. All the while
feeling his life, his remaining family, his work, his sanity,
even, collapse around him. Upset himself any further. He
didn't think that was possible.

'Does my wife know?' he asked, throat as dry as glasspaper.

'Not yet, Mr Donovan. If you'd like us to inform her
instead—'

'No, don't. Not her. Not yet. I'll go. I'll do it.'

Alison spoke again, counselling him.

'And don't say there's no need to go. For me, there's
every need.'

The deal he had made with himself. With David in
dreams. Any lead, no matter how small, how seemingly
pointless, he would pursue. Because it was his son. He owed
it to his son.

There, then gone.

There, then gone.

Gone.

'Every need,' he said again, almost to himself this time.

Alison sensed that any more words would be wasted. She
promised to email him contact details of the police detective
dealing with the inquiry plus information on how he could
be reached. She gave more professional solicitations, offered
him the name of a good counsellor, which Donovan refused
and rang off.

Donovan pocketed the phone, looked back at Albion.
Sharkey standing in the doorway looking over at him, a
puzzled expression on his face.

Anger rose within Donovan on seeing the lawyer. He crossed the street, shouting as he went.

'Where were you, ay? Where the fuck were you?'

Sharkey's initial look of surprise at the words soon became the look of a man waiting for an electric storm to break over him. He flinched in anticipation.

Donovan reached him, his heart pounding, seemingly too large for his ribcage to hold. He could hear nothing but the blood in his head, the air in his lungs. He grabbed Sharkey by the lapels of his handmade suit.

'Why didn't you tell me? Why the fuck didn't you tell me?'

Sharkey's eyes darted about. Fear creased his face. 'I don't know what you're—'

'That was the Missing Persons Hotline. They've found a boy. I'm going to give a DNA sample.'

Sharkey, for once, was genuinely at a loss for words. His jaws moved up and down, but no sound came out. Donovan pressed on.

'So where were you, eh? You've got people on it. You've got people looking for him. Weren't looking hard enough, were they? Eh? Eh?'

His hand was back ready to strike the lawyer. It never connected. He felt a restraining arm around his. Peta was there, pulling him back as hard as she could.

Donovan looked around. The whole team was there, staring at him, hardly able to believe what they were seeing.

Donovan dropped his arm, the fight, the anger, leaving him as suddenly as it had come. He took his hands from the lawyer, who backed away as quickly as he could. A wave of emotion built up inside Donovan. He felt it about to break, didn't want the others to witness it. He turned away.

'Get him inside,' he mumbled. 'All of you, inside . . .'

He staggered away from them and away, down the alley at

the side of the offices, made sure they weren't following him, that he was alone. Stood there, eyes seeing past the buildings in front of him, took a deep breath, let the tears come.

'So why didn't you tell me?' said Decca, standing over the moon-faced man sitting on the sofa. 'Didn't you think it was that important?'

Noddy looked up at him. Shrugged. Then went back to the TV. 'Not really. Nothin' to do with business.'

'Not really?' Decca looked around. The front room of the brothel Noddy ran looked no more cheerful in the daylight. Or what passed for daylight; the filthy windows and nets in the front room operating a strict selective policy as to what could be admitted. The room that Noddy called home was so lived in it was worn out. Fake veneer units, cheap, stuffing-spewing sofa and chairs, ten- or fifteen-year-old Argos chic. A tabloid on the arm of the chair, opened and folded to the form pages, spider scribbles in the margin. A TV, the screen reflecting greasy handprints and dust, dominated one corner, the racing turned down by Decca. Noddy trying to see around Decca, watch the race.

Decca kneeled down, got right into Noddy's face. 'I'm talking to you.'

Noddy's eyes flicking between the two, torn as to which to look at. The racing won out.

Decca stood up, angry. 'Oi. I'm talking to you.'

Noddy looked at Decca, a clear lack of respect in his eyes. 'I've told you what happened.' He pointed to the screen. 'That's that. Now I'm—'

Christopher had him from behind, arm locked around his throat, pulling him up by his neck. Noddy's eyes bulged out, his glasses dislodged themselves, his face going redder than an overweight businessman in a sauna. Decca smiled to himself. Fear, even reflected, was a powerful thing. He leaned over Noddy once again, eye to eye.

'That's better. Got your attention now, haven't I?'

Noddy made a strangulated noise in the back of his throat.

'You a gambling man, Noddy, eh? That why you didn't tell us about what happened at this place the other night? Eh? Thought we didn't need to know?'

Christopher pulled tighter. Noddy turned from red to purple.

'So, what d'you reckon your chances are of walking away from this unharmed if we don't get what we want out of you?' Decca was pleased with that line, pleased with Noddy's gurgling, red-faced reaction. 'Let's go over it again,' he said. 'Just to make sure we've got it right. This guy, Joe Donovan, and this whore come in to talk to a working girl. They say they're from the police . . .'

Noddy gesticulated that he was ready to talk. Christopher eased the pressure.

'No,' said Noddy, his voice sounding like Lemmy after a European tour with Motorhead, 'No. They said they were part of an investigation. A murder investigation.'

'Murder. Now Gyppy and Weird Beard and Chainsaw and probably every other pimp in Newcastle know about it, but you didn't think murder was serious enough to tell us?'

'Nothin' to do with us. Keep out of it, I'd say. It's that student, not one of ours.'

His flickering eyes told Decca there was more to Noddy's evasion than just wanting to watch the racing. Decca thought hard. Then had an idea.

'You were gonna keep the information, weren't you?' he said, looking down at Noddy. 'Keep it and take it to the media, is that it?'

The racing commentary played quietly beneath their

words. Pounding hooves building up tension in the small room. Noddy, struggling hard, resisted the temptation to look at the TV. To look anywhere.

Decca leaned in. 'Is that it?'

'Yes,' said Noddy, shaking. 'We thought with all the papers an' TV an' that, we could make a bit o' money, like.'

'We? Who's we?'

'Me an' Sharon.' Noddy's eyes lit up as a desperate, duplicitous thought struck him in such an obvious fashion that he should have had a light bulb above his head. 'It was Sharon's idea. All of it. I just . . . went along with it.'

'Sharon.'

'Sharon. Sharon Healy. One o' the freelancers.' Noddy rubbed his neck. 'The S&M queen. That's who they wanted to see.'

Decca looked around, as if expecting her to walk into the room. 'And where is she now?'

Noddy shrugged. It seemed to hurt him. 'Dunno. Doesn't come on until tonight.'

'You've got a phone number. An address.'

Noddy nodded, coughing, his hands massaging his throat, his face reddening again. He pointed into the back room. 'The table. By the phone.'

Decca walked into the back room. It was equally as depressing as the front one. He leaned over the table, rummaged through a pile of old newspapers, porn magazines, bills and junk mail until he found an address book, held it up.

'This what you mean?'

'Yeah,' said Noddy, breathing roughly. 'They're all in there. In case we're raided, then I just say they're friends o' mine.' He almost smiled. 'Clever, eh?'

'Brilliant.'

Decca leafed through. Found Sharon Healy's name written in semi-legible script, a half-formed row of numbers next to it. He keyed the number into his mobile with her name next to it, wrote the address down as a text message for himself. Went back into the front room, faced Noddy.

'Now what was so hard about that?'

The race had finished. Noddy said nothing. He looked between Decca and Christopher. No idea whether he was a winner or a loser.

Decca and Christopher moved to the door. Decca turned. Noddy had been reaching for the paper. His hand froze in midair, his face looked up, fearful. Decca liked that. Prepared a suitable line to exit on.

'There was no need,' said Noddy. 'No need for that.'

Decca looked at the man. Tears began to well.

'No need . . .'

Decca opened his mouth to speak his prepared line, but it wouldn't come out.

Christopher left the house.

Decca, with one last look at the crying man, followed him.

The pub was a squat, squalid square-roofed construct on an inexorable downward slide that no amount of lottery makeover money could ever halt. It sat at the bottom of a long, characterless bank in Bensham, among a run-down pit of half-demolished warehouses, neglected old terraces and closed garages that seemed a world away from the Sage Music Centre and Gateshead Hilton that nestled on the south bank of the Tyne less than a mile away. The wooden slats that ran along the front of the pub had been painted black and white, probably in allegiance to the football team over the river but now probably all that was holding the place together.

Decca hated the area on principle. It was the kind of area he was from. The kind that he would do anything to avoid going back to.

He parked the car in a patch of rubbled gravel that claimed to be a car park and got out. He looked around, worrying about what would happen to his car, saw Christopher getting out of the passenger seat, drawing any potential young criminal's eye, and felt his worries abating.

He was beginning to enjoy having a henchman. When this was all over he'd have to get himself one. But one he could get on with. One that talked English. One that talked.

They walked into the pub. It was exactly as he had expected it to be. A place for drinking, for escape. Although the drinkers must have been escaping something very bad to seek refuge there. It smelled of stale beer, fried food, dead tobacco air. Monday afternoon. The lunchtime rush long gone. Decades gone.

Decca looked around. There she was by the pool table. Bending her bulk over, lining up a shot. Chatting to the fat, bald, middle-aged man standing next to her. Giving him a lascivious look. An audience of unattractive, badly dressed, unwashed men who seemed to be more drunk than the hour should have allowed for, and she played up to them. She took a long time lining up her shot, wiggled her large arse as she did so.

Decca walked over to her, spoke before the cue connected with the ball.

'You workin', Sharon?' he said. He ran his eye up and down her ample figure, took in her Newcastle United top from several seasons ago and black stretch leggings. 'You don't look dressed for it.'

'Fuck off,' she said without looking up. She took her shot. Missed. 'Now look what you made me do. Bastard. Who are you?'

'You know who we are,' said Decca, feeling anger rise at being ignored. 'You work for me.'

Sharon looked up. Her eyes darted between Decca and

Christopher. Her attitude of seconds previously dropped away.

'We want to know why you didn't tell us about your little visitation last week.'

She looked around as if her audience would give her help. None was forthcoming. With little option, she seemed to arrive at a swift realization that truth would be best. She placed the cue at the side of the table, waited for her opponent to line up a shot. He alone had briefly seemed to be about to jump to Sharon's defence, defend her honour, but one look at Christopher had decided him against it. Instead he held his eyes on the table, found the old, scarred, once-green felt intensely fascinating.

'Noddy thought we could make some money out of it,' she said.

'Noddy said it was your idea.'

Sharon gave an angry sigh. 'Noddy would.'

'Shall we go somewhere quiet an' talk about it?' asked Decca.

'Let's talk here,' said Sharon, fear giving her voice an angry edge.

Decca shrugged. 'Let's sit down, at least.'

They found a booth away from the table. Split faux leather and a table with uneven legs. Their arrival had given a focus to Sharon's male audience that they might not have otherwise had. They all tried to crane their necks to see what was going on. Christopher's bulk blocked out their view of her, like an eclipse of their sun.

She told him everything. The visit from Donovan and the girl. Russian, she thought. Something like that. Used to be on the game.

She told Decca what Donovan and the girl had wanted. To talk about Michael Nell. Even asked her to sign a statement if it came to that.

'And did you?'

'I said I would. So long as I wouldn't be implicated in any way.' Sharon looked at the pool table. It seemed several miles away, well out of reach. 'But it was that girl.'

'What about her.'

'I've worked with her before. Stroppy lass. Wouldn't do what she was told. Didn't think she'd last five minutes.'

'Did she say what she was doing with this Donovan?'

Sharon shook her head.

'Do you know how we can contact this Donovan bloke?'

Sharon was about to shake her head but remembered something. 'I've got his card.'

She shouted at one of the men to pass her handbag over. He did so, approaching the table timidly, gingerly stretching his arm around Christopher's muscle-hardened bulk. She took the bag, began rummaging through it.

Decca threw a look at Christopher, who didn't return it. He might as well have not been there for all the interaction Decca got from him, he thought.

Sharon brandished a dirty, bent business card.

'Here. It's got his address and phone number on. Give him a ring.'

Decca looked the card over, saw a company name: Albion. An address and phone number. He pocketed it.

'Thanks.' He looked back at Sharon. 'You want a lift? We're goin' back over to the town.'

She looked between the two of them. From her expression, she didn't like what she saw.

'I'm not on until later.'

Decca and Christopher didn't move.

'You got everythin' you want?'

Decca nodded. 'Yeah.'

Her eyes were on the scarred table. 'Then leave me alone. Please.'

Decca looked at Christopher, hoping for a response. Christopher didn't seem to have moved since he last looked at him. Or even drawn breath.

'Come on,' Decca said, standing up. 'Let's go.'

Christopher looked at Sharon. 'Don't go to work tonight. Or for the next week. Until we tell you. If anyone asks, you never heard of Joe Donovan.'

Sharon didn't argue, just nodded meekly.

Christopher turned away from her as if she wasn't there, went out of the door.

They walked out of the pub. Behind them, Sharon almost ran over to her admiring audience with a speed that said she thought she would never see any of them again. Her cue was handed to her, along with a drink. She gulped it down.

Outside, the car was where they had left it. They walked towards it, gravel crunching underfoot.

'You hungry?' asked Decca. 'You wanna get somethin' to eat?'

Christopher shrugged.

'You want me to drop you off somewhere?'

'I have to stay with you,' Christopher said.

'What, that means you're comin' back to my flat? You're goin' to sleep with me?'

Christopher's eyes flared. He took a menacing step nearer Decca. His arms stayed at his sides. 'Have you heard of Serbian necktie?'

Decca frowned.

'You slit throat. Side to side. Pull tongue out of hole. Leave to die.'

Decca swallowed hard.

'Do not speak to me like that again. Ever.'

Decca felt himself shaking. 'OK,' he said. 'OK, cool.'

He tried to get his car keys out of his pocket but his hands were shaking too much. Christopher took them from him.

'I drive.'

Decca didn't know if Christopher could drive, had insurance, had a driving licence, anything. But above all, Decca didn't argue.

Christopher got behind the wheel, Decca in the passenger seat. Christopher turned to him. Almost smiled. 'Nice car.'

Decca swallowed hard. 'Thank you.'

'Now we eat,' he said, turning on the ignition. 'Then we work.'

The car roared away.

Darkness fell, covering the city like an old grey blanket, the city centre turned Monday-night quiet. Sparsely filled buses operated on near-empty streets. Pubs did slight business, restaurants likewise. No one went to the cinema. People would go out only to things they had booked for, things they would lose money on if they didn't attend. It was as if the first working day of the week had proved too much. The blanket too heavy to lift.

Quiet extended from the centre of the city out to the residential areas. Through urban to suburban, where Jill Tennant walked down Fenham Hall Drive on her way to the uni to see Wilco with her lecturer, the Prof.

She smiled, felt slightly giddy at what she was doing. An illicit thrill ran through her; she tried to admonish herself for that. She was a grown woman. He was a grown man. Slightly older than herself, granted, but still two consenting adults. There was nothing wrong, nothing illegal in what she was doing. Who she was seeing.

She hadn't told Ben where she was going. None of his business.

Past Fowberry Close.

Ben. She sighed. Maybe she should give him one last try.

Perhaps he wasn't so bad after all. Bit of a rugby-playing git, and a sneery Tory, but that could be explained away as the influence of his parents. He hadn't started to think and experience things for himself. He even read the *Daily Express* because his parents did. Maybe he still had potential. He needed sorting out, admittedly, needed a few truths explaining to him. And maybe she was the girl to do it. Maybe. Besides, Ben was well fit from all that tackling, and running had given him real stamina. And he was surprisingly good in bed. There hadn't been a huge amount to compare him with, but there had been enough. Enough to know what she liked. And she liked what he did with her. Just a shame about the rest.

Straight down towards Nuns Moor. The silhouetted trees edging the Moor bordering the larger Town Moor seemed to both absorb the darkness and suck away what light remained. The Moor looked like it held secrets in that darkness. Unpleasant ones. Took them and swallowed them and wouldn't give them up. Like an inner-city black hole. She shivered. It would be quicker to cross over the Moor, but she wouldn't take that route. Not with a murderer going uncaught. She would stay under the streetlights, on the residential streets. Where nothing could happen. Where it was safe.

Down along Wingrove Road.

A night out to see Wilco. With her lecturer, no less. She smiled. Wondered if any of Ben's friends would be at the gig. She hoped so. Might do him good to know he had competition.

She had never been out with an older man before. At least not as old as the Prof was. And Wilco. She'd heard of them vaguely, thinking they were the kind of band only the serious student boys and dad rockers liked. Alt country. But the Prof had given her an album to listen to and it had been quite good. Not, perhaps, what she would have rushed out and bought, but not bad at all. She liked going to gigs, and the Prof had assured her they were good live. Which was fine. The gig would take care of itself. But what happened afterwards? She sighed. What did she want to happen afterwards?

I am trying to break your heart. A refrain from one of the songs on the album the Prof had burned for her. It stuck in her mind. She thought of Ben. Smiled. Hoped he had heard it.

Footsteps behind her. Voices. She stopped.

Turned. A couple of lads in hoodies walking down the pavement towards the end of the street, towards her. She looked straight ahead, swallowed hard. Unused to the sudden swell of fear within her. Not like her to be scared, but with a student's murderer uncaught perhaps it was right to be cautious. She gave a quick glance around. No one else on the street. The two lads crossed the road, kept level. One kept looking at her.

Really looking at her.

She kept her eyes straight ahead. Pretended that if she didn't look at them, they couldn't see her.

But the hoodied youth was still looking at her. She could feel it. She knew without looking, without even asking, what he was doing. His eyes exploring her body, imagining her without clothes. Openly leering. She began to feel self-conscious. She had worn jeans, a thin, strappy T-shirt, an even thinner jacket on top. She had chosen her clothes carefully, knowing it was going to be warm in the gig, even if the weather outside wasn't. But the youth's eyes made her feel as if she had too much flesh on show. Like a Western tourist in some medieval Muslim country.

At the next street corner, just beyond the shadow cast by a streetlight, a man was pushing a woman in a wheelchair.

Dressed in an old overcoat and hat, he was struggling. Having trouble getting the wheels of the chair off the pavement and over the road, as if the woman in the chair was old, heavy and sensitive to the slightest jolt.

Jill felt a wave of relief wash through her. At least there was someone else there. The youths wouldn't dare put their thoughts into practice while there were others about.

She slowed her pace, hoping the youths wouldn't do likewise. They didn't. They kept on walking. Crossed the road, went on to the Moor. Jill stopped walking, watched the darkness swallow them up. She breathed a sigh of relief. Turned, kept walking.

She drew level with the small man, still struggling with the wheelchair. It seemed to be caught on a high paving stone. He was trying to ease it over as smoothly as possible, talking, murmuring words of supplication all the while. He looked up at her, smiled a long-suffering smile.

'Excuse me,' he said.

Jill stopped, returned his smile. He was small, middle-aged. Nondescript, she would have said. Inoffensive. The overcoat made him look bigger. The hat gave him an air of the Prof. But those glasses were so out of date they were laughable.

He gestured to the chair. 'I'm sorry about this. I need a bit of help with Mother. She's very—' his voice dropped '—sensitive.'

Jill nodded, as if the two of them were sharing a secret.

'Would you mind?'

'No,' she said, 'not at all.'

He gestured for her to go around to the front of the chair, help to take the weight when it left the pavement. She did so. She looked at the wheelchair's occupant, readying her smile for the elderly, sensitive woman she expected to find there.

Jill stopped. Confused. She looked up, frowning, about to speak.

And he was on her.

The small, inoffensive, nondescript man was gone. In his place was a rabid, blood-crazed feral animal. It was those features Jill saw descend on her.

She put her hands up as fear rooted her to the spot. Her fists caught his glasses; she saw those unfashionable frames fly off his face, saw his rage increase. Saw a flash of blue light, felt a great numbing pain.

Then she saw nothing.

Felt nothing.

24

Donovan stood alone on the empty beach, looking out at the sea.

He watched waves form in the distance; huge white horses that came noisily crashing towards him, threatening to take lives in their furious gallop to reach land. He knew they were capable of it, knew they had done so. He looked down at the sand, expecting them, daring them, to wash him away. But those fearsome life-takers just lapped placidly around his feet, their power fizzling away with a soft-fried-egg sizzle. Anger now spent, just harmless white noise. Then the sea reclaiming them, pulling them back, readying itself for another assault.

Behind him, around him, the massive cliffs rose out of the vast, flat, sandy expanse of beach. Time-carved slopes and coves, they stretched towards the dipping clouds that floated over the upper reaches. A monochrome day: the colour-bled grey of sand giving way to the harsh grey of stone gloved by the soft grey of mist.

Wind flapped his jacket against his body, blew his hair in his eyes. He squinted as sand and dead vegetation, beach debris, swirled all around him.

He took it all in. He took nothing in. Just wanting to see it for himself. Look into the past, discover how the present had been created. Donovan just a small, slight figure standing there, dwarfed by cold nature.

Llangennith Sands, Rhossili. Wales.

Where the body had been washed ashore.

★

He had left Newcastle as soon as he had recovered his composure. He had made an attempt to tie up loose ends, but a shaken Sharkey had smoothly stepped in. He had informed the rest of the Albion team what was happening. They were all as empathic as could be.

'What about Katya?' Donovan had asked.

'We'll move her somewhere else. Keep her separate from her brother in case anything goes wrong. You don't need to know where.'

'The other thing, for Janine Stewart—'

'Will be put on hold until you return.'

'If she needs you for anything,' said Peta, appearing by Donovan's side, 'one of us will deal with it.'

Donovan nodded, moved by the understated, low-key concern that the rest of the team were showing. Tears threatened to well up inside him again; he pressed his palms into his eyes to stop them, face twisting with the effort. He felt an arm around his shoulder, allowed himself to be led into the front room to one of the leather sofas. He was dimly aware of the room emptying. He heard a voice speak to him. Couldn't make out the words. He looked up. Peta was next to him, eyes choked with concern.

'I said, d'you want me to drive you down there?'

Donovan said nothing, just breathed. Eyes closed. He didn't trust himself to speak. Eventually he nodded.

'OK,' she said in a soft voice. 'OK. D'you want to go straight away?'

He nodded.

She would take him back to his place, let him get some things together, she would do the same. He tried to thank her.

She gave a small smile in return. 'What friends are for.'

Jamal skulked in the doorway. He had been standing back from the others, waiting for them all to leave, wanting

Donovan on his own. Donovan looked up, saw the boy standing there.

'Hi, Jamal.'

Jamal took that as his cue, came in, sat next to him. His hands were restless; he squirmed in his seat. He was trying to do or say something that would comfort him, show him he was cared for. It was a self-appointed task he felt hopelessly ill-equipped for. He opened his mouth, hoped the right words would emerge. 'You'll know for soon, then, yeah?'

Donovan sighed. 'I don't think so. I don't think this is him.'

Jamal frowned, genuinely puzzled. 'So why you goin'?'

'You've got to try. Explore every avenue. I owe it to him.'

Jamal nodded. 'Wish I had someone like you lookin' out for me.'

Donovan smiled. 'You do.'

Jamal nodded. Couldn't speak for a while.

'You know all that shit before,' he said eventually.

'It's OK,' said Donovan.

'Yeah, man. It's OK.'

The two sat there, neither speaking. Silently drawing comfort from each other.

Two hours later Donovan and Peta were on the A1 heading south. Peta driving Donovan's Mondeo, trying to get the kind of performance out of it she managed to extract from her Saab, Donovan slumped in the passenger seat, hand over his face as if trying to stave off a headache.

He sighed. Looked out of the window. Barely noticed the anonymous countryside blurring past him. 'I don't know which I want more. It to be him or it not to be him.'

Peta said nothing, the silence encouraging him to speak more.

'He's been there, all this time, these years, hardly ever

away from the front of my thoughts . . .' He sighed. 'I've tried to forget him, to get on with things, but he keeps coming back. Like a ghost. An echo. And I feel guilty for letting him slip away . . .' Another sigh. 'And I don't know. I just never know for sure . . .' His fingers fluttered, as if forming a net to catch some invisible entity, coming apart as if it was too intangible to hold. 'It's not him. I know it's not him. But you've got to . . . you've got to . . .'

They drove on in further silence.

'Look,' said Peta eventually. 'About the way I spoke to you on Saturday. About Katya. I'm sorry.'

'It's OK.'

'No, really. I'm sorry. It's none of my business. Work's work and that's that. And sometimes attachments get formed through work.' She kept her eyes on the road. 'And that's OK. As long as they don't interfere.'

Donovan sighed. 'I don't think I can talk about this now.'

'OK.'

'OK.'

Another silence. Peta kept her eyes on the road.

'There's not . . . not much left of him, I'm afraid.'

Donovan and Peta had stood up from the moulded plastic chairs they had been sitting on in the entrance to Morriston Hospital, Swansea. Donovan knew what DC Davies was about to say.

He looked at the paper he had held all the way down, read from it even though he had memorized it, crumpling and uncrumpling it in his hands as he did so. The body found was that of a small boy. About eight years old. Washed up on the shore. Llangennith Sands, Rhossili. On the Gower. Jeans, T-shirt, one trainer on his left foot. Enquiries had been made. No reports of a missing child either from holidaymakers or locals. Post-mortem put time of death at anything from a week to a fortnight previous. In the water all that time.

Donovan put down the paper, hands shaking. Eyes closed. He was breathing hard, struggling not to give in. Peta gently took the sheet of paper from him.

DC Davies was a small man who looked as if he had just cleared the police force's minimum height entry requirement. He was balding, which he had disguised by that twenty-first-century version of a comb-over: a shaved head. A small, neatly clipped goatee blossomed on his lower face. He was dressed in khaki combats, boots, a plaid shirt and a padded denim jacket with a faux sheepskin collar. He walked through the entrance of the hospital. Donovan and Peta stood up.

'Sorry we had to contact you at home,' said Peta.

Davies sketched a smile. 'No problem,' he said. 'Parents' night at school. Glad of the excuse to get away, really.'

Peta, making small talk, asked him how many children he had.

'Three. Two girls and a boy.' Sensing Donovan's discomfort, Davies said nothing more on the subject. He and Peta shared uncomfortable glances. He looked at Donovan.

'No one locally came forward with any information, so we put out a national appeal,' said Davies. 'The usual missing persons organizations get involved at that stage.'

'Has anyone else contacted you about this?' asked Peta.

'Not yet,' he said. 'You're the first. And we appreciate you coming.' He looked at Donovan, unsure how to proceed. 'Do you want to . . . take a swab first? Or view the body?'

Donovan felt his chest constrict even further. 'View the body,' he said, his voice small. 'Might not need the DNA.'

Davies nodded. 'Down here, I think, then,' he said, gesturing.

He set off down a corridor. The other two followed him.

Peta put her arm around Donovan's for support. He clung to her like a drowning man to a life raft.

Down anonymous, supposedly sterile corridors. Glimpses of illness, death and reprieve from the corners of Donovan's eyes. Further down. More corridors. Donovan felt like they were moving inexorably towards the heart of something. He began to shiver. A cold heart.

'Always chilly down here,' said Davies. 'Even in summer. Has to be, though.'

They reached the mortuary.

Through two heavy plastic doors and into a room with steel chambers lining the walls. Strip lighting rendered everything and everyone pallid, leached life even from the living. Somewhat incongruously, Foo Fighters were playing on a sound system.

'Just like on TV,' said Peta. She swallowed hard, her face drawn.

''Fraid so,' said Davies. 'Apart from the music, of course.'

Donovan said nothing. Just clung harder to Peta. She felt him shaking, hoped he wouldn't collapse.

A white-coated, latex-gloved technician came over. Davies showed his warrant card, explained who they were and which body they wanted to view. The technician, brown hair tied back into a ponytail, turned the music off.

'Sorry,' he said, his Welsh accent tempered by a university education. 'I'm the only one here. I wasn't expecting company.'

Under different circumstances and probably in the course of work, Donovan would have responded to a line like that by asking with a raised eyebrow what other things the technician got up to in the mortuary when no one else was there, but he couldn't. This wasn't about anyone else. This wasn't an enquiry in the name of work. This was his life.

His son.

The technician checked the note that Davies gave him, opened the corresponding drawer. He pulled out a plastic-sheeted body.

Donovan trembled.

The technician unzipped the plastic, looked up before opening it.

'It's, uh . . . the body's been in the water a while. It's not . . . like it is on TV, you know.'

Peta nodded.

'Just, y'know, prepare yourself for a shock, like, is what I'm saying.'

He unfolded the plastic back. The body lying there had once been a human boy. But that seemed a long time ago. It had since become the property of the ocean, its plaything; buffeted, tossed and swollen up by the waves, gnawed and chewed on by fish and other marine creatures. Eventually given up and returned to shore, all further possibilities exhausted.

But there was one thing the body wasn't.

'It . . . it's not him,' said Donovan.

The other three looked at him.

'It's not him.'

Donovan looked again at the body. It was a mess. But the basic shape was still there. And even allowing for the intervening three years and the treatment of the sea, it wasn't David. He could see that.

Davies frowned. 'Are you sure, Mr Donovan? The body's in a bit of a state and there's still the DNA tests, but—'

'It's not him.' Donovan's voice became stronger. He didn't know whether to be relieved or despondent. 'I can feel it. I know it. It's not him.'

Davies nodded at the technician, who re-covered the corpse and sealed it once again in the wall. He looked at Peta, who gave a shrug, then at Donovan.

'Thank you for coming down,' he said. 'Hope we haven't wasted your time too much.'

'It hasn't been a waste of time,' said Donovan. 'At least there's . . .'

He was about to say '*hope*' but stopped himself.

Davies caught the unsaid words, nodded.

Another technician was called and a DNA swab taken from Donovan's mouth with a cotton bud. The results would be ready within forty-eight hours at the earliest, Donovan was told, and he nodded. But he knew what the answer would be. He gave a sigh. Whether of relief or any other emotion he couldn't tell.

'What will you do now?' Peta asked Davies.

'Continue with our lines of enquiry. Perhaps someone from another mispers organization will get in touch. We'll continue asking around in the boating community, see if they've heard of anyone going overboard.'

'He could have fallen off a cruise ship,' said Peta.

'Or off a trawler or a merchant ship. Could have been people smuggling. An illegal immigrant.' Davies sighed. 'Someone knows, somewhere. I just hope they can let us know.'

They thanked the technician and left the mortuary. He nodded. Before the heavy plastic doors had swung shut behind them, the Foo Fighters were rocking the place out again.

Davies walked them to the front door of the hospital. He gave them the names, locations and directions of a couple of chain hotels that he could recommend, shook hands with them both, wished them well and walked back to his car.

Peta and Donovan watched him drive off.

Peta looked at Donovan. He was watching Davies's red rear lights disappear, merge anonymously with all the other red rear lights on the roads. Become lost in the crowd.

There, then gone.

There, then gone.

She tugged on his arm. He looked at her with eyes that seemed to have aged several years in the space of hours. She dredged up a smile for him.

'Let's go and find somewhere to stay for the night.'

Donovan appreciated the effort she had made with the smile, returned it.

'OK.' His voice more of a sigh than a sound.

They walked back to the car. Arm in arm.

They found a Holiday Inn, booked two separate rooms.

'You going to be OK on your own?' Peta asked.

Donovan looked at her. Peta's eyes held so many questions; some she wanted answers to, some she didn't dare ask, some she couldn't even articulate. He knew all this because he wanted to put many of the same questions to her. But he also knew the overriding reason for her question because he still remembered what had happened the last time they had booked in to separate rooms in a hotel.

Donovan had tried to kill himself. And Peta had had to stop him.

'Yeah, I'll be fine,' he said. 'You don't have to worry about me.'

'Not much, I don't.'

'I do want a drink, though.'

'I'd better keep you company.'

Donovan looked at her. He knew the last thing she wanted to do was watch him drink and not be able to join in.

'I won't have one, then,' he said. Peta began to argue but he cut her off. 'But I'm hungry. Fancy something to eat?'

She did.

They ate at the hotel restaurant. The food was passable,

the drinks studiedly non-alcoholic, the conversation light and diversionary. Like two ice skaters dancing on an unsafe, cracked lake, wilfully ignoring the huge elephant sat in the middle.

Donovan and Peta walked along the hall, reached his bedroom. She turned to him, caught his eye with hers, held it.

'Is it a relief,' she asked. 'or not?'

Donovan sighed, grateful for the opportunity to talk, pleased she had waited until he was almost turned in for the night. He didn't want to say more than was necessary. 'I don't know,' he said. 'I looked at that body, that swollen, chewed body . . . and it wasn't him. I'd been expecting the worst, bracing myself for whatever. But when I saw it wasn't him . . .' Another sigh. 'I don't know. Part of me wanted it to be him. Because then I would know. For definite. I could plan, one way or the other. But it's not, so I can't . . .'

Peta nodded.

'I don't know what's worse,' he said. 'The knowledge he's dead, or the hope he isn't.'

He shook his head. Yawned.

'Go to bed,' she said. 'Get some rest.'

'I want to see, though. Where they found him. I . . . I want to see.'

'Get some sleep.'

Donovan nodded. Turned to enter his room. Before he could, Peta hugged him.

'Thank you,' he said, voice muffled by her embrace. 'Thank you.'

He felt her smile as she pushed against him. He nodded.

They separated while the embrace was just one of mutual support.

Donovan entered his room, closed the door behind him,

stripped, climbed into bed. He was more tired than he had felt for ages.

But it still took him hours to get to sleep.

Donovan stood alone on the empty beach, looking out at the sea.

Looking for boats.

For answers.

But neither came.

Donovan sighed. Became aware of someone standing at his side.

'Hi, Peta.'

She was pulling her clothing around herself, shivering.

'God, it's freezing here.'

'I won't be long.'

He kept staring out to sea. She kept shivering. Neither spoke. Eventually Peta sighed.

'Let it go, Joe,' she said, teeth actually chattering.

He looked at her. 'What d'you mean?'

'You know. We don't know the boy's identity, but we do know he isn't David. Just let it go at that.'

Donovan shook his head. 'I can't.'

'You have to.'

He sighed again. 'I just wanted to see this place for myself. Where the boy was found.'

She stamped her feet, willed the blood to move around her body. 'What for?'

'I don't know.' Donovan almost smiled. 'Yes, I do. It sounds stupid when I say it aloud. But I just wanted to see if I could pick up any . . . I don't know . . . resonances of what had happened to him. Clues to his life.'

'Why? What would that prove?'

He shook his head, unable or unwilling to articulate the voice that emanated from deep within him, that forlorn and desperate voice whispering to him, telling him that if he found out what had happened to the boy he could use those clues to guess what had happened to David.

And perhaps be able to find him.

'Nothing,' he said.

Peta sighed. 'Some things you just can't solve, Joe. Some things you just have to give up.'

Donovan said nothing, just kept staring out to sea.

'Like they tell you in AA,' she said. 'Sometimes you just have to admit you can't do everything, give things up to a higher power.'

'Then what?' he said without taking his eyes off the horizon.

She shrugged. 'Get on with things. Let life go on.'

Donovan thought for a long time, saying nothing, then nodded. He turned to face her. Peta wasn't sure if the drops of water on his face were tears or sea mist.

Donovan pretended not to know the difference either.

'Come on,' he said. 'Let's go home.'

They walked back to the cliff, made their way up the path and back to the road together.

25

'Shit. Shit, shit, shit, shit, shit . . .'

DI Nattrass stood in the women's toilet in Market Street police station, gripping the wash basin so tight she threatened to pull it from the wall, her head down and avoiding her own eyes in the mirror.

Water trickled from the tap in front of her, ran unnoticed down the plughole.

She sighed, clenched her eyes tight shut until galaxies imploded on the backs of her eyelids, opened them again.

Two days.

Or, strictly speaking, two nights and a day. Since the disappearance of Jill Tennant. Another female student missing. Another high-profile, high-grade case.

The inquiry room was in overdrive: bodies drafted in for door to door, to follow up leads, to man the phones. All ranks and levels. Anyone and everyone doing anything and everything. Whatever it took to find Jill Tennant.

Detective Chief Inspector Bob Fenton was working hard at stillness, at being the quiet eye of the storm. And failing. The team was working hard around the clock to find the girl, Fenton more so. He hadn't slept, had only eaten when his body had threatened to stop functioning. Personal responsibility for the inquiry was his. With regular briefings and talks with his team, both for information and inspiration, he was leading by the front and the members of his team responded to that. They, too, gave it their all.

Including Nattrass. The first briefing, called early on

Tuesday morning, had given them the news. Jill Tennant missing. Michael Nell disappeared. Join the dots. Let the clues speak for themselves. Other avenues, Fenton had explained, were going to be investigated. But the inference was that it was pretty clear who their main suspect was. Not only that, but the post-mortem results and forensic evidence in the Lisa Hill case have been re-examined and, due to findings of strange, unexplained bruising on the body, a definite link drawn between her death and that of Ashley Malcolm. Michael Nell's whereabouts at the time of Lisa Hill's disappearance were to be looked into. But they had to move fast. Or Jill Tennant would be his third victim.

Nattrass had then been called into Fenton's office after the briefing.

'Where's Paul Turnbull?' Fenton had asked before she could sit down.

'I don't know, he's . . .'

A shiver ran through her. The Bacchus on Sunday night, Turnbull, drunk, telling her he was going to go after Nell, make him pay for what he had done.

I'm ganna have him. Have the cunt . . . The picture of Ashley held pathetically in his hand . . .

Then another girl abducted. Then Nell disappeared. And Turnbull also.

'He's what?'

'I . . . don't know. Sir.'

'When did you last see him?'

'Saturday, I think. Didn't turn up yesterday. Thought he must be sick or something.' Sweat trickled down her spine. She wanted to scratch the itch in the hollow of her back but didn't dare move. 'Didn't think anything of it.'

Fenton stared at her, laser beams seemingly searing into the part of her brain responsible for truth and lies. 'You didn't think anything of it?'

The urge to scratch the itch was becoming overwhelming. She wished she had sat down. She shook her head. 'No. He'd been working pretty hard. We all had. And I think he had some trouble at home. Just thought . . . might have been exhaustion.'

Fenton kept up the stare. Now her legs felt hot and prickly. She felt twelve years old again, reporting to the headmaster to answer for indiscretions.

'What if I told you,' he said, his eyes unblinking, unflinchingly locked on hers, 'that DS Turnbull turned up outside Michael Nell's house and relieved the surveillance team of their duty, taking over from them?'

Nattrass swallowed, her throat hot and dry. She opened her mouth. No words emerged.

'And while doing this he was reported as being drunk?'

Nattrass shook her head. 'Shit . . .'

Fenton nodded. 'Shit is right. And he's in it. One way or the other.'

Nattrass was curious at his choice of words despite herself. 'One way or the other?'

Fenton sat back in his leather armchair, relaxing his posture but not his intention. 'One way or the other,' he said. 'Sit down, Diane.'

Nattrass gratefully took the offered seat.

'The two surveillance boys have been reprimanded,' said Fenton in a tone that made Nattrass glad she hadn't been one of them. 'But we are left with both a missing main suspect and an investigating officer.'

She nodded, said nothing.

'Comments? Ideas?'

She had heard those two words many times before. Usually at the start of one of Fenton's brainstorming sessions, the investigating officers around the table throwing out theories as to what could have happened in whichever crime they were investigating. She had enjoyed them at first, felt they were a useful part of the process in the apprehension of dangerous criminals. Exercises in getting inside a deviant mind. But lately she was beginning to feel they resembled nothing more than a bunch of blokes – and they were usually blokes – sitting in a pub trying to work out what had happened with only a supply of tabloid facts to base any motives or assumptions on. Plus her ideas were always ignored: the older dinosaurs treated her as if she was invisible; the younger ones ignored her because she was past the age group they wanted to shag.

But this was different.

'Well . . . could Nell have surprised Paul? Injured him? Killed him, even?'

'And then run? Finding another victim along the way? Possible.' Fenton nodded. 'But not very plausible. This feels planned.'

'Could Paul have followed him? Gone undercover?'

'Why? Why not call in if he saw something?'

'Because . . . because he lost his phone. His battery died.' Fenton looked at her. Try harder, the look said.

'He knew he shouldn't have been there and knew he would be reprimanded?'

Fenton gave a thoughtful nod, as if he was processing the information. 'Possible. Anything else?'

She knew what he was waiting for her to say. Fenton wasn't stupid. He had seen how Turnbull had been the last few days, the state he was in. He must have done.

I'm gonna have him. Have the cunt . . . The picture of Ashley held pathetically in his hand . . .

Could he have done it? Could he have crossed the line . . . ?

'What about Nell's father?' said Nattrass with a deliberate change of thought. 'Can he shed any light on the subject?'

She felt sure that Fenton had noticed her ploy, but he didn't mention it.

'Claims to be just as worried as we are about finding him. Now believes him to be innocent and wants to help him. Protect him. Still leaves us no further forward in finding Paul Turnbull.'

'No.'

Fenton leaned forward. 'I think if we find Paul Turnbull we find Michael Nell. If we find Michael Nell we find Jill Tennant. That's my feeling. My gut feeling.'

Nattrass nodded. Her mind fleetingly flashed on an image of blokes in a pub sharing tabloid insights, leaving her excluded. She quickly banished it.

'Unfortunately I can't spare you at the moment to follow that chain of reasoning. I want you to re-interview that university teacher she was supposed to be on the way to meeting when she disappeared.'

'Is he a suspect?'

'As I said, we're looking at different lines of enquiry. Two students. Both at the same university. Someone with his colourful past might be worth looking into. Perhaps you might get something different from him than a male officer would.'

'Colourful past?'

Fenton's cheek twitched. He almost smiled. 'Read up on him. You'll see what I mean.'

Nattrass nodded and stood up. 'I'll get on to it right away, sir.'

She made for the door.

'Diane . . .'

She stopped, turned.

'Yes, sir?'

'This is the time to tell me.'

'Tell you what?'

'Anything. Anything to do with Paul Turnbull that could help us find him, Nell and the Tennant girl. Anything. No matter how delicate. In confidence. This is the time.'

Nattrass looked at him, her hand on the door knob.

Have the cunt . . .

'There's nothing else I can think of, sir. I've told you everything.'

Nattrass left the room, closing the door behind her.

Whatever else, Turnbull was her partner. He deserved the benefit of the doubt.

For now.

She made her way straight to the women's lavatory.

The Prof was behind his desk in his office, fingers playing nervously, eyes unable to hide the apprehension. Jacket off, dull light glinting from his wire-framed glasses. Nattrass looked at him, let her eyes wander around the room.

A small, airless, breeze-block cube, he had done his best to personalize it. Shelved psychology textbooks gave way to the spines of old 1950s pulp paperbacks. Postcard copies of their lurid, thrilling covers dotted the wall behind his desk. Just the titles were enough, thought Nattrass, to put together a composite of the man before her: *Demented, The Flying Saucers Are Real, Teen Temptress, The Marijuana Mob, The Body Snatchers.*

Some were blown up to poster size. She picked out three of them as her immediate favourites: *I Married a Dead Man* – a picture of a bride and groom at the altar, the groom in a state of advanced decomposition – *A Hell of a Woman* – a *femme fatale* tempting a weak man to what was surely certain doom – and the most bizarre of all, *The Gods Hate Kansas*, which showed a picture of a spaceman with a raygun standing on his spaceship battling with a squid-like alien.

'Nice designs,' she said when she became aware of him watching her.

'Thank you,' he said. 'One of the ways to take the temperature of a society is by its popular culture, I always think.'

Nattrass nodded.

'However, this is something of a blind alley for me. A passion, I'm afraid.'

'Makes you imagine what the stories are like inside them,' she said.

The Prof smiled. 'Some were excellent. Most of Faulkner's work appeared like this; Zola, even. And there were indeed works of genuine brilliance within their genres. Thompson and Willeford, for instance, Day Keene, vastly underrated. Even William Burroughs. But for the most part the contents were disappointingly prosaic,' he said. 'Impossible to live up to that kind of billing.'

Nattrass, just about lost now, nodded again.

The Prof picked up on it. 'Too much detail.'

'Right,' she said and waited an appropriate amount of time before continuing. 'Jill Tennant. Her disappearance.'

The Prof's mood changed. The room seemed to darken. The postcards, books and posters no longer seemed like a quirky affectation; they took on qualities of creepy compulsion.

Demented.

Teen Temptress.

The Body Snatchers.

Nattrass sat back, her face a blank, studied him. Waited for him to speak.

'I was due to meet her, you know,' he said eventually.

'Yes, we know.'

'She didn't turn up. I thought nothing of it. Changed her mind. Something she'd agreed to in the moment, regretted later.'

'Why would she have regretted it?'

'Do I mean regretted? I don't know. I'd bought the tickets for . . . someone else. They couldn't go. And I bumped into Jill. One lunchtime after a seminar. We got talking, I offered one to her. I didn't know her . . . personal situation. I just had two tickets and I liked her company. Nothing more than that.'

'There was no . . . relationship between you?'

'No. Nothing like that.'

'Did you want there to be?'

The Prof looked uncomfortable. 'Relationships between lecturers and students are still frowned on. Even in this day and age.'

'You haven't answered the question.'

The Prof frowned, thought hard. 'I don't think I know the answer.'

Nattrass referred to her notebook. She questioned him on his personal history. His past relationships, his lack of marriages. She ascertained he was straight but uninterested in any long-term partner.

'Perhaps my ego takes up too much space to admit anyone else,' he said, attempting levity.

Nattrass looked at him, studied him. Waited for her instincts to tell her – yes or no. Nothing came.

'We've talked to her friends, her boyfriend—' the Prof flinched at the word '—and we're looking into everything they've told us.' Which wasn't much, she thought. 'Did anyone see you either before, during or after the Wilco gig?'

'Yes,' he said. 'Lots of people. They're a very popular band among both students and lecturers. I had a couple of drinks with students, met another lecturer. In the university bar. Waited for Jill to turn up. When she didn't, I went to join the others.'

'I'll need names, please.'

The Prof sighed, nodded.

'And have you a list of the other students in Jill's group? Perhaps I could ask around while I'm here.'

The Prof began to complain, tell her he had already handed one over to someone else on the inquiry, but did as she asked. She glanced down the list. One name stood out.

'Peta Knight.'

The Prof swallowed. 'What about her?'

'I know someone of that name. What a coincidence. Wouldn't be the same one, would it?' Nattrass described her.

The Prof nodded. 'Mature student. Ex-policewoman, I believe.'

Interesting, thought Nattrass, but she wasn't sure why. She pocketed the list, gave the Prof her full attention. 'One last thing. Graham McAllister. That's your real name, I take it?'

The Prof nodded warily.

'Only we've got a file back at the station on a Graham McAllister.' She looked directly at him, unblinking. 'Wouldn't happen to be you, would it?'

The Prof's eyes darted nervously, as if unsure whether to speak. Mind made up, he opened his mouth.

And her phone rang. It cut the air like an air-raid siren.

'Excuse me,' she said. She put it to her ear, ready to answer. The phone went dead. She frowned, looked at the number in the display.

Turnbull.

She returned the phone to her pocket, looked again at the Prof. 'You were saying?'

He shook his head. Whatever it was, the moment had passed. 'Nothing. That file. If it is the same one, that's all long in the past.'

She sighed, stood up, tried not to let her agitation show.

Handed him a card. 'Give me a ring if you think of anything. Should be like old times.'

The Prof said nothing.

Outside the office she felt angry with herself. Regretted her parting line to him. It had been a cheap and unnecessary shot. She shook her head, phoned Turnbull's number. Got his answerphone, left a terse message telling him to phone her, walked away.

Demented.

Teen Temptress.

The Body Snatchers.

She felt she had missed something, but she didn't know what.

26

Peta opened the door to her house in Walker. They stepped in, shook off the cold and the dark.

'It's late,' she said. 'Might be better if you stay here tonight rather than driving back to Northumberland. Jamal'll be OK. He's at Amar's.'

Donovan agreed. He hadn't felt like being alone, and Peta's company was better than most. And he enjoyed being in her house.

It was relatively small – two up, two down, with a small back yard – and she lived there alone, but she had worked hard to make it comfortable. It felt like a home. In the front room, where Donovan dropped his holdall, kicked off his boots and shed his jacket, the sofas were soft and welcoming, the shelved books wide-ranging and interesting, the art prints striking, the lighting tasteful and subdued. It was the kind of room where a couple could have curled up together, either on the sofa or the rug, shared a bottle of wine and watched a DVD. Something witty but adult. *Lost in Translation*, say, or *Sideways*. Donovan corrected himself. Not wine. Coffee, perhaps, for Peta. Hot chocolate to be daring.

'You're not leaving them there, are you?'

He looked up. Peta was pointing to his bag, boots and jacket.

'No, Mum,' he said, standing and scooping them up. 'Where d'you want me to put them?'

'Upstairs,' she said.

He looked at her. She looked at him. Neither spoke.

'In the spare room,' she said eventually, her face reddening slightly. 'I know it's my office, but there's a futon in there. You can have that.'

She turned away. Donovan took his things upstairs, deposited them in the spare room. Went back downstairs again and went into the kitchen. Peta was taking things out of the freezer, looking at them. An unplunged cafetière of coffee sat on the side. Donovan took over, got mugs, milk and sugar out, made the drinks.

They settled back in the living room, waited for microwaved lasagne to thaw, cook and ping.

'How d'you feel?' she asked.

Donovan slowly shook his head. 'I don't know . . . Relieved? That it wasn't him? Then guilty for feeling relieved. Then thinking of that other boy . . .' He sighed. 'I dunno. I really don't know.'

Peta nodded understandingly. Then stood up. 'I'd better check my messages.'

He heard her out in the hall, listening to her answerphone. He was right: he didn't know how he felt. He didn't know how he was supposed to feel. Emotions churned painfully inside him, like a washing machine full of bricks on a fast spin. He heard Sharkey's voice filtering in from the hall. Picked up the remote and pointed it at the TV. The news was on. Something about global warming, a condemnation of Bush's wilful ignorance and downright lying in allowing the situation to become so bad. He should have been angry, he thought, but he just didn't have the energy. Then the next item made him sit up.

'Peta,' he called, 'get in here.'

She did. Just in time to hear the news about Jill Tennant.

'Oh, my God . . .' She looked at Donovan. 'I knew her . . . Oh, my God . . .' She sat down next to him. 'Oh, fuck . . .'

Fenton's face appeared next, looking drawn and tired. He made the usual noises, but neither Donovan nor Peta were listening. They were still letting the shock sink in.

Peta moved close to Donovan. She began to cry. Donovan looked at her, surprised. This wasn't like her, he thought. He gently placed his arm around her and she folded into him, sobbing quietly. They sat like that for a while, the bouncing rays from the TV illuminating the dimly lit room, an island of warmth.

'That was Sharkey,' said Peta eventually. 'He's got some work for us.'

Donovan said nothing.

'Janine Stewart wants us to find Michael Nell.' She sat up, stared Donovan in the eye. Her tears seemed to have hardened, crystallized to sharp, freezing icicles. 'Let's find him, Joe. Let's fucking find him.'

Donovan watched the shape of her mouth change with each word she formed, the movement a sensuous, undulating riff on the letter 'o'. Expensive, expertly applied gloss gave her lips a rich, crimson lustre, the teeth glimpsed behind a perfect white. Again, he was fascinated and again he figured that was the intention.

'So that's the situation,' Janine Stewart said. 'My client has disappeared, another abduction of a young, female student has taken place. And they are also trying to link the death of a prostitute to him from last year.'

'And Paul Turnbull's gone too, I hear,' said Donovan, proving he was following her this time. 'Becoming a regular Bermuda Triangle around here.'

Janine Stewart graced him with a smile of enough dazzling power to light up a small town, showing off her expensive dental work in the process.

She sat back in her chair, seemingly waiting for him to

speak. She reminded Donovan of a beautiful queen in one of those old Hammer lost-world epics from the 1960s: beautiful, much desired, but with a core of ice.

He spoke. 'And what's my part in this?'

'We want to track down Michael Nell before the police do. My client has always maintained his innocence. We're worried the police may have a slightly skewed version of this.'

'Right,' said Donovan, slowly nodding. 'Father Nell's had another change of heart, has he? Decided to dip into the old handbag again?'

'The father–son bond is a very strong one. And very glad we are of it too,' she replied, seemingly immune to his sarcasm. 'As should you be. Since you'll also be benefiting handsomely from this.'

'What d'you want me to do?'

She passed an envelope across the table. The same size as before but heavier than the last one. Donovan guessed what it contained. 'More of his models?'

Stewart nodded. 'The full portfolio. If you could track them down, see if they know where my client is. See if any of them are harbouring my client.'

'And if they are?'

She shrugged. 'Negotiate his safe passage back to us.' She straightened her body in her chair, smoothed down her blouse and skirt. The effect wasn't unpleasant. 'Since Michael Nell has not been charged with any crime, we have to assume his innocence. We just want what's best for our client.'

They discussed money, how impressed the company had been with Donovan's previous work with them, and then it was time for him to leave. Janine Stewart stood, offering her hand to be shaken. Donovan did so, finding it, unsurprisingly, cool and smooth.

He left the building, stood in the street and looked around. He hadn't thought about David for nearly an hour. He looked at the envelope in his hands.

Grateful for the diversion.

The university looked the same but felt very different.

Radically different.

She walked over the main square, coat and scarf pulled close against the biting wind, bag over her shoulder, ready for her afternoon seminar. The tension all around her was almost palpable, a physical constriction in her chest making her unable to breathe. Students eyed each other warily; girls walked in pairs and stared at boys with outright hostility. No one was smiling. Home-made, quickly assembled banners had been tied to the walls:

RECLAIM OUR STREETS
RECLAIM OUR BODIES

Some girls were sporting quickly manufactured badges with the same slogan.

There was an increased security presence from bought-in guards. All ages, shapes and sizes, with their uniforms smartly pressed and their erections almost visible, they strolled, eyes darting around corners, into doorways, anyone caught in their cross-hairs vision a potential troublemaker, rapist, murderer. Demanding ID as they performed illegal stop and searches. Peta noticed that the black and Asian students were primarily singled out for this treatment. No one stopped these rent-a-cops, questioned their actions. No one wanted to be singled out as a troublemaker, a protester with too much to hide, a target inviting a thorough investigation of their life.

The university was a society in microcosm, a society with

fear and anger in the ascendancy. Never a good way to live, she thought.

She reached her building, showing her ID to a security guard on the door, unwinding her scarf and opening her jacket as she did so. He glanced idly at her photo, his eyes more interested in trying to see down her top. She felt the anger rising, couldn't stop herself.

'Had a good look?'

The man was middle-aged and small. Bespectacled. His eyes widened as if he had been jolted out of a pleasant reverie.

'And you're supposed to stop us being abducted, raped and murdered, is that it?'

The guard reddened. 'I don't . . . don't know what you mean . . .'

She gave an angry shake of her head. 'Pathetic.' She strode off.

Still angry when she reached her classroom, she almost missed the notice on the door informing her that the day's seminar had been cancelled. She wasn't surprised. She should have phoned before coming in.

She sighed, anger subsiding. She thought of Jill. Sighed again.

'Bit old for this lark, aren't you?'

Peta turned quickly. DI Diane Nattrass stood behind her. Peta was too surprised to speak.

'I'm not stalking you,' said Nattrass. 'Saw your name on the register. Gone back to college?'

'Yeah.' Peta didn't feel like explaining. 'Unfinished business.'

'Know what you mean. Happiest days of your life.' Nattrass almost smiled. 'Or they were mine.'

'Not for Jill Tennant, though.'

'No. Did you know her?'

'She was in my year,' said Peta, pointing to the classroom. 'First-year psychology. Got on well with her. She was a nice girl.'

'Don't say "was", Peta. Don't make my job any harder.'

Peta nodded. 'How's it going?'

'We're looking at several lines of enquiry, following several leads. That sort of thing. I'm sure you remember the drill.'

Peta nodded. 'And you don't tell the public what they don't need to know.'

Nattrass gave a sad smile. 'Exactly.' She frowned, looked around before speaking, made sure they were alone. 'I'm glad I ran into you. Want to ask you something.'

Peta felt wary. 'What?'

'Your lecturer. The Prof. Is that what he calls himself?'

Her sense of wariness increased. 'What about him?'

'What d'you make of him?' Nattrass tried to make the question neutral, casual, even. Peta wasn't fooled. She had asked the same kind of question in the same kind of tone many times.

'Is he a suspect?'

'Would he be walking around free if he was?'

'If you didn't have enough to bang him away, yes.'

Nattrass sighed. 'That sounds like Joe Donovan talking.'

Peta smiled. 'Taught me everything I know. And Northumbria Police, of course.'

'You haven't answered my question.'

Peta thought. 'He's . . . a one-off. Hopefully. Eccentric, certainly. But you're asking me if he's capable of abduction and murder?'

Nattrass looked at Peta. Her blank face gave nothing away.

Peta returned the unyieldingly blank look with interest. 'I doubt it,' she said.

Nattrass kept her eyes on Peta as if checking her words for veracity. Eventually she nodded. 'Thanks, Peta.' She looked around, ready to leave. 'I'll be off. Which way out?'

Peta showed her. Nattrass walked away. Peta watched her go. She opened her mouth to call out, stop her, talk to her, confide. But she didn't. Instead she pulled her jacket about herself, rewound her scarf, readied herself to leave. Nattrass had gone through the door, closing it behind her. Peta turned the other way, not wanting to bump into her again. She began walking.

Music echoed around the walls of the near-deserted corridor, got louder as she walked. She looked around. The Prof's office was directly in front of her. The sounds emanated from there, seeped out from under the door. She couldn't place it; something dark and sinister; twanging guitars, baleful drums, mournful saxophone. A voice intoning, imploring over the top. Something to do with fires and eyes, blood and poison. She couldn't be too clear. She stopped, glanced in.

There were no lights on in the room and for a second she thought it was deserted. She looked closer. The Prof was sitting at his desk, head down, hands propping his chin up as if studying something, brow furrowed. He hadn't seen her. She continued to watch, fascinated. He still didn't move. The music played on, crescendoed and crashed into some apocalyptic cacophony. Still he didn't move. Energy spent, the song died away. She watched him sigh heavily, move his arms to the side, ready himself to get up.

Not wanting him to see her, she moved quickly away from the glass. Hurried down the corridor without looking back. Behind her, the music started again. She found the door, pulled it open and was outside.

The cold air hit her like an icy slap in the face, the winter daylight interrogation-room bright. She stood for a few seconds getting her breath, thinking. She considered going to the refectory, seeing if there were any of her fellow students there. But decided against it. She couldn't see the point. Besides, she had work to do. She set off across the quadrangle.

She kept her eyes straight ahead, tried to avoid eye contact with anyone else in case their paranoia infected her, bubbled up into fear, broke out as anger. As she walked, she couldn't lose the feeling that she was being scrutinized by unseen eyes, that she was being followed. She tried to shake the feeling off, dismiss it as irrational. But she walked faster, trainers squeaking and scuffing, almost running.

She reached the corner, turned around. No one behind her. She sighed, let go a breath she didn't know she had been holding. Looked around again. Saw the old security guard she had argued with on her way into the building. Even with the square between them she could see he was staring at her. She could sense the anger coming off him in waves.

She turned around, ready to walk back over there, mouth open to let fly some insult, give vent to her own anger. She stopped herself. She couldn't see the point. Insulting a pathetic old man hiding behind a uniform. Instead she turned around, kept walking.

Feeling his laser-like eyes firing into her back, burrowing all the way inside her, until she knew he could see her no more.

Jamal concentrated hard, stared straight ahead, breathed heavily. He heard a screech of tyres, reacted quickly. He jerked the steering wheel sharp left to avoid collision with the car snaking out of a blind alleyway on his right side. As he did so, he pushed down the accelerator, brakes squealing, rubber burning. He knew the car could only be bad news.

It was. It gave chase behind him. He only became aware of that when the bullets began to zing.

'Shit, man . . .'

Then the whomp of helicopter blades. Two, one on each side, both after him. He needed some fancy driving to get out of this one.

He did some.

He pulled the steering wheel tight, sent the car into a 180-degree handbrake turn; the shockwaves juddered up his forearms. He raced back up the hill he had just come down, mounting the pavement as he did so, sending pedestrians running, darting left and right to avoid hitting them.

His pursuers were still on him, still spewing out bullets. He saw a turn-off on his left and, without slowing down, pulled hard again on the steering wheel, sending the car skidding around.

Too far.

Out of control, it hit the side of a building. He tried to straighten up but it was too late. With a huge, retina-searing Technicolor explosion, the car blew up.

'Aw, man . . .'

Jamal stared at the screen, shook his head. Took his hands off the steering wheel.

A steering wheel. To play the game properly. Well cool.

He liked staying at Amar's. It was the kind of flat – overlooking the city, cool and modern, proper urban – he dreamed of having when he was older. And he would have the same kinds of games and shit in it that Amar had. The day when he had the disposable income to make his dreams a reality couldn't come quickly enough.

His dreams. He looked at the screen, watched the flames begin to subside. They would be gone soon. He'd get his second chance.

His second chance. That's what he had. What Albion

and particularly Donovan had given him. A life where he didn't have to sell himself for money to get drugs and booze; those brief highs and temporary blackouts chasing away who he was and what he did. A life where he wasn't on the run all the time, where he didn't have to hide – either externally or within himself. Sometimes the realization of this would hit him like a slap in the face, and the emotions it released would just pour out in one huge, unstoppable torrent.

He never drank now, never took drugs. He didn't need to.

He was lucky to have these people around him who wanted him and liked him. Loved him, even. They were like family to him. But better than his biological family: a family unit that worked. Things were good. And he didn't want them to change.

But.

Joe was still looking for his son. And that was cool, that was right. Jamal could understand that. In fact, when he was younger, he used to hope that his father was looking for him, even though he knew, deep down, that he wasn't. And Joe had called him last night to tell him the dead boy wasn't David. He sounded upset, choked, even. And Jamal had felt sorry for him. Sorry but confused.

Because he didn't know if that was a good thing or not. And he didn't know why he felt that. Just like he didn't know why he was so unhappy about Joe sleeping with Katya. Maybe he should talk to Amar about it. He could always talk to Amar.

But then maybe this was what being part of a family was all about. You sometimes argued and felt confused about each other, but you all loved each other. Maybe that was it. Maybe all the other shit didn't matter.

Amar entered the room. 'Jamal, Peta's phoned and—' He stopped, looked at the boy. 'You OK?'

Jamal turned away, unaware that tears had begun to fall down his face. He hoped Amar hadn't seen them.

'Yeah, man, I'm good.' He grabbed the wheel, head still averted, and began to play with the controls. 'Love this steering wheel, man. Give it a real arcade feel, you . . . you get me?'

'Glad you like it.'

Jamal smiled. 'Yeah. Safe.' He looked at the wheel, gave it a couple of twists, tried to think of something to say to fill the gap. 'Hey, Amar, you reckon Joe'll let me drive his car now I been practisin' with this?'

Amar looked at the screen, the dying flames, smiled. 'Driving like that? In his car? I doubt it.'

'I've done it before. For real.'

'And you were lucky not to get banged up for it.'

Jamal seemed about to argue, thought better of it. Amar was right. He noticed he had his coat on.

Jamal stood up. 'Joe called?'

'Peta called. Said Joe was staying at hers another night. So you've got me again, I'm afraid.'

'Fine,' said Jamal. He looked at Amar, waiting for him to speak again. Saw he was wearing his coat and scarf, pointed to it. 'So? We workin' then tonight, yeah?'

Amar looked away. 'No. I'm . . . off out. You'll be OK here on your own. I know you will. You've done it before.'

Jamal's eyes narrowed. He frowned. 'Where?'

'Just out.' Amar couldn't quite meet his eyes. 'Doesn't matter.'

Jamal scrutinized him, unblinking. It was something he had learned to do on the street. It was an intimidation trick that had never failed him yet. 'Where?'

Amar's eyes flared. 'Look, I don't have to explain myself to you as well.' He sighed. 'Jesus.'

Jamal knew where Amar was going. And what he was

going to do. He broke eye contact, looked away. 'Can't say nothin', man. You do what you gotta do. Or what you think you gotta do.'

Jamal sat down again, looked at the screen. He put his hands on the steering wheel, readying himself for another attempt. He was aware of Amar standing behind him, unmoving, wanting to say or do something but not having the words or actions. Jamal heard him walk away, heard the front door close as he left. He stared at the screen.

He was lucky, he told himself; he had a second chance.

And all the other shit like Joe and Katya, and Joe looking for his son, and what Amar was doing with his life, maybe that was just how families were. Maybe none of it mattered.

And then again, maybe it did.

He gripped the wheel, readied himself to ride into hell once again.

Night fell cold and hard. Black ice hid in long shadows.

Black ice. And something else.

'This is it?'

'This is it.'

Decca and Christopher sat in the BMW, parked unevenly on the cobbles, around the corner of the overgrown playground in Summerhill Terrace. Through denuded branches of stunted trees, crumbling stone and rusted ironwork, they could see their target: the Albion office.

'Is this the only entrance?' asked Christopher.

'Yeah. I've checked out the back. There's a kind of yard thing backin' on to another kind of yard thing. Whole row of them. No real way in.'

Christopher nodded. 'A kind of back yard thing . . .'

Decca flushed. The night hid it. 'Well?' he said tetchily. 'We doin' it or what?'

'We are doing it,' replied Christopher. 'But remember. Once the alarm is taken care of, no talking. No excuses. Right?'

Decca nodded. 'Yeah, I hear you.'

They got out of the car. Christopher looked around, checked for eyes behind curtains, pedestrians. Found none. Began walking towards the Albion office, Decca following. Christopher had put on a huge overcoat, Decca noticed, a heavy one by the look of it, weighing him down as he walked. Christopher stopped outside, looked at the front of the building. Decca watched; he knew what Christopher was looking for. Burglar alarms, CCTV, elaborate locking systems. They had been past during the day, appearing as inconspicuous as possible, checking the place out. They had found nothing too hazardous. Christopher had given it a medium security rating. Decca had just nodded.

Christopher walked up to the front door, looked at the lock, his face granite-like, thoughtful.

'Keep watch,' he said.

Decca turned, scoped the street. Still no one about. From a reinforced inner pocket in Christopher's large overcoat, he produced a scarred, heavy metal bar with two grips welded along the top of it. He grasped it, pulled it back, his body tense, and swung it forward, putting all his considerable strength behind it.

The door crashed open, the alarm sounding simultaneously. Decca and Christopher hurried inside, Christopher throwing the metal bar to the floor.

'The alarm,' said Christopher above the din.

Decca saw the box mounted on the wall, moved over to it. He looked at the numbers on the keypad, fingers poised above them, thinking of what the successful combination could be. Before he could press anything, Christopher knocked him out of the way and, grunting only slightly, ripped the box off the wall. The noise stopped. He threw it to the ground.

Christopher pointed at the front door, made a closing motion. Decca hurried to it. It was ruined, uncloseable. He pushed it shut, found a heavy stone vase in the hallway, dragged that against it.

Christopher had already moved into the first room. Decca followed him. They looked around, saw large leather sofas, a central coffee table. Christopher pulled the sofas away from the walls, looked behind them. Nothing there. A door led to a further back room. He motioned to Decca to open it.

Decca tried. It was locked. He took a step back, lifted his leg, brought his booted foot down on the handle. It opened. He entered, grinning. Buzzing off his head. The most fun he'd had in ages. A bigger kick than gear, booze or sex. He wanted to kick something else, smash the place up, rip it apart. Put his print on things. Show them he'd been here.

They were into the main office. Desks, filing cabinets, computers, phones. Christopher had already made his way to the nearest filing cabinet, had a metal bar out and was forcing the lock. The top drawer sprang open. He motioned for Decca to come across, rifle through with him. Donovan's file was near the front. Decca removed it, opened it. Home address, bank details, car, everything. Decca waved it about, grinned.

'Fuckin' jackpot.'

Christopher pushed his finger angrily against his lips, glared at Decca like he was about to hit him. Decca flinched, closed his mouth immediately. Christopher still glared at him. Decca looked at the documents he held in his hands. They just looked like bits of paper. His heart sank, his adrenalin plummeted. Suddenly this wasn't as much fun any more.

He handed them over to Christopher, who silently pocketed them.

They looked through the rest of the filing cabinet, through the desk drawers, rummaged in the wastebin, working efficiently. Found nothing pertinent. Christopher motioned to the two computers on the desks. Both iMac G5s, neither had base units, just a screen, keyboard and a mouse each. Christopher nodded towards one, picked up the other. They both pulled out wires, disconnecting the machines from electricity and Ethernet, hefted them up and, with a last look around the office, left with them under their arms.

They walked slowly back towards the car, neither being stupid enough to draw attention to themselves by running, making sure to close the front door of the Albion office as well as possible on the way out. Decca opened the boot, and they placed the computers inside. They got in the car, Decca again behind the wheel. Decca breathed a huge sigh. He was sweating, hands shaking, chest pumping.

'Can I talk now?'

Christopher just looked at him, his gaze lizard-eyed, his face stone. He didn't seem to have broken into a sweat.

Decca swallowed. He couldn't remember what he had been about to say. 'Those computers'll be encrypted,' he said, panting, just so he didn't look foolish. 'Passwords an' shit.'

'We have someone for that. Drive.'

'Whatever you want,' he said. 'You're the boss.'

If Christopher heard the sarcasm in Decca's voice he didn't remark on it. Decca, without looking at him, turned the radio on. He had it set at certain times of the day and night to find hip-hop and RnB stations. Clattering beats came tumbling out of the speakers. Decca picked up the rhythm straight away, felt it bring back some of that nasty-edged euphoria he'd had in the Albion office before

Christopher had taken it away. Yeah, he thought, nodding along, things weren't so bad.

Christopher, without looking at Decca, leaned forward and retuned the radio to a classical station. Strings immediately replaced beats. Happy that this was what he wanted, he sat back comfortably in his seat, letting the operatic music wash over him.

'Drive,' he said.

Decca was pissed off. He had been looking forward to turning those offices over and Christopher had gone and spoiled it for him. Now he was dictating what Decca could listen to. In his own car. He felt anger flare within him. He was about to argue, tell Christopher what he thought of him. He turned, mouth open, ready to let go. And caught that stone lizard face looking back at him.

Decca said nothing. Just silently turned the engine over, put the car in gear.

And drove away.

They rounded the curve in Summerhill Terrace, came out on to Westgate Road. Decca indicated, turned left, drove carefully away.

Once they were out on the main road, Christopher turned the opera up.

Decca said nothing. There wasn't a single thing he could do about it.

Just keep driving.

27

Jill lay there, naked and shivering. Beyond crying, beyond screaming.

Tied to his worktop. Beyond hope.

She tried opening her eyes, felt only pain. She couldn't. Tried again. The same. She stopped trying. Like picking at a wound that hadn't had time to heal. She didn't know if the wetness running down her cheeks was tears or blood.

She lay as still as she could, listened. He wasn't there.

It didn't matter: his voice still resonated in her head. Those words, going around again and again . . .

'I'm sorry about this,' he had said, his voice frighteningly calm and reasonable. 'I really, really don't want to hurt you. You might feel some pain, I'm afraid. It's quite necessary. There's no other way, unfortunately.'

He had advanced towards her. She had seen the needle in his hand, the light glinting off it.

'It's time for the first step. It's time for you to stop looking at this world and start looking at the next.'

He had knelt over her. She had struggled, tried to pull herself away, got nowhere.

'It's the first stage on your journey . . .'

The needle had come towards her.

She had felt pain.

And remembered the first time she had opened her eyes and found herself tied there. It felt like months, years ago.

Not just days . . .

★

She had opened her eyes to find herself tied down flat. Naked, cold. And to find him standing before her. Naked also, except for his glasses and, she noticed, his socks. Under other circumstances she would have found that amusing. Then she saw his erection, guessed his intention and found her breath coming in even shorter gasps. He had smiled at her.

'You're still with us? Good. Thought we might have lost you. And we wouldn't want that to happen, would we? At least not yet. Not before you've answered my questions for me.'

She tried to take in her surroundings. It was an airless, windowless room. Wires trailing, hanging, lamps on stands like a film set, trained on her. Behind the lights, grey lumpen shadows and razor-light glints. Like figures standing, holding poses.

He came nearer to the table. She struggled all the more.

He shook his head slowly, almost sadly. 'I'm afraid there's no way out of those bonds. I've done them properly. The more you struggle, the tighter they get.'

She tried to scream. Couldn't force the words out because of the gag in her mouth.

'Don't make work for yourself. Don't make things worse than they already are.' His voice: all little man ordinariness, the filing clerk given centre stage, the office party bore allowed to assume power.

'I'm sure you don't see it this way at the moment,' he had continued, 'but you're in a very privileged position. You're going to tell me the answers to questions that have plagued philosophers and religious leaders for centuries.' He giggled. 'Yes, you.'

He walked around the table, his erection incongruously hard against his flabby, old skin. She found it repulsive.

'I chose you for this specially. Because you're a student.

But not just any old student, a psychology student. And you must be a bright girl to do that, mustn't you? Mind you, I thought the last one was and she wasn't. But I'm hoping for better from you, Jill.'

She flinched.

'Oh, yes, I know your name. Jill.' He rolled the word around in his mouth, luxuriated in the pronunciation. He knelt down, his face near hers. 'I know all about you.'

He stood up, continued walking. 'The others I tried it with, they were no good. Rubbish. Useless. Animals.' Rage entered his voice; he spat the words out. He smiled, dispelled it. Leaned down and touched her hair. 'But you're different. Special.' He sighed, gave out another madness-tinged giggle. 'We're going to get to know each other in the next few days. Before I hand you over to my friends you see all around me.'

He gestured with his arms, looked around the room. Jill could see nothing. He nodded, smiled, as if being told jokes no one else could hear.

'Mm. Get to know each other.' He walked over to the side of the room where there was what looked like a workbench. Picked something up from it. Jill craned her neck to see, heart almost in her mouth. It was a condom. He was opening the packet, rolling it on.

He smiled. 'I shouldn't do this. Very unprofessional. But—' he shrugged, looked at her naked body '—what can you do?'

He moved towards her.

She wished she could have passed out.

But she didn't. She experienced everything.

The next time she opened her eyes it was from a dream of safety that had become a nightmare of hopelessness. She had found tears running down her face. And realized it was no dream.

She didn't know how long she had been there. Whether it was day or night. She had wanted to go to the toilet but was still gagged, unable to express the words. With no alternative, she had evacuated her body where she lay. And he had watched and laughed. The commission of that act and his response took her beyond degradation.

He had raped her again. And again. At least he hadn't lasted long. That was the only positive she could find in the experience.

She no longer felt like a person. Her previous life felt like some fantasy she had imagined in a dream. A dream of safety. Her body ached from lying still so long. She had gone beyond noticing it. She was all cried out. All screamed out.

He had entered the room then. He must have heard she was awake.

'Still here?' he had said, and laughed.

She started struggling again.

'Look, you'd better get used to it. You're not going anywhere. This isn't Hollywood. There's no hero to rescue you. No one's going to come in and save you. No one knows where you are. Except me. So why not make the best of it, eh?'

Jill stopped struggling. Instead she tried to talk, communicate with him, let him see her as a person, not just a victim, a slab of meat to be experimented on. But the gag wouldn't allow her. He had taken no chances. She flopped back, sighed.

That was when she saw the needle. Heard his words about pain. About the first step. About the journey.

And in that moment she realized he was right. There would be no hero. No rescue. The good didn't survive. The bad wouldn't get punished.

'You see, your previous life was just fantasy,' he said. 'Just living in the here and now. Safe and boring with a security seal. Well, I'm going to remove that.'

This wasn't Hollywood. This was real life. Nothing, no one, could help her now.

'I'm going to reveal to you the past, the present and the future. I'm going to give you reality in all its squirming, gory glory.'

The needle came closer.

'I'm going to make you see . . .'

She closed her eyes.

'. . . everything.'

She couldn't even scream.

28

The phone rang, startling Jamal's eyes open, his body out of sleep. He listened, waited for Amar to come and pick it up, expecting to hear his voice any second. No response. The phone kept ringing.

Jamal threw back the duvet and got out of bed. He padded down the hall of the flat to the front room, opened the door and stopped dead.

Amar was lying, half-on, half-off the sofa, the remains of some takeaway food and a fifth of vodka spilled around him.

The phone shrilled insistently.

Jamal sighed angrily, crossed to the table by the window, picked it up.

'Yeah?'

There was a pause. 'Jamal? That you?'

Joe. 'Yeah, man, it's me.'

'Good. Look, is Amar there?'

Jamal looked down at him. His clothes were dishevelled, dirty and partially open. Dark flecks of vomit splattered his trousers, like blood spray from an automatic weapon wound. Hair on end, nose crusted with dried blood. He stank of so many things it was impossible to single one out.

'He's, er, he's still asleep.'

'OK. Well, listen. The Albion offices have been broken into.'

Jamal was stunned. 'Wha'?'

'Yeah, I know,' said Donovan, his voice grave. 'The place is a state.'

Jamal began to stammer out questions. Donovan cut him off. 'I don't know anything yet. What they were looking for, whether they got it, or if it was just kids.' He sighed. 'I'm here with Peta right now. The police are on their way, but I doubt there's much they can do. I just need Amar there.'

'What for?'

'Because he installed all that high-tech hidden CCTV stuff. And no one else can operate it.'

'I can.'

Donovan's voice stopped, surprised. 'Yeah?'

'Yeah. I helped him install it. He showed me.'

'Good.' Jamal could tell Donovan was smiling. That pleased him. 'Well, you come down with him. Case he needs his apprentice. But I need you both down here right now.'

'Yeah, yeah, man. I hear you.'

They said their goodbyes. Jamal replaced the handset.

He looked down again at Amar, who hadn't stirred throughout the call. Jamal loved the man, his surrogate uncle as he thought of him, but right now he was so angry with him he wanted to hit him.

He stood there in his shorts and T-shirt, thinking what to do next. He would have to clean him up, get him focused, make him presentable. He had done it before. He remembered his mother before her breakdowns, before she sent him to the children's home. Soaring through the stratosphere on one of her binges, screaming and singing and laughing like the world held no fears or pain or problems for her. She would pick any passing male as a dancing partner to share her euphoria. It could go on all night. Days and nights. But the comedowns, when she would hit the deck harder than Frank Bruno under Mike Tyson's fists, would always be endured alone but for Jamal. He would clean her up, get her fed. Put her clothes in to wash. Tell her things were going to be OK. Like resetting a scrambled jigsaw. Like re-mending a broken heart. Looking after her as best as a six-year-old could.

After he had done all that out of love she had left him, splitting his family up. Worse than a scrambled jigsaw. Worse than a broken heart. And he wasn't about to let it happen again.

He kicked Amar's foot, got no response. He kicked harder, careful not to let too much anger go into it. Amar groaned, threw his arms uselessly about.

'Time . . .' Jamal cleared his throat. 'Time to get up, man.'

Amar groaned again. Jamal kicked again. Amar opened his eyes, closed them immediately. Gave another groan.

'Come on, man, don't do this . . .' Jamal's kicking was getting angrier. 'Come on.'

Amar made a noise that could have been a question.

'You got to get up, man. We got work to do.'

Amar found his voice, in part. 'Not . . . today. No . . . work . . . day.' He turned over, sighing, on to his side.

Jamal knelt down, pulled Amar up by the front of his shirt.

'Look, man, don' fuck about. You're wasted an' we need you. Don' do this to me, yeah?' His voice was angry and desperate in equal measure.

Amar's eyes opened. He frowned. 'Jamal?' He looked around, clearly unsure of where he was. 'How'd I get back here?'

Jamal had no time for this. 'I dunno, man, maybe you flew. Maybe that shit you stuck up your nose gave you superpowers, yeah? Come on, man.'

'Whassa problem?' His breath stank. Jamal recoiled from it.

'Joe wants us.' He told him about the office being broken into, the need to check the CCTV.

Amar groaned. 'Not today.' He slumped to the floor, turned over again.

Jamal saw the red mist descend. It was no longer Amar on

the floor but his mother. He picked him up again. 'Look at you, man! Look at you! You a state, man! Where's your fuckin' self-respect, eh? How you meant to look after people like that? Eh?'

Amar's eyes opened. He frowned.

'This how you show you're meant to care? Yeah? Is it?' Jamal's face was up close, spitting in Amar's eyes.

'Jamal?' He spoke slowly, quizzically.

Jamal blinked, looked at Amar strangely, as if unsure who was lying before him. He let Amar drop, stood up, turned away from him. Amar struggled up into a sitting position, put his head up.

'Shit . . . I'm spinning . . .'

Amar looked around, seeming to see more than just what was in front of him, take in more than just his surroundings. 'What a wreck . . .'

'Yeah, man,' said Jamal. 'You said it.'

'Shit,' Amar groaned. 'Oh, shit . . .'

Jamal turned around, faced Amar again. 'Yeah, shit is right. Look at you, man. What's wrong wit' you, you got to get fucked in the head like this? What's so fuckin' bad wit' what you got?'

Amar just stared at him. 'Nothing. It's nothing. It's just going out, having fun.'

'Havin' fun?' Jamal gave an involuntary suck of his teeth, kept going.

'Man, we like family here, yeah? You an' me an' Peta an' Joe. Family. An' families, right, they look after their own, right? Well, you, man, you're wrong. Well wrong. Look at you, man. The state of you. Check yourself.'

Amar opened his mouth to argue, stopped himself. Saw tears forming in the corners of Jamal's eyes. Jamal, aware of what he was doing and not wanting anyone else to witness it, turned away.

Amar sighed. 'What's so bad, Jamal? You used to get like this. You told me. Told me how much you used to enjoy getting high, having fun. When you were . . .' Amar stopped, aware of what he had been about to say.

Jamal could barely speak, he was so angry at Amar's words. 'You need me to tell you?' he managed to say. 'You really need me to spell it out for you?'

'No.' Amar's voice was almost whispered.

'When I was on the street? When I . . . I sold myself? I got high when I did that? You wonder why, man? You wonder?'

Jamal turned away again, shoulders hunched, shaking.

'Sorry,' said Amar quietly.

'Yeah,' said Jamal. 'Fuckin' sorry. That'll cover it.' He sighed angrily. 'Was it worth it?'

Amar knew the answer but couldn't say it out loud. He couldn't admit it, not even to himself.

The silence between them stretched further than the space of the room.

Eventually Amar prised himself off the floor, stood unsteadily on his feet.

'I'll go and get a shower. Get ready.'

Jamal, without looking at him, nodded.

Amar padded out of the living room. Jamal heard him entering the bathroom, taking off his clothes. Then the unmistakable sound of someone being violently sick.

'Good, man,' said Jamal under his breath. 'Hope it hurts.'

He swiped angrily at the tears that were starting to tumble out of his eyes.

Later, they sat side by side in Amar's battered old Volvo estate, no radio, no CDs playing. Just one long, uncomfortable silence. Amar pulled up at the car park on the corner of Blandford Street. He took his shaking hands off the wheel, turned off the motor, but made no attempt to leave the car.

Jamal waited.

'Sorry,' said Amar.

Jamal said nothing.

'You were right, OK? Right.' He took a deep breath, held it for a thoughtful length of time, then, mind made up, let it out as a long sigh. 'It's . . . I've got a problem. A problem. I know I have. And I've . . . been lying to myself. For a long time. It's . . . I'm going to get some help. It's not fair on you or the others. Some professional help. It's what I need.'

Jamal nodded. 'OK.'

'I will.'

'I said, OK.'

'Good.'

Another silence stretched between them.

'We'd better go,' said Amar eventually. 'We've got work to do.'

Jamal nodded, got out of the car.

They walked up Westgate Road together, not speaking. Jamal felt that the pavement was made of eggshells. One wrong step and he would disappear, the world collapsing around him.

Joe Donovan was standing against the wall watching the police SOCO team go about their work: moving studiously around, coming in and out, carrying plastic-bagged objects, placing them in the back of a police van. Watching his new business venture, the thing into which he had invested time, effort and above all money, the thing which he was most proud of in his life, be broken down and dismantled. Sharkey stood next to him, puffing on a cigarette.

'Lot of fuss for a break-in, isn't it?' Donovan kept his

eyes on the scene, his arms rigid at his sides. 'Usually just send one guy out.'

Sharkey pulled on his cigarette, moved it away from his face. 'At least they haven't got their paper suits on.' He extravagantly released the smoke. It plumed up and away. 'Look like we'd been the victims of a chemical attack if they'd done that.'

'If we'd been Joe and Vera Public and our DVD player had been nicked they wouldn't have gone to all this trouble.'

Sharkey curled another plume of smoke. 'But we're not and it hasn't been.'

'Meaning?'

Sharkey shrugged

Donovan turned, looked at him. 'What have you told them?'

Sharkey's eyes were on the disappearing smoke, smile curling on the corners of his lips. 'In and of itself, nothing.'

Donovan stared at him.

Sharkey cleared his throat. 'But I may have, however, mentioned a couple of names. Janine Stewart. Michael Nell. Does help to speed things along, don't you find? One tends to get taken more seriously that way.'

Donovan felt his hands begin to shake, his breathing become heavier. 'Taking referrals from you is one thing, Sharkey. Employing you is one thing. But this is my business. And don't you fucking dare presume to take it over.'

Sharkey tried not to flinch. Donovan didn't trust himself to stand with the lawyer any longer. He detached himself from the wall, let his anger carry him over the road.

'Just stay out of the way until we've finished, sir.'

Donovan ignored the woolly suit, walked straight in. 'How much longer you going to be? I've got work to do.'

The SOCO team were going about their tasks: dusting, shining what looked like ultra-violet lights on surfaces, photographing. They barely gave him a glance. He suddenly felt foolish at his outburst. It was misplaced anger that should have been directed at Sharkey. A uniform came over to talk to him. But he had already turned and gone back out through the broken front door.

He stared at Sharkey who couldn't hold his gaze. Felt the wave of anger rise and subside. He looked back at the useless front door, saw the trail of damage, the empty places where the computers had been, the files strewn all over the floor. Knew it wasn't Sharkey he was angry with.

He walked up the street.

'Gonna get a coffee,' he mumbled, not knowing whether Sharkey heard him but sensing he understood.

Later, Donovan was allowed back inside. The police had cleared up their mess as much as possible, leaving only the aftermath of the break-in itself to deal with. He stood in the office looking around, trying to find the positives in the situation. Well, he thought, it could have been much worse. They had taken things, they had wrecked things, they had disrupted things. But they hadn't torched the place. They hadn't defecated anywhere.

A locksmith had been called to deal with the door, along with the insurance company to assess the damage and value of missing items.

Amar and Jamal had turned up, Jamal seemingly tightly wound and either angry or scared about something, Amar looking fragile and wasted. Donovan didn't have time to deal with either of their problems there and then; sorting out the future of Albion had to take priority. On their arrival Sharkey had disappeared, citing a prior business appointment. Peta had then joined them, appalled at what she saw. She looked straight at Donovan to see how it had affected him. He couldn't return her look of concern.

'Did they find the CCTV?' asked Amar.

'No,' said Donovan. 'You did a good job there.'

Amar gave a tentative smile. 'Undetectable and therefore undetected. I'm very good, aren't I?'

They decided to relay the footage in the upstairs room. It was only the ground floor, the office, that had been disturbed. Their planning room had been left untouched. Amar set his laptop up on the desk. They clustered around to watch it. He punched in commands, hit keys.

'Here we go,' he said. 'Last night. Think we need only concern ourselves with these cameras.' The screen split into four: the outside door, the hallway, the meeting room, the office. All in sharp colour.

'Good picture,' said Donovan. 'Usually this stuff has the same quality as 1970s home video porn movies.'

'Of which you are a serious collector,' said Peta.

Donovan said nothing but knew he was blushing.

'The CCTV's on an HD Wi-Fi system. Top of the range. Called in a lot of favours to get this.'

'Ooh, get you,' said Peta.

Amar smiled. 'You don't have to be straight to be a techno gadget fanboy.'

'No,' said Donovan, 'just sad.'

They kept their eyes on the screen, collectively pleased that their wisecracks were helping them cope with the situation.

Amar pressed a button. 'Let's just fast forward here.' Bars appeared across the screen. The picture speedily swapped daylight for streetlit darkness. Nothing happened quickly. Then a movement.

'There,' said Donovan.

Amar moved his fingers, reversed the picture in slow motion, let it start in real time.

'Here we go,' he said.

'We got sound on this?' asked Donovan.

'What do you think?'

They saw two overcoated figures stand at the door, one bulky, one medium-sized. They watched as the bigger one pulled out a mini battering ram and smashed the door open.

'Jesus . . .' said Donovan.

They heard the alarm go off, saw the action switch to the hallway. The medium-sized man fumbling with the alarm box, the bigger one ripping it off the wall.

'One way of disarming it,' said Peta, trying to hide her horror.

They watched them enter the front room, pull the sofas about.

'They bein' real gentle,' said Jamal curiously. 'When I broke in somewhere, man, I went apeshit.'

'When you broke in somewhere?' Donovan said.

Jamal felt his cheeks colour. 'All in the past, man, all in the past.'

To a collective gasp from those watching, the two thieves smashed their way into the office.

'Recognize them?' asked Peta.

Donovan frowned. 'Don't know, something . . .'

They prised open the filing cabinet, took out Donovan's file.

'That's my stuff!' he said, pointing at the screen. 'They've taken my stuff!'

They all looked at him, eyes off the screen for a second.

'Listen!' said Amar.

He punched in some keys, rewound the action.

'Watch. Don't speak.'

They watched silently as the two burglars broke into the office again, crowbarred open the filing cabinet, took out Donovan's details. One of them waved the file about, spoke.

'There,' said Amar.

'What did he say?' said Donovan.

Amar rewound, played with the sound filters. The action played again.

They heard it loud and clear: 'Fuckin' jackpot.' But more than that: the man had looked directly at the hidden camera when he had said it.

'Got you,' said Donovan.

'D'you recognize him?' asked Peta.

'Yeah,' said Donovan. 'Decca Ainsley.'

Amar froze the picture. Decca looked at the camera and smiled.

'Decca Ainsley. Gotcha, you bastard.'

They watched the remaining footage, saw Decca and his associate make off with the desktops. Then sat back on the office chairs, looked at one another.

'We gonna tell the police?' asked Jamal.

Donovan thought it over. 'Not yet, I don't think.' He looked around. 'Feel free to contradict me, but this is the way I see it. If Decca Ainsley is breaking into our offices, that means Kovacs knows we've got Katya and her brother and is trying to find out where. And to do that they're following me.'

'Or bypassing you and looking through the computer databases,' said Amar.

'You reckon they could do that?' asked Jamal.

'I reckon,' said Amar.

'True,' said Donovan. 'Either way, they're on to us. We'll have to get on to Sharkey, get the Tokics moved to other safe houses. Hotel, anywhere.'

'And then what?' asked Peta.

Donovan whistled out a stream of air. 'This is what I think. Again feel free to shoot me down if you disagree. Or chip in with other ideas. I'll keep doing what I'm doing.

Looking for Michael Nell through the prostitute photo trail. We've just been burgled. We've got insurance, but it's a well-paying job and we need the money. So we go on with that, show we're professional about it. That OK?'

The others nodded in assent.

'Good,' said Donovan. 'Peta, you keep going to college. The girls all disappeared from there. There might be a connection with Michael Nell.'

Peta nodded, face blank. Whatever thoughts she was having were kept hidden.

'Amar and Jamal. Why don't you two see if you can pick up a trail on Decca Ainsley?'

Amar nodded. Donovan looked at him, deciding whether to speak to him in front of the others or not.

'I'm OK. I can handle it,' he said, pre-empting him.

'You sure?'

'I'm sure.' He looked at Jamal. 'We can both handle it, can't we?'

'Don' worry 'bout him,' Jamal said. 'I'll look after him. Ain't nothin' happen to him with me there.'

Amar gave him a smile of gratitude. Jamal broke into a smile of his own for the first time that day. Donovan noted the fact. He would have to talk to the boy soon, set things straight between them. But not now. When this was all over.

Jamal nodded.

'Good,' said Donovan.

'Now remember,' said Peta, before he could speak again. 'We're not police. We're just doing our jobs. We're making a good reputation for ourselves and we want to keep it. The best way to do that is to be professional. Any questions?'

'Yeah,' said Donovan, patting his pockets. 'You seen my mobile? Must have left it somewhere.'

There were no other questions.

They all went to work.

29

'Listen . . .'

The Historian stood still, hand in the air, head cocked to one side.

'Listen . . . Can you hear them? I can.'

Jill couldn't see him, her eyes sewn tight shut. She couldn't respond to him either. Her breath was expelled as a kind of wheezy keening, like the death rattle of an old, pained, dying dog.

He threw words at her, talked incessantly. Sometimes to her, sometimes to others. At first she had listened, thinking someone else was in the room with them or nearby; a collaborator of his who would take pity on her, perhaps a potential helper or even saviour. But gradually she had tuned out. There was no one else there, she realized. He was talking either to himself or to people only he could see. Now she paid him no attention at all.

'Shh, they're here. They're with us. I wish you could see them.' Then a laugh. 'But you will. Soon enough.'

He moved around, caught the light of one of the swinging overhead bulbs, stood before it. Jill felt rather than saw the shadow fall across her. The sudden absence of weak heat on her naked, bruised body.

'Bet you wonder where we are, don't you?' The air swished as he moved around her. She felt his breath on her ear. Excited, rasping. Smelling like earth from an age-rotted grave. 'Mm? Don't you? Well, this is my chamber. My world. My home. And it's secret. No one will ever come here.' He stood up. She heard him laughing to himself again. 'No one.'

The air moved and swirled around her again as he walked around the table.

'What are you studying? Psychology, is that it? A pretendy science. Think you know what makes people who they are. I've seen you all, walking around like you know all the answers. Like you're the first ones ever to be here, to experience life, to . . . to know things.' He spat. 'Self-important, arrogant. You don't have to go to university to show you're smart, you know. I'm just as clever as you. Just as clever. More so, in fact.'

He breathed hard, bringing himself under control.

'You know nothing. You don't even know your history, do you? What happened before you got here. Can't say you've forgotten because you don't know; you never knew, did you?'

Jill continued to struggle for breath.

'There used to be a gaol here. Not jail, gaol, g-a-o-l. And a big one. Yeah, right in the middle of town. Right in the middle of Newcastle. Fancy that.' His voice took on a distant, whimsical aspect. He huddled down close to her. 'Newgate Street gaol. For over four hundred years until the eighteen hundreds. Eighteen hundred and—' he tried to think, the exact date eluding him, making him angry at forgetting '—until the eighteen hundreds. And they had dungeons. Lots of them. Under the streets. Now when they pulled it down, the gaoler's house they turned into a pub, but d'you think they got rid of the dungeons? Hmm?' He laughed. She felt him move in closer, that dead breath on her ear. 'There's more than rivers hidden under these streets. Much more. And I found it. But it wasn't empty. Oh, no.'

He stood up. She heard him move over to the far side of

the room, heard him touching something, his voice crooning, muttering words too low to hear, holding a conversation she wasn't privy to.

'Occupants, inhabitants . . . to be expected, really. We didn't get on at first.' He gave a snort of laughter. 'Imagine that. Wouldn't believe it, would you? To see us now you'd think we'd always been the best of friends.'

He stopped talking. Jill thought he had left the room, left her alone. She let out a ragged sigh. She preferred being left alone. Her mind created vistas, Cinemascope visions of open fields, sunsets, happiness. She was in Ireland, where she had holidayed with her family several times as a girl. The Mourne Mountains. The beach. She could feel the sun on her shoulders, the gentle breeze ruffling her hair. Hear the susurrating fizz of the tide lapping the shore. And she was there, away from him. Away from this. Her heart, in desperation, in madness, clung on to the fantasy, willed it into reality.

'Ghosts,' he said. 'The souls of the departed.'

And hearing those words, her spirit crashed once more. The involuntary keening sound came raggedly from her once more.

'Course, I didn't believe it at first. Well, you wouldn't, would you? You see, I'd found this place by accident just before my mother died.' He sighed. Shook his head. 'What a difficult time that was, I can tell you. Well, I was brokenhearted, as you can imagine. I stopped taking my medication, even. Oh, I was a handful. And then I found this place. But it wasn't easy. Shall I tell you how I did it?' Pride rang through his words. He told her the story. All the while she was trying to return to Ireland while he talked.

He told her of his mission, his quest. The Hidden Rivers project giving him the idea. He went to the library, the Discovery Museum. Pored over old maps and plans. Looked at the rivers, charted their courses. Thought about the

prison. Tried to work out where the old tunnels, passage-
ways and dungeons would have been. He had a head start.
Somewhere to dig from without anyone watching. He
pulled open the manhole cover and, armed with a torch, a
pickaxe and a pair of strong boots, down he went.

At first he hit the sewer. It stank. Made him throw up.
Several times. Wasn't like you see it on TV. But he kept going.
Kept walking. Looking at the walls, feeling his way with his
fingertips, following the map he had memorized. Eventually
he found the spot he was looking for. A patch of wall with
different brick. This was it. He didn't know how, just felt it.

He began to chip away. Took him ages. But that was
OK; he had ages. All the time in the world. The first brick
came out. He felt behind it. Nothing. Just stale air. He does-
n't mind admitting he wet himself with excitement. He was
right. There was the tunnel.

He got to work in earnest, chipping away in a frenzy.
Pulling out bricks with his bare hands. Throwing them, one
by one, into the filth at his feet. He kept going, ignored
hunger, ignored the tiredness of his arms. Working until he
had created a big enough gap to crawl through. With the
torch held out in front of him, he crawled in.

It was just big enough to take his body. Pitch black, filthy
dirty. He breathed in cobwebs and their spiders. Dust and
dirt. Knocked rats out of the way, scared them off with his
light. But he kept going, pulling himself along with his arms
now beyond feeling, beyond tiredness.

There was an incline; it took him down. Never once did
he doubt what he was doing, never once did he fear it would
go wrong and he would be left there under ground to rot.
He was right. He knew he was right.

And eventually his hard work and perseverance were
rewarded. He found what he was looking for.

A dungeon.

Deep, deep under ground. Further down than the cellars and basements of shops, the foundations of buildings, the tunnels for the Metro. The hidden rivers. Deeper than all of them.

A dungeon. *His* dungeon.

He swung his torch around, pleased he had remembered to pack extra batteries. It was a small room. Stone, rather than brick, with old, rust-perished manacles and chains still attached to the walls. Still, the only air coming from the passage he had just entered by. It stank of rot, of corruption. A thrill went through him. He loved it. Felt instantly at home there.

'And then the voices started again . . .' He pounded the sides of his head, reliving the experience before Jill. 'All around me, deafening me . . .' He swung his head around to emphasize the point. 'But I didn't give in, didn't let them overwhelm me. I thought it was just the voices, you know, the ones I was supposed to take my medication to stop hearing. But then I thought for a bit. And I realized it wasn't. And I knew who they really were.'

He came close to Jill again, his voice right in her ear. 'Ghosts.'

She increased the volume in the sound she was making.

'Yeah, ghosts. The men and women who lived here. Who died here. It was their space, their room. I was an intruder, an interloper. It was time to leave. But I knew I'd be back. I was determined to remember the place.'

He told her how he made his way back up the tunnel, through the sewer and back on to the street.

'And the journey didn't seem half as bad on the way back. I suppose it's that old thing where people say that it only seems a long way if you don't know where you're going. Well, I did. And I would be back. And the sewer — even that didn't smell as bad. Funny what you get used to.'

He laughed again, chuckling as if recalling a joke from the previous night's television.

'Mind you, when I got up top again I didn't half get some looks. It was the next day and folk were going to work. I must have looked a sight, stinking and filthy. But I didn't care. It was them who was wrong, not me. I'd found something special, something different. I had more than they had.'

He sighed, trailing off into a self-satisfied hum.

'I went back. Course I did. Loads of times. Well—' he laughed '—look around you.' His laughter trailed away. 'But we came to agreement. And here we are.' He smacked his lips. 'Here we are.'

Silence fell. Jill knew he was still there. She could hear his breathing. It began to get heavier.

'You're a good-looking girl, you know. Bet you have all the boys after you.'

She felt his eyes explore her body, imagined the look on his face.

'Yes, you're a looker, all right. Not my usual type but you know. Needs must and all that.'

She felt his fingers, cold, clammy and trembling, on her stomach. She recoiled at his touch, even though she had nowhere to go to.

'Needs must . . .'

Her mind created vistas, Cinemascope visions of open fields, sunsets, happiness.

It was all she could do.

It wasn't enough.

30

The bruises still showed. Even underneath all the make-up. She looked in the mirror, sighed. Maybe it didn't matter, she thought. Maybe they were just the first in a long line. Something she should get used to.

Anita sat in her dingy room in the hostel in Shieldfield, took a drag on her cigarette, flicked the ash into a saucer. Sighed and exhaled.

The room was basic, almost office-supply functional. Bed. Table. Mirror. Wardrobe. All chipped Formica and cheap boxwood and none of it new. Her bed linen had been washed but still retained traces of previous occupants. It told its own history, the aromas trapped in the fabric like ghosts in an old haunted house.

She was lucky to be in there. That's what she told herself. That's what the staff told her. Lucky to be in there.

Lucky.

She stood up, smoothed down the front of her skirt, undid another button on her blouse, pushed her breasts up. She checked her watch. Five o'clock. Too early. They wouldn't be out yet. Drunk enough and brave enough to attempt to take out their rage on her body.

Another drag, another exhalation. The radio played songs she sang along to in words she didn't fully understand. It made her feel more alone than she had ever felt in her life. The songs were catchy and poppy and bright, but her heart felt like lead in her chest.

She sat down again, drank another mouthful of vodka

and tonic. A large mouthful. Rinsing out any fairy-tale champagne residue that she might still be harbouring. She sighed.

Alone.

She had to do something, get out of the room. Look around the shops, even, before going to work. She stood up, grabbed her handbag, checked it had everything she needed, the tools of her trade. She drained her vodka and tonic, ignored the shaking of her hand, resisted the temptation to pour herself another one just for luck.

Lucky.

Took one last, deep drag on her cigarette and stubbed it out in the saucer, crushing it down hard like it was a dream that needed to be broken.

Closed the door softly behind her. The radio still relentlessly churning anodyne chirpiness into the dead, empty air.

Katya had waited. Planned. She knew what to do. Her chest was tight, her breathing hard. This was the night.

She looked around her room, pacing the floor, measuring, unconsciously counting steps.

The safe house. She had tried to memorize the journey from the Albion office to where she was now, somewhere in a place called Shiremoor. A grim, desolate place, she thought. The kind she had wanted to go to university to escape from. It was flat land, open, spare, semi-industrialized. Dying. Not at all like the countryside surrounding Donovan's place.

The couple downstairs were watching TV. One of the soap operas that seemed common the world over. They were being paid by the lawyer, Sharkey, to look after her, keep her safe. He had mentioned they were a couple who owed him a favour after some legal work he had undertaken for them. A couple who could care for her and keep their mouths shut.

'Look at them as foster parents,' he had said on the drive there.

She didn't know what he meant but had smiled anyway.

She gingerly pushed open her bedroom door. It creaked slightly: old, like everything else in this draughty old terraced house. She stepped carefully on to the landing, hoping the carpet would muffle her footsteps. She was wearing a new pair of trainers that she had bought on her shopping expedition with Peta; jeans, a sweatshirt and a heavy leather fleece-lined jacket. She didn't know how cold it was outside or how long she would be out there, but she wasn't taking chances.

She moved, step after careful step, down the stairs, stopping each time the wood creaked beneath her, listening for any response from the closed door of the living room. None. The TV was on loud, cockney voices loudly venting stunted emotionalism on each other. She moved quickly, almost at the bottom.

She looked around, deciding quickly which door to take: front or back. Back.

Katya turned away from the front room, with its blaring TV, and walked cautiously down the hall towards the kitchen. It was warm in there, the smell of the evening meal still hanging in the air. Spaghetti bolognese. Or at least a local version of it. She crept over to the back door. It led out into a small rectangle of concrete with a wooden shed at the side and a double gate at the far end. The back door, she had noticed previously, tended to stick in the frame. She turned the handle and pulled hard, trying not to overexert herself and pull the door so far back that it clashed against the wall. With a small grunt of effort, the door gave way and opened. She sighed her relief then stepped outside.

The night air was cold, wind biting immediately at her face. She pulled the door to, not closing it completely but jamming it in the frame, and walked towards the back gate.

She turned the handle. Locked. And she didn't know where the key was.

Katya swore in her mother tongue, looked up at the top of the gate. It was about seven feet tall. She could climb it easily.

She pulled herself up, using the angled wooden bars as leverage, trying not to rattle it too much. Reaching the top, she risked a peek over into the back lane. Up and down, both ways. No one there. Not waiting for the situation to change, she pulled herself up and over, landing easily and safely on the other side.

She looked around. Working out which way to go. She took Donovan's stolen mobile from the inside pocket of her jacket, speed-dialled a number she had memorized and inputted. The person answered.

'I'm out,' she said to the voice at the other end.

The other person spoke. She listened.

She nodded. 'OK, I'm on my way. See you soon.'

She ended the call, turned the phone off, pocketed it. Looked around again.

Remembered the route they had taken to get there, began to walk back towards Newcastle.

Anita sat in the same bar she had sat in for the last few nights. Not her personal choice, but one that catered for business people staying at the hotel opposite.

The barman walked past on the way to serving someone, winked at her. She returned a smile. He had barely tolerated her presence at first, threatening to throw her out after her second appearance there. Now he couldn't be more different. He even gave her the nod for potential clients. Supplied her with free drinks. Amazing what a couple of blow jobs in a dank pub cellar could do.

She looked around the bar, scoping for customers, hoping

for good-looking, high-paying ones. It was near closing time and it had been a slow night. She had only had two punters. Neither of them good-looking. One with breath and body odour that stank like the devil's own. But they had paid her adequately and not hurt her. That, she was beginning to believe, would have to be enough for her.

She would have to live with that.

She looked over into the far corner. It was kept deliberately dark there, perfect for couples who weren't necessarily with their own partner and could enjoy a bit of semi-private alcoholic foreplay before moving over the road to give the hotel bedsprings a good pounding.

But there were no couples there tonight. Only a single drinker. Tall, thin and young, as much as Anita could gather, who seemed content to let the shadows claim him. His hair hung down over his face but occasionally he would look over at her and his eyes, catching a steely reflected glint from the bar lights, would connect with her.

This sent a *frisson* through her. Her heart skipped a beat the first time it happened. She didn't know why, just felt like there was some kind of connection.

She watched him on his rare excursions to the bar. His lanky, black-clad frame moving slowly, almost ghost-like through the half-empty bar. Like he didn't want to be touched or seen. He would silently pay for his drink, then resume his position in the shadows. Taking slow sips. Pulling on a cigarette, the glowing tip like a demon's eye in the gloom.

Watching Anita.

She went out with her two punters, returned. He remained there throughout. She should have been scared, she thought the way he was looking at her. But she felt no fear. Only a sense of thrilling inevitability.

She downed the last of her drink, placed it on the bar.

The barman was hovering nearby, hopeful for another free-
bie, she thought. She gave a small shake of her head. Not
tonight. He shrugged, walked away.

She got off the bar stool, gathered up her cigarettes and
lighter, put them in her bag. Two punters. Good in one
respect, not in others. She walked to the door, then outside.

The cold air hit her but the alcohol inside her body both
warmed her and numbed her. She walked along the street
towards the Tyne Bridge, thinking she would treat herself to
a taxi home. Maybe stop for some food on the way.

The street was weekday-deserted. The only sounds she
heard were the faint music trails coming from closing bars,
distant cars, the occasional rumble of a Metro train overhead
and her own shoes clacking along the pavement.

And something else.

She stopped, sensing more than hearing another person
behind her. She turned, knowing, in a way she couldn't
explain, who it would be. There, tall and lanky and smelling
of cigarette smoke and alcohol, was the young man from the
bar.

'Hello,' she said, slipping into business mode. 'Did you
want me?'

He thought for a few seconds, then nodded.

'Good,' she said. 'Your place or a hotel?'

He laughed. She didn't know what at. Must have been a
private joke.

'What about your place,' he said.

She thought for a moment. They often tried that one.
She usually had a few quickly learned lines she could trot out
to put them off. But not this time. He was different somehow. Again she couldn't explain. It was something she just
sensed.

'OK,' she said, surprising herself as the words came out.
'Mine.'

He looked at her. She returned the look. She felt that if she touched him electricity would arc between them. She wasn't even thinking of money. Neither of them moved.

'So,' she said, 'what's your name?'

'Michael,' he replied.

And Michael Nell smiled.

Nattrass was tired. Beyond tired. She should have gone home hours ago, as she had been told several times, but she couldn't. There was something on her mind, something infuriatingly beyond her grasp. A connection, a solution. Every time she reached for it, tried to bring it forward, it danced off into the dark recesses.

She sat at her desk, poring over witness reports. Statements. The results of door-to-door enquiries, eyewitness accounts taken from homes, volunteered from passers-by, anyone. All of this came through the inquiry coordinator, DC Stone, and he was a very good gatekeeper, but Nattrass couldn't shake the feeling that there was something he had missed. Something everyone had missed, including herself.

She didn't know what it was, wouldn't know until she found it.

She sat back, rubbed her eyes, stretched her arms over her head. She wouldn't give in, wouldn't give up. She couldn't go home; this would just haunt her, stop her relaxing.

She picked up the next statement, started to read. Not expecting this one to yield more than the last, beginning to believe she was imagining things.

She read down. And there it was.

She read over it again, checked it against another statement she had pulled from an earlier pile.

There it was.

She sat back, light-headed, the information buzzing

through her. She made notes in a pad at her side. She kept going.

It was going to be a long night.

But, she felt, a fruitful one.

Antony sang, his plaintive, haunting voice filling the car with songs of loss and desolation, asking questions of hope. The music matched the landscape: dark, spare. Denuded winter trees sketched charcoal black before grey night skies.

Donovan sighed, kept his eyes on the road. He was on his way home, winding through the B-roads of Northumberland. Late. Well past midnight.

He was tired, and it had been a fruitless night. Trailing around the brothels of Newcastle, clutching pictures of beaten-up prostitutes, clutching at straws. His mind wasn't on the job; his heart wasn't in it. What with the boy who wasn't David, the break-in, his behaviour with Katya and Jamal's and Peta's reaction, he couldn't give the task his full attention. Phrases he would have normally used, incisive questions he would have usually asked, charm that he thought never failed, all deserted him. He was stonewalled at every turn, doors slammed in his face, women refusing to talk.

He had tried explaining, saying who he was and what he was doing, but the women, the pimps, sensed vulnerability about him and closed down. No one talked. Eventually he gave up, came home.

He pressed a button, ejected the CD, paged along to find something else. Beautiful though the music was, he felt he needed his dark mood lifting, not reinforcing. He chose the Magic Numbers, waited for the upbeat, retro 1960s guitar combo sound to kick in and lighten him up. Even their songs of loss were upbeat. The music started but it didn't lighten him, just irritated him. With another sigh he turned the CD player off, continued in silence.

His house wasn't far off, and he looked forward to getting inside, pulling the door closed behind him. Collapsing on the sofa with a generous measure of Black Bush. Keeping the night out, the darkness at bay.

He approached the ridge before his house, crested it and continued down. He could see it now, a welcoming light glowing from behind the curtains of the sitting room.

Donovan's eyes narrowed. That wasn't right. He hadn't left a light on and Jamal, he recalled, was still at Amar's flat.

He remembered: Decca Ainsley had taken his file. Knew everything about him.

Donovan had argued against moving out, against his house being put under surveillance. Once Decca Ainsley had taken his details, Donovan had claimed, they would have obviously moved Katya somewhere else. He wouldn't be a target.

Now he wasn't so sure.

Breath beginning to come quicker and heavier, he slowed the car down so the engine sound wouldn't carry and turned his lights off. He knew the road well, let the Mondeo coast down the last few metres with the motor off.

He pulled up outside his house as quietly as he could, leaving the car door open as he slowly got out, pocketing the keys so no one could steal it for a quick getaway. Kneeling down, he felt under the seat. He stashed an American police torch there in case of emergencies. As heavy and hard as a truncheon, and just as effective. And if he got caught with it, he could quite rightly claim it wasn't a concealed weapon. He took it out, felt reassured by the heavy heft of it in his hand, looked around. No other cars in sight.

He walked towards the house, staying on grass so his feet made no sound on gravel or pavement. Almost tiptoeing, he reached the front door, listened. The TV was playing quietly.

He checked the front door. It had been opened but with minimum force. A professional job. Then closed again. Donovan frowned. That didn't feel right somehow.

He took his house key out, hands wrapped tightly around the rest of the keys in the bundle to stop them jangling, carefully inserted it into the lock, turned it.

The door opened. Silently. He was glad Jamal had insisted on oiling it when they were renovating the house together. Donovan held his breath, braced himself for the worst, looked inside.

A figure sprawled on the sofa, snoring lightly, empty bottle and glass of whisky on the floor at his side. The TV, unwatched, was showing Argentinian football.

Donovan sighed, slammed the door loudly. With an incoherent shout of either disorientation, distress or both, the figure jumped, sat bolt upright, eyes fluttering, seeking focus.

'Jesus fuck . . .' The figure focused on Donovan. 'Oh, it's you. Wondered what time you'd turn up.'

Donovan put the torch down and stared at the sight of DS Paul Turnbull. Drunk on the last of Donovan's whisky.

Donovan wasn't happy.

31

'So this is it? We're in?'

'We're in.'

Kovacs looked at the computer screen. It was scrolling up through an address book. He pointed at it. 'What is this?'

His computer expert, Goodge, looked up. Small and overweight, he seemed to be on a quest to turn his body into the perfect sphere. Hunched and wheezing, with greasy hair and greasily smudged glasses, his skin was the colour of tobacco and had a translucent appearance, like his recreation consisted of sitting in front of a screen and smoking. Which it did. His working life too. He stank of sweat, stale roll-up smoke and several bodily secretions, none of them too fresh. He looked like one of the most unhealthy specimens of humanity Decca had ever seen, and he had seen quite a few.

But he was good. That was a given. Probably the best freelancer in the area, if not the country. Kovacs wouldn't use him if he wasn't.

'Address book,' Goodge said, returning his gaze to the screen. His voice sounded just like he looked. 'Got some kind of encryption on it. Nothin' I can't break.'

'Will it take you long?' The merest tic in Kovacs' cheek displaying impatience.

'Shouldn't think so. Though I'm more of a PC than a Mac man. Wanky posers' machines.'

Decca, standing behind Kovacs, looked around. They

were in a converted warehouse on Lime Street just beside
the Ouse Burn, part of a development that was being
reclaimed and turned into shells for small businesses in what
was once one of the most derelict and neglected areas of
Newcastle. Kovacs had similar bolt-holes throughout the
city, all hidden behind an untraceable papertrail.

The windows were boarded over, completely blocking
the morning light. Computer equipment surrounded them.
Looping and trailing wires led to stripped-down base units,
which in turn fed screens of various shapes and sizes, which
in turn excreted yet more wires. The walls looked like a
solidly dark, living, malevolent thing, with half-hidden eyes
of blinking red and green. It was like a cluttered version of
the Batcave with two crucial differences: no sense of aes-
thetics and no big car.

Or like a huge web with Goodge the spider at the centre.

Christopher stood next to Decca, watching proceedings,
giving small nods of his head at every verbal exchange
Kovacs made. Decca still couldn't read him. Kovacs had
appeared almost deferential to him when they had returned
with the computers and files. Perhaps he was scared of him,
thought Decca. That wouldn't surprise him.

Goodge was still talking. 'I just connect this here . . . run
this . . .' He looked at the screen of the stolen iMac on the
workbench before him and pressed a button. 'There you go.'
The screen started scrolling a list of figures, stopping occasionally, the cursor flashing like a body pants to get breath,
then off again.

'How long?' asked Kovacs again.

'Depends. Could be a minute, could be days. Depends if
we hit the right combination at the right time.'

'I don't have days.'

Goodge shrugged. It looked like the most exercise his
body had taken for days.

'I have other business to attend to. A new shipment coming in.'

He looked towards Christopher, who slowly shook his head. Kovacs fell silent.

Decca frowned. A shadow of something had passed across Kovacs' eyes at that moment. It looked to Decca, who fancied himself an expert in finger-breaking and intimidation, like fear. That unnerved Decca. If Kovacs was scared of Christopher, he thought, then everyone should be.

'Just do it,' Kovacs said. He pulled at his lapels, straightening his already straight, immaculately tailored jacket, turned away.

The screen stopped scrolling. Goodge gave what passed for a smile. 'You're in luck.'

Kovacs turned back to the screen.

'Here you are,' he said. 'Now take it away and do with it what you like. Just remember to pay me.'

'Bank transfer this afternoon,' Kovacs said, staring at the screen. 'Can you give me a printout?'

Goodge nodded, pressed a button, sat back. Paper began flowing out of a printer at the opposite end of the room. He made no move to get it. Decca, realizing that would be his job, did so. He collated it in his hands, looked through it. A list of names and addresses.

Goodge turned away from them, waiting for them to leave. He wasn't the kind of man for small talk.

'What now?' asked Decca, thumbing through the pages.

'You go back to work,' Kovacs said. 'I am not a gambling man, but I am betting she will no longer be at this Donovan's place. You have the list of where she might be. Her and her brother both. Go and look. Find them.' He handed the list to Decca, who pocketed it. Smiled at him. 'Come with me,' he said.

He led Decca, with Christopher bringing up the rear,

through a locked door and down into the building's basement. The room was freezing. Decca pulled his jacket around him. Then looked ahead. And felt even more chilled.

In the centre of the room was a chair. Sitting on the chair was a man, stripped to the waist. Covered in blood and bruises. Before him stood one of Kovacs' imported hard men, wearing a sweat- and blood-stained T-shirt, jeans and boots. And a huge, darkly glittering mass of hard, sharp metal on his right hand. As Decca watched, he swung his fist into the seated man's face. His head went back but he didn't fall. He screamed, blood, snot and spit arcing from his face.

'Soundproofed,' said Kovacs to Decca, smiling. 'Just as well. Our friend here is a policeman. He has been telling his superiors about my business. And I don't like that.'

Another fist, this time to the chest. Another scream. Decca flinched as if they were happening to him.

'He has been telling the police when my next shipment is coming in. So we have to do something about that, do we not?'

Decca, thinking it was his turn to speak but finding no voice to use, nodded.

'Good. We move the shipment forward. Tonight.'

'I will be there,' said Christopher. 'Take charge personally.'

Kovacs frowned at him. When he spoke, the composure of a few seconds ago seemed dented. 'Do you think that wise? What if they are waiting—'

Christopher looked at the man in the chair. 'We would have heard.' He looked directly at Kovacs. Something passed between the two of them, a kind of understanding Decca was not privy to. Kovacs cast his eyes down, nodded. Again there was that look, again it seemed to be fear.

'Good.' Kovacs seemed relieved. 'Good.' He reached

underneath his jacket, handed Decca a gun. 'Take this. You may need it. If you do, use it.'

Decca took the gun, weighed it in his hand. Felt a thrill course through his body. This was it. No matter what was going on behind him, or around him, this was it. The real deal. He pocketed it, happy to feel it pull down one side of his jacket.

Decca looked between the two men, waiting for further instructions, but neither spoke. He took this as his dismissal cue and walked out, patting both the gun and the folded piece of paper. No one called him back.

Outside, the tarmac-grey clouds overhead were threatening biblical weather conditions. The air was cold and carried on it the fetid, post-industrial stink of the Tyne. Decca looked around, breathed deeply. Fresh air had never tasted so good.

He was a real-life gangsta.

Clint would be proud.

Nell watched her sleep, the weak sunlight pushing its way around the thin, ancient curtains.

He had never seen a more beautiful woman than Anita. He knew in the bar that there was some connection between them, had felt it across the room. And then afterwards in her room. It had been sublime. He had never experienced anything like it.

Her body was perfect. He had watched her undress, tentatively at first, nervous about revealing herself to him, then with growing confidence as she saw how appreciative he was of her.

And then he had seen the bruises. And that did it for him.

'You like it rough?' he had asked her.

She had stared at him, her eyes wide and doe-like, as if trying to imagine what answer he would want to hear.

'Like a bit of pain, do you?' He pressed his thumb on one

of her bruised ribs. She gasped, squirmed under his hand. 'Like that? Yeah?' He pressed harder. She went down on the bed.

'I like . . . whatever you want to do to me . . .'

And that was it. In that moment he knew he had her.

And he wasn't about to let her go.

He looked at her again, sat on the bed next to her. Her chest rising and falling with her sleeping breaths, showing off the extra bruises and hurt he had given her. He felt his erection rise.

She was the best. She was perfect.

He had been looking for a woman like this all his adult life. And now he had found her he wasn't going to let her go. He still had a stolen credit card that hadn't yet been traced, so he was good for a little while yet. And when that ran out he would get another one. He knew how to do that, who to go to. Had done it before.

But that was in the future. Right now he had things that needed doing. Something taken care of. He placed his hand on her ribs, moved them slowly up over her breasts, stopping to touch her nipples. His movement wakened her. She opened her eyes, smiled. Said something he couldn't identify that sounded like 'Dec,' then stopped, realizing where she was and who she was with.

He smiled at her, continued to caress her body.

'Good morning, Anita,' he said, pointing to his erection. 'Look what I've got for you.'

She looked, summoned up a smile.

He continued to caress her.

The smile turned to a grimace as his fingers found the sore, broken parts of her body and pressed down hard on them. She gasped, writhed.

That was all the encouragement he needed. He took her then, as hard as he wanted to.

'You're mine now,' he said, grunting the words out. 'You know that? Mine. I love you.'

And Anita let out a cry that could have been pain or pleasure.

Nattrass walked briskly through the corridor towards the incident room at Market Street police station, a file of papers clutched tightly in her hand. She tried very hard not to run. She reached Bob Fenton as he was taking off his overcoat, placing it on a hanger, putting it on his coat stand. His actions were mechanical, no life to them.

'Sir.'

He looked at her, a weariness in his face and body that was impossible to hide. He looked nearer the end of the day than the start of it.

'Diane.' He tried not to sigh as he said her name. She knew it wasn't anything personal. 'You're very bright and breezy this morning.' He looked at her again. 'I take that back. You look like you haven't been to bed.'

'Got a couple of hours' kip in the office, sir.' The word 'overtime' began to form on Fenton's lips so Nattrass hurriedly continued. 'I think we may have a breakthrough.' She was breathing so hard she could barely get the words out.

A light went on in his eyes, a small kindling. He uncurled his tired shoulders, stood upright. 'Tell me.' He perched on the edge of his desk.

'The last girl who disappeared, Jill Tennant. We've been focusing on trying to trace the youths who were seen walking along the road beside her.'

Fenton said nothing, waited.

'I think we've been looking at the wrong people.'

'Explain.'

Nattrass took a big breath, went on. 'I checked some of the eyewitness statements from Jill Tennant's disappearance.

Yes, there were two youths carrying on. But a lot of them also mentioned an old couple. Or what they took to be an old couple.'

She paused, tried to get her breath back. She felt dizzy, light-headed.

'This is how we didn't get it first. How it slipped past. Witness statements this time say an old couple and then leave it at that. They don't seem to have been pressed on it. Except one. This witness—' she checked the name on one of the papers in her file '—Hazel Blaine, says it wasn't an old couple walking down the street, but a man pushing an old woman in a wheelchair. So I checked the statements for Ashley Malcolm's disappearance. Same thing. Man pushing a woman in a wheelchair. And then I contacted forensics about the Ashley Malcolm crime scene. The snow was melting that night, so they couldn't get a definite print, but they found tracks on the pavement—' she consulted another piece of paper in her file '—"consistent with a pram or a wheelchair".' She closed the file, looked at Fenton. 'I'm willing to bet there'll be something similar in the Lisa Hill files. I think that's our man.'

Fenton stood up, tiredness gone from his body, eyes alight once more.

'And you've been up all night?'

She shrugged. 'More or less.'

He shook his head. Smiled. 'Jesus, the overtime. Right,' he said. 'We need to trace this eyewitness, re-interview her. See if she can put together an e-fit. Then re-interview all the witnesses, see if we can get a better description of this man. Right. Meeting in the incident room, five minutes. The whole team, detectives and uniforms. No one starts anything until they've heard it.'

'Right, sir.' Nattrass turned to leave.

'Oh, Diane,' he said as she was nearly through the door.

'Sir?'

'Heard anything from DS Turnbull?'

At his words, the elation she felt began to leak out of her like air from a punctured balloon. 'Not yet, sir.'

Fenton nodded. 'I see. Well, we'll deal with him later. In the meantime, well done.' Fenton smiled. 'Good police work. Very good.'

'Thank you, sir.'

She left the office, went to make arrangements for the meeting. She smiled to herself, a quick speed grin. Not all of the air had leaked out yet.

32

'She's not there.' The Historian sighed. 'No matter how hard I look, she's not there.'

Jill felt herself ebbing away. No longer a part of the world.

'The one spirit I thought . . . I knew . . . I knew I'd see . . .'

His words had long ago stopped meaning anything to her. They were just part of what she existed with, like the cold air on her naked skin, the pain, the regular abuses he carried out on her.

'When she, when she passed over, I thought she'd still be with me. All the time. My father I didn't care, but her . . .' He sighed. 'And I couldn't find her. Not anywhere. I tried silence, hoping she'd come to me, I tried looking for her, actively seeking her out. You know, mediums and such. Nothing.' His voice took on a deeper degree of sadness. 'Nothing. And I do miss her so. Not a day goes by . . .'

Jill tried to move, found it too painful. The end, she felt, couldn't be far away. His last attack on her had been the most frenzied. He had used knives. Taken out his rage and lust on her with knives. And she couldn't even scream.

'You know,' he continued, his voice conversational, low. 'Sometimes – and I shouldn't say this, should I? – but sometimes I wonder. I really do wonder. Are these really ghosts around us? Spirits of the long since departed? Or is it . . .' He stopped. 'Is it . . . me?' He continued speaking, voice clearly choked with emotion. 'Because if I can see *them* then I should be able to see *her*. But if it's not that, well . . . I'm not saying I'm mad . . . but that would mean there's no such thing, wouldn't it? No ghosts. No spirits. No . . . soul. Do you understand? Because this is important. This is what it's all about. It would mean there's nothing else. Us. Now. Is all there is.'

Jill felt a different kind of blackness dancing around her eyes. Starbursts of dark light played in front of her. She tried to breathe deep, felt her body take in only pain, not air.

'And I have to know. I have to know. If the body has a spirit, a soul. If it leaves at the time of death. Because if it's not, if there's no such thing . . . then, what's the point? Why do anything?' He stood up, began pacing the room.

Jill just wanted it to end. Everything to end. One way or another.

'I mean, that would make us nothing more than, than bone machines. Just slabs of meat that think. Just another component in this, all this. The city. The world. Just one huge machine built on bone, kept going by bone. And flesh. Just . . . *cogs*. D'you understand?'

His words a buzzcut blur, his voice a chainsaw hum slicing through her dimming brain.

'We're born, we live, we die, we go under the earth. And sometimes we're remembered, but most often those graves become forgotten or lost or hidden. And the living don't care, they just keep going, walking over the dead, not knowing who or what is underneath them. All those lives, all those deaths . . . Just . . . food for the bone machine. To keep it going. *Why?* It doesn't make sense, does it? No, we must be something more. We have to be. And I have to know.'

Jill felt him climb on top of her. Even unrestrained she would have been too weak to fight him off.

'I need to know. And you're going to tell me. You're going to show me the truth.'

She felt the knife, pain on pain. Again. And again. She

knew the pain wouldn't last. Couldn't last. Knew that the torture would end soon. Knew also that whatever took its place couldn't be worse than this.

'Show me . . . show me . . .'

Holding her hard. Another stab.

'Show . . . me . . .'

The Historian sat in the corner of his room, hunched up. Foetal, like a newborn: naked and red with blood not his own. Not born again in light and understanding, just continuing on in darkness and ignorance.

The voices were swishing and swirling around his head like so many sonic kites. He ignored them, focused only on the body on the worktable, now just an empty, bloody husk. A slab of useless meat.

It had been so close. So close. That rising, her body bucking . . . him pressing down against her, that final judder . . . and then . . . nothing.

He would run the camera back, check the tape later. But he knew what he would find. Nothing.

And it made him feel impotent, like when he couldn't come in front of the whores no matter how much he strained and panted, and they would laugh at him behind their hands. They would pretend they weren't, but he could see it in their eyes. They couldn't hide their eyes. And he remembered the anger he felt those times. How he had lashed out. Gone too far, one time. But that had been OK, then. That had worked out, opened up a whole new avenue. Gave him something to spend his money on and a thrill of achievement. But that anger he'd felt then, that was how she made him feel now.

So close. And this one, he had felt, would be the one. But she wasn't cleverer, more intelligent or better than any of the others. She was just a whore, like all the rest. A useless, disappointing whore. A carcass to be used, then discarded.

He looked around the room. The lights. The figures. No longer necessary totems for an important ritual, now just so much useless set dressing for a play missing an ending. A joke without a punchline.

A joke.

And that embarrassed him, angered him further.

And it was all her fault.

Leaping to his feet, he grabbed his knife, lunged at the empty shell before him. He slashed at it once, twice, further and again; screaming incoherent abuses, exorcising his pain and anger.

Eventually, spent of energy and rage, he tired, dropped the knife and slumped to the floor once more. He sighed, sat completely still, barely breathing. For how long he didn't know.

The voices were still there, attempting to talk to him in soothing, reassuring tones. Telling him she was there, that he had missed her, that he wasn't to worry. He didn't listen. Didn't trust them. He had to make up his own mind, find out for himself.

This was no longer satisfying him. His experiments were no longer satisfying enough. He needed more. He felt impotent rage fluttering within, feeding on his stillness, growing again. Knew what he needed. Another test subject. And quickly. And he didn't care how he got her or who she was.

He looked again at the carcass.

But first he had to get rid of that. And in doing so, teach them a lesson.

A history lesson.

He smiled widely. It was like opening a door to winter.

He didn't have to consult his books this time. He knew just the place.

33

'Here bastard, drink this.'

Donovan shoved a mug of hot coffee at Turnbull's prone form. Turnbull moaned and burrowed in further. He was curled up, his face pressed into the back of the sofa, still wearing his clothes, his backside sticking out from under a duvet that Donovan, in a moment of weakness, had thrown over him the previous night.

Donovan dragged over a small table and placed the mug on it, half-hoping Turnbull would knock it over and scald himself with it. He sat down on the armchair and looked across at him.

'Oi, sleeping policeman, wake up,' he said, louder than was necessary.

Still no response. He picked up the remote for the hi-fi, pointed and clicked. The Drive By Truckers burst into action, their angry-hearted, Jack Daniels-fuelled, southern-fired stomp boogie kicked up to eleven. Turnbull shouted incoherently and jumped up as if on fire. Donovan, smiling, watched, his amusement tempered by the fact that the mug of coffee was still upright.

'What the fuck . . . ?'

'Good morning,' said Donovan above the din. 'Sleep well?'

Turnbull's eyes roved the room. It took him several seconds to place where he was and who was talking; once he had, his body hit the back of the sofa and slumped down as if he'd been shot.

'Bastard,' he said with his eyes closed.

'No way to talk to your generous host. Most people who find an intruder pissed and passed out on their sofa would call for a policeman.'

'Fuck off.' Turnbull's words seemed to come from a mouthful of pillow.

Donovan laughed and, victory won, turned the music off. The abrupt silence seemed just as deafening. Turnbull sighed.

'Oh, God . . .' He breathed through his mouth, head held at one side, eyes screwed tight.

Donovan knew the feeling well enough. As if the laws of physics had ceased to operate and you'd been made aware of the nauseating, dizzying speed of the universe. 'If you're looking for sympathy you've come to the wrong place,' he said. 'In fact, you're lucky you found the right place. They take the Tony Martin approach to burglars around these parts.'

Turnbull's head flopped forward, his breathing increasing.

'If you're going to be sick, the bathroom's upstairs. Anywhere else and I'll be fucking annoyed.'

Turnbull nodded and rose from the sofa like a Hammer horror zombie from the grave. He stumbled and staggered upstairs and soon Donovan heard the unmistakable sounds of vomiting. He smiled to himself, taking pleasure in the other man's obvious discomfort.

Shame the coffee was still standing, though, he thought.

Nattrass looked around, wondering what colour to describe the building before her. It had once been 1980s beige with red trim but years of natural and man-made wear and tear had leached that to something more muted. Some kind of dirty yellow, perhaps: pub ceiling? Old computer monitor? She didn't know. And didn't want to spend any more time speculating. That wasn't what she was here for.

The offices of the Blood Transfusion Service stood just off Barrack Road between the BBC Television Centre and a BMW dealership on the fringes of Leazes Park. The washed-out slab-fronted building was enlivened by appropriately blood-red lettering announcing what it was. A car park sat in front. And, on a lamppost in the car park, hung a body. Naked. Female. Mutilated. Dead.

Even without tests they all knew it was.

Jill Tennant.

DI Nattrass pulled her coat around her. She had showered at the station and changed into the spare set of clothes she kept there. She knew her unit were required to dress more smartly; suits and ties, as if the murder squad were a judicial accounting team for balancing the body count, but she had no option. She wore jeans and boots, a waist-length faux-fur-trimmed parka and a scarf. Her hair was pulled back and tucked down the neck of her hood. No one would say anything about her violation of the dress code. Just let them try.

That morning's briefing never took place. Instead, a call had come through from a security guard at the Blood Transfusion Centre saying something had been left hanging on a lamppost. He had seen it on his CCTV screen from inside the building and thought it the work of students from the halls of residence nearby having a laugh. It was only after a sustained period of observation that he had decided to leave his cosy office and brave the cold night air to look at it and plan to take it down. On approaching he had thought it was very realistically done. On getting close enough to touch and smell it, he had thrown up, run back inside and called the police.

SOCO had cordoned the area off and, along with forensics, were trying to pick up what clues the security man hadn't trampled away. They weren't expecting to find many.

And yet . . .

There was something different about this one. The body just strung up and left. Not so carefully arranged. More hurried. Less planned. And if that was the case, if he was getting more slapdash, then he was more likely to make mistakes.

She gestured to DS Deborah Howe, the SOCO senior manager. She crossed over to Nattrass, a couple of vermilion and mahogany spikes sticking out from behind her white hood, and waited impatiently for her to speak.

'Yes?' Making it quite clear she was in the middle of something important.

'You found anything?'

'Not much, not so far.' She looked around, anxious to get back.

'From here it looks more rushed. Like he just dumped the body and ran.'

Howe nodded. 'We're checking for footprints on the bank side and in that mud up there. Don't worry, whatever we find, we'll let you know.'

'Check for wheel marks,' Nattrass said in response to an urgent hunch.

Howe was trying to establish an insulted look. 'We always do.'

'No, smaller ones. Like, like a pram. Or a wheelchair. On the path, the bank side, wherever.'

Howe nodded, walked back over to the rest of her team, resumed her work.

Nattrass looked around again. Questions were forming. Why here? Why now? He was sending a message, she was sure of it. Something to do with blood? Death, in some way? She didn't know. She wished Turnbull were with her. He'd be good to bounce questions off. Admittedly he was an annoying bastard at times but a good copper and a loyal member of the team.

Or had been.

She looked again at the body. Wondered, not for the first time, just what would drive someone to do that to another living person. What horrors had been inflicted on an individual to make them see other human beings as just slabs of meat to be carved up. She shook her head. Those were dangerously liberal thoughts for a DI, and there was no Turnbull to temper them with his tabloid logic. She thought she had better keep them to herself in case they got out of hand.

Her train was broken by the hurried arrival of DC Stone. He was almost running in his haste to reach her.

'Ma'am,' he said, almost out of breath.

She turned, irritated. She hated being called 'ma'am'. Made her sound like Jean Brodie. 'Yes?'

'We've got him, ma'am. We've got him.' He couldn't keep the excitement out of his voice.

He hurried back to the main building.

She didn't need any invitation to follow him.

'So to what do I owe this pleasure?'

Over an hour had passed. Philip and Fern were soothing the nation on the TV. Donovan was sitting in the armchair. Turnbull had followed his vomiting session with a shower. He had emerged, found the combats, T-shirt and fleece Donovan had left on the landing for him and, despite the fact that he was smaller than Donovan, had put them on. His own clothes were stinking and filthy. The gesture wasn't completely altruistic: Donovan had deliberately dug out his old Kurt Cobain T-shirt just to see Turnbull wearing it. Turnbull seemed too semi-detached to realize he was having the piss taken out of him. He sat on the edge of the sofa regarding a replacement mug of coffee with suspicion.

Donovan turned the TV off. He didn't feel that his life would be particularly enriched by hearing gossip from the set of *Coronation Street*. Turnbull wouldn't have come to his house if it wasn't serious. If it wasn't the last resort. The policeman had the look of someone who needed to confess. Donovan, with no attempt at niceties, ploughed on.

'I presume this isn't a social call,' Donovan said.

Turnbull's eyes were downcast. He looked at the floor and when he spoke his words were mumbled.

'I'm in trouble,' he said quietly. 'Big trouble.' His voice sounded scratched and crackly; he took a sip of coffee, realized he wasn't about to bring it up again, took another. Said nothing more.

'What kind of trouble?'

Another mouthful of coffee, then he replaced the mug. 'I nearly stepped over the line.'

He said nothing more. Donovan waited.

'Michael Nell . . . I was gonna . . .' He sighed. 'Gonna have him.'

'Did you?'

Another sigh. Turnbull shook his head. 'I wanted to. I followed him. But I lost him. Looked everywhere for him, everywhere . . . But . . . I was pissed. Too pissed to see. I collapsed. Somewhere. A bus shelter, I think.' He gave a short, humourless laugh. 'Lucky I wasn't picked up, put in a cell for the night by one of my lot.' Another sigh. 'My lot . . .'

'You sure you didn't do something to Nell? Did it in a raging, drunken, blackout?'

'That's what I thought at first. I went over and over it. Checked me hands, me clothes, nothing.' He looked up, briefly caught Donovan's eye. 'There would have been marks, believe me. Lots of them.'

'So what happened next?'

Turnbull took another mouthful of coffee. 'I was going to go back to work, turn up at the station and face the music, even if I got kicked off the investigation. But by the time I'd found my car and put the radio on, they were saying that Michael Nell had disappeared. Well, I knew I couldn't go back then. Couldn't go back anywhere.'

'Why didn't you go home?' As Donovan asked the question he realized how little he knew of Turnbull outside of work. He presumed he had a wife, probably a family, but the subject had never been raised.

Turnbull gave another humourless snort. 'Home? What home? There's nothin' left there. The wife hates me, she's turned the kids against me . . . What the fuck would I go there for?'

Donovan nodded, realizing now why Turnbull had never spoken about it.

'I thought of going to Peta's.' He gave a quick, shifty glance at Donovan to see how he took that one. Donovan said nothing. 'But I didn't. Thought I'd get the same reception there.'

'What about Di? Didn't you contact her?'

'I tried. Phoned her mobile. Got no answer. I knew she'd phone me back but I . . . didn't know what to say. What I could do. So I turned the phone off. Bottled it. I had nowhere else to go. Nowhere.'

'So you turned up here and let yourself in.'

'I had nowhere else to go . . .'

'And drank all my whisky.'

'I'll replace it . . .'

'Yeah, with cheap shit, probably.'

Turnbull gave another sigh. 'I'm fucked. Completely fucked . . .'

Donovan regarded the sad lump of humanity before him, left slumped and broken on the sofa like an old sack of decaying potatoes. He had always felt that underneath the right-wing, chauvinistic, alpha male bluster, Turnbull was a more fragile construct than he was letting on. But Donovan still hadn't been prepared for the depth of self-pity the man was currently wallowing in. Drowning in, even.

'So what you going to do now?' Donovan asked.

'I don't know. I really don't know. I can't . . . I don't . . .' He slumped further down in the sofa, almost unrecognizable now. And then the tears started.

Donovan couldn't leave him like this. Someone would have to do something, and if there were no other volunteers it would have to be him.

Oh, joy, he thought.

He mentally flicked through several approaches on how to talk to him, decided on one that was likely to work best.

'And you can stop that feeling sorry for yourself shit right now,' said Donovan.

Turnbull looked up. His eyes looked wet and startled, like headlamps in a muddy pool.

'Pull yourself together. You're no use to me like that.'

Turnbull frowned. 'Use to you? Fuck you talkin' about?'

'You've got to move on.'

The tears were halting, drying on Turnbull's cheeks. 'Move on? Fuck you talkin' about?'

'I've got a job on. Need some help. Don't know if I can pay you, though, might be on a volunteer basis.'

Turnbull seemed to be mulling over the offer. Then his head dropped, his face cradled by his hand. 'I should be out there doin' somethin'. I should be back at work . . . not this . . .'

'Yeah, you should. But you're not. And you can't. And you can't stay here and wallow in your own self-pity. So d'you want to help me or not?'

Turnbull looked at the coffee mug, at the near-empty whisky bottle Donovan had deliberately left on the floor as a reminder of the previous night. He swallowed hard, breathed out through his nose.

'OK, then,' he said. 'What we doin'? What kind of job?'

'Missing person.'

'Who?'

'Michael Nell.'

It took a few seconds for the name to sink in, but when it did Turnbull let loose a broad grin.

'Lead the fuckin' way,' he said.

DI Nattrass bent over the desk, watching the screen intently.

It was grainy, blurry: the early-morning/late-night rain rendering the image a static-filled bad TV reception, any figures moving like ghosts.

'There.'

DC Stone pointed. The machine operator pressed the pause button. The image on the screen froze. A blurred figure, a dark blob of grey against a slightly lighter background stood before them.

'Now advance, slowly.' DC Stone again.

The operator complied. The figure moved ahead in jerky slow motion. Like watching a flicker book with the pages missing.

'There!' Nattrass almost shouted. 'Look!'

She could barely contain the excitement rising inside her. They watched: as eyes became accustomed to what was on the screen, the figure became more distinct. It was a man, dressed in a hat and a long overcoat.

Pushing a wheelchair.

'Yes!'

Both the operator and DC Stone cast her a quizzical look. She was too pumped with adrenalin to give a coherent explanation, breathing too heavily to care if her words made sense.

'Went through the witness statements. Found him there at every scene. Knew it. Knew it . . .'

The picture advanced, frame by frame. The overcoated figure pushed the wheelchair and its covered, seated occupant up to the lamppost, then looked around.

'Get a frame grab of that, get it blown up. See if we can get some detail off it.' See if it resembles Michael Nell, she thought.

Stone nodded. The picture advanced.

The figure, satisfied that no one was watching him, pulled the covering back from the prone, broken body of Jill Tennant.

'That poor girl . . .' said the CCTV operator. 'Got a kid about her age meself. Makes you think, all this.'

Nattrass nodded, urging him to keep going. He did so.

Jill Tennant's body had been rigged to hang and tied with rope. The hatted figure threw the coiled rope up and over the curving top of the lamppost, made sure it didn't slide off and threw it around again to make a second loop. He pulled the rope tight, heaved down. Jill Tennant's body left the chair and began to be hauled up. It was slow going; he didn't seem to be very strong and the body looked heavier than anticipated.

'Wimp,' said Stone. No one argued.

He kept pulling until he had the body hoisted up.

'Persistent wimp, though,' said the operator.

Eventually the body hung there. He tied the rope off, stood back to check his handiwork, gave an admiring nod, turned and quickly made his way back up the street with the wheelchair. He was soon out of shot and gone.

Nattrass sat back, heaved a huge sigh of bitter vindication. She turned to Stone.

'See if there's any footage from other cameras in the area. Try to get a picture of where he came from, where he went back to. Get forensics on the moor over the road. Maybe he went that way, maybe he left tracks. Then if that's the case start a door to door with the houses over the other side of the moor. We've got a description now, maybe a face shot. Someone'll remember those clothes. Get him tracked down, get him found.'

She turned to the tape operator. 'Thanks for your help. We really appreciate it.'

The man seemed to be in shock. He nodded numbly.

She looked again at the screen. At the figure, frozen before his victim. She tried to guess his features, see the expression on his face. She was still breathing heavily.

'We'll get you, you bastard. We'll get you.'

34

Peta looked at the empty coat stand. No hat, coat and scarf. No sign of the Prof.

The seminar room had a dark, depressing atmosphere. Some might have said funereal, but not Peta. Funerals, in her experience, involved families consisting of relative strangers standing around in curtained living rooms eating curled sandwiches and making the smallest of small talk.

Perhaps that's just me, she thought. Or perhaps I haven't lost anyone who was really close to me.

This room was nothing like that. There was a space where Jill should have sat, some empty chairs and the remaining ones filled with students wearing numbed, fear-deadened expressions. Things like this didn't happen to them. Or to their friends.

News of the discovery of a body was doing the rounds. Details were vague or non-existent but that hadn't been allowed to get in the way of a good story. By the time the news had Chinese-whispered its way around to Peta's group of Jill's fellow classmates, the body was definitely that of Jill and all manner of unspeakable acts had been committed on her before she died.

Let them speculate, thought Peta. Can't be any worse than what actually happened to her.

Peta felt like she had a rock inside her. Jill. She kept thinking of her. She hadn't known the girl long but had come to really like her. And now she was gone. Peta knew that, felt it. The same way Donovan had known the body in

Wales wasn't that of his son. She had cried before coming to college, tears for Jill. Sadness had turned to anger, though, and now it sat like a knotted ball of razor wire in the pit of her stomach. She was going to use that anger. She was going to get payback for Jill.

The campus was awash on a sea of horror and revulsion, fear and excitement. And on a state of high alert. The extra security guards were still throwing their weight around with extra gusto; stopping any infraction of imagined rules and regulations, forcing people to take the most circuitous route possible, examining student passes with the same rigorous attention to detail that they would use if they were trying to stop terrorists entering the UN building.

Peta had seen the guard she had had the altercation with a few days previously. He was stationed at a different doorway from the one she wanted to enter. She looked at him and in return felt his eyes follow her across the quadrangle and into the main building.

Sad little bastard, she thought. Probably how he gets his rocks off.

She turned the corner, didn't give him another thought.

In the seminar room, they all waited. Conversation peaked and troughed about Jill until the subject was just about exhausted. Peta tried not to join in, kept her feelings for the girl to herself. Then speculation turned to the no-show of the Prof. They were collectively building up to nominating someone to go down to his office and see if he was there when the door opened and in he came.

'Apologies, apologies, one and all . . .'

He began the ritual of taking off his hat, scarf and coat.

'Some . . . some other business which . . . demanded my attention.'

He sat down behind the desk. Normally he would have been removing textbooks from his antique briefcase but he made no effort to do so. Instead he looked out at his class. Individually. One by one his eyes fell on them, his lips moving silently as if making an incantation, giving a blessing.

He came to Peta, looked straight at her. There was a well of sadness, tiredness there. And something else. Something she couldn't read. She tried to catch the words on his lips but failed. He moved on.

The move had spooked her. Glancing around, she knew she wasn't the only one.

He reached the end of his students and with a sigh let his head drop until he was looking at the desktop.

'I don't believe,' he began, addressing the veneered surface before him, 'that under the present circumstances we may be able to wring a useful lesson out of today. Neither you nor me. So take the rest of the day off. Go home. Reflect. Grieve. Get drunk. Whatever.' He sighed. 'Imagine it's half-term. Or a week of Sundays. It doesn't matter which. Just . . . just go.'

He put his head up. He didn't bother to hide the tears. 'Go.'

Looking and feeling uncomfortable, the students rose and, not without hesitation, made their collective way to the door. Some attempted to stop, talk to the Prof, but he seemed off in a place they would find unreachable.

Peta was one of the last ones to leave. She looked at him as if expecting him to say something. He said nothing. Just stared ahead. She joined the exodus.

She walked down the corridor, heading towards the refectory. She could have a coffee, go to the library. Do some work. She could phone Joe, see what was happening with him, maybe help him in his work.

But she didn't.

She thought again of the Prof and how he had looked, his eyes when they locked with hers . . .

*A well of sadness, of tiredness, and something else . . . something
she couldn't read . . .*

Something was going on with him, she thought. Her old
police instincts told her so. But suspicions weren't enough.
She had to find out what it was.

She felt that ball of razor wire in her stomach. That anger.
And headed for the refectory. Not because she needed a
coffee. But because it had a clear view of the main door. The
one the Prof would enter and exit by.

She would watch him leave.

And then perhaps engage in a spot of office-breaking
again.

Katya was walking.

She had walked for most of the night, headed in the
direction of the city. She had walked as cars had pulled into
driveways, come to rest for the last time that night, their
engines cooling and ticking as she passed. As lights and
TVs had been switched off in houses and flats, generating a
silence and stillness that sometimes reached her on the
street. As buses with no destinations had gone by, depot-
bound.

The air had turned cold around her. Small predators
moved in the bushes and hedgerows to the side of her. As
the night wore on, lone cars would slow as they approached
her, hesitate and be gone again. She knew what the drivers
were thinking, what they were planning to do with her.
She knew she was taking a risk just by walking lonely streets
and roads by herself in the dark. She knew there were other,
bigger, predators out there. But she didn't care. She was lit
by an inner light, driven by a sense of purpose. She knew she
would reach her destination; no one would stop her from
getting there. That wasn't going to happen tonight.

Just in case someone was tempted to approach her she

repeated her plan to herself, aloud, over and over in her native language, like a mantra. Something to ward off evil spirits. Keep her heart and mind focused on where she was going, what she had to do.

The words were old, familiar. She drew strength from them, companionship. The words and what was behind them made her feel she was no longer alone. Made her feel that others were walking with her. Offering her the rough magic charms of old comforts, old protections.

And it worked. No one stopped. No one approached her. She was left alone.

Dawn broke like a sickly egg over the city skyline. By that time tiredness had come and gone, struggled to claim her as the devil in the desert struggled to claim Jesus Christ. But she won. She spoke her mantra aloud, chased the demon of fatigue away. It left with no claim on her. She had felt good after that struggle, calm. She had rewarded herself with a rest, watching the sunrise.

Katya was sitting on a wall in one of the town's suburban outer circles. She had taken her new trainers off, saw the damage for herself in the morning light. Her feet had turned to lumps of painful stone, the skin rubbed away in places leaving her socks soaked with blood and sweat. She found an unused tissue in her pocket, split it and inserted the halves into each sock. It was temporary, it wouldn't hold, but it would have to do. She rubbed them, tried to ignore the pain, concentrate on what was important to her. Only a little longer and that pain would be gone.

Or at least transferred. Permanently transferred.

She pulled her trainers back on. Her feet cried out in silent agony. She ignored them. She had to keep walking. Time was precious.

Standing up, she resumed her walk. Not far now. Soon it would be time to make another call. Then they would meet.

Then, and not until then, so many souls could finally be at rest.

She smiled. Took herself once more to the place where pain couldn't touch her.

And kept walking.

The day wore on. And Donovan and Turnbull found they were having very little luck.

'Course, it's the wrong time of day for this kind of stuff,' said Turnbull knowledgeably. 'Should be here at night. That's when most of them come out. When a man's most base desires demand satisfaction.'

'Speaking from experience here, are we?' Donovan couldn't keep from laughing.

'Fuck off. You know what I mean.'

Donovan did, but he wouldn't admit it to Turnbull. They were sitting in a café off the West Road in the west end of Newcastle. Once-red moulded plastic chairs and well-worn Formica-topped tables, wiped down so often there was virtually no pattern left. Dark walls and tinny Radio 2. Plates of sausages, chips, eggs, beans and bacon in various combinations set before them. Tea so strong it turned stomachs to acid. Turnbull had begun tentatively but was now wolfing his food down, a hangover kill or cure. Donovan was picking at his, risking the safest, most edible pieces, leaving the items of more dubious provenance alone.

They hadn't had a successful morning. Donovan had a list of prostitutes Michael Nell had persuaded to model for him together with photos. They had addresses, or approximations of addresses where the women worked or perhaps lived. The two of them had knocked on doors, attempted to strike up conversations with whoever answered. They sensed Turnbull for police, even in the clothes he was wearing, and

Donovan to have no legal authority. The brothels were on shift work. No one knew, or claimed to know, the pictured women. Certainly no one could tell them where the photos had been taken.

And Donovan still hadn't found his phone. He had picked up his old one from the cottage and, after hastily texting Peta, Amar, Jamal and Sharkey his temporary number, was carrying it. They were used to it – he was always losing and misplacing his mobile. He hated the things but had other things to concern himself with. He would worry about its whereabouts later.

'It's difficult,' said Donovan, contemplating a chip. 'I came out last night and couldn't get anywhere.'

'On your own?' asked Turnbull, his mouth wrapped around a virtually whole sausage.

Donovan nodded.

'Not surprised. Should have had Peta with you. Or that bird you had in the car that time. Eased your passage, so to speak.'

'Maybe my head's just not in the right place.'

Donovan wasn't even aware he had spoken aloud until he saw Turnbull stop chewing and stare at him.

'What d'you mean?'

'Nothing,' said Donovan. 'I didn't say anything.'

'Yes, you did.' Turnbull took a few gulps of tea. 'Your head. Not in the right place. Why?'

Donovan sighed, found his half-eaten lunch fascinating. 'Nothing. Doesn't matter.'

Turnbull laughed. 'Fuckin' 'ell. After all the shit I came out with this morning? Thought we were helpin' each other here. Don't have to like each other to do that.'

Donovan said nothing. Turnbull shrugged. 'Please yourself, then. I don't care.'

'I've just got back from Wales. I thought I'd found David.

I thought I'd found my son.' Donovan spoke without looking up.

Turnbull stopped eating, looked at Donovan. 'Shit,' he said. 'You mean . . . you mean dead?'

'Yeah, I mean dead.'

Turnbull looked hard at him, the unasked question on his lips.

'No,' said Donovan, returning the stare. 'It wasn't him.'

'Oh.' Turnbull nodded. 'They know who . . .'

Donovan shrugged. 'Who knows? A boy washed up on the shore. Another unsolved mystery. Another report in another file somewhere.' He stopped speaking, thought. About everything else that was causing him concern. Katya. Jamal. 'And then to come back and find the office ransacked . . .'

Turnbull put down his knife and fork. 'What? Your office?'

Donovan had done the same thing again, speaking without realizing. He nodded.

'You didn't tell me that.'

'We're not married. I don't have to tell you everything.'

'But still . . .' Turnbull started to question Donovan on the break-in. Proper copper's questions. Donovan wished he had kept his mouth shut.

He managed to tell Turnbull as little as he needed to know, keeping Decca Ainsley and his unidentified friend out of it. Turnbull seemed satisfied by what he heard, finished his lunch, threw his knife and fork down with a clatter, wiped his mouth with his waxy napkin, drained the toxic tea from his mug, sat back.

'Feeling better?' asked Donovan.

'Oh, yes,' he said. 'Much better. More like me old self.'

Great, thought Donovan.

'You know,' said Turnbull, sitting back and lighting

himself a fag with no regard as to whether Donovan had finished eating or if he was offended by it, 'we've been going about this all wrong. No wonder you weren't gettin' anywhere.'

'And I suppose you know a way to do this that'll get results.'

Turnbull grinned what he assumed was a supremely confident grin, completely unaware of the baked bean husks and lumps of unmasticated sausage that lay nestling in the front of his teeth.

'Oh, yes,' he said. 'Stick with your uncle Paul, you can't go wrong.'

'I knew this was a bad idea,' said Donovan. He stood up, began to pull on his leather jacket. 'If you're so sure of yourself, then, you can get the bill.'

Donovan turned and walked to the door without looking back or stopping. Turnbull's grin fell slightly, but he still made his way to the till and paid, then followed Donovan outside.

The Historian had locked himself away, not for the first time that day, in a toilet cubicle. It was where he came to find solace, no matter how temporary, during his working day.

The adrenalin high had been and gone, the racking, aching guilt had been ridden out, the panic attacks had subsided. Anyone watching his actions would have thought him to have a bad attack of the runs. And that was the excuse he had ready to give if anyone should ask.

But they hadn't. And now he was breathing regularly again, in control once more. He thought back to his early morning's work.

The husk had been deposited according to plan. He had been worried it wouldn't work, that the planning and positioning were too hurried, not thought through enough. But it was fine. He hadn't been spotted; he had walked up to the lamppost and walked away unharmed. And left them a conundrum that was childishly obvious to him but painfully obscure for the thick, uneducated heads of the police force.

And he liked that. Drew power from that feeling.

Not only that, but he had even been able to go to work afterwards.

There was one thing that rankled, though, one thing that niggled. As he was walking away, he saw the blinking eye of a CCTV camera. The sight of it had almost brought on a panic attack there and then in the street, but he had kept himself together, kept walking away.

That CCTV camera. He had told himself there was nothing to worry about. He was familiar enough with security systems to know that nine times out of ten there would be no tape in the camera or that, if there was, it would be wiped over on the next shift. And anyway, he was sure the camera hadn't been on him.

Pretty sure.

Panic has risen again at that. He had managed to hold it down. It kept recurring all day but, with frequent trips to the toilet, he had managed to cope with it. Concentrate on the important things. Get the voices to talk to him, tell him things were OK. They were going to be OK. It would all work out in the end. Because inside him, that familiar need was gnawing, that hunger growing. Quicker this time, the gap between test subjects getting shorter. He needed another one, fast. He had to know, had to find out.

He stood still, tested his body with a deep breath: in, hold steadily . . . and out slowly. Good. And again, just to make sure. In, hold steadily . . . and out slowly. Good. His breathing was fine.

He flushed the toilet, stepped from the cubicle and up to the mirror. He ran his hands under the water, just in case anyone should walk in, dried them on his trousers, then walked out, back to the rest of the world.

He walked, watched. Felt strong and secure in his power over those he saw, felt the familiar stirrings of an erection in his trousers. Good. He walked with his hips thrust out, enjoying the feel of the fabric against his engorged skin.

Cup of tea time.

He made his way into the rest room he had been using for the last couple of days, nodded to some of the others in there. He brewed up, took his mug to one of the easy chairs, sat down before the TV. The local evening news was on.

And there he was.

Blurred and grainy but unmistakably him.

He jumped, spilling hot liquid over his thigh. He glanced furtively round, hoping none of the others had seen him do that. They hadn't. Their attention was riveted on the screen. He joined them.

The reporter was wrapping up, talking about how the killer had made a mistake that could prove to be fatal. His last one. He gave that grave, middle-distance stare that they all did at the end of serious news items, then it was back to the studio. The anchorwoman was looking equally grave. His picture flashed up on the screen again, blown up as big as it would go, with a phone number underneath.

He heard voices behind him: his colleagues giving their opinion of what they would do with the killer, how they wished he was in the room with them right now. How he wouldn't get out alive, how they would take their time, make him suffer like he made all his victims suffer.

He wanted to turn, look at them, shout out what they had wrong. That it wasn't about the suffering. That it was a carefully controlled medical experiment. How they didn't understand. How they would never understand.

Hoping his hands weren't shaking too much, he stood up,

placed his near-untouched mug of tea on the draining board
and left the room.

They were on to him. It was only a matter of time. He
had been careless, hurried, and now it was only a matter of
time. But not now. Not yet. Not when he was so close to
finding out the truth. It couldn't stop now, otherwise it had
all been for nothing.

He had to plan. Find his next test subject. And fast.

But not straight away.

First he had to go to the toilet.

35

Katya was waiting.

She sat in the Intermezzo coffee bar nursing her third cappuccino. The caffeine was starting to give her the shakes now, but she didn't know what else she could do. Walking around town was out; she had walked enough for today, had to save her feet for the final bit of walking she would do later. So she had found somewhere Donovan had taken her. Somewhere she felt relatively safe. Somewhere to be anonymous, to drink and watch the world go by.

Shoppers, office workers, unemployed. Going by and carrying their cares and worries with them, their loves and hatreds. Thinking of themselves as civilized. Cultured even, some of them. None of them realizing how thin the web was holding them in check. How easily the mask of respectability could be removed. Just slightly educated animals. Each carrying an in-built receiver that just needed the right signal, the correct permission and the bloodlust would begin. She had seen it happen. With her own eyes.

She sipped her coffee, shook her head. She didn't like spending so long on her own, because once her mind began travelling down that lost, dark highway, unwanted thoughts would arrive in her mind. Unbidden ones, unpleasant. And as difficult to dislodge as concrete monoliths.

The massacre.

Her family.

The gangsters and what they did to her.

What they forced her to do.

Another mouthful of coffee, another shake of the head.

At Joe Donovan's she had tried to blot those experiences out; relax, luxuriate even, in her new-found freedom. Focus on the future: reuniting with her brother, getting official papers to stay in the country. Making a new life for themselves. A better one. A happier one.

She had tried not to give in to depression and despair, tried not to sleep all day, help herself to his alcohol. Follow the old, well-worn routes: numb herself, desensitize herself. Then take a knife to her skin and carve pain into her body. Create manageable pain, controllable pain. The kind that reminded her she was alive, but on her own terms.

It had been a struggle, one that at times she didn't feel she had the strength to win. But that fire inside her kept her going, kept her strong. Those words of hope, those thoughts. The plan. And the burning desire to see that plan implemented carried her through.

And Donovan had helped too.

Poor Joe Donovan. A good man with a good heart. Under different circumstances she might have enjoyed her time with him. Her intimate time. Seen it as more than just a means to an end. She wished she could feel sorry for using him. But sorrow for others was a luxury she could no longer allow herself. Not after what she had been through, what had been done to her. Not when she needed to focus on what remained to be done.

She had tried to delve deep within herself, retreat into the distant past, rekindle the spirit of that optimistic little girl she had once been. The happy girl who played with her friends, her neighbours, and believed in wishes and miracles. Who found her home, the village and the world itself to be a good, safe place.

It was a huge effort. That little girl barely existed any more.

Instead other images came to mind. Her village after the soldiers came, after the police. After people she had believed were her friends and neighbours joined them in killing and hurting those they had lived side by side with all their lives. Killing her father. Raping and torturing her mother before finally killing her. Raping and torturing her little sister before finally killing her. Torching her house after looting and ransacking it.

Right before their eyes.

She and her brother had been away on an errand. They heard the commotion on their return and something, she still couldn't say what, had forced her to grab her brother and jump into a nearby cellar where they hid and watched. Watched with uncomprehending horror as the safety net was removed from her world, as hell and all its demons spewed forth to claim the earth.

She couldn't believe what she was seeing. Conflicting emotions ran through her like an electric current. She wanted to run to her family, help them. But she knew it would be futile. There was nothing she or her brother could do. Except stay as silent as possible if they wanted to live.

Later they emerged and her new life began. She came to regard the old one as some kind of fantasy, a made-up fairy story to help troubled children sleep at night. And the ending a fable of what would happen if they didn't. She and her brother went forward from that day carrying equal measures of guilt and relief of survivors like monkeys on their backs.

And carrying something else.

A picture in her mind of the man responsible for the deaths of their family. The man in charge of the unit who destroyed their village. Who laughed as he killed and raped, whose eyes glittered with an evil light reflected from the burning homes. Who looked like the devil personified.

Marco Kovacs.

It was getting dark outside, the day slipping away, the shadows claiming all around.

Katya sipped her coffee. She had switched on the stolen mobile in her pocket an hour previously waiting for the call. Saving the battery, minimizing the possibility of any calls for Donovan of which there were plenty on voicemail. She hoped it would ring before she got to the bottom of her mug. Her money was running out; she couldn't afford another one. And they were closing soon.

It did.

She could have cried with relief. This was a sign. A sign that the plan was the right thing to do, that God was on their side, that it would be a success.

She scrambled for the phone, checked the display in case the call was for Donovan. It wasn't. She answered it and heard that familiar voice again. She could have cried at the sound.

She listened. Instructions were given, plans were made. She hung up, turned the phone off, pocketed it. She mouthed the directions of where she had to go. The book-shop next door was still open; she could go and look at a map, memorize the route she had to take.

She drained the frothy dregs from her mug. Her head was spinning now from more than just caffeine. She slid off the window stool. As her feet touched the floor, pain shot up her legs, reminding her of the walking she had done in the previous twenty-four hours and complaining about any fur-ther exercise. She didn't care. It had to be done. Just a little more time, a little more pain, then she could rest for as long as she wanted.

She made her way to the door, heading for the bookshop.

Taking the first step towards the endgame.

★

Donovan and Turnbull were finally making headway. Of a sort.

The darkness had brought the women out, and their punters. The two men were standing on an anonymous, run-down terraced street in the west end of Newcastle, trying to read the situation. On the opposite side of the road, working girls were beginning to appear, bracing themselves for whatever the evening would throw at them. The wind carried ice and the sky the threat of rain, but the girls were showing more flesh than was seasonally prudent. Miniskirts and crop tops to attract the punters, spike stilettos to give them an approximation of a sexy walk.

Or to stop them running away, thought Donovan.

Skin the colour of old mashed potato or plucked goose flesh. Shivering, drawing on their fags, hoping the smoke would fill their bodies with warmth.

'You see there,' Turnbull was saying, 'there's the girls. Now look at the ends of the street.'

Turnbull flicked his finger, trying not to attract attention to himself. Donovan followed his gaze. In the shadows stood a couple of men. Big, burly and shaven-headed, wrapped in leather and sheepskin. Eyes like attack dogs.

'See them? They're the minders. In case the girls get any ideas about runnin' away. Or refusin' punters. They remind them who's boss. What they're there for.' He spat on the pavement, like the words had given him a bad taste in his mouth.

'The girls I've been talking to are all indoors,' said Donovan.

'Yeah, the brothels. Hard to touch them, or at least the people who own them. They're protected by papertrails and front men. Always someone to take the rap. Mind, some of the girls have been doin' this for years. Got a set of clients, work for themselves, manage to make a decent living out of it and know when to get out. Some of them.' He turned to Donovan. 'That girl we met you with in the brothel that night. What was she? Russian or somethin'?'

'Bosnian.'

Turnbull nodded. 'Figures. Eastern Europe, Africa. There's no shortage. They're taken to the brothels by their minders, given a room that they have to pay rent for, told which shifts to work. Told they have to service everyone. Everyone. Whatever they want, no matter how horrible, they have to do it.'

'And if they don't?'

'Like I said, there's no shortage. They're commodities. They're meat. They'll throw old meat out that's past its sell-by date, bring in some fresh stuff. Got to make their profit.'

'Where do they throw the old meat out to?'

Turnbull shrugged. His shoulders were tight. 'Who knows? The girls never officially existed here anyway, so they can disappear just as easily. Take a guess. Any one is as good as another.'

'Sound like you know what you're talking about.'

Turnbull kept his eyes away from Donovan when he spoke, but he couldn't keep the anger from his voice. 'Pimps. Fuckin' hate them. Men who prey on women. Men who live off women. Turn them on to drugs, on to drink, turn them on to the streets to earn money. Turn them into somethin' less than human. Scum. Fuckin' scum.'

'I'm surprised.'

Turnbull turned to Donovan, faced him then. Fire danced behind his eyes. 'Why? You think bleedin'-heart liberals've got the monopoly on stuff like that? Think all coppers are just loudmouth bastards, takin' freebies on the side and turnin' a blind eye? Eh?'

'OK, OK, fine, I'm sorry. I was just surprised at how . . . ferocious your response was.'

Turnbull turned away, moved his shoulders as if releasing a stiff muscle or something more pent up. 'Ferocious.' He said the word as if he was trying it out for size. Decided he liked it. 'Yeah. Ferocious. Think you know everythin'. Sometimes you're so fuckin' wrong.'

They continued to watch in silence. Cars approached, slowed down. Cars that all looked as if they belonged in a more affluent area. As they approached, the girls, as if on some kind of radar, knew which ones to walk up to. They leaned into the windows, pushing their breasts at the drivers, dredging up smiles, negotiating. A repositioning of the cleavage if the price wasn't to their liking and then, sale agreed, they would climb in and off they went.

'Taking their lives in their hands,' said Donovan.

Turnbull nodded. Donovan couldn't read what he was thinking.

A car pulled up to the kerb and disgorged a prostitute, who tottered away on high heels. She offered a little wave to the departing driver, but he sped off too quickly to even acknowledge it. She laughed, shook her head. Took a hip flask from her handbag, took a swig and joined the other girls.

'There she is,' said Turnbull. 'There's Claire.'

He gave a surreptitious wave at the girl, trying not to attract the attention of the minders. Claire saw him and sighed. She gave a couple of surreptitious glances of her own, then crossed over to meet him.

'Keep walking,' she said as she approached the men. 'Round this corner here at least.'

Donovan looked at her as they walked. She wore the standard whore uniform along with caked make-up and bigger-than-life hair. Cosmetics couldn't mask the tiredness in her eyes or, as they passed under a streetlight, the unhealthy pallor of her skin. She looked at Donovan, suspicion in her eyes.

'Who's this?'

'This is Joe Donovan. He's a . . .'

Donovan hid his smile. Obviously Turnbull couldn't bring himself to say 'friend'.

'. . . work colleague. We're workin' on somethin' and we thought you could help us.'

Claire smiled. 'You gonna pay us, then?'

A look of genuine hurt passed across Turnbull's features. He nodded, eyes averted. 'Yeah, I'm goin' to pay you.' He dug into his pocket, brought out his wallet, handed her two twenties and a ten. The money disappeared on Claire's person so fast that Donovan could have doubted it had ever actually been there.

'What d'you want to know?'

Donovan had the envelope of photos in his jacket inside pocket. He brought them out one by one, handed them to Claire. She stood under a streetlight looking at them.

'We want to know if you recognize any of the girls in the pictures,' Turnbull said.

Claire made a face. 'S&M. Don't go in for that if I can help it.'

Another wince from Turnbull.

'But d'you recognize any of them?' asked Donovan.

She frowned as she looked. Paused a couple of times over some shots. Donovan looked at her expectantly, but she passed them over. She finished, handed them back over.

'Sorry,' she said.

'D'you mind looking again?' asked Donovan. 'You might have missed someone; something might come to you.'

Claire obliged by looking through them again. As she did so, she asked questions.

'So what happened to all these girls? They disappeared or something? No, course not. You lot wouldn't be wastin' your time on a load of missin' prossies.'

'They didn't disappear,' said Donovan. 'We're just trying to find them. Do a lot of girls go missing?'

Claire shrugged. 'Kind of job it is, innit? Don't get a pension with this. Some just pass through, say they're on their way to London or Edinburgh or wherever. Had one girl said she was goin' to Carlisle. Talked about it non-stop. God knows what she expected to find there.'

'And you never hear from any of them again?'

Claire shook her head.

'What about the Eastern European girls? The Africans? Do they disappear?'

A shadow crossed over Claire's face. 'Don't be askin' about them. Those bastards that look after them are hard fuckers. You don't cross them. Don't even mix with them if we can help it. Those girls suffer.'

'Why doesn't someone say something? Do something?'

'Get real. Who wants to get involved with that lot?' She looked at Turnbull. 'Not very bright, your mate, is he?'

'No,' said Turnbull, 'he's not.'

She handed the photos back to Donovan. 'Sorry.'

'That's OK.' Donovan pocketed them.

'Maybe you should try the other side of the water. Plenty of girls there. Mind, sometimes they seem further away than Eastern Europe or Africa.'

Donovan nodded his thanks.

Claire looked around. 'Listen, I'd better be gettin' back. Nice to see you, Paul.' She gave Turnbull a kiss on the cheek. He gave her a hug that, Donovan thought, he would rather not let go from. She pulled away, made her way down the street on her tottering heels.

'Oh, well,' said Donovan when she had rounded the corner, 'it was a good try.'

Turnbull nodded, his eyes pools of private sadness.

'How d'you know her, then?' asked Donovan.

'Mind your own fuckin' business.' He began to walk away.

Donovan decided to leave it. He hurried along, caught up with him.

'Fancy a pint?'

Turnbull nodded.

'Come on, then.' They walked off. Further along the street, a thought occurred to Donovan. 'Disappearing girls.'

'What?' grunted Turnbull.

'Disappearing girls. I wonder if it's anything to do with the case you were working on.'

Turnbull shrugged.

Donovan made a mental note: ask Katya. When he next saw her.

Turnbull stopped walking, looked at Donovan, something building inside him. 'What d'you want? Ay? Now. What d'you want?'

Donovan looked at him, taken aback. 'Now?' he replied. 'I want to find Michael Nell, or at least the girls in the photos. Then I'll have done my job. Then I can go home.'

'That's it? Do your job and go home?'

Donovan shrugged. 'Yeah.'

'Thought you were one of those glory boys. Want to be there in the thick of it, showin' us how to do our jobs, getting the adrenalin rush. That's how you used to be. How you were when I first met you. You're tellin' me you don't want to be out there, huntin' for Nell? Findin' the killer?'

It was an honest question and it deserved an honest answer, Donovan thought. About past cases he had worked on. The adrenalin rush he had experienced from them. From being tied to a chair facing a killer.

Then he thought of David, his lost face swimming into vision.

Then Jamal, the boy he had to look after now, bring up as best he could.

'Just do my job and go home,' he said.

Turnbull looked at him as if not trusting in the answer he had heard. 'Thought you had passion. Commitment. Whatever else, thought you had that.'

'I do,' said Donovan. 'But I've also got responsibilities.'

Turnbull stared at him.

'You don't believe me?' Jamal's face dancing before his eyes.

Turnbull shrugged. 'Let's go to the pub.'

Donovan nodded.

They kept walking, each in their own silence.

Donovan thinking about Turnbull's words, wondering whether the answer he had given had been the true one.

Turnbull thinking about something too deep for Donovan to fathom.

Peta looked up and down the corridor, checking for security guards, students, lecturers. Anyone who would find her actions suspicious. Her actions of breaking into a lecturer's office.

When night had fallen, the campus had emptied as if in response to an unspoken curfew. Outside, occasional beams from security guards' torches swung over the courtyard, like searchlights in an old Second World War POW film.

Peta had sat in the refectory, watching the main door until activity around it had eventually ceased, including the departure of the Prof. In what had been a moment of almost *Casablanca* loneliness she had been the last to leave. Chairs were placed on tables, the floor mopped, meaningful glances were exchanged between herself and the serving staff. All the scene needed was some minor chorded Hoagy Carmichael tinkling piano and it would have been complete. The fact that the furniture was all plastic and Formica, the mop stank of some industrial cleaner that was probably declassified MoD baby deformer from the Gulf War and the server was one of two scowling migrant women who just wanted to finish up and go home all spoiled the illusion somewhat.

She had left the refectory and, dodging the searchlights, made her way to the main building. Inside, the corridor was striplit and long-shadowed. Peta's footsteps had given out lonely echoes as she had walked slowly and warily up and down, satisfying herself that she was alone in this stretch of the building.

She turned off the overhead lights in the section containing the Prof's office, continued in darkness. Seen from outside, the darkness would look accidental – a power failure or a blown bulb. She stood outside the door, lightly perspiring, shaking slightly from adrenalin. She took deep breaths, controlled herself, channelled the adrenalin, worked with it.

The Prof hadn't been back to his office in all the time she'd been watching it. He had gone home, she was sure of it.

She hoped she was sure of it.

Her fingers dexterously worked the lockpick. A career burglar she had once been professionally acquainted with had provided her tools. He had felt she had been honest and fair with him and had taken a bit of a shine to her. When he found himself facing a sizeable stretch, he had asked her to take care of his tools for him. She had been surprised at the request but pleased and even honoured to do so. When the burglar had died after a year in prison from a particularly virulent cancer, she had held on to them, teaching herself how to use them, for fun at first but eventually in memory of him. She had an aptitude for it. And she enjoyed it, carried them in her bag always.

And she had never been locked out again.

She slowly and delicately probed, felt metal move against metal, teeth fall gently into place. She tried the handle. It turned. She opened the door and was in.

She looked around the room. It was as she had last seen it: a pop culture/psychology car crash shrine. She checked the desk: nothing out of place. She checked the drawers: locked.

She scanned the room, unsure what she was looking for: something that would jump out at her, something that would feel wrong. She didn't find it.

Taking out the lockpicks again, she crossed to the desk and sat down at the chair. Putting the desk lamp on and pulling it close to minimize any light seeping into the corridor, she opened the top drawer. Stationery, Post-It notes, pencils and dust. The usual top-drawer clutter. She worked her way down, tried the second drawer. Papers, work-related files, assessments. She resisted the temptation to look at her own. The third drawer. More of the same. The fourth.

Something different.

A file, the elastic bands around it setting it apart from everything else. A typed label on the front cover: THE HIS-TORIAN.

Curious, she looked at it. Was it a plan for a novel? Case notes? She drew the file out, undid the band wrapping, settled back and began to read. A shiver ran down her spine as she did so. This was something important. This could even be the smoking gun.

The first page detailed the first victim. Lisa Hill. A photo snipped from the paper was clipped to a detailed description of the girl, her background, her life, her disappearance and her death. There were even psychological notes as to her state of mind. The whole thing read like a report combining analysis and forensics. Peta took a while to think who this girl was. She remembered. There had been speculation after

Jill's abduction that this girl had been the killer's first victim but no official confirmation. This was more than speculation, Peta thought. This looked to her like evidence.

Her heart was beating fast, her breathing becoming laboured. She turned the page.

Just as Peta had suspected, Ashley Malcolm was next. The familiar, cheerful face from so many newspaper reports. She flipped it over, read what was underneath. Another detailed description of another life and death.

Peta was beginning to feel light-headed. This was a kind of sensory overload. Almost too much to take in.

She turned the page.

Jill Tennant. The same thing again. The only difference: the piece about her death more hastily written, unfinished. As if he had been disturbed.

Very disturbed, she thought.

She turned the next page, almost too scared to read what she would find there.

She never got to look at it.

'Enjoying yourself? Found something worth reading?'

Peta looked up, startled. There stood the Prof, in coat, hat and scarf, silhouetted in the doorway, like a shadow detached from the darkness. His eyes glittering with cold, hard anger.

He closed the door behind him.

Her heart was pounding, her chest hammering. She opened her mouth, but no sound came out.

He made his way towards her.

36

Katya rounded the corner. And there it was. Perfect. Just as the map had said it would be.

The street names were unfamiliar and difficult to pronounce; saying them aloud made them sound like stones or lumps of clay in her mouth. Likewise the symbols and descriptions. But she had persevered, committing them to memory, ignoring the looks from the staff in the bookshop, and then begun what she had hoped would be the last part of her trek.

As instructed, she had taken the Metro. It was a risk, as she had no money left after the coffee for a ticket, and potentially ruinous if she had been caught, but there was no other option. She had watched from the window as the train had emerged from the tunnel into the electrically illuminated evening darkness, going first over a huge bridge, past some high-rise housing that seemed to be constructed from one long brick wall. Cranes had appeared next, towering over streets of poor old houses, etched against the night sky like the skeletal remains of huge lumbering beasts from an earlier era.

The doors opened and closed, people got on and off. The areas stayed poor-looking. They seemed hard-faced, these northern people, she thought, short-haired and not given to smiling much. Wearing leisurewear to accentuate their lack of employment. Overweight yet still looking malnourished. They looked like any peasant stock anywhere in Europe. They looked like her own people at home.

She shook her head, looked out of the window, waited
for her stop. It arrived.

North Shields.

She stepped off, exited the station and looked around.
Shops and businesses had closed up for the night. Papers,
fast-food wrappers and other detritus blew down the streets.
It was low-level; it was poor. People hurried home as if not
wanting to risk some invisible curfew. In doorways and on
corners youths were beginning to congregate, watching
from beneath their hoods, their eyes reflecting the streetlights
in razor glints, looking like apprentice wizards casting spells
of dark magic.

Katya knew that their sharp eyes were on her, could
almost feel their ugly thoughts being transmitted. She turned
away from them, got her bearings from the street names,
walked off. She hoped they weren't following, but she didn't
look back to check. She didn't want to show weakness, be
marked out as a victim. There had been enough of that in
her life.

She followed the street names, comparing them with the
memorized grid in her head. Her walk led her to a row of
old terraced houses down an unspectacular street. Flat-
fronted, some of them had been pebbledashed and painted
in an effort to distinguish them from each other. Two storeys
tall but the dark, flat expanse of sky above still seemed to
bear down on them oppressively.

She checked for the number she wanted, thought of
going around the back, finding a way to break in, but
thought better of it. The time for stealth, for creeping around
in shadows, was over. The time for confrontation was on her.
She dragged her weary body to the front door, rang the bell.

Anita lay there on the bed. It hurt to move her body. But
hurt, she was beginning to feel, in a good way.

They had had to move, Michael had told her, and the hotel was old, run down. The greasy old couple who ran it had stared at them when they had booked in, the fat man running his eyes up and down her body. He obviously found her to his liking because when he gave her his rotten-toothed smile the corners of his mouth were gummed with white, oily spittle.

He had given them their room key, followed them up there and stood in the room not in any hurry to leave. She had expected Michael to say something, do something, but he hadn't. Eventually the man had left, but she could still feel his fetid breath, see his bloodshot eyes looking at her from every corner of the room.

Michael hadn't seemed to notice. They had sat on the bed.

And had sex.

And now she hurt. Again.

Her bruises, wounds, were still raw. Michael wouldn't allow them to heal. He poked them, prodded them, played with them until they changed colour or the blood trickled once again from them. His hands were all over her, in her, his body pressed against her, her own forcibly restrained, bound up. Until she was no longer the person she used to be, until she had given her will up to him. Until she had no option but to take whatever he flung at her and love him for it.

Then she came.

Later, lying side by side in bed, they had talked.

'So why are we running?' she had asked.

Michael Nell had smiled. Anita felt something sharp and hot stir within her when he did that.

'I'm a wanted man,' he said, relishing the words. 'Haven't you seen the papers?' He laughed. 'No, of course you haven't.'

She frowned. 'Wanted for what?'

'Murder.' The smile widened, his eyes glistened.

'They want you for murder?' she had asked, inching away from him across the bed.

He stayed where he was, shrugged.

'Did you . . . did you do it?'

He looked at her, eye to eye. 'Do you think I did? D'you think I could kill someone?'

She moved her body, felt her bruises ache, saw fresh blood as she rubbed against the sheets. 'I . . . don't know . . .'

He laughed.

'Did you?'

'Well, they think I did. That's why they're chasing me. That's why I'm on the run. And you're with me. My moll. Like Bonnie and Clyde. Outlaws. Cool, isn't it?'

'What if . . . if they catch you?'

He leaned over towards her. 'We'll have to make sure they don't, won't we?'

He saw she had retreated into her own thoughts. 'Don't run out on me, Anita. I've waited a long time to find you. You're perfect. I won't let you go.'

'No, no, I am not . . . But what do we do for money? How do we live?'

Michael Nell laughed. 'Well, I can't go out to work, can I? It'll have to be you.'

She frowned again. 'What can I do?'

He moved up close to her. She felt his stale breath, his sweat. His need of her. He was turning her on despite the situation. 'What you were doing when I met you.'

Her heart sank. She closed her eyes. 'No. No.'

His hands were on her, holding her down. He straddled her, becoming unmistakably erect.

'Yes. We've all got to contribute. Bring something in. And you can do that. Be a whore. My whore.'

He was fully erect now. She said nothing.

'You can start with the old bloke downstairs. Bet his wife hasn't serviced him in years. Bet he'd let us stay here for free if you did that.'

'No.'

'It's just a start. Just to help out. You can go back out on the quayside. Service all those high-flying, well-paying businessmen again.'

She shook her head.

She felt him holding her down harder, his body pressed tight against hers. 'We've both got to contribute, Anita. Now, I've been waiting for you all my life but if you're not prepared to contribute to the family finances, you're not one of the family. And then where would you be?'

Anita saw herself back on the plane to Lithuania, stepping off, her family hurt and disappointed. The end of a fairy tale.

Michael Nell smiled. 'What's your answer?'

She nodded, eyes averted from his.

'Good.' He smiled. Put his hands behind his neck. Undid the chain that was hanging there, placed it around her neck, fastened it. Sat back and smiled at her. 'There. We're engaged. My princess.'

And as his body moved over hers, she thought she could forgive him anything.

Because he had just said the right word.

Decca checked the house in front of him against the one on the list and the one in the A to Z, made sure they all matched. They did. He sighed. This wasn't what he had signed up for. This wasn't him. This wasn't what Clint would do. He was a man of action, a gangsta. Not some creep who ticked off names on a piece of paper. Christ, anyone could do that.

But still, he wanted to prove himself. Show he had the

smarts to be a major player. And if this was what it took, then this was what it took. He could play the game Kovacs' way if he had to.

He looked over at the front door in a row of boring, nondescript old houses. The kind he had grown up in. The kind he had run away from. The kind he had vowed never to go back to.

He looked again at the list, saw all the crossed-off addresses. The safe houses he had checked out looking for Dario Tokic. As he looked down the list he thought of the ways he had tried to get information out of the people who had answered the doors to him. He had been cunning, he had used guile, as they said in *Match of the Day*. He smiled at the thought, remembered the clipboard, the fake marketing questions. Gas supply, electricity supply. He had bought a daily paper, read the headlines, clued himself up. Asked what they thought of the government's approach to whatever. There had been some who wouldn't say anything no matter what he said to them, but in general he had been surprised at how much people had wanted to talk. A question here, a question there, a bit of flattery, a twinkly smile and he had them eating out of his hands. He was good, even if he said so himself. But they were mostly women. And he knew how to talk to women. Get what he wanted out of them.

A few questions about how many people lived in the house, were there any lodgers. If not, then they were off the list and he was out the door. A few weren't in, and he noted them down for a callback, and a couple of lonely housewives had even given him their number. Maybe he would call. He liked older women. They always seemed more grateful.

But that was for later. This was about work. The place in front of him was unremarkable in every way. Even its pebbledashing to distinguish it from the other houses in the street was mundane. He stifled a yawn, got out of the car, crossed the street.

Rang the doorbell. And waited.

He heard noise from within. Someone was there, but they were in no hurry to answer the door. Voices were raised as if in argument. Perhaps the TV was on too loud. Perhaps they were eating.

He rang again.

Footsteps came down the hall. A light was put on. The door was opened. A timid face looked out. A woman, late twenties, Decca reckoned, with mousy-brown hair, stared at him. He looked back. It wasn't timidity he saw in her face, he thought. It was fear.

'Ye-yes?' she said in a voice that matched her features.

Decca, smile in place, began to talk. 'Hi, we're doing a survey on . . .'

The door was yanked open wide, almost knocking the woman off her feet. She gave a yelp and jumped out of the way, losing her footing and falling backwards into the hallway. Decca moved forward to help her up. Stopped in his tracks when he felt a knife at his throat.

'In.'

He moved inside. The door was slammed shut behind him. He heard it being locked.

He looked at the man who had spoken. Dark-haired, dark-eyed. Wearing a sweatshirt and jeans. He looked familiar. Then it clicked into place.

Dario Tokic.

'We've been waiting for you,' Tokic said, keeping the knife pressed at Decca's throat. He gestured with his head towards the kitchen. 'Hands on your head. Move.'

Decca did as he was told, walked down the hall. He was aware of the automatic in his jacket pocket, equally aware that there was no move he could make to get it out.

'No tricks.'

'How did you know I'd be coming here?' asked Decca.

'You've been looking for me. For us. Even broke into their offices looking for us. It was only a matter of time.'

Decca said nothing, kept walking. Into the kitchen. The table had been laid, and a smell of spoiled food was in the air. Katya Tokic was holding another sharp-looking kitchen knife to a man's throat. Two young children cowered in the corner.

Tokic kept the knife pressed hard on Decca's throat, addressed the family.

'I am truly sorry to have to do this, believe me. Truly sorry. We mean you no harm. This is the man we wanted. We knew he would come. As soon as they moved me here I knew he would come.' The knife was pushed harder. Decca wanted to swallow, felt he would break the skin if he did, so refrained. 'Please accept my deepest apologies. We will be going soon. Gun.'

Katya moved over towards Decca, began searching his pockets.

This was the moment, he thought. When Clint would make a move, when Bond would distract her, get the gun out and shoot them both. The moment. He tensed, ready to move.

'Don't.'

The knife was pushed harder. A small pain, then Decca's neck felt wet. His breathing became heavier, his legs too. He stayed where he was. She found the gun, stood back, pointed it at him.

'We will leave now,' Tokic said. He stood back beside his sister, looked at Decca. 'Your car. You will drive. We will be behind you. No funny business or we shoot you.'

'Then . . .' He tried to find a brave voice. 'Then you'll die too.'

Tokic shrugged. 'What's death when you've been through what we have been through?'

Decca said nothing. Knew he meant it.

Tokic turned to the family. 'Please accept my apologies once again. We are not bad people. Just good people driven to do bad things. We will bother you no more. Please, I implore you, do not phone the police. Please. And I know you may not believe me, but I thank you for your hospitality.'

He turned to Decca, indicated that he walk down the hall. Decca did so. Katya handed her brother the gun, opened the front door.

They crossed the street, got into the BMW, Decca in the driving seat, Katya and her brother behind him.

'Whuh – where're we going?'

Decca felt more than saw Tokic smile.

'To see Kovacs. And make him pay.'

37

Amar was tired. His limbs ached, his stomach groaned and his head hurt. His body was filmed in dried sweat, the smell mingling with that all-too-familiar post-drug comedown odour. His skin felt like it belonged to someone else. And, he thought with a kind of twisted pride, he was still working.

He let out a groan. Jamal, in the passenger seat, looked at him, concern in his eyes.

'You OK, man?'

'Yeah. Yeah. Just tired. You know how it is.'

'Don't I? This stakeout shit. Ain't like on TV. Never see those cops from *The Shield* pissin' in no bottle.'

Amar gave a weary smile. They had spent the day looking for Decca Ainsley. Without any success. They had tried Decca's café, sitting there in turn nursing cappuccino after cappuccino, eating croissants until Amar thought his skin would turn into flaky pastry and Jamal got sugar rush after sugar rush, Amar reading every page of every newspaper they had in there, Jamal with his head stuck in gaming magazines. No sign of Decca Ainsley, just a host of office workers being served by a bevy of pretty girls for whom English clearly wasn't a first language.

After that they had driven around what they had been assured were Decca's haunts. The bars he frequented, the places he was known to eat lunch at. All the time observing only. Amar did most of that as Jamal was underage for the bars. The boy sat in the car, sullenly playing games on his mobile. Amar spotted Decca's friends, or known associates as he was required to call them, but couldn't speak to any of them, ask any of them where his target was. He couldn't come up with some story, invent an official reason for his visit. That would arouse too much suspicion. Neither could he pass himself off as a friend of Decca's. He doubted Decca was the kind of person who had any Asian friends. So he had to content himself with just watching, straining to pick up any snatches of dialogue that would give him a clue to Decca's whereabouts. He heard plenty of other stuff, but nothing to do with Decca.

So now they sat in Amar's battered Volvo outside Marco Kovacs' house in Ponteland. It was a last resort, but they didn't know where else to go. Amar certainly didn't want to go home. And he certainly didn't want to go out. He had made a promise to Jamal. And he had to stick to it.

So they sat and watched, flattened down in the seat so as not to attract attention, ignoring the rumblings of their stomachs, the ache of their bladders. The car was pulled away from the house slightly, positioned in a small patch of semi-darkness between two streetlights but still with enough of a view of the main gate. It was a private road, and Amar was surprised that no one had called the police, or whatever rent-a-cop outfit patrolled the place, to report an unknown car in their street. It was a good job they didn't know he was Asian, or Jamal was a light-skinned black boy, he thought. It was the kind of area where things like that still mattered.

He looked at the house and wondered again what kind of defences Kovacs had installed. He could see the CCTV cameras on the high wall by the front gate, sweeping the street every so often, the sharpened staves above the wall, the huge double gates. He wondered how many people patrolled the grounds, what they were armed with. How many dogs.

He broke off his calculations, yawned and stretched, careful not to extend his arms too far over his head. He couldn't play the stereo in case it ran the battery down, couldn't read in case he missed something happening before him, couldn't talk to Jamal because boredom had dried up conversation to post-I Spy levels. He could do nothing but wait and watch.

And then they saw it.

'Who's that?' Jamal was sitting up.

Amar joined him. Watched. A car pulled up to the gates, stopped before the intercom and the driver spoke into it.

'Camera,' he snapped at Jamal. Jamal handed it over. Amar grabbed it off him, focused through the telephoto.

'It's him. Decca Ainsley.'

A thrill of adrenalin ran through Amar's body. His body no longer ached, his bladder no longer felt full. He felt like he was in his own skin again. He kept watching, caught a movement from the back seat of the car, swung the lens towards it. A figure sitting behind Decca, holding something to his neck. Focus in further. A gun. An automatic with a man's finger on the trigger. Amar trained the lens on the gunman's face.

Dario Tokic.

'Shit.'

Amar swallowed hard, ran his tongue over his lips, tried to quell the rising excitement within him, let his professionalism take over. He refocused the lens, looked along the back seat. Next to Dario Tokic was his sister Katya. Holding a knife.

Amar couldn't believe his luck.

Jamal grabbed the camera off Amar, looked for himself.

'Fuckrees, man, look at that . . .'

The gates swung open. Dario Tokic said something to Decca, Decca gave a solemn nod and drove in. The gates began to swing shut behind them.

Without pausing to think his course of action through, Amar started scrambling out of the car.

'Where the fuck you goin', man?'

'Over there. Got to be quick. You stay here. I mean it, stay here.'

'You can't. You ain't fit enough today, bro. Your head ain't together.'

'Yes, I can. Yes, I am. Yes, it is. Now, stay here.'

And Amar was running across the road.

He didn't think about the guards, armed or otherwise; he didn't think about the dogs or the CCTV cameras or any potential booby traps within. He just knew he had to get into the grounds of that house. He would deal with everything else as and when it happened.

He reached the gates just as they were swinging shut and squeezed himself between them. He fell to his knees, feeling the sharp gravel through his jeans as the gates clanged behind him. He stayed like that for a few moments, getting his breath, assessing his options. He looked up the driveway. Decca's BMW had reached the front of the house and Decca was parking it. Amar stood up, looked around, listened. No dogs, no sirens, no sounds of running feet. He was undetected. For the moment.

Decca was getting out of the car, Katya and her brother following. Walking towards the front door.

Amar gave one more quick look around, then, using the evergreen foliage for cover, made his way cautiously up the drive.

Decca was scared. It wasn't something that happened often, not something he had much experience of or knew how to cope with. So scared it was taking all his willpower not to wet himself.

He had driven to Ponteland from North Shields as carefully as possible, keeping well within the speed limit. He had seen films when the hero had been in a similar situation and had gunned the car as fast as he could, throwing it around the road, dislodging the villain's gun, gaining the upper hand and after a struggle throwing him bodily from the vehicle. The cold metal of the gun against his neck, the cold, dead eyes in the mirror and the words by Tokic before they had driven off reminded him just how far his Hollywood fantasies were from real life.

He had pulled up before Kovacs' house, stopped before the intercom.

'No tricks,' said Tokic. 'No code words, nothing out of the ordinary. Do that, you die.'

Decca didn't doubt it. He spoke into the intercom, asked to be admitted, told them he wanted to see Kovacs. The gate swung open. Decca expelling a breath he wasn't aware he had been holding, drove in.

He parked before the house.

'Feeling brave, Mr Gangster?' asked Tokic, pressing the gun harder on his skin.

Decca couldn't find the words to answer him with. He shook his head instead.

'Good. Let's keep it that way.'

Decca fought hard, found his voice. He felt there were words he had to say. 'Whuh . . . why d'you . . . What d'you want with . . . with Mr Kovacs, anyway? Is it him, or is it me . . . me as well?'

'Kovacs killed our family.' Katya's voice. A voice filled with damage and resolution yet also softness. 'While we watched. While we hid and watched.'

'Killed. Raped. Our whole family. Our whole village. And we saw him. And we will never forget him. And now we come to make things even.' Tokic's voice was laden with conflicting emotions; he was clearly struggling to keep them in check.

Decca nodded. 'So . . . so it's not with me, then?'

'You traffic girls. You exploit them.' Katya again. 'You use them. And when you have no use for them, you kill them.'

'Aw, no, now, not me. I don't do that.' Decca was sweating again. The urge to empty his bladder was becoming overwhelming.

'Maybe you don't kill them. But you give them over to someone who does.' Katya's knife glinted in the night light. 'I know this. For fact. You have someone to dispose of the bodies.'

Decca said nothing. Kovacs' 'efficient disposal scheme'. Decca knew all about it. He could see that anything more he said or did was useless. Their minds were made up. His fate rested entirely with them.

'Let's go,' he said, getting out of the car.

They followed him. He walked up the steps, rang the bell. A shadow from the other side of the door was approaching. A slight hope rose within Decca. Kovacs usually had a staff of two or three on duty guarding him. And they were always armed. And this was one of them coming now.

The door opened. Before them stood one of Kovacs' inner retinue of bodyguards, a huge, hulking mountain of muscle who was surprisingly quick on his feet. Decca could attest to that; he had seen him in action. Hope rose further within Decca as he opened his mouth to speak. He could see the guard taking in the scene. His eyes spotted the gun and he swiftly went for his own.

Too late.

Decca felt the automatic pulled from the back of his neck, heard the deafening crack of a bullet being fired, and again, and felt the heat as they whizzed past his cheek and saw them connect with the bodyguard's head and chest, sending him sprawling backwards in a spray of blood, bone and brain.

Decca stood as if rooted to the spot. His heart was pumping fit to burst, his ears ringing from the blasts. He was aware of Tokic's face next to his.

'We are not playing games here.'

Decca felt the prod of the gun. He walked into the house like a sleepwalker, stepping over the prone, lifeless body before him.

'Where is he?' Tokic again.

Decca pointed towards the vivarium. 'Through there.'

'Will he have heard the shots?'

Decca shook his head. 'Soundproofed. He likes to be alone in there. With his snakes.'

Tokic laughed. 'Zmija. The Snake.' He looked at his sister. 'Fitting.'

A sudden noise came from the back of the house. The sound of a heavy-footed man running. Another bodyguard. He rounded the corner and stopped in his tracks, trying to process what he saw before him. He looked up and, mind made up, went for his gun.

Tokic was quicker than him. Three bullets, four, made the bodyguard give a final, grisly dance of death before collapsing on to the floor.

He waved the gun at Decca. 'Are there any more—' he looked down at the dead bodies '—like them?'

Decca was close to fainting. 'There might be another one. I don't know. Depends.'

'On what?'

'On . . . on whether there are three or two. Usually two. Usually.' He swallowed hard.

'Where would he be?'

'I don't know. Anywhere.'

Tokic looked around, made a decision. 'We will deal with him if we find him. Katya, get their guns.' She did so. He turned to Decca. 'Lead.'

Decca could barely walk. With great effort he managed to place one foot in front of the other, leading them to the double doors of the vivarium. He placed two shaking hands on the handles and gripped. The handles were cold and hard. Solid and reassuring. He wanted to keep on gripping them. Never let go. Just stand there for ever.

'Move.'

The gun was prodded against his back. Decca had no choice. He opened the doors, went in.

Amar crept up the gravel drive as slowly as possible, trying not to let his feet make too much of an audible impact. He stayed close to the conifers, feeling the rainwater from that afternoon's downpour against his face and hands, soaking into his clothes. Tried hard not to be seen.

He reached the side of the house as Decca and his two passengers were closing the car doors. He looked up: a motion-sensor light was mounted on the corner of the house. If he rounded it while they were there the light would go on. He would have to sidestep it or be spotlit by it. He flattened himself against the brickwork, began edging his way along to the corner hoping not to come into the ambit of the sensor.

Then he heard them: the unmistakable sound of gunfire. Two shots. Amar knew from experience that real guns didn't sound like they did in the movies, particularly Michael Mann movies, but that the results were more messy and dangerous than could be shown. He heard gasps and stifled screams followed by the sound of people moving quickly into the house.

Time for a calculated risk. Thinking they were gone inside, he walked swiftly around the corner of the building, becoming spotlit as he did so. There was no one in front of the house and the door was open. He hurried towards it. What he saw there stopped him.

A dead body blocked his path.

He heard voices from inside, flattened himself against the wall. Then more gunshots.

His breathing felt heavier, his heart began doing overtime. They weren't playing games, this lot, he thought. This was the real deal.

Voices again from inside, then the sound of feet moving off somewhere else inside the house. He waited until all was still, then slowly made his way up the steps, over the dead body, being careful not to get blood on his shoes and into the house.

He saw the other body lying on the floor.

'Jesus . . .'

He hadn't meant to speak. He looked around quickly, seeing if he had been heard. No response. He looked around again, listened hard. Heard voices coming from down a corridor on his right. Walked slowly down that way.

He came to a set of double doors. Closed. He leaned in close, put his ear to them. Tried to make out what was being said.

Kovacs was at the far end of the room looking through the glass at one of his prize specimens. The snake was curled around a tree, its flat, unblinking eyes staring back at him. It was hard to tell whether the snake was regarding him fondly, with hatred, as a potential meal or not regarding him at all. Kovacs was dressed in his usual business suit, his tie removed, his shirt buttoned up to the neck. He turned when he heard the doors open.

'Derek.' He frowned. 'Why are you here?'

Dario and Katya Tokic stepped into the room, closed the door behind them. Kovacs' eyes widened.

'What are they doing here? Derek, remove them.'

Kovacs moved to a central antique table, made as if to press a button.

'Don't do that.' Tokic pointed the gun at him. Kovacs stopped moving, looked at him.

'I have men in this house. They will be here in seconds.'

Tokic couldn't keep the grin from his face. It was the grin of the powerless suddenly given power. And revelling in all the cruelty that comes with it. 'They will not. I have dealt with them.'

Kovacs looked at Decca as if seeking confirmation. Decca nodded. Kovacs tried to keep his face from showing anger, or indeed any emotion. He spoke. 'What do you want?' he said flatly.

'Marco Kovacs,' said Dario Tokic. 'Where is he?'

'Here,' said Kovacs. He seemed to be having the same trouble as Decca in swallowing.

Tokic looked around. 'Where?'

Decca pointed at Kovacs. 'There. In front of you.' Desperation was showing in his voice.

Tokic and Katya exchanged glances.

'That is not him,' said Katya. 'That is not the man who killed our family.'

'Who are you?' asked Tokic, taking a step towards Kovacs.

'Marco Kovacs. I am Marco Kovacs. A legitimate businessman.'

'Marco Kovacs was a member of Arkan's Tigers. Marco Kovacs was known as the Snake. A warlord. Marco Kovacs was the person who tortured and killed our family. We know what he looks like. You know him. They show me photo of you and him. So who are you?'

Kovacs looked as if he was about to expire before them. 'I have told you. I am . . . am Marco Kovacs . . .'

Tokic stepped in front of him. He pulled his arm back, ready to bring down his fist holding the gun on to Kovacs' face.

There was a noise. From behind the double doors.

Tokic stopped, arm aloft. He turned to Decca. 'What was that?'

Decca shrugged. 'I . . . I don't know . . .'

Tokic turned again to Kovacs. 'You have more than two bodyguards in this house tonight? The truth.'

Kovacs shook his head. 'No, no. Just two . . .'

Tokic looked between Kovacs and Decca, deciding whether they were telling the truth. He turned to Katya. 'Go and look.' He gestured with his eyes at the automatic she was holding. 'Kill whoever is there.'

Katya nodded and left the room.

Tokic turned back to Kovacs. 'Again. Who are you?'

Fuck, thought Amar. Fuck.

He had tried to straighten up. The door was heavy, old. Not much sound travelled through it. He had tried to move to the centre, put his ear on the gap. In doing so he had caught his sleeve on the handle. Pulling it away had made the noise.

He heard footsteps coming towards him, looked around.

He couldn't run back to the main door he would be seen. And shot, if the other two bodies were anything to go by. He looked for somewhere else to go, a hiding place. Saw an entrance to what he presumed was a cellar under the staircase. He ran towards it, pulled at the handle.

Locked.

He looked around again. The footsteps were getting nearer, the handle being turned.

An alcove, shadowed, just along from the cellar doorway. That would have to do. That was all there was. He ran to it, pressed himself up against the wall, hoped to melt away into the darkness.

The door opened. Footsteps on the polished wooden floor. They came nearer.

Amar pressed himself harder into the wall.

Nearer.

He tried to stop breathing, willed himself invisible. In desperation he closed his eyes.

The footsteps stopped.

Amar opened his eyes. There was nothing else he could do.

Before him stood Katya. Pointing a gun at him.

Amar breathed out, accepting his fate. There was nothing he could do now.

Katya looked at him, shocked to see him there at first. Then she recognized him. The gun wavered.

Amar waited. Neither spoke.

Then a voice came from the double doors.

'Katya. Find anything?' Dario Tokic. Impatient.

Katya looked between the sound of her brother's voice and Amar. She opened her mouth to speak. Amar held his breath.

'No,' she said. 'Nothing.'

'Get back in here, then.'

She turned, ready to go.

Amar looked at her, opened his mouth, whispered thanks, ready to come out. She shook her head, crossed to him again. Put her mouth against his ear. Whispered gently. 'Say nothing. Do nothing. Stay hidden. And you will live.'

He nodded. She gave a slight nod in return, turned, walked back down the corridor.

Closed the door behind her.

Amar, body shaking all over, let out a silent sigh.

'Liar.'

Tokic picked up where he had left off. He raked the gun across Kovacs' face. Kovacs twisted backward away from the blow, lost his balance, fell to one knee. Blood was beginning to seep from the ragged wound on his cheek. 'Who are you?'

'I, I told you. Marco Kovacs . . . You bastard . . .'

Tokic looked around as if looking for something to earth him, something that would stop him exploding. He seemed almost incandescent with rage. His eyes fell on the snakes. Rows of them. Behind glass. Behind mesh. Primeval forces of survival barely contained. He smiled.

'You have the key for these cages?'

Kovacs nodded.

Tokic looked around, let his eyes alight on a particular pit of snakes. 'These are cobras, are they not?'

Kovacs nodded again.

'Dangerous to man. Fatal. Am I correct?'

Kovacs said nothing.

'Open the door.'

Kovacs didn't move.

Tokic stretched out his arm, pointed the gun at him. 'Open the door.'

Kovacs, his hands shaking, took a set of keys from a drawer in the desk. He crossed to the glass-fronted cage on unsure legs, found the lock and, with a great, trembling effort, opened the door.

The snakes coiled and uncoiled, sensing something happening, or about to happen.

'Now get in.'

Kovacs turned to him. 'Please . . .'

The gun was waved once more. 'In.'

Tears were starting to well in Kovacs' eyes. He opened his mouth, ready to implore.

Tokic aimed the gun at his feet, shot. The bullet went into the polished wooden floor, throwing up splinters. Kovacs jumped back, got his feet out of the way just in time. The snakes recoiled and reacted.

'In.'

Kovacs, trying not to let the tears show, stepped inside.

Tokic walked over to the cage, closed the door behind him, turned the key in the lock and removed it. He stood before the glass, watching. The snakes sensed another presence. Began circling it, deciding whether it threatened their territory or not.

Kovacs pressed himself against the glass. 'Please . . .'

'Where is Kovacs?' Tokic's voice flat, inflectionless.

Kovacs shook his head.

'You will be dead soon if you do not answer. If you do not tell me the truth. Where is Kovacs?'

'At . . . at the dock. Waiting for a new shipment.'

Katya bristled as she heard the word. She knew what it meant.

'Which dock?'

'There is only one here. One that takes ships from Baltic. Tyne Dock. We know you knew. We moved the date forward. In case you told authorities, tried to stop us.'

'Why are you pretending your name is Marco Kovacs? Who are you?'

'No one. No one. Just an accountant playing a part.' The man calling himself Kovacs looked behind him. The snakes were becoming interested in him. 'Just a front man. An accountant from Belgrade. Please, I've told you, let me go. Please . . .'

'Which one is Kovacs?'

'He's . . . he's calling himself Christopher.'

Tokic frowned. 'Why?'

'In case . . . in case something like this happened.' He swallowed hard. 'Christopher. He's the one you want. You will know him when you see him. Now, please, I beg of you, let me go . . .'

Tokic turned to Decca. 'Do you know where this Tyne Dock place is?'

Decca wasn't sure but he nodded. He could see the

alternative in front of him. 'Yeah, yeah. I can take you there.'

'Good.' Tokic looked at Katya, nodded. Katya looked away. 'Let's go.'

Decca turned around, saw the man he had known as Marco Kovacs pressed against the glass, the snakes slowly coming towards him. 'What about him?'

Tokic looked at him, unblinking. Decca had seen eyes like that before. On the snakes.

On Christopher.

That war must've really fucked them all up, he thought. 'We leave him.'

Decca was about to speak. Tokic stopped him.

'He made his choices. He takes the consequences.' He waved the gun at Decca. 'Go.'

Decca walked out. As he crossed the threshold, the first screams began to ring out. Decca didn't look back. Decca knew that could have been him there.

The double doors opened. Amar, still in the same hiding place, pressed himself against the wall, hoped none of them would look his way.

They didn't. He imagined rather than saw Katya look in his direction, but none of the others did. He listened until they were outside the house and the car was revved up and away before moving.

He walked towards the double doors. They had been left open. He peeked in.

'Oh, no . . .'

Marco Kovacs' body was slumped against the inside of the cobra cage, snakes writhing and slithering all over him. Amar's first instinct was to cross to the man, open the door, help him. Another glance and he knew the man was beyond help.

He left the vivarium, consciously trying not to touch

anything. He walked down the hall, avoiding the bodies, and went outside. He saw the gates closing, breathed a sigh of relief.

Amar stood against the side of the house, ignored the security light coming on, dug into his pocket, brought out his mobile. Dialled Donovan.

'Joe?' he said when it was answered. 'We've got a fucking situation here, mate . . .'

Amar tried to keep himself together, told Donovan the facts he needed to hear, then hung up. He placed another call after that, an anonymous 999 one, ringing off before they could get a trace.

Amar walked quickly towards the gate, looking for the manual switch at the side that would open it. He felt something on his body, looked quickly up. The rain was starting again. He breathed a sigh of relief, hit the switch. The gates swung open.

He looked back at the house. It looked so ordinary, banal even. Hard to believe what horror had taken place there. He turned, walked through the gates.

And stopped.

Dario Tokic was standing right in front of him, his automatic pointing directly at Amar's stomach.

'My sister means well. She has a good heart. But sometimes that is not enough.'

Amar opened his mouth, tried to speak. He didn't get the chance.

Tokic fired.

Amar was flung backwards, hitting the glistening pavement with a wet thud.

Tokic turned, ran back to the waiting car. Amar watched him turn but didn't see him reach the car. It was like a black-velvet curtain had been draped over his vision.

Soon he saw nothing.

38

'Come any closer,' said Peta, body automatically falling into a tae kwon do stance, 'and you'll be sorry. I mean it.'

The Prof stopped moving, looked at her. There was anger in his eyes, and his hands were twitching, clasping and unclasping, as if he couldn't decide what to do with them.

'Hmm,' he said, as if assessing the situation. 'I believe I should be the one saying that to you. This is my office. And you appear to have forcibly let yourself in.'

'Yeah?' said Peta. She moved around to the front of the desk, facing him, controlling her breathing, finding strength and focus for what she believed was coming next. 'I think once people see what I've found that's not going to matter at all.'

The Prof looked behind her, down at his desk. Saw what she had been reading. A wave passed over his face. Of shock, embarrassment, even fear, Peta didn't know. She couldn't read it but it wasn't what she had expected. Then his body posture relaxed. He smiled.

'Ah. You found it, then.'

'Oh, yeah.'

The Prof sighed, expelling it as a laugh. He shook his head. 'Should we both sit down? Talk things through like rational adults?'

'That won't work,' she said. 'Don't try and be my mate. You think I'm stupid? Is that what you did with the others?'

The Prof frowned. 'Others?'

'Your victims. The ones in the folder. Jill.' Peta felt her voice wavering. She tried to calm herself, channel her emotion as a thin blade of anger straight at the Prof. 'For fuck's sake, she was your student. She was my friend.'

The Prof smiled again, shook his head. 'Peta, I assure you. The deaths of those girls are tragic events in the extreme. Tragic. And believe me when I say I had absolutely nothing to do with their deaths. And certainly not that of Jill. Certainly not.'

The look on his face suggested the mere thought appalled him. Peta wasn't convinced.

'Then why are you keeping a file on them? Why do you seem to know so much about them? And the murderer. The Historian. That you, is it? Bigging yourself up with some grand name?'

The Prof shrugged. 'I had to give him a name. Something that seemed fitting. In keeping with what I sensed he was trying to achieve. It was purely a research tool based on standard FBI procedure. It wasn't my intention to create melodrama.'

'Fitting.' Peta nodded. 'Fitting. What, like a . . . an alter ego? A secret identity? It's not you that does this, it's the other fella?'

Another sigh. 'It isn't me, in whichever manifestation you claim I have assumed, that's responsible for these murders at all. Allow me to explain.'

Peta didn't speak, didn't move.

The Prof gestured to his desk. 'May I come in? Sit down? It would be easier to talk if I were at my desk.'

Peta kept staring at him.

The Prof sighed. 'I'll put the big light on. You can keep the door open. Make a run for it at any time. I won't stop you.'

'That's kind of you.'

'If I had a gun I would gladly let you hold it on me. Well, perhaps not gladly.'

Peta remained unmoving.

The Prof sighed again. 'I'm afraid I'm at a loss as to what more I could say to reassure you. But if you indeed think I'm responsible for these girls' deaths, why aren't you on the phone to the police now?'

'Perhaps I've already phoned them. Perhaps they're already on their way.'

'Perhaps. But I doubt it. You would have mentioned it sooner. Look, Peta, I'm as upset as you about Jill's death. I honestly am. It cuts into me. Really.' He gestured to the file open on the desk. 'That's why I've been trying to do something about it. Now, please. Allow me to explain. I shall abide by whatever constraints you impose.' He gestured again at his desk. 'Please?'

Something in the sincerity of his words touched Peta. She didn't feel able to trust him, but she decided she would at least hear him out. 'Go that way,' she said, pointing at the wall furthest from her. The Prof squeezed himself around the corner of his desk, trapping himself against the bookcase in the process. He extricated himself, took off his hat, coat and scarf, hung them up, sat at his desk. Peta stood before him, one eye on the open door.

'Why don't you sit down? You'll find it much more comfortable.'

'That what you said to all of them? That how you lulled them into a false sense of security?'

The Prof looked pained. 'Please, Peta, can't we move beyond that? I am not a murderer.' He shook his head. 'A sentence I never believed I would have to utter.'

Peta looked around, checked for accomplices, tricks and traps, checked she had a clear path to the door.

Satisfied there was nothing there, she sat. But perched warily on the edge of the chair, ready to run at any moment.

'Thank you,' said the Prof. He turned his attention to the file open on the desk before him. 'This, you may have gathered, is a psychological profile of our killer. I've been building it.'

'Why?'

He shrugged. 'I'm a psychologist. It's . . . what I do.'

'Why didn't you take this to the police? They've been in here. They've questioned you. You've had the perfect opportunity.'

The Prof gave a shy smile, verging on embarrassment. He focused on the desk instead of Peta's eyes. 'The police and I . . . we haven't always viewed life from the same perspective. Suffice it to say I doubt I'd make their approved list of registered profilers.'

'Why not?'

A small smile played at the corners of the Prof's mouth. 'You may find it hard to believe, but I wasn't always the shining example of academia you see before you. I am that most tediously clichéd of people. A man with a past.'

Peta, despite the situation, smiled, then checked herself straight away. The Prof affected not to notice, continued.

'I used to embrace what might accurately be described as the most chemically enhanced of lifestyles. And embraced it both fully and enthusiastically. Dropped out of university, much to my parents' horror, to embark on what I believed would be a quest for even greater knowledge. A Tyneside Carlos Castaneda, if you will.'

'And did you find it?'

The Prof's gaze became distant. Beyond, even, his kitsch film posters. 'Those are stories I would like to be permitted to tell on other days. Suffice to say, I found a world I never knew existed. And soon became a part of. In fact, sold up here and moved there.'

He settled back, into his story now. Peta responded in kind, relaxing her body posture slightly, then again checked herself.

'And lived there for years. Surviving by doing odd jobs, sometimes selling small amounts of dope, speed. Purely among friends, to make ends meet, you understand. But always careful to operate below the radar. Known but never touched by the police. Now, in this world I also got to know a lot of things, became a repository for a lot of certain kinds of information. Information that certain people wanted to know. And would pay handsomely for.'

'You mean you were a police informer?'

'Sometimes. If that information did no harm to myself or my friends. If I believed it contributed to society's greater good. But I lived in a two-way world. Others were given information too. People whom the police would perhaps find conflicts of interest with. Again, a moral decision.'

Peta got the picture. A low-level druggie who had moved on and justified his actions by retaining a selective, self-justifying memory of those times. Whatever gets you through the night, she thought.

'What stopped all that, then? How did you get from there to here?'

'I had what might be described as a life-changing experience. A chemically unenhanced one, I might add. I was assisting a journalist friend of mine with some kind of . . . exposé, I suppose you would call it, on some very nasty dealers who had moved in to town. Providing him with background and suchlike.' The Prof sat back, looked at the ceiling. Back in time, back in his story. 'Unfortunately they found out about what I had learned and whom I was telling it to. And decided to make an example of me.'

He leaned forward, placed his deformed right hand, the hand he usually kept hidden, on the table.

'They left me, among other things, with this.'

Peta leaned forward, examined it. 'Jesus . . .'

He nodded, looked at it as if seeing the wounds being re-created anew. 'Not an experience one would forget in a hurry. Or ever want to repeat.' He withdrew his hand, hiding it once more. 'Of course, the police were unhappy because I refused to tell them who had done it. Or why. My personal morality forbade it. They never forget a thing like that. Or forgive. So, I sensed the end of one chapter in my life had come, and another was about to start. I made peace with my family, resumed my studies as a mature student.'

Peta knew that feeling.

'And worked hard. Very hard. As religious converts are the most fervent. Perhaps I was, to all intents and purposes, born again. And I enjoyed it. Discovered an aptitude for it. That led to working my way into this job. A job which I love more than anything else on this planet.' He steepled his fingers, became thoughtful. 'But your past stays with you. We are all the sum of our actions. Especially where the police are involved. Because they believe we can never change. Detective Inspector Nattrass mentioned as much when she spoke to me.' He sat back, looked at Peta. 'So that is a rather long answer to why I will never make the police's list of approved psychological profilers.'

He stood up. 'And with that established, let us move on to important things. Tea? Or would you prefer coffee? Or something stronger?'

Peta looked at him. He smiled.

'I am not a murderer.'

Peta weighed things up in her mind, made a judgement call. 'Tea, please. That would be perfect. But keep your hands where I can see them.'

He didn't seem to be much of a murderer, she thought. But she would keep a clear getaway to the door just in case.

Anita closed her eyes. Pretended she was somewhere else. Someone else. The girl she used to be. The girl she thought she should have been. The girl, when all this was over, that she perhaps could be.

She stood in the bath, scrubbing away at her skin. The bath was as new and clean as the rest of the hotel. It suited her mood. It suited her. What she had become. What she was now.

But at least she had made Michael happy.

'That's it,' he had said on her return to the room. 'You just had to let him fuck you. You didn't have to enjoy it. Or even look at him. You've just paid our rent and stopped any awkward questions.' He had smiled then. 'You're contributing.'

She stepped out of the bath, towelled herself dry. She looked at herself in the mirror. At her bruises. Scars. Badges of love, Michael had called them. Forget-me-nots. And his words as he had delivered them, his actions. Pleasure and pain intermingling until she didn't know what hurt and what felt good. Just taking his word for it.

She dropped the towel, dressed in the clothes Michael had left out on the floor for her. Her whore's clothes. She looked again in the mirror.

'You ready yet?' he called from the bedroom.

'Nearly . . .' It wouldn't do to keep him waiting.

'Hurry up. You've got to go out.'

She stepped out. He looked at her, ran his gaze appraisingly up and down her body. Smiled.

'Perfect,' he said.

His eyes gave him away. They contained more than just lust for her, she could see that. Love, whole oceans of it.

That was what made him different. What made her stay. She stroked the metal of the necklace he had given her. Smiled. Why she would continue to please him.

He got up from the chair, crossed to her. He grabbed her, roughly put his mouth over hers. His hands all over her, pulling her into him, trying to consume her.

'You're beautiful,' he gasped. 'I love you.'

She kissed him back, started to enjoy herself.

'My whore. My beautiful whore. My slut. I love my slut . . .'

He pressed even harder. She pressed back. His fingers exploring, grabbing, twisting. She felt herself falling, giving in to it.

'Michael, I have . . . I have to, to go . . .'

He pushed her back on to the chair he had been sitting on. It was old and worn, hard and unyielding. He pressed himself down on her.

'In a while,' he said. 'In a while.'

She gave herself up to him willingly.

'There is something I haven't told you.'

Peta replaced her mug of tea on the desk, readied herself to run.

'Don't worry,' he said. 'Not a bad thing. It's just . . . the night of Jill's . . . When Jill disappeared. I was supposed to . . . to be seeing her.'

Peta relaxed, nodded. 'Wilco,' she said. 'The Wilco gig.'

He looked surprised, nodded. 'Right. Ah, yes, of course. Because I . . . Yes.'

'Because you asked me to go.'

'Yes.' The Prof blushed. Sipped his coffee. 'The police, they know. I told them. It was a social affair. Many of us there. Not just . . . the two of us.' He gave a weak smile. 'You might have enjoyed it.'

Peta nodded, said nothing.

They sipped their drinks. Peta pointed to the file. 'So this is your profile of the killer?'

The Prof nodded.

'Why the Historian?'

'In good time. Now, I'm sure the police have come up with their own profiles. I have a contact on the investigation, left over from the old days. In a lowly position, I'm afraid; just one of the foot soldiers. He has provided me with access to information not available to the press or the general public.'

'Why?'

'So I could come up with a profile. Present it to him.'

'And he would take the credit?'

The Prof nodded. 'If it was right. If I was wrong . . .' The Prof shrugged. 'No harm done. Having said that, some of this is still guesswork. Educated mostly, because that's what I do, but occasionally requiring a leap of faith. This is what I've come up with. The killer knew all his victims. Perhaps not closely, but he was certainly in some form of contact with them.'

'So he works at the university?'

'My first thought. But then there was the first victim. Lisa Hill. I don't believe it has been officially confirmed, but I do believe she was one of his victims. But not a student. So he had to know her another way. That fact must have thrown the police initially, stopped them connecting the three. But the thing that binds them together is the positioning of the bodies. All the clues are there if looked at in the correct way.'

Peta waited. The Prof got up, crossed to a shelf, took down some well-thumbed books and a full document file, placed them on his desk. He opened the file, took out photocopied sheets. Peta leaned over, looked at them.

'What are they? They look like . . . maps.'

'They *are* maps, Peta. But not current ones. Antique. Now, the past is one of the two connective things this killer is interested in.'

'What's the other?' asked Peta.

'Death.'

'Well, no prizes for guessing that.'

'I'll explain what I mean in a while. First, the past. The places the bodies were left should have set any profiler's alarm bells ringing. Lisa Hill was found at Barras Bridge. Ashley Malcolm in Westgate Road cemetery and Jill . . .' He looked around his desk for the piece of paper.

'The car park of the Blood Transfusion Service.'

The Prof nodded. 'Proves my point.'

Peta frowned. 'How, exactly?'

The Prof smiled, happy to be showing off his knowledge. He reached for the photocopied sheets, fanned them out on the desk, arranging them in some kind of order. Peta looked at them.

'Maps, as you so correctly identified,' he said. 'Old ones. Of how the city used to be. Its past configurations.' He pointed to somewhere on his left. 'Westgate Road cemetery.' He rifled through to the end of his file, picked up a sheet Peta hadn't reached in her reading, continued. 'Constructed in the 1820s, modelled, believe it or not, on Père-Lachaise in Paris. Obviously without Jim Morrison.'

'And Edith Piaf.'

'Quite. Disused since 1960.' He looked directly at her. 'Disused. Old. Obsolete. That's the key. And the next one.' Head down again, he ran his finger over the map, in a line from Westgate Road cemetery to Barras Bridge. 'Here. Barras Bridge. Between the Civic Centre and the Newcastle Playhouse on St Mary's Place. And just down the road from where we are now.'

'And there's a church there, St Thomas's, isn't it?' asked

Peta, warming to the theme. 'That's why he left her there.'

The Prof gave another one of his enigmatic smiles. 'One would think, wouldn't one? But no.' His fingers traced the map again. 'Look here.'

Peta looked. The map was even older than the one relating to the cemetery. It showed a completely different layout for the town. Very old, hard to read. She squinted.

'Barras from the word barrow. Meaning grave mounds,' he said. 'Twelfth century. The Hospital of St Mary Magdalene. For lepers.'

'A burial ground for lepers?'

The Prof nodded. 'Initially. As leprosy died out it was used for victims of plague or pestilence. Poor, obviously.'

'And the Blood Transfusion offices? What's buried under there?'

'Nothing,' he said sitting back, looking at her.

'Nothing? Then doesn't your theory fall apart?'

'Not at all. Look here.' He leaned forward, traced his finger in a line from the medieval map of Barras Bridge to the third one. 'What d'you see?'

Peta looked. 'Gallows Hole . . .' She looked up, barely able to contain her excitement. 'Jesus! Gallows.'

The Prof nodded. 'I had a suspicion, something I read about once. In a book on the history of death in the northeast.' He gave a shy smile. 'My esoteric, eclectic tastes are well documented. I decided to follow it up. That's where I've been today, getting these copied. The old public execution site is off the old Turnpike Road, past Gallowgate, now the car park of the Blood Transfusion Service. I don't know the facts, but I'm willing to bet the body was found hanged.'

A shadow crossed the Prof's features leaching the triumph out of him as he realized whom he was talking about.

Peta shared the feeling, looked at the maps, tried to find something constructive to say.

'This is brilliant. If you're right.'

'Yes, if I'm right. But I believe I am.'

'So he's the Historian because of his interest in the past?'

The Prof nodded. 'Partly. There's something else. Death. Or rather the ritual of death. That's what I think appeals to him. My contact told me the bodies were found with their eyes and mouths sewn up.'

Peta's face held a look of disgust. The Prof continued.

'That led me to believe the bodies were all laid out in a certain fashion, possibly utilizing the ritual trappings of an antiquarian culture.'

'How d'you mean?'

'Even before I heard that, I believed he would have done something like that to the bodies. Pennies over the eyes, perhaps. But sewing up the mouths and eyes – that confirmed my way of thinking.'

'Why?'

'Because he's sending us a message. This man, and I think we can safely say it *is* a man, has gone to a lot of time and trouble, and he wants people to know what he's doing.'

'He's a vicious, psychopathic killer, don't forget.'

'Indeed he is. But I'm sure he won't see himself in those terms.'

'They never do.'

'He believes he has a higher calling. Is on a mission.'

'What?'

The Prof shrugged. 'That I haven't yet discovered.'

'What about Michael Nell? Would this fit him?'

The Prof sat back, steepling his fingers across his chest, assuming what seemed an academic position. Peta could see no trace of the self-justifying druggie she had talked to earlier. His journey was obviously complete.

'This is an angry man, obviously,' he said. 'Clever but not educated, I would say. Self-taught. That, I think, would tend to rule out Michael Nell. This man feels that the expression of his intellect has been thwarted in some way. He wants us to know how clever he is. The body positioning is his way of showing it.'

'I'm sure the police will have considered this.'

'I'm sure they have. But at the risk of sounding arrogant, I don't think they're using the correct parameters. And unless they use the right parameters as a cross-referencing tool, they won't get the right results. That's why my contact came to me. He thought the investigation needed someone to think outside the box.'

'You've got to take this to the police. Tell them what you've told me.'

'My contact will take it.'

'No, you. Now. They have to see this.'

The Prof shook his head. 'And be dismissed as some crackpot? Especially an ex-druggie crackpot? Walking in off the street with a connection to one of the victims? What if I turned out to be wrong?'

'Do you think it's wrong?'

'No.'

'Then do it.' Peta pulled her mobile out of her bag.

'No. I won't.'

Peta looked at him. Felt anger rising again. 'All right, so you don't want to risk being made a fool of. Have the police dredge up your past again. Fair enough. But what about doing this for someone else?'

'Who?'

'Jill.'

The Prof sighed, put his head in his hands. His body seemed to sag. Peta couldn't tell if a great weight had been applied to him or lifted from him.

'Do it,' he said.

Peta didn't wait for him to change his mind. She dialled Nattrass.

Michael Nell stood on the street corner, watching.

Anita was back in the bar, working. He felt a thrill run through him, the like of which he had hardly experienced before. The power he yielded. The sweet power he had over her was immense. He was like Superman. No, not Superman; someone equally powerful, but darker. Lex Luthor. Or Neo in *The Matrix*. The one.

He was having the time of his life. For the first time ever he was in control. Complete control. And it gave him a hard-on he could barely shift, a need he could hardly satisfy. Away from his father, from university. *From expectations*. He was himself. He was free.

He laughed to himself. On the run, but free.

And then there was Anita. He had never met a girl like her. She fitted him so perfectly she could have been designed for him. His soul mate. He had never felt such all-encompassing love for another human being, especially in such a short space of time, as he did with her. He had never felt love before. When they met, when they touched, it was like electricity passed between them. They didn't need to talk: the understanding went deeper than that.

Soul deep.

She was his life, his love, his heart.

His perfect victim.

And he knew nothing would ever force them apart.

His erection was twitching again. He wanted her. Right then and there. But she was working. Giving her body to other men. For money. And that just made him want her all the more.

His whore.

His love.

The door of the bar opened and she emerged, walking arm in arm with a punter over to the hotel. She looked over to him. He blew her a kiss. She turned back to the john, pretended to find what he was saying really interesting. They went through the double doors.

Michael Nell sighed. He could imagine what they were doing in there. But he didn't need to. Later he would ask her and she would tell him. And he would take her again.

His erection was threatening to burst out of his jeans now. He should wait until later, but he couldn't. He looked around for a secluded spot where he could go. Away from pedestrians, CCTV cameras. Somewhere he could relive his fantasies, imagine Anita all over again.

He turned and walked away, his heart full of love.

39

Donovan snapped his old, bulky phone shut, slid it back into his pocket, where it left an unsightly bulge. He didn't have time to care about that now.

'That was Amar,' he said. 'And shit is happening.'

Donovan repeated to Turnbull what Amar had just told him. Kovacs. Katya and Dario Tokic. Decca Ainsley. The cobras. Tyne Dock. He sat back, scarcely able to believe the words that had just come out of his mouth.

'Tell him to stay there,' said Turnbull. 'Wait for uniforms to turn up.'

'He'll be long gone, Turnbull. Phoned 999 anonymously, then he'll have split with Jamal. You think they're going to hang around there? Now?'

Turnbull opened his mouth to answer. Donovan cut him off.

'And, anyway, you're in no position to go issuing official orders.'

Turnbull said nothing, sat staring at Donovan, simmering in silent, dangerous resentment, like a dried-out pan left on an electric hob. Ready to go at any time.

They were sitting in a pub in Bensham, Gateshead. One of a dying breed of literal street-corner pubs. Small, old and with no attempt at décor beyond the basics, it was as familiar a part of the lives of the regulars as their living rooms or bathrooms.

The streets around were old dirty red-brick terraces, front doors facing out directly on to the street. No gardens at the back to speak of. No great treasures inside. A wide-screen TV and Sky Sports the height of luxury. That kind of area.

Donovan and Turnbull sat at a corner table, the rest of the pub giving them a wide berth. They were outsiders, but even worse: one, if not both, was a copper. They could sense it, despite how he was dressed. Years of practice. So pints in front of them, they sat.

They had taken a break from looking for the elusive women in the photos after having come across what could have been a promising lead. By chance, they had found a working girl standing alone on a street corner just off Bewick Road. Rounded more than curvy, her tight, skimpy clothes either an approximation of what she thought would attract the punters or an exercise in self-denial about her actual size. She wasn't doing a very good trade, and her smile had been fixed in place by the time the two men had approached her, hoping against experience that it meant double money. Turnbull had started talking, introducing himself, flashing his warrant card, ignoring the light dimming in her eyes. Donovan had stepped in.

'It's OK,' he said. 'You're not under arrest or anything. You're not going to be moved on. We just need a bit of help.'

The woman, not missing a trick, asked, 'You ganna pay for it, like?'

'Depends if you can help,' said Turnbull. 'We just want you to look at some photos, see if you can identify anyone in them.'

'That's it?'

'That's it.'

'I'm not ganna have to pick anyone out of a line-up, am I? 'Cos if I am I'm not doin' it, like.'

'You won't have to pick anyone out of a line-up,' said Donovan, taking the photos out of his jacket pocket. 'Here.'

He handed them over, looking at her face when she took them. Her eyes had a look he'd seen before, simultaneously sharp and unfocused. A druggie's eyes. Hunger and need balanced with numbing pain relief.

The woman looked through the photos, nothing registering on her face. Then she stopped.

'I know her. Met her before.'

'Where?'

The woman wrinkled her face as she looked closer. 'They're a bit rough, these, aren't they? Tried that. Didn't like it. But sometimes you've got to do what you don't want to do in this life, don't you?'

'Who is she? Where d'you know her from?' Turnbull letting his impatience show.

The woman sighed. 'She used to work this side of the water. In one of the . . .' She cast her eyes down, closed her mouth.

'You can say it,' said Turnbull. 'Nothing's going to happen to you for it.'

'Fuckin' better not, an' all.' She nodded, not quite believing him, but continued. 'In one of the brothels. Down on Saltwell Road. Nice house. Posh. The kind you wouldn't think. She used to have a room next to me. Used to work the same shifts.'

'Can you remember her name?' asked Donovan.

The woman shook her head. 'She was Russian or somethin'. Serbian. Somewhere there. The blokes mindin' her, they were bad bastards. You didn't want to tangle with them. They told her what she had to do. Like it or lump it.'

Donovan interjected, tried to keep her on track. 'D'you know a name? Where these photos were taken?'

The woman thought hard. 'I remember . . . somewhere in Newcastle. There was a few girls went there. Let's see them photos again.'

Donovan handed them back to her. She looked hard at them this time, really studied them.

'Yeah,' she said, pointing to another picture. 'Knew her.' Another one. 'Her an' all. And her.'

Donovan and Turnbull exchanged glances, shrugs. Not knowing if she was telling the truth or off in a fantasy world. 'Do you know where these might have been taken?' Donovan trying to keep her on the right track again. 'Any idea?'

Her eyes were screwed up tight. She could have been thinking hard, or she could have been suffering withdrawal symptoms.

Turnbull waded in. 'Think, please. You could help to catch a killer here.'

Her eyes opened wide. 'A killer? Are all these dead? I never saw them again, like. But then I don't work in the brothels any more. Can't afford the rents. Better off here, like.'

'Please,' said Donovan, 'just think. For a moment. Then we'll be gone. Do you know where these photos were taken?'

Her face brightened, as if a light bulb had gone on in her head. 'They asked me once. If I wanted to go have me photo taken. This must have been it . . .' Behind her, Turnbull shook his head, began to walk away. Donovan persisted.

'Well, where was it? Can you remember?'

'Never stayed in the brothel long enough. Came here before I could go. Don't like it, but, like I say, you've got to do things you don't like in this life.'

Donovan felt like joining Turnbull. 'Can you remember?' He grabbed her shoulders, felt flabby, clammy goose flesh. She looked at him as if in shock, as if seeing him for the first time. 'Can you remember?'

'Somewhere beside the Grainger Market,' she said, her voice like that of an automaton. 'A disused old shop that'd been turned into a studio. On the corner, they said. You can't miss it. Boarded up. Used to sell clothes. An' wool. Fabric. Threads an' that. On the corner.' She shook her head. 'Never went there meself . . .'

Donovan and Turnbull exchanged a glance, nodded.

'Thanks for your time,' said Donovan. 'You've really helped us a lot, er . . .' He frowned. 'What's your name, by the way?'

Fire flashed in her eyes as she stared at him. Like she was a different person. An angry one. 'Fuck's it to you?' She looked between Donovan and Turnbull. 'Yous ganna pay me, then?'

Donovan drew out his wallet, peeled off two twenties, handed them over.

She took them, and they disappeared about her body with practised ease. 'That it?'

Donovan opened his wallet again. Turnbull interjected. 'Yeah,' he said. 'It is.'

He turned away from her, walked off. Donovan followed.

'Bit harsh on her there?' said Donovan.

'Junkie,' said Turnbull, as if that explained everything. 'Only smoke it, stick it in her veins. Time they've reached that stage there's not much you can do.' He looked back. She was still standing there. 'Don't know who's got it worse. Her or them who wants to fuck her.'

They found the pub, entered.

'Who you phonin'? You're meant to be takin' me to Tyne Dock. Now.'

'I'm calling Peta. Since our plans have changed for the evening I'm asking her to pay a visit to the photographer's studio.'

Turnbull snorted, eager to dismiss it, ready to go. 'Think she was telling the truth? She was so fuckin' raddled she could hardly remember who we were. Or who she was. Come on. Tyne Dock.'

Turnbull had called it in. Asked for an armed response team, gave them his name. Told them, with a sly look towards Donovan and a casual glance down at his Kurt Cobain T-shirt and combats, that he was working undercover. Told them exactly what was going down. Told them who they would catch red-handed. Hung up and was ready to go. Wanting to be part of the action, eager for that righteous adrenalin rush. Donovan knew that and still he wouldn't get up.

'It's a lead,' Donovan said. 'Probably better to look at it in the daytime. Doubt there'd be anyone there now, but it wouldn't hurt. Peta's probably in the area. Just ask her to swing by.'

Turnbull drained his pint, gathered his coat about him, made impatient gestures behind Donovan. The phone was answered. Donovan started talking. Peta cut him off, told him what she had discovered.

'I'm with the Prof now,' she said. 'Just phoned Nattrass. Told her.'

Donovan was stunned. 'That's incredible. You sure it's genuine?'

'I think so. Only one way to find out.'

'So you sure he's not . . .'

'I'm sure. Well, I think I'm sure.' There was a pause. He could imagine her smiling. 'Pretty sure.'

'Good. Well, look. Got something for you when you've done that.' He told her about the studio, Turnbull huffing and puffing behind him. Donovan took the hint and started walking. They left the pub. He imagined a huge, collective sigh of relief as they went.

He walked to the car, Turnbull trying to make him hurry, talking into the phone all the while, exchanging information. The rain had started, painting the shabby streets with a greasy sheen. They reached Donovan's Mondeo, got inside.

Donovan finished his conversation, turned to Turnbull. 'Guess what?'

'Tell me when you're drivin'. Come on.'

Donovan put his hands by his side.

Turnbull looked ready to explode. 'What's the matter with you? Come on!'

Donovan passed him the phone. 'You've got to call someone first.'

Turnbull could barely believe what he was hearing. 'The fuck you on about? Come on, we've got to go!'

'Di Nattrass. I think she deserves even a courtesy call. Don't you?'

Turnbull was tightly wound, looked like he was ready to lash out. But the words hit him, connected. 'Fuck off, Dear Deidrie, I'll do it later.'

'Longer you put it off, the harder it'll get. Phone her now while that undercover story you invented still stands up. Tell her what's happening. Damage limitation, Paul. You've got to do it. Sooner or later. Sooner's best.'

Turnbull looked at the phone as if it might bite his hand off if he touched it. Reluctantly, with a sigh of resignation that sounded like an angry growl, he picked it up, punched in a number he knew by heart. Waited.

Donovan turned on the ignition, put the car in gear.

The phone was answered.

'Hello,' he said in a voice that seemed too small for his body. 'It's me.'

Donovan drove away, trying not to listen.

But not able to help himself.

40

Jamal was crying like he had never cried before.

'Hold on, man, just hold on . . .'

He held Amar's body, pressing his jacket against the bullet wound, trying to stanch the flow of blood. Amar's face was twisted in pain, his eyes rolling back in his head. He was shivering from more than just the cold. Shock was setting in.

'Come on, man, it's me. It's Jamal. You can't die, man, you can't die . . .'

Jamal had watched Amar get shot from the other side of the road, powerless to do anything about it. As soon as he saw what had happened, he had jumped behind the steering wheel of the Volvo, revved it up, hit the headlights and, in his best *Grand Theft Auto* style, moved it forward. Tokic had been poised to fire again but had run back to his car on hearing the noise. Leaving Jamal cradling Amar.

'Jamal . . .' Amar tried to grip Jamal's arm. Jamal took his fingers, held them tight.

'I'm here, man, I'm here. I'm not goin' nowhere.'

Amar's breathing became heavier. Jamal held him harder.

'Don't go, man, don't go. Stay. Stay with me.' He clung on to him, tried to find the right words. Words that would comfort, soothe. Heal. Save his life. 'Who'm I gonna play *Grand Theft Auto* with, eh? Who?'

Amar gave a weak smile.

'That's it, man, hold on. Hold on.' Impotent emotion welled inside him. He looked at his friend lying there, help-less. Willed him to get up. 'Come on, Amar. You can do it, man. I made a promise, didn't I? A promise to Joe. That I would look after you. Let no harm come to you. I made a promise . . .'

He heard sirens: distant, getting quickly nearer.

'Just hold on, man, hold on. They're coming . . .'

Donovan sat in the Mondeo, stared at the road in front of him. The rain rendered the windscreen liquid, making what few cars went past little blurs of wet, rushing sparkle against the night.

Tyne Dock. The Port of Tyne Authority car park. This far, for Donovan, and no further. Low-level, red-brick administration offices behind him, interior lights sparse. The dock itself a huge, sprawling complex with areas for containers, rail, an enormous amount of warehouse space and a sea service that covered, among other places, Scandinavia and the Baltic. And all the action, Donovan thought, was happening on the dock front itself. It felt like it was miles away. It could have been miles away.

He sighed. Played Turnbull's last conversation again in his head.

'Fuck off.' Donovan was getting out of the car.

'I said you're staying here. Last thing we need is a fuckin' civilian messin' everythin' up.'

'Oh, so I'm a civilian now, am I, is that it? You were keen enough for my help earlier. When no one else wanted to know you.'

Turnbull reddened slightly. 'Sorry. But that's the way it is. You have to wait here.'

'OK,' said Donovan. 'Makes sense. After all, you're in enough trouble already without me turning up. Might say something embarrassing. Don't want that, do you?'

Turnbull got hurriedly out of the car, actually growling. Donovan couldn't let that one slip past.

'Were you growling? Actually making bear noises?'

He received a mumbled 'fuck off, wait there' as his reply, and Turnbull walked off.

So Donovan had waited. And he wasn't happy.

He looked around, saw nothing, heard nothing. The adrenalin rush was still there, running around his system, waiting to be utilized. He had to do something. He hadn't come all this way to sit in a car park.

The security guard in the gatehouse looked as bored as Donovan felt. He had seen Turnbull talking to him, assumed he was issuing him with instructions not to let Donovan into the main area.

Well, fuck that.

He pulled his old mobile out of his pocket, put it to his ear. Started the car at the same time, swung it towards the barrier. The guard was a round, grey-haired cheerful man smelling of mints, on the wrong side of middle age and with a strawberry nose to match. He got up from his portable TV, crossed to the window. Donovan stopped, held up the mobile.

'Detective Sergeant Turnbull,' he said. 'Just got a call from him. Got to go through. Now.' He revved the car up.

'I'm sorry, sir,' the guard began. 'I've got orders . . .'

Donovan extended his arm, waved the phone out of the window, pumped up the urgency in his voice. 'Do you want to tell him? He said now.'

The guard, obviously not one for confrontation, opened the barrier. Donovan waved the kind of thank you a man would if he was in a hurry and went through.

Once inside, he realized he had no idea where he was going. It was massive, much bigger than he had imagined, with long sheds down one side of the road, great piles of scrap metal on another. Tractors and JCBs parked further along, what looked like metal feed silos behind them. He tried to think rationally: where would Turnbull be?

Containers. That would be how they were getting the girls in. Import–export, wasn't that Kovacs' official job title? Containers. And cranes to get them off and on the ships. That's what he would look for.

He would drive around until he found them, decide what to do next when he was there.

Turnbull sat in the observation room at the Port of Tyne Authority. In front of him was a bank of screens relaying, at regular intervals, CCTV pictures from around the dock. He had particularly asked for attention to be focused on the container areas.

Beside him sat Bob Grant, a sandy-haired, fit-looking DI in his mid-thirties. Dressed in combats and an army parka, he was off duty but on point. Turnbull had been put through to him with his information. Turnbull was impressed: Grant had been off duty, but in the time it took Turnbull to drive from Bensham to Tyne Dock he had managed to get permission for and assemble an armed rapid-response unit and position them at strategic places, with the help of several Port of Tyne staff, around the docks on standby.

The security manager had gone to great lengths to describe how it was impossible for smuggling to take place on a modern dock such as this one. Anxious to be believed, he had repeated the information over and over until Turnbull had asked him, politely but firmly, to shut up. He had done. The two policemen then concentrated only on the screens.

'You sure this tip-off is genuine?' asked Bob Grant, not for the first time.

'Absolutely,' replied Turnbull. 'No doubt about the source.'

Grant had already asked how it could be coming in at this

time. There was no workforce, no one to unload. No ship down to be unloaded.

'Maybe they're bringing their own help,' he had said, becoming irritated. 'Look, you believe it or you wouldn't be here.'

Grant, having no reply, had fallen silent.

Turnbull's call to Nattrass had gone surprisingly well, he thought. Donovan, he grudgingly admitted, had been right. He was glad he had done it. There was still some way to go, some serious bridge building to be done, and she hadn't for one minute believed him when he had said he had gone undercover and been working on his own initiative. He hadn't believed that himself. But it was something to be worked out later. Right now, he had a job to do.

He and Grant kept concentrating on the screens.

In the surrounding darkness, the containers, stacked neatly on top of one another, colour and size coded, and with road-width alleyways in between, looked like a city in miniature. Both simultaneously permanent and temporary. Half brutally futurist, half shantytown. The rain, the overhead lighting, the screen relay, increased the feeling of grimness and foreboding. Looking from screen to screen, the containers were stacked for what seemed like miles, the driveways and alleyways offering a variety of shadowed concealment.

Turnbull wondered how long some of those containers had been there. Wondered just what might have been left inside. Secrets lost or buried.

They kept looking, eyes flickering from one screen to another.

Grant sighed, rubbed his eyes. Getting ready to speak again.

'Look,' he said. 'Are you sure . . . ?'

Here we go, thought Turnbull.

★

Decca was finally on the right road.

It had taken some time, unfamiliar as he was with being south of the river, but more by luck than judgement he had seen a sign pointing to Tyne Dock and followed it, like a drowning diver clinging to his final air line.

He had driven up to the gates, aware all the time of Tokic's gun sticking in his back. BMWs were good, he thought, but he doubted that their upholstery would stop a bullet. He stopped, leaned across to the glove compartment, opened it. Felt cold metal on the back of his neck.

'What are you doing?' Tokic's voice.

'Getting my security pass,' Decca said in a voice that he didn't recognize as his own. 'Won't let me in without it.'

'No tricks.'

No tricks, thought Decca. Did people really say that?

He got his pass out, let the window slide down. Ignored the rain being blown on to his face. He showed the pass to the elderly guard, smiled.

The guard nodded, then leaned closer and said, 'Who've you got with you?'

Decca blinked at the fumes. Whatever the guard was drinking it clearly had clinical applications. 'They're with me,' he tried to say in as breezy a manner as possible. 'No problems.'

'They need passes too,' said the guard.

Decca felt the gun being moved away from his back, heard a click. Knew it was pointing at the guard in his box.

'OK,' said Decca, trying to quell the panic in his voice. 'Have you got some I could use?'

The guard smiled. 'You gotta check with the office for them. An' they're closed.'

Decca felt the gun being moved, the target being focused in the sights.

Decca reached into his pocket, brought out a crumpled twenty, handed it over. 'What about that? That OK?'

The guard laughed. 'That'll do nicely, sir.'

The barrier was raised. Decca put the car into gear, drove through.

Felt the gun being repositioned against his back.

Thought seriously about seeking another career.

41

'So what d'you think?'

Peta looked between the two detectives, waiting for an answer.

She sat next to the Prof in DCI Fenton's office, papers, books and files spread out before them. The Prof had just finished explaining his theory to both Fenton and Nattrass. The two glanced at each other, faces impassive.

'You say,' began Nattrass, not proceeding before receiving a nod from Fenton, 'that there should be some kind of ritualistic aspect to the way the bodies were left?'

The Prof nodded. 'If my hypothesis is correct, it would make logical sense.'

'And what do you think that would be?'

The Prof shrugged, looked uneasy. He had talked with Peta on the way there. Reluctant to divulge his source to Fenton and Nattrass, he had decided to claim that the whole thing was his idea. 'I can only speculate,' he said. 'As I said, pennies over the eyes, mouth sewn shut. Some kind of embalming, mummification, I don't know.'

Another glance between Fenton and Nattrass.

'Just out of curiosity,' said Fenton, 'do you have a contact on this investigation?'

The Prof looked down, shook his head. 'No.'

Peta was beginning to share the Prof's uneasiness; they exchanged glances of their own. Peta had called Nattrass, asked her over to the university. Nattrass had insisted they meet at Market Street police station as she couldn't leave her desk at present. Peta had put that to the Prof. Reluctantly, and after much persuasion, he had agreed to come to the station. But she knew he was unhappy about it. More than unhappy.

'You know how some people have a fear of hospitals?' he had said to Peta in his office before leaving. 'How they think once they go into hospital they'll never come out again?'

She had nodded.

'I feel the same about police stations.'

Peta had thought that was just an old stoner's paranoia, but listening to the way the questions seemed to be going, she wasn't so sure.

Fenton sat behind his desk, hoping, it seemed to Peta, that it would give him a natural air of authority. 'And the night of Jill Tennant's disappearance,' he said, 'you were . . . where, exactly?'

The Prof cleared his throat. 'At a Wilco concert. Waiting for Jill. As you know. As I've been cleared for.'

Another look between Nattrass and Fenton.

'There's quite a file on you here, Mr McAllister,' said Fenton, his gaze steely and even. 'From way back.'

'Look, are we suspects here?' asked Peta angrily.

'Suspects?' said Fenton. 'What makes you say that?'

'You just seem to be ignoring what we've actually brought you. And wasting our time with pointless questions.'

'Those questions aren't pointless,' said Fenton. He seemed to regret the words as soon as they escaped his lips.

'Yes they bloody are,' said Peta, jumping on them. She stood up. 'There's a killer out on the streets. We've brought you something that could be a big help in catching him. And all you can do is sit there behind your desk and play "My Cock's Bigger than Yours". Well, fuck you. We'll go.' She began gathering the papers on the desk together. 'Take our theory somewhere else if you're not interested. The papers, perhaps.'

Another glance between the two police. A more worried one this time. Nattrass came forward.

'Don't do that, Peta. Please.'

Peta stopped, looked at her.

'Yes, we are interested.'

'And?'

Nattrass turned to Fenton, who gave a sigh, an irritable nod.

'You're not suspects.'

Without looking, she knew the Prof was breathing a huge sigh of relief. 'Thank you. Apologies all round, I think,' she said. She looked at Fenton. He couldn't hold her eyes.

'That was unprofessional of me under the circumstances,' he said to the desk. 'And I apologize unreservedly.'

Peta gave a brittle smile. 'So now we're communicating. What next?'

Fenton looked at the two of them, clearly unhappy at having his authority attacked in his own office, but not risking upsetting them any further. 'It's a good theory,' he said. 'I like it. Think it has weight. Leave it with us. We'll follow it up.'

'That's it?' said Peta.

Fenton looked genuinely puzzled. 'What were you expecting?'

Peta let it go, said nothing.

Fenton pointed to the papers on the desk. 'May I?'

'They're to be returned to me afterwards,' said the Prof, his voice slightly uncertain.

Fenton nodded.

'I'll see you out,' said Nattrass.

She saw them to the main door. Outside, the rain was getting into its stride. Nattrass stopped and turned, offered her hand.

'Sorry about that,' she said, her tone conciliatory. 'To

both of you. But especially you, Mr McAllister. And for what I said the other day. It was uncalled for. I'm sure what you brought us will be a big help.'

The Prof shook hands without looking at her. Said nothing. Peta made goodbyes on his behalf. Nattrass turned and walked away.

'Hate police stations,' he said, once she was out of earshot.

'I can see why.'

'But thank you.'

'No problem.' Peta allowed herself a small sigh.

Joe Donovan would have been proud of me, she thought.

Nattrass made it back to the office as fast as she could. Fenton was waiting for her, poring over the Prof's notes.

'What do you think?' she asked.

'Fucking dynamite,' he said, more animated than he had been in front of the two members of the public. 'That's what I think. Worth having to kowtow to that old hippie to get this. Di, get a team in and on to this straight away. Don't worry about overtime. Our academic friend has saved us the expense of calling in a profiler, so we can afford to be a bit more generous. As long as it gets results.' He looked at the file, sifted through the sheets. 'And I'm sure it will,' he said, 'I'm sure it will. Parameters, he said. The right parameters. Well, we've got them now. I feel sure of it. It's only a matter of time, Di. Only a matter of time.'

Nattrass turned, left the office. Buzzing once again.

She could feel it too.

The Historian was hunting.

Down on the quayside, making one last desperate trawl. They were on to him, he could feel it. The net was closing in. He had always thought that phrase was just so much tabloid cliché. But that was exactly how he felt. Like an invisible net was encircling him, his would-be captors just waiting for him to step out of line, press the hidden switch that would activate the trap.

When he realized that was what was happening, his first reaction was to do nothing. Stand immobile like a statue, play dead. Bury his head in the sand. Whatever, just wait for them to go away. But that was just as bad as doing something. That would be like waiting for them, welcoming them with a cup of tea, almost. Anything, looked at it that way, would be the wrong thing to do.

And there was his work. His research. He had to finish it, had to find definitive answers. Yes or no. Yes or no. Had to. So the decision almost made itself. He prioritized. The work was the most important thing. It was what he had to do. It was what the spirits were telling him to do. Urging him on. He had to honour them. He had to keep going.

So there he was, walking slowly along the quayside, pushing his wheelchair. People all around him, bar hopping, going to and from restaurants, Baltic and the Sage music centre. Relaxed, looking for pleasure, entertainment. And him standing out. The only one of them with a purpose, an agenda.

He pushed his way through them, not caring that they could see there was no one in the wheelchair, nothing but a bundle of old clothes wrapped around a dummy. Hurrying as he went, knocking the strollers left and right.

He didn't care. Let them see him, let them gawp. He didn't care.

He had the angry hiss of the spirits in his ears. Cajoling, shouting even. He had the weight of history bearing down on him.

He had work to do.

He moved past the end of Dean Street, past the old

Guildhall, down under the High Level Bridge. The lights became more sporadic at this point, the crowd thinner. It would be easier to pick off the stragglers, the ones who might not be so easily missed.

The bars and clubs petered out. Only one bar left and a hotel. A businessman's hotel.

He knew what kind of women hung around those places. He smiled to himself. Almost like old times.

He stopped on a corner, the entrance to Long Stairs behind him. The winding, badly lit old stone steps that led from the quayside to the old Keep. He pulled the chair in and waited.

But not for long. A girl came out of the hotel, made her way across the road. She seemed to be headed for the bar but stopped, looked around. As if she was waiting for someone.

The Historian took her in. Blonde, slim, young. Whorishly dressed.

She would do.

He made up his mind, crossed to her. Satisfied there was no one else about. He would have seen them while he was waiting. He had to catch her while she was still undecided about what to do next.

'Excuse me,' he said in his mildest, most inoffensive voice, making a big production out of pushing the chair up and over the pavement, hand already tightening on his hidden stun gun. 'Could you help me, please?'

The girl gave one last look around, shook her head, crossed to him.

'Yes?' she said, her accent Eastern European.

He smiled, readied the gun.

He had her.

Peta stood on the steps of Market Street police station, looked at the rain, putting off moving out into it. She pulled her coat around her. The Prof stood next to her, unmoving.

'Listen,' she said. 'I feel I should apologize. For breaking into your office. And suspecting you of being a murderer.'

The Prof laughed. 'Forgiven.'

She nodded. 'Thank you.'

He nodded in return.

'Your mate's going to be pissed off,' she said. 'Missing out on handing his theory over.'

'I'm sure he'll get over it.'

They both looked at the rain.

'Listen,' the Prof said. 'Would you care to get something to eat? Or a drink, perhaps?'

It was Peta's turn to smile. 'I would love to. But,' she said quickly, before he got his hopes up, 'I'm still working. I've still got a job to do tonight.'

The Prof nodded. 'How many knock-backs can one man take?'

'It's not that. I do have to work. Honestly.'

'So,' said the Prof to hide his obvious embarrassment, 'what is it you do, exactly? As well as being a student, of course.'

Peta smiled again, looked him in the eyes. 'I'll tell you sometime. Maybe when we go for that drink.'

'Right.' The Prof laughed, understanding her words. 'Right.'

'But I really have to go.' She extended her hand. 'See you tomorrow.'

He shook it. 'Tomorrow.'

She turned, walked off into the rain, pulling the paper out of her pocket which had the address Donovan had given her.

Probably be no one there, she thought, not at this time. But still, worth a try.

Just one last thing for the night.

And then home.

42

Turnbull kept watching.

They had trained the CCTV cameras on the warehouse section of the dock. One in particular. Kovacs'. As an importer-exporter he had his own dedicated warehouse on Tyne Dock.

Turnbull and Grant had focused initially on the containers, thinking something was about to happen there, but when nothing did they turned their attention to the warehouses.

They didn't have to wait long.

'Here we go,' said Grant.

They watched as a soft-top BMW pulled up to a stop outside the warehouse. Both men sat forward, as if that would make them see better. The driver got out, closed the door behind him. As he looked around, checking the area, they got a good look at him on the CCTV.

Grant smiled.

'Decca Ainsley.' He laughed. 'You're nicked.' He reached for his radio. 'Time to rally the troops.'

Turnbull put a restraining hand on his arm. 'Wait.'

Grant looked at him. 'What for?'

'Decca Ainsley? He's nobody. And he's done nothing. We can pick him up any day of the week. We want what's inside. We want who's inside. Just wait.'

Grant looked at him, ready to argue. Although it was against his core instincts, Turnbull knew he was going to have to use diplomacy.

'Get him and we've got nothing. The rest'll probably run. Then wriggle out of it in court if we catch them. Just wait a little while and we'll have them bang to rights.' He smiled, said words that didn't come naturally to him. 'Patience. 'It'll be worth it.'

Grant sat back, replaced the radio.

'Fuckin' better be,' he said.

Decca got out of the car, looked around. No one about. The rain had really started now. Coming down in wind-whipped lashes, catching exposed skin like a slap from icy stinging nettles. He pulled his leather jacket around him, made his way to the main door. Weighed up his options.

He knew what was about to happen, tried to formulate the best strategy for his personal survival.

He could run. Hope whoever survived wouldn't come after him. Hunt him down. He rejected that idea. No good. Too many chances.

He could walk away. Have nothing to do with any of it. Again, a rejection. Spend the rest of his life living looking over his shoulder. He doubted he could run far enough from Kovacs.

Third option: he could walk in there, brave out the shitstorm that was about to hit. Find somewhere to hide, come out when the fighting was over. No good. Too many variables. Of the stray bullet variety.

Last option: walk tall into there, tell Christopher what was about to happen. Make the signal to Dario and Katya, lure them in. Get him ready, prepared. Good one. Only problem with that: Christopher might make him fight back. Still, it was a chance he'd have to take.

The only chance he had. Was that what Clint would do? No. But then Clint wouldn't get his gun taken off him so easily either.

He knocked. Waited. Heard a muffled response.

'Decca,' he said, looking up at the camera mounted above the door. 'Open the fuckin' door, it's freezin' out here.'

The door opened. Too slowly, Decca thought, like they were taking the piss.

Like they knew something was up.

He swallowed the thought as the door rolled open. Went inside. It rolled shut behind him.

He shook the water from his arms and head, tried not to let his nervousness show.

The warehouse had a wide, central striplit area with shelves on all sides rising high up to the ceiling, going back deep into shadow. Filled with all manner of appliances Kovacs' company imported: consumer electricals, household items. Restaurant fixtures and fittings. Anything and everything that could be bought and sold. All neatly racked, compartmentalized and catalogued. The whole thing screamed 'legit', invited inspections.

In the centre of the space sat an articulated lorry rig, a container fixed to the back. Next to it a large, Transit-sized people carrier, the windows tinted to blackness. Decca knew the container would have been loaded on to the lorry from the ship earlier in the day then driven around to the warehouse and parked up until nightfall, when it could be safely dealt with. That was how they usually did it.

Leaning against the shelves, not bothering to hide the guns they were carrying, were two of Kovacs' most trusted thugs. Milo and Lev, Decca knew them as. Both Bosnian, he presumed, both wearing Kovacs' unofficial henchman uniform of black-leather jacket, jeans, sweatshirt, steel-toe-capped work boots. Both swarthy and unshaven, with thick black hair. Like an evil Tweedledum and Tweedledee, distinguishable only by the fact that one's mullet was slightly shorter than the other's. Decca had tried, unsuccessfully, to hold conversations with them, but they had just nodded and smiled, claiming not to speak English. He had taken their claims at face value, but at times he had caught smirks and nods between them from the corner of his eye that made him think they understood more than they were letting on. He could work with them. But he didn't trust them.

'Where's Christopher?' he asked one of them. Lev, he thought. The one with the shorter mullet.

Lev shrugged, made a vague gesture to the back of the warehouse which was both directional and dismissive.

Decca swallowed hard. 'Is he here?'

An imperceptible nod. Mocking eyes fixing him with a condescending look.

'He says get doors open,' said the other one. Milo, thought Decca. His mullet was longer. 'Get going.'

Decca looked around, saw no sign of Christopher. 'I want to speak to him. Now.'

Milo detached himself from the shelf he had been leaning against, started a slow walk towards Decca. There was menace in it. Danger. He stood next to Decca, face to face. Close enough for Decca to know what he had been eating. Close enough to know it wasn't very fragrant.

'Open doors,' he repeated.

Decca swallowed hard. Opened his mouth to speak again then thought better of it.

Milo turned, walked towards the back of the lorry, started to undo the locks.

Third option, he thought.

Everyone for himself.

Michael Nell was becoming frantic.

He emerged from the shadows feeling refreshed. His libido wasn't diminished; if anything it was heightened. He couldn't wait to see her. He hadn't felt excitement like that for years. Like a kid with a new toy.

But there was no sign of Anita anywhere.

He checked his watch. Surely she should have finished by now? It couldn't have taken him that long. He ran into the bar, had a look around. No sign of her. He stood in the middle of the road, literally not knowing which way to turn, barely aware of the rain lashing down on him. Taking ragged, panic-filled breaths. Running between the hotel and the bar.

Had she run away? Was she still in the room? He didn't know. And the not-knowing was beginning to consume him.

He looked at the hotel doorway. Anita's client was coming out, heading back to the bar across the road. He ran towards him. The man saw him coming, a look of fear spreading over his face. He turned, tried to make it back inside the safety of the glass double doors. Nell was too quick for him. He reached the man, grabbed hold of his jacket lapels.

'Where is she?' He almost spat the words into the man's terrified face.

'Whuh – who?'

'You know who. The girl you've just fucked. Where is she?'

'I . . . I don't know. She came out ages ago. I . . . I let her go first. Phoned home afterwards, talked to my wife . . .'

Nell let him go, turned away from him.

Panic was rising, threatening to engulf him. He looked over to the badly lit street corner, an old, disused ware-house, which the quayside's gentrification process hadn't yet reached, bordering the steep incline of Forth Banks. Saw something lying on the pavement, glinting in the meagre streetlighting. The rain making it glisten like a diamond. He crossed over, picked it up.

Felt his legs go weak.

Anita's chain. The one he had given her.

You belong to me now . . .

He gripped it hard, felt the wet metal dig into the palm of his hand. Turned left and right, hoping for a glimpse of her, a clue to where she could have gone.

He ran to the end of the block, looked up Long Stairs. No one there. He listened: no footfalls.

He ran to the other end of the block, looked up the steep slope of Forth Banks.

Saw a figure near the top, pushing a wheelchair. Hurrying.

Like he was trying to get away. Make an escape.

'Hey, stop . . .' he shouted.

The figure didn't stop. If anything, he ran faster.

Nell, with no option left, began to run up the hill.

Nattrass was buzzing. Almost physically vibrating. So much and so fast she felt she could levitate from the earth.

She stood in the incident room, the majority of the murder investigation team around her. They had come in bleary-eyed, disgruntled, several of them smelling of post-work alcohol. All of them resentful of the hours, all of them grateful for the overtime.

She had talked to them, told them what they would be doing, set them in motion. Now there were no more bleary eyes, no more disgruntled faces. And they all had a better buzz than the alcohol had given them. They shared the same one as her.

The anticipation of being close to catching a murderer.

The righteous thrill of nailing a killer.

And they would. Soon.

She could feel it.

They had taken the information the Prof had supplied

them with, cross-referenced it with what she herself had learned, plus records they had already been working through. Sifting through names, addresses, looking for previous form in a specified geographical area. It felt to her like they were lining up the cross-hairs on the scope of a sniper's rifle. Framing the suspect, just looking for the final trigger.

'Got one.'

The whole team looked around. A PC on secondment, Davy Hutton, she thought his name was, looked up. He was sitting at his computer, connected to the National Crime Computer. 'Got him,' he said again. 'This is him. I bet this is him.'

Nattrass felt she should say something, advise caution, but she didn't. Swept up in the atmosphere, she joined the rest of the team in gathering around him.

'Tell us,' she said.

Davy Hutton looked at the screen, read off what he had found.

'Graham Harris,' he said, barely able to keep the excitement out of his voice. 'Lives in the west end of Newcastle. The triangle you said, boss. Shares a home with his crippled mother.' He looked harder at the screen. 'No, wait a minute, she died. Two years ago, nearly three. Still lives in the same house, though.'

'What have you got on him?' asked Nattrass, trying to read the screen.

Hutton scrolled the information down, read it off. 'Exposing himself. Got off with a caution. That was a bit ago, mind. Low level. But he's been building himself up. Here's another. Attempted rape. Dropped. Another caution.'

'Sounds like our man.' Nattrass struggled to keep the triumphalism from her voice.

'Why hasn't he been flagged up earlier, then?' asked a DS

at the back, not bothering to hide the anger in his voice. 'Why isn't he on the register?'

'No charges, no record,' said Nattrass, looking at the screen, reading. 'The attempted rape . . . What about that . . . ?' She read on. Knowing there would be a reason why they hadn't looked at him sooner. Hoping the screen would show her it.

'Don't think . . . Here. Yes, here it is. Altercation with a prostitute. Charges dropped. Well, one word against another there. How hard are those cases to prove? But look after this. Schizophrenia. Mental illness, history of it. Hearing voices, the lot. It's all here.' She gave a grim smile. 'Referred for psychiatric help. Given medication.'

The same DS snorted. 'Can't be much good.'

'Or he hasn't been taking it,' said Nattrass. 'That's how he kept under the radar. No further charges. Let's see if he's got a job . . .'

Hutton scrolled further down.

A *frisson* ran through Nattrass.

'Centurion Security,' she said. 'Didn't have to declare a criminal record because he hasn't got one. Centurion Security . . .'

Hutton frowned. Then got it.

'Centurion Security. They provide security guards for—'

Nattrass finished the sentence for him. 'The university.'

That news ran around the room like an electric current.

'Crippled mother . . .' Nattrass frowned. 'Fuck . . . Crippled. She would have had a wheelchair.'

Nattrass took deep breaths. She straightened up, felt suddenly light-headed. Fenton appeared next to her, looked at her. She could see he was feeling the same way too.

'Let's get the t's crossed and the i's dotted,' he said,

addressing the room. 'Do it properly. No room for error. We don't want to fuck this one up.'

'And we won't,' said Nattrass, addressing both the room and Fenton. 'Let's get it sorted. Let's go get the fucker.'

It was an order she wouldn't have to make twice.

Jamal stood at the front desk of the Accident and Emergency Department at Newcastle General Hospital. He looked around anxiously, hoping to catch a glimpse of Amar.

He had ridden in the ambulance, the paramedics not asking too many awkward questions, just concentrating on keeping Amar alive. He imagined the police would arrive sometime, would deal with that when it happened.

The paramedics had stretchered Amar, attached various drips and tubes and moved him into the back of the ambulance, taking off, sirens and lights going, for the General.

Then it was straight through the double doors and away. Jamal had tried to follow, but his route had been barred. The desk staff had fired questions at him, and he had answered as best he could, writing down his answers. Then pointed him to a seat, left him alone to wait.

He looked around at the other people waiting, sitting on plastic chairs, balancing boredom with pain. Most of them, with bloodied clothes and wadding held against their faces, looked like the results of pub fights. Some of home accidents. A couple of children sat there, younger than Jamal, looking very scared. They were waved through before the others.

Jamal waited. He played over the scene again and again in his mind. Each time thinking of something he could have done, a way he could have saved Amar. If only he had been quicker. If only he had been able to warn Amar. If only. If only. Every permutation until he had just about driven himself insane with it.

A nurse was crossing the floor, striding purposefully towards him. She looked as if she would have been pretty under less stressful circumstances. He stood up immediately.

'Mr Miah is in surgery,' she said.

'Is he . . . ?' He couldn't bring himself to complete the question. Not caring how much like a cheap TV cliché he sounded.

'He's critical but stable.'

'Right.' He had heard those words used on TV too. He knew they could mean anything.

'Can I see him?'

'Not yet, I'm afraid. He's still in surgery.' She reached over the desk, produced a clipboard. 'We'll need to get some more information.'

'OK.'

'Right. First off, next of kin?' she asked, looking directly at him.

Jamal thought. Remembered words from earlier in the day. About how families were more than just biology.

'Me,' he said. 'That'll be me.'

Felt his heart swell with pride when he said it.

43

'What was that? Down there?' Turnbull pointed at the screen.

Grant followed his finger. 'Where?'

'Side of the warehouse. Thought I saw something. Or someone. Movement. In the shadows.' He turned to Grant. 'One of our boys?'

Grant shook his head. 'Too close. Embedded further back. Waiting for the call.'

The two of them kept looking. Hard. Eyes screwed up, squinting.

'See it again?' asked Grant, blinking.

Turnbull shook his head, kept his eyes on the screen.

'Keep looking, then.'

Turnbull bit back his reply.

He didn't need to be told what to do.

Katya and Dario Tokic made their way through the alleyways between the warehouses. Katya had Decca's gun clenched tightly in her fist, her brother his. They hadn't spoken since Dario had made Decca pull over and they had got out, walking to Kovacs' warehouse, using shadows and the night for cover. The rain hid their footsteps.

They reached the warehouse they wanted. Dario risked a glimpse around the corner. He pulled back into the darkness quickly.

'It is there,' he whispered. 'The car is there. He did not run away.'

'Do we go in yet?' asked Katya, breathing shallowly, hard.

'We wait. For the signal. Then we go in.'

Dario looked around. Took in the cranes, the river beyond. Rain hit hard, drops smashing down like machine-gun spray, making the water jump as if in an agonizing dance of death.

'We wait,' he said again, his hot breath turning to vapour in the cold. 'We wait.'

The double doors of the container were opened. Inside, packed floor to ceiling and seemingly front to far back, were cardboard boxes containing flatscreen plasma TVs. Decca climbed up, pulled out the box nearest to him, handed it down to Milo. Or Lev. Then another box. Then another. Until a makeshift walkway had been created leading to the back. He walked along it.

Three-quarters along the length of the container he came to the back wall. Hidden by the boxes and looking to an enquiring eye like a seamless part of the interior was a concealed door, overlapped by the metal corrugations of the wall. Decca knew where it was, felt along for the latch. Found it. Flipped open a concealed lock, was presented with a padlock. He reached into his pocket, brought out the key. Undid it and, not without effort, pulled the door open.

The stink that hit him made him recoil. A mixture of unwashed, confined bodies and all the human smells associated with them. He swallowed hard, tried to breathe shallowly, put a defensive hand across his mouth.

'Come on, ladies, out you get.'

One by one they emerged: slowly, cautiously. Fearfully. Made their way down the cardboard box passage on unsteady legs, were helped down from the container by Milo and Lev. They stood on the concrete floor, squinting in the harsh striplighting, holding their small bags, the sum total of their possessions, before their bodies like shields.

Decca followed them out, stood on the ground before them. Did a head count. Twelve. The correct number.

'Welcome to Britain,' he said, starting his usual spiel. 'Please hand your papers to my two associates.'

Milo and Lev translated. Not for the first time, Decca wondered what they actually said to them as they forcibly removed passports and identity documents from the girls. They would be kept, collateral against the debt they had incurred by getting out of the trailer. A debt that would never be paid, would be always rising, no matter how long and how hard they worked for Kovacs. And Decca knew they would be worked hard.

Decca looked at them. Tried not to see them as hungry, tired, scared girls, many not yet out their teens, dehumanized and broken as they tried to make a better life for themselves, but the way Kovacs encouraged him to look at them. The way he had to look at them if he wanted to survive in this business. As commodities. Meat to be bartered, traded. And above all used. He tried. Succeeded.

And in that moment he saw his way out. He smiled to himself, wondered why he hadn't spotted it earlier.

'Well, ladies,' he said, 'if you would be so kind as to get into this.' He gestured to the people carrier. 'Bit of a squeeze, I know, but nothing like what you've been used to.'

He knew they barely understood a word he was saying, but that didn't matter. He enjoyed the sound of his own voice. Should have been a ringmaster, he thought. All he needed was his top hat and whip.

Milo and Lev roughly herded them into the people carrier.

Brilliant, thought Decca. Get in, drive out and be miles away from the docks when anything kicks off.

But one girl obviously hadn't read the script. As Milo and Lev tried to force her into the back of the car, copping several rough feels as they did so, she resisted. She pulled her arm away from them, screaming at them to let her go.

Amazed, they momentarily dropped their grip on her. In that instant she made a bolt for the door, clawing at the frame, frantically trying to find a switch, a lever, anything that would open the door and let her out.

Decca stood there, too surprised to move. Milo and Lev moved towards her but didn't reach her.

A shot rang out. Then another. And another.

The girl jerked, hit the door three times, then fell to the cold concrete floor. Dead.

Decca looked at her body. Blood fountained and pooled, arced and sprayed. Flesh and chipped bone came to rest around and about her. He looked up.

Christopher had detached himself from the shadows, was walking towards the centre of the warehouse, gun extended.

'Shift that,' he said to Decca, pointing at the body.

Decca, not wanting to but not daring to argue, tentatively pulled the girl's body to one side, left her there.

He turned, his need to get out of there even more imperative. He would drive them away as fast as he could. He didn't care if he got stopped. He could claim they were workers for the café. Let the lawyers work it out. Just get out of there.

The girls were in the people carrier, cowering and cowed. Some had screamed, some were sobbing. Some were beyond both.

'Right,' said Decca, looking at his watch, 'let's go.'

Katya and Dario heard the shots, looked at each other. They didn't have to speak. They knew the sound.

For a few seconds Katya was back in her village with

Dario, watching their family being butchered, hiding from the Snake. She felt the tightening in her chest, tingling in her body as terror began to overtake her.

She breathed hard and fast. Felt like she was going to collapse.

'Dario . . . Dario . . . I can't . . . I can't . . .'

'Yes, you can,' said Dario. 'Yes, you can. That was him. In there. Doing that. Someone has died. That could have been us he shot. Or our mother. Our father. We have to do this. Understand? We have to.'

He grabbed her by the shoulders as he spoke, eyes boring into hers. He kept them on her, unblinking, holding her fast, his fingers digging in to clothing, skin. Held her until she sighed, relented.

'Yes?' he said.

She nodded. 'Yes.'

'Good.'

Then came the sobbing: muffled by the thick walls of the warehouse but again unmistakable.

And Katya was back somewhere else. Somewhere closer. The warehouse. *This* warehouse.

It was where she had come when she first arrived in Britain. Stepping out from the back of a container that had been her residence – she couldn't call it home – for the previous few weeks. She had thought there was nothing else they could have stripped her of. But she was wrong. They took every last vestige of her humanity. She was only now getting it back.

She broke away from Dario, tears beginning to well in the corners of her eyes. 'No . . .'

Dario turned, looked at her, exasperation etched on his features. 'We have been through this . . .'

'No,' she said again. 'Those screams, those girls . . . that was me. In there . . . My God, me . . .'

It hadn't been Decca then, but someone like him. They were all the same. Herding and prodding, using, abusing. Casually and cruelly crushing what dreams remained. She couldn't go in there. Not again.

'No,' she said, shaking her head, 'I can't do it. I can't go through with it.'

'Katya . . .' Dario grabbed her shoulders again. 'We were both there. I remember too. That's why we have to do this. Take the power of those memories away. For ever.'

She shook him off, close to hysteria. 'No, Dario, I cannot do it. Please, please do not make me . . . no.'

He sighed, expelling angry exasperation. Bit back what he wanted to say. Instead said, 'Give me the gun.'

She meekly handed it over. He turned away from her, keeping whatever opinions he had of her to himself. Looked around, took a couple of deep breaths.

'Wait here. Be safe. I go.'

He began to move, guns ready. Face set hard as granite, eyes as hot as lava. Katya remained where she was.

Dario stepped from the shadows. And stopped.

A car was pulling up right in front of the warehouse. Headlights on full, dazzling him.

He put his arm before his face, squinted. His depth of vision gone.

He could see light.

Blinded by light.

In the control room Grant was off his chair and on his feet.

'Who the fuck is he?' he shouted. Then pointed at the car on the screen. 'And who the fuck is that?'

Turnbull said nothing. He didn't know who the first man was but he knew who was in the car.

Joe Donovan.

44

Peta pulled her jacket around her, close to her body. But the gesture was futile: the rain had already penetrated the fabric. She felt as if her joints were squeezing out water as she walked.

She stopped by Grey's Monument, looked around. Tempted to just go home, leave it until the morning. But she couldn't. She had given Donovan her word. And besides, she was a professional. It was her job.

Down Grainger Street, past the Grainger Market. She loved that place. It reminded her of Saturday-afternoon shopping trips when she was a little girl, her mother dragging her around the shops, keeping her from whining by buying her a toy and an ice cream from Mark Toneys. She smiled at the memory. The toys were cheap and barely lasted the journey home or the Saturday-evening play with them, but the ice cream stayed with her. Thick and white, out of the tub and sculpted around the top of the sugar cone with a wooden spatula. She loved it, could still taste it. And then there was the market itself. Old, neoclassical in design, it smelled and sounded like a proper market should.

The rich aroma of café coffee, the hot whoosh of steamed milk and water, the clink and chink of smoke-grey glass cups and saucers. The fragrance of the fruit, the earthiness of the veg. A sugar rush as the sarsaparilla and sherbet got in her nostrils passing the sweet shop. The natural, cloying perfume of the florist's, the sprays, drips and trails of water as stems were taken from tin vases to be wrapped in paper. And most overpoweringly of all, the cheerful whistling of the porters carting whole animal carcasses around, the thunk of the cleaver on the butcher's block as they were sliced up before her eyes. And all around them the smell of blood and sawdust.

But it wasn't special any more. Mark Toneys was gone, as was most of the central, open-plan area and the Green Market backing on to it. It was a prime site for redevelopment in the insatiable corporate hunger to house the city's young, urban professionals. The shops and pubs skirting its back alleys were boarded up already as if in surrender.

She rounded the corner. The street was surprisingly empty. She had noticed that crowds just didn't seem to gather in the city centre as much lately. Probably not safe to with a killer going uncaught.

Ducked into a doorway to keep the rain off, checked the address again.

The back of the Grainger Market.

Nearly there.

The street deserted.

Feeling the cold, she made a token gesture of pulling her coat around her once more. Do this quickly, then home to a hot bath.

Nattrass looked at her team: six of them including herself. Another team of five led by DC Stone were heading around the back of the house.

Ravensworth Gardens in the west end of Newcastle. Fenham. An anonymous, solid-looking 1930s semi in a street full of them. Perhaps less well cared for than the others, but then that was to be expected. He had other things on his mind, she thought.

They moved slowly, stealthily, using the darkness as cover. Vehicles out of sight, radio chatter to the minimum.

Communication by hand signal only. All in protective body armour.

A light in the front room, none in the hall or upstairs.

Nattrass stopped, two doors down, crouched behind a hedgerow. Her team did likewise. She spoke into her radio. Waited. Got an affirmative answer. Turned to her team, nodded. They were all in place. A sudden gust of wind blew rain into her face. She squinted, rubbed it away. She was energized, on fire. The tiredness of earlier forgotten, the surprise of Turnbull's phone call put out of her mind. She was focused, blinkered to anything and everyone else but the task in hand. This was what she did.

This was what she loved.

She would go first. As senior member of the team, that was her prerogative, but also because she wanted to. She opened the metal gate as slowly as possible, thankful that the hinges let out only a tiny squeal, hidden beneath the wind and the rain, moved cautiously up the path, positioned herself at the side of the door. The other three did likewise, taking their places on either side, behind her, as prearranged.

She looked at them, making eye contact, getting visual assent of their preparedness. They nodded in turn.

She felt her heart beating, the blood pumping around her body, the breath coming out of her lungs in hot clouds.

Gave the final nod.

Reached over and knocked on the door.

The Historian froze, hands in midair.

Knock, knock, knock.

He looked around: fear lanced him like a bolt of lightning.

The blonde was before him, propped upright in the wheelchair. No time to lay her out, no time to even strip her. He was still in his coat and hat, water dripping down his glasses.

And again: knock, knock, knock.

He looked around the room madly. Nowhere to hide, nowhere to hide the body. This was it. The end. Maybe that's how the end came, he thought grimly. In the middle of something. When you weren't expecting it. With all your questions still to be answered.

He turned from the girl, walked towards the door, undid the locks. Opened it.

'Oh, you're in. Sorry to disturb you at this time of night.' She smiled.

So did he. In recognition. But she hadn't placed him yet.

'Yes?' he said, smiling, putting on his most inoffensive, unthreatening voice. 'What can I do for you?' He stepped back into the shadow of the doorway, masking his face but careful to keep himself between the girl's body and the eye-line of the woman at the door.

'I believe,' she said, gesturing to the building, 'that this is a photographic studio. Is that right?'

Another wave of fear ran through him. She knew. She knew. *The bitch knew.* This changed everything. He had to do something.

He kept the smile in place, the voice mild. 'It is, yes. Of sorts.'

'Good. I have come to the right place. I believe someone called Michael Nell took some pictures here. Ring any bells?'

He frowned as if in concentration, hoped his inner turmoil didn't show. 'Michael Nell . . . Michael Nell . .' The name did it. He had no choice now but to act fast. And decisively. He felt in his coat pocket, fingered the stun gun. It was still there. Charged up. The decision was made for him. 'Perhaps. Would you like to come in?'

He opened the door wide.

'Warmer inside,' he said, hint of a chuckle in his voice. 'And drier.'

Peta Knight smiled. 'Thank you,' she said and walked in. He shut the door behind her.

She stepped into the room. Saw the wheelchair. And froze.

She turned.

The stun gun was in his hand, the blue light arcing down towards her.

45

A split second of indecision: Turnbull didn't know what to do. Donovan had complicated matters no end.

'Is he one of yours?' asked Grant, looking frantically around as if searching for answers anywhere.

'No, he's not,' said Turnbull.

'What, neither of them?'

'Neither,' he said, then, looking at the Mondeo on the screen, muttered under his breath: 'Stupid bastard.'

'What did you say?' asked Grant, turning to him. 'What did you call me?'

'Nothing,' he replied, much stronger now, squaring his body up in case there was going to be some action. 'Didn't call you anything. I was lookin' at those two. On the screen.' The words sounded weak even to his own ears.

Grant held his eyes, unblinking for a few seconds, then turned away, shaking his head. Mouthing dark mutterings of his own, no mistaking who they were directed against. He focused back on the screen.

'Jesus Christ,' he said, reaching for his radio. 'He's got a gun.' He looked closer. 'Fuck a duck. Two guns.'

The radio was at Grant's lips. Turnbull reached across and pulled it away.

'No,' he said.

Grant stared at him, as if he was about to explode. He slammed the radio down on the desk, kept it in his fist like a weapon. 'This your arrest, eh? You in charge now?'

Turnbull felt the familiar red mist rise once again. Fought

hard to keep it down. 'No, I'm fuckin' not. But if I was I wouldn't lose sight of why I was here and what I was doin'. Unless those two are the targets, we're not after them. I think we should wait. Just a little while longer.'

Grant stared at him, looking like the only things holding him back from attacking Turnbull was a thin veneer of professionalism and a desire for the collar. 'We've got someone we don't know waving a gun around. You think that doesn't fall into the remit?'

'We don't know what's goin' on in there. We don't know who those people are. But we know something's about to happen. So we don't move in yet, pre-empt it.'

Grant's stare was unwavering.

Turnbull attempted a smile. He grimaced as if he had been impaled on razor wire. 'Get the top guy, be a bigger collar for you.'

Grant, despite everything, saw the sense in that. 'And what do you get out of this?'

My career back, thought Turnbull. My pride and self-respect.

'Satisfaction of a job well done.'

Grant slowly placed the radio on the desk, put his eyes back on the screen. Still wary of Turnbull. 'We'll wait,' he said. 'A little while longer.'

Turnbull nodded. 'Good.'

Yeah, he thought, I'll get my career back. If I can stop that interfering twat Donovan from making this go tits up. He looked at the screen again, gave a grim smile.

Maybe the bastard with the guns will do it for me.

Dario shielded his eyes with his forearm, turned away from the headlights, guns still clutched in both fists.

He had no idea who this was, ally or enemy. And he didn't have the luxury of carefully reasoned contemplation.

He had to assume the driver was hostile to him and act accordingly.

He took aim and, squinting against the blinding, widening light, fired.

Donovan saw the figure jump out from the side of a warehouse, stand in front of the car. He couldn't place the person – he had his arm over his face – but he looked familiar in some way.

Donovan slowed the car.

Then his right headlight went out.

The windscreen to his left cracked, splintered.

He looked again at the figure ahead. Saw the gun.

Shit, he thought, fear and surprise vying for equal attention within him, the bastard's trying to kill me.

Dario cursed. The shots had gone wide. Those fucking headlights. And now the driver knew what was happening.

The car speeded up.

Dario jumped out of the way.

Donovan pulled the car over to the left, desperately trying to avoid the shooting man. His foot became lodged on the accelerator. Panic held it there.

Time moved at different speed, both faster and slower than normal.

The big, wide, metal doors of a warehouse loomed up before him.

His speed increased.

Time warped. He had what seemed like an age to study the approaching door in minutest detail yet was still travelling too fast to change his course.

He braced himself, closed his eyes.

The car hit.

★

It was like a bomb had been detonated inside the warehouse.

It shook with the impact, sound amplified, echoed and boomed all around, vibrating discordantly off the corrugated-metal walls, like a thousand different Hendrix guitar solos played at concert pitch in surround sound. The doors buckled, split like tinfoil in a fake circus strongman act. Chaos broke out.

The girls screaming and running, anywhere and everywhere, survival instincts kicking in, not knowing what was happening but looking desperately for cover.

Decca looked around, too stunned to speak. He thought of Dario and Katya, thought they must have had something big planned. Was suddenly more scared than he had been all night.

Christopher recovered his composure first. He was barking orders at Milo and Lev, telling them to round up the girls, get them into the people carrier and away. Milo and Lev did as they were asked, running and reaching out, trying to grab the terrified females, hold on to them and drag them back. It was like an episode of Benny Hill out of *A Clockwork Orange*, thought Decca. He would have laughed if the situation hadn't been so potentially ruinous for himself.

He looked at Christopher again. He was standing in the centre of the warehouse now, no longer skulking in the shadows. Issuing orders, commands, expecting to be heard, obeyed. Everything else happening around him, taking their cues from him. Like an old-school Shakespearian actor giving his Macbeth.

Like a general on a battlefield fighting one last war.

Christopher was lost to the moment. Decca watched as he produced a huge machine gun from underneath his long overcoat. His eyes somewhere else, fighting another war in another place, full of rage, hatred.

Full of joy. Exhilarated.

And in that second came realization to Decca: he would never be a gangster. Not like in the films. Because real life was different. Pimping, drug dealing, throwing his weight around and getting respect for it was one thing. But Christopher was another. Christopher was different.

And Decca didn't want any part of that.

Christopher raised the gun.

Decca didn't intend to wait around to find out what he was going to do with it.

The spirit of Clint had well and truly deserted him. He turned, ran to the double doors, pressed the button at the side to open them. Hoping that whatever had happened outside hadn't damaged them too much. Felt in his pocket for his car keys.

The doors began to open. Gears and metal creaked as they were prised apart, squealing like some giant wounded mechanical animal in its death throes.

Nearly there. Moving with agonizing slowness. His heart was pounding, pulse racing. Breath coming out in ragged gasps, like he had just run a marathon. A bit more and he could squeeze through, run, put miles between himself and here.

And Clint Eastwood be fucked.

A bit more.

The night was appearing through the gap now, big enough to get through. He ran to that gap.

'Derek.'

He froze at the voice. Didn't want to turn.

'Derek. Where are you going?'

The breath came out of Decca like a punctured football that had been kicked one time too many. He turned. Christopher was standing there, legs apart, machine gun held before him, eyes lit by that manic light.

Evil. That was the word to describe it. Evil.

'You aren't running away, are you?'

Decca opened his mouth to speak. No sound would come out. It didn't matter. No answer would be right.

'There is only one way anyone leaves my employment.'

The bullets hit his body. Forcing him to dance, blood spraying and arcing upwards and outwards like cut, red marionette strings.

Dancing to someone else's tune. I'm always—

His final thought. Half-finished.

The firing stopped. Decca's body, with nothing to hold it up, slumped to the floor. The door slick and shining with dark red.

The girls had stopped screaming.

Christopher looked around.

'Time to go,' he said. 'Torch it.'

Turnbull and Grant looked at each other. They had seen the car plough into the doors, heard screams and firing from inside.

Grant picked up the radio.

'Go! Go! All units! Go!'

There was no argument from Turnbull.

Peta saw the light, didn't know what would be following it, but knew it wasn't going to be pleasant. She dived out of the way, hitting the floor hard with her left shoulder, the impact sending a jolt of pain down her arm, a loud gasp from her lips. She ignored it, moved quickly out of the way of her assailant, scuttling across the floor like a cornered spider.

He made a frenzied exclamation that she couldn't understand, but there was no mistaking the rage behind it. She risked a look at him. A nondescript man in raincoat and glasses. His hat had fallen off and there was something familiar about his features. Familiar, but not particularly memorable. She couldn't place him. She shoved the thought out of her mind. That was for later.

He was advancing towards her, hand outstretched, holding a long black object, the end of which was both giving off light and fizzing. Some kind of stun gun, she thought. He was clearly angry that he had failed to subdue her and was making his way towards her, ready to try again.

She looked around. The place was an old shop, medium-sized, the plate-glass windows boarded from the outside with wood, smashed in places. Old display cabinets, sturdy, of heavy wood, had been piled into one corner by the glass. A shop counter with a huge old-fashioned till in front of them. The far back wall had been painted white, with various hooks and other attachments mounted on it, a space cleared before it for camera equipment. A camera-less tripod stood, flanked by two large lamps. They provided the only illumination to the room. At the back wall was a girl in a wheelchair, her arms and legs strapped to the frame by plastic disposable handcuffs, her mouth taped over. An old, rain-wet blanket wrapped around her. She seemed only barely aware of what was going on, eyes flickering slowly between half-wakefulness and sleep, her head lazily lolling, pulling away from the bright light.

Peta's assailant was running now.

She jumped over to the tripod, picked it up and, ignoring the complaints of the muscles in her damaged arm, swung it towards him in one smooth movement. It connected with his arm: he screamed, dropped the weapon.

She pulled it back to try again but didn't have the same strength. He blocked it this time, caught it with his hand. She pushed it towards him, tried to make a break around him.

It fell at his feet. He tried to make a move for her. His feet found the tripod; he twisted and fell. But his reflexes were good: he stuck out an arm as she passed, missed her.

She jumped over him, made her way to the door. Had he locked it? She couldn't remember. She fell against the door, grabbed the handle with shaking hands, twisted and turned.

Locked.

She pulled hard, again ignoring the pain in her shoulder. Stopped.

It was a Yale lock. He had only put it on the snib. Manually locked it from inside. It was just a question of pressing the button, turning the knob. She pressed the button, felt the lock mechanism free up. She turned the knob.

And he was on her again.

Pulling her back from the door, the force of his attack taking her by surprise. He pulled her backwards, on to the floor.

And was on her.

Pounding at her body, tearing at her clothing. Ripping, rending. Growling.

She was being suffocated by malevolence. Peta couldn't get free, couldn't lever her body from the floor to try anything that would get him off her. Insane rage had more than doubled his strength. She felt his hands scrape her, his teeth bite her skin. Her face was forced into the dirty, bare, cold boards. She couldn't breathe.

But she had to survive. She couldn't die here. Not like this.

She would have to fight him on his own terms.

She pushed against his weight, forced as hard as she could, managed to snake an arm free of his body. He tried to shift his weight, trap it again, but she wouldn't let him.

If insane rage was giving him strength, then the will to live was doing the same for her.

Her arm free, she found one of his hands that was scratching away at her cheek, digging his nails in, seemingly trying to rake the flesh from her face. She grabbed one finger. Just one finger. And pulled. Away from her face. All the way back. Until she heard the snapping sound in her ear.

He howled, took his hand away from her. She tried to press the advantage. Where his arm had been, where there was now a space, she pushed her elbow back as hard as she could, felt it connect with something. His face.

He yowled again.

She felt his weight ease up on her, and twisted round. Managed to pull herself out from underneath him.

He made a desperate grab for her with his good arm. But missed. She risked a look at him: one eye was closed. It had been a lucky shot.

Pain and anger were still twisting his features. He pulled himself up off the floor.

Peta made a dash for the front door, but he was there before her.

She turned, looking around frantically for another exit.

Saw a door at the back of the shop. Ran for it.

He saw what she was doing, where she was going. Ran after her. Peta reached it first, turned the handle. It was open. She ran through, almost tripping as she did so as the floor disappeared beneath her. She stopped. Felt around with her foot. A set of steps leading down. A doorway to a basement.

She turned. He was right behind her. She had no choice.

Hitting her arm against the side wall to find a light switch, she ran as fast as she could down the steps, lights coming on as she did so.

She reached the bottom of the stairs and stopped, the air taken from her lungs.

She couldn't move.

Couldn't speak.

Because of what she saw before her.

Behind her, footfalls on the steps. Slow. Heavy. No need to hurry.

He knew what she was seeing. What she would be experiencing.

Knew there was no escape down there.

He reached the bottom of the steps.

Peta turned, looked at him.

'I know who you are,' she said, chest heaving from exertion.

He smiled.

'Yes.'

He came towards her.

46

Christopher was gone. Kovacs was gone. Now there was only the Snake. And the Snake was back where he belonged. Back in the war.

A healthy way to live. A natural way to live. Survival of the fittest, the best.

And he was the best.

He strode through the warehouse holding his gun before him. Milo and Lev's fires beginning behind him. And he was back on the streets, in the towns, the villages. Houses, barns burning behind him. Fearful crying and angry shouts all around him. The satiation of all desires. Life and death at his fingertips.

The power. The fear.

There was no need for pretence now. No need to hide behind false names, assumed identities. The war proved that to him. Gave men licence to be themselves. Their true selves. And he knew who he was.

His empire here was crumbling. No matter. He would get away, start somewhere else. He was resourceful. He was strong. He had plans in place. And he had to leave now.

He looked around. Smiled. Felt the comforting heaviness of the gun in his hands. It was cold. It was the power of life or death at his fingertips.

He stepped over the body of Decca Ainsley. Another one who promised so much yet delivered so little.

Of the screaming girl whose name he had never learned. Another expendable in a whole list of them.

He bent down, picked up Decca's discarded car keys. As he stood up, he looked at the flames. They were starting to take hold. The girls were sitting in the people carrier, too terrified to do anything else. Expendable.

He smiled. He should have some fun now.

Really give them something to remember him by.

Donovan opened his eyes. He was still alive.

He undid the strap of his seat belt, pushed at the door of the car. It was jammed, wedged into the frame. A couple more strong pushes and he had it. It swung open. He got out of the car. The front was crumpled where it had ploughed into the doors, the windows gone. A complete write-off. It wouldn't need a mechanic to get it going again; it would need a priest.

He looked around. Listened. Heard screaming and what he took to be gunfire from inside the warehouse.

'Oh, shit,' he said aloud.

He looked through the partially open doors. Saw flames licking their way up the back wall, building in intensity, the fires being fed by two identikit dark-mullet-haired thugs in leather jackets. He turned away, back to the dockside. Caught a glimpse of movement in the shadows to the side of the warehouse. He ran towards it.

And was greeted with two .45s pointed at his face.

Donovan stepped back, kept his arms by his side. The man holding the guns spoke.

'Please stay where you are. I do not want to kill you.'

'Oh, good,' said Donovan. He looked again at the man, recognizing the accent. 'I know you. Dario? Dario Tokic?'

The man moved uneasily. 'Yes. And I know you, Joe Donovan. You have been a good man to my sister. I am going to go around to the front of the warehouse. Do not try and stop me. I do not want to kill you. But I will.'

'OK,' said Donovan. 'Where's Katya? Is she with you? Is she all right?'

'I am here.'

She stepped out of the shadows behind Dario. Even in the half-light Donovan could see she looked traumatized. Donovan made to cross towards her. Dario stopped him with the gun.

'She comes with me.' Dario held her by the hand. 'There are things we must do. She and I.' He looked at her. Placed one of his guns in her free hand. 'Together.' She made no reply. He pulled her with him. She allowed herself to go. She was too tired to argue.

Donovan stood aside, let them go.

They went around to the front of the building. Donovan stayed where he was. He cocked his head, heard something: sirens. Police. Saw a shadow flit across the front of the warehouse that belonged to neither Katya nor Dario. He waited a few seconds, then followed the path Dario and Katya had taken.

Katya reached the front of the warehouse with her brother. She looked between the double doors. And gasped.

The people carrier was still in the centre of the floor, unmoving, flames moving closer towards it. She saw terrified faces inside it, heard screams. The women were trying the doors: they had been locked. She turned to her brother.

'Dario, you must do something!' She pointed.

He ignored her.

She pulled at his sleeve. 'They will die in there! Do something!'

He shrugged her off. 'No. We have things to do first.'

He walked away from her, eyes darting all the time, a hunter looking for his prey.

Katya looked again at the people carrier. Two men got in the front seats. A shiver of recognition ran through her. Milo and Lev. She remembered them. Remembered what they had done to the girls. Done to her.

They started the engine, drove the carrier towards the doors. She moved out of the way, back into the shadows again, as it sped past her and away. Breathed a sigh of relief that the women had got out alive. Then stopped herself.

She knew where they were going.

She tried to shake off the thought, join her brother.

An arm around her neck stopped her.

She tried to kick, to scream. Couldn't. Tried to run away. Couldn't. The grip was too strong, too powerful. She could do nothing to resist.

Her assailant plucked the gun she was holding from her grasp, flung it behind her.

'Well.' A voice spoke to her. A shudder went through her. She knew who it was. Just from that one word she knew who it was. 'Don't struggle. Don't scream. We're going to have some fun, you and I.'

She knew.

The Snake.

Dario, on the other side of the doors, looking down the other side of the warehouse, turned. Saw what was happening. Raised his gun.

'I wouldn't do that if I were you,' said the Snake. 'You might hit your precious sister. And you wouldn't want that to happen, would you?'

'Let her go,' shouted Dario. 'Just you and me. Man to man.'

The Snake laughed.

'Kovacs is dead,' said Dario. 'The little man I saw in the photograph with you. The snakes took him.'

The Snake smiled. 'Then you have destroyed my business here, see? Look around. Congratulations. Is that enough for you?'

'Never enough for what you did to our family.' Dario was shouting now. 'For what you did to our lives.'

The Snake said nothing. The sirens were getting louder, coming closer. He stepped forward. Dario stepped back, collided with Donovan's abandoned car. He quickly righted himself.

Too late. The Snake fired a single shot from his gun. It hit Dario square in the chest. He fell backwards against the Mondeo, blood fountaining from the wound. Katya screamed, tried to run to him. The grip around her just tightened.

'Are you still alive?' shouted the Snake. 'Eh? Good. I want you to watch what I do to your sister. That can be your final image you take with you into death. When you see the devil, send him my regards.'

Dario struggled to get up, anger powering his body. He couldn't.

The Snake laughed.

Then stopped dead.

'Touch her or make just one move and I'll blow your fucking head off.'

Donovan pointed Katya's discarded gun at the base of the Snake's skull.

Pressed in hard.

Peta stared. Eyes unable to comprehend the full horror of what she was seeing.

The room was laid out as if for a film or theatre set. In the centre was a heavy table, the wood matching the old cabinets in the shop upstairs. On it were what she assumed were wrist and ankle restraints. The wood was old, scarred. Darker in patches than in other places.

She knew what the dark patches were. She felt nauseous.

Around the space were mannequins, posed in different positions and decorated with dried, lumpen objects. She couldn't make out what the objects were. At strategic intervals were arc lamps, increasing the feel of theatricality. All centred on the table. A workbench ran along the back wall. On it were various bladed instruments, all home-made-looking. Next to them were several bobbins of heavy black thread and large needles.

She stepped closer to one of the mannequins, examined the misshapen objects draped around it. Recoiled once she realized what they were.

Body parts. Skin. Internal organs.

'This is my room,' said a voice behind her. Oily, quavering with barely suppressed twisted joy. 'This is where I do all my experiments.'

'I know who you are,' said Peta. 'The Historian.'

He frowned, puzzled. Then smiled. 'Yes. I suppose I am. The Historian. Yes.' He seemed proud of the description.

'I know who else you are,' she continued. 'That weaselly little nobody of a security guard who kept trying to stare at my tits.'

Anger flashed across his face. Hot and bubbling. He looked about to lunge but held himself in check. Peta watched him, braced to run again. His head was cocked to one side as if listening to something only he could hear. His lips were moving as if in conversation. He was nodding. Talking. He stopped, looked back at her.

'They say you should be my last experiment,' he said. 'Instead of that whore up there.'

'Do they?' she said, edging away around the table.

'They do,' he said. 'They also say you'll be the one to tell me for definite. You'll give me the answers I'm seeking.'

'Is that right?' she said, playing for time, trying to humour him. 'And what answers would they be?'

'The answers I've been trying to find,' he said, as if it was obvious. 'Life. Death. What happens to us when we die. Where our spirit goes.' He looked around, gestured to the room, gave a snort of a laugh. 'What else do you think all this is for?'

'I have no idea,' she said.

She edged her way around the main table. He followed her.

'They told me. Just now. That you're the one who would tell me for sure.'

'That's nice of them.'

'Oh, it is. Now, I'm willing to forgive what you've done to my hand.' He held his hand up. The finger Peta had broken had been snapped back into place. It now hung uselessly, like a swollen, mutant appendage. 'And my eye. Because yours will be the supreme sacrifice.'

He lifted up his other hand. It was holding the stun gun once again.

'You're a worthy opponent.' He smiled. 'But you won't get away from me this time.'

Peta kept slowly moving.

The Historian kept stealthily advancing.

He gestured to an alcove on her right. 'You see in there? There's all my previous experiments. The ones who failed to make the grade, shall we say?'

Peta looked. Three walls of the alcove were lined with deep chest freezers. Her knees threatened to give way once she realized what was in them.

'Want to see?'

Peta shook her head.

'Never mind.' Closer and closer. 'This place used to be part of Newgate Street prison. Did you know that?'

Peta said she didn't.

'I had to tunnel under the city to find it. We're miles away from anywhere. Too deep down for anyone to hear you scream.'

Peta reached the workbench, stood before it. She couldn't feed his delusions any more.

'No, we're not,' she said. 'We're in the basement of a shop.'

Anger flashed again in his eyes. He raised his stun gun. The electrodes crackled.

'You're just like all the others,' he said, his voice rising in pitch. 'Just another lying bitch.' He smiled. It was like an annexe of hell opening. 'But you're still going to be my final experiment. You're still going to give me all the answers. Just like they said.'

'You're pathetic,' she said with a conviction she wished she felt. 'I said that last time I saw you, and I'm saying it now.'

He lunged at her.

She dodged out of the way as the stun gun came harmlessly down on the workbench.

Peta picked up a knife, tried not to look at the blood encrusted and rusted along the blade, and turned to face him.

He lunged at her again. She dodged, swiped with the knife. It caught the back of his hand. She pushed deep, forcing it down as hard as she could until it hit the wood of the workbench, became embedded.

He screamed, tried to pull it out. Couldn't.

'That's for Jill,' she said, and ran.

Around the table to the bottom of the stairs. Up the stairs as fast as she could go. Through the door at the top.

She slammed the door shut behind her, turned into the room.

And there, bending over the girl's body in the wheelchair, stood Michael Nell.

He jumped on seeing her, then stood up, angry.

'What have you done to her, you bitch? What have you done?'

47

'So what do you intend to do?' asked the Snake. 'Stand here all night?'

'Just until the police come,' said Donovan. 'They're on their way now.'

The Snake gave a slight rolling chuckle. 'And what if I don't want to wait?'

Donovan pushed metal harder into skin. 'I'm the one holding the gun. I'm the one who makes the rules.'

'So you are,' said the Snake.

Before Donovan knew what had happened, he had felt a pain in his chest, another in his leg and he was slumped against the side of the warehouse, gun missing from his hand.

The Snake stood over him, still clutching Katya.

'Amateur,' he spat.

The siren sound intensified in volume. They were taking their time, thought Donovan. He knew the dock covered several miles, but how far away had they stationed themselves? Wherever, they couldn't come soon enough.

The Snake heard them also, looked around.

'Get up,' he said.

Donovan began struggling to his feet.

'I said get up.' He kicked Donovan in the thigh.

Donovan got up.

'This woman—' he gestured with the gun at Katya '—she means something to you?'

Donovan didn't reply. The Snake smiled.

'Good.' He nodded towards Decca's BMW. 'You will drive me away from here.'

'And if I don't?'

He pushed the gun tighter against Katya's face. 'She and I will be in the car with you. Do I need to say any more?'

He didn't. He handed Donovan the keys. Donovan crossed to the car, got in, turned the engine over. The Snake threw Katya in the back seat behind Donovan, got in the front next to him.

The fire had reached the front of the warehouse now. Gaining in strength, the rain would not stop it spreading.

The Snake put the huge machine gun between his legs, pointed the automatic at Donovan.

'Drive,' he said.

Donovan did so. As they pulled away, Katya looked out of the window. Her brother lay sprawled across the bonnet of the Mondeo. He had stopped moving. She tried to bite back her tears. Failed.

'Shut up,' said the Snake. 'Stop wailing or I give you something to wail about.'

Katya screamed, leaned forward. She grabbed hold of the Snake with both hands, raking the skin off his face with her fingernails, shouting curses and profanities in her native tongue. Her fingers reached for his eyes, tried to claw them out. Her right hand found his right eye. She squeezed.

He turned, swatted her back. He twisted around and fired the gun at her. The sound nearly deafened Donovan. He stopped the car.

'What the fuck have you done? You fucking animal!'

The Snake swung the gun on to Donovan. 'You want the same? Eh?'

Donovan said nothing.

'Then drive, amateur.'

Donovan turned around to look at Katya. The shot had hit her somewhere in the chest. She hadn't screamed, just put her hand to the wound, held herself as if she had a bad muscle ache, moaning with the pain. The blood seeped between her fingers.

'She is not dead,' said the Snake. 'Get me safely away from here, then you can get her to a hospital.'

Donovan was seething. His hands were shaking as he gripped the wheel. 'You cunt.'

'Whatever.' The Snake pointed the gun at him. 'Drive.'

Donovan gunned the car into gear, drove. He had no idea where he was going, whether he was taking the way out or a route that would lead him to Turnbull and his officers. Just round and round.

Containers were piled high on both sides of him. He drove down the centre. Crates and pallets were waiting at the dockside to be loaded or stored. Huge open-top trailers full of metal sat beside cranes waiting to be lifted on board.

'Drive.'

He drove.

He knew what was going to happen. As soon as he had driven away he was going to be killed. And Katya, if she wasn't dead by then. He was under no illusions. Anger rose all the time. He wanted to scream, to shout. To pummel the steering wheel in rage. He wanted out. He couldn't believe this was happening to him. He was angry. He was terrified.

His desperation increased as he tried to think of something, anything, that could get rid of his passenger, get Katya to a hospital.

He turned a corner. And saw it before him. Something only the truly mad or the truly desperate would attempt.

At the end of the road was a forklift truck, the forks

about a metre off the ground. He looked at the Snake, back to the forklift. It would be just about right.

He pushed his foot down on the accelerator, checked his seat belt was on, gave a glance in the back. Katya was lying down, curled up in agony along the leather.

Donovan pushed harder. The car gathered speed.

The Snake looked at Donovan, frowning. Then straight ahead. Realized what Donovan was about to do.

He pushed the gun towards Donovan, shouted something. Donovan ignored him, pushed harder, his world shrunk down to the two prongs sticking out before him, coming ever closer with each second.

Get it right. Or go down too.

The Snake tried to prise Donovan's hands from the wheel. Donovan didn't budge.

The forks loomed up.

No going back.

Donovan pushed harder.

Shouted to Katya to brace herself. Had no idea whether she heard him.

Gave himself the same advice. Hoped that God, if He existed, was with him.

The car hit.

Donovan turned his head to the right, closed his eyes. Brought one arm up to shield his face.

The windscreen shattered. The thick steel blade of the forklift punching through the glass, catching the Snake in the chest as he made a lunge for the door. The blade impaled him to the seat, as thousands of glass razor shards rained into the car.

The car skidded away to the right, the weight of the forklift pinning the Snake's body in place, the force of the car pulling his body along, ripping him open as it went. A piercing wail sounded out louder than the screech of metal on metal as the Snake struggled to detach himself from the impaling fork, as it tore both himself and the seat out of the car.

The car smashed sideways into a container and, with a squeal of metal, came to rest.

Donovan opened his eyes. Shook his head. Shards of glass fell from his hair. He felt his face, looked in the mirror. Cuts and slashes where the windscreen had exploded, but pretty superficial, nothing too deep. Nothing that would leave him scarred for life.

He felt his chest. Tender. The seat belt had saved him from too much damage but bruised his ribcage. He would ache for days. He checked his body. Still in one piece. He flexed his legs. Still attached. And unbroken.

He looked out, saw the Snake's ruined body, now just a ragged collection of used flesh, hanging from the front of the forklift.

Donovan exhaled deeply, checked the back seat. Katya was curled up foetally, arm wrapped protectively around herself, jammed in between the back and front seats. Tiny shards of glass glittered like diamonds on her body.

Donovan got out of the car, pushed the seat forward, leaned in.

'Katya? Katya?'

She turned slightly, wincing from the pain, opened her eyes.

She was alive.

Donovan smiled. 'Katya . . .' He put his arms around her, cradled her.

She tilted her head up.

'Did you . . . Is he dead . . . ? The Snake? Is . . . he dead?'

Donovan glanced at what was hanging from the fork-lift.

'Yeah,' he said. 'He's dead.'

Katya closed her eyes. Relaxed against his arms.

The sirens were almost on them.

Michael Nell stood before Peta. She recognized him straight away. Cries of pain and anguish came from the basement. The Historian trying to pull the knife out. Her eyes darted between the man in front of her and the door at the top of the staircase.

'What have you done to Anita?' screamed Nell again. Then heard the screams coming up the stairs. 'And what have you done to him?'

'I've not done anything to Anita,' said Peta quickly. 'Nothing at all. It's the guy who owns this place. It's him. He did this.'

Nell frowned. 'Graham? Graham did this?'

'Yes,' said Peta. 'Graham.' The screams abruptly stopped. He must have managed to pull the knife out. Peta had no time. She decided to push it. 'Your friend. He did this. That's him downstairs. He was going to kill her.'

'Don't talk shit.'

'He was, Michael. He was going to kill her and he was going to kill me. He kidnapped her.'

Footsteps began on the stairs. Slow, painful ones, accompanied by dark mutterings. He was coming up. And she doubted he would be unarmed.

'You've got to believe me, Michael. He zapped her with a stun gun, tied her to the chair. He was going to kill her. Like he's done with all the other girls. The one's you got blamed for.'

Nell looked as if his head was about to burst. He looked frantically from the door to Peta, to Anita.

'I . . . I used his studio . . . I took photos here . . .'

The footsteps got louder.

'I know you did. But that's all. Just photos. He did the rest. Graham. He killed them. Used them for his experiments, he said. He killed my friend Jill. And that's what he was going to do with Anita.'

Michael Nell flinched at the words as if they were physical blows.

'Kill her. Slice her body up.'

'No . . .'

The Historian reached the top of the stairs, flung the door open, knife in hand. He stopped, confusion etched on his face. Saw who was there. Opened his mouth to speak.

'You bastard!'

And Nell was on him. Fists, kicks rained down on him. The Historian backed away towards the basement. In his haste to get away, he lost his footing, stumbled backwards down the stairs. Nell gave him no quarter, was straight down after him.

Peta slammed the door shut behind them, turned the key in the lock, slumped to the floor in front of it. Looked at Anita, who was beginning to stir.

'In a minute,' she said, 'I'll have you out of there in a minute.'

She dug out her phone, put in a 999 call. Told them all the details, asked for Nattrass by name. Pocketed the phone, sat back.

Sounds travelled up from the basement. Unpleasant, violent ones. Peta tried to block them out.

She closed her eyes.

Snapped them open again.

Her phone was ringing. She answered it.

'Oh, hi, Jamal.'

Listened.

'Oh, no. Oh, shit . . .'

48

Donovan stood in the centre of Albion's ruined office. The weak sunlight was having trouble penetrating the closed blinds. He was alone in the shadows. Trying to find respite, peace. He looked around.

Spaces where computers should have been, files strewn all over the floor, broken doors left hanging. Then the next strata of upheaval overlaid: SOCOs' remains. A sign on the front door read: CLOSED FOR THE FORESEEABLE FUTURE.

He couldn't see very far into that future. All he could see was the past. Playing it over and over in his mind. Tyne Dock and its fallout.

It was like some mad nightmare. No matter how many times he played it over, he was still unsure of the correct order of events and his part in them. Memories came back to him like snapshots of dreams, were fired towards him like acrobats out of cannons, tumbling and changing.

Standing in the rain, wreckage all around him, sirens getting louder, he had called Sharkey for protection. Then he remembered being strapped and boarded into the ambulance, taken to the Queen Elizabeth Hospital in Gateshead. Prodded, poked, examined for spinal injuries, concussion. None found, he was advised to go home and take painkillers for the pain that would strike him in a few hours' time.

Asking the doctors about Katya. Being told the bullet

had torn mainly through muscle, miraculously missing lungs and major arteries. She was expected to be up and around within a week. Sharkey telling Donovan she was then likely to be sent home. Since the criminal she was going to testify against was no longer alive. Donovan didn't have the strength to argue.

He remembered trying to sleep after that, but seeing only Tyne Dock, death, the impaled body of the Snake. Seeing him again when he opened his eyes.

Seeing the news, Nattrass and Fenton talking about apprehending Michael Nell and their capture of the killer who had been terrorizing the city. Then hearing who the killer's two final, intended victims were. And dropping the coffee mug he was holding.

Then getting a phone call, hurrying to the General Hospital. Peta and Jamal waiting at the front desk, Peta white-faced and red-eyed, Jamal a frightened child. The nearest thing he had to a family. His heart ached to see them like that, ached even more when Peta told him about Amar. Donovan not being able to take it all in, having to sit down. Still critical but stable. Still unconscious. They didn't think the bullet had caused any spinal or nerve damage, but it was too early to tell. They would have to wait.

Shaken and damaged, the three retreated to Peta's house. None of them could talk. But all of them sharing the pain. Eventually their bodies, drained and tired, couldn't function any more. They slept, slumped on sofas and armchairs.

Donovan couldn't sleep for long. When he closed his eyes he saw Christopher's body explode again next to him. He looked around. Had to get out. Not wanting to disturb the others, he rose and left the house, slipping the lock into place as quietly as he could. He needed to get some fresh air, some perspective. He thought his walk was aimless, but found himself standing outside the Albion offices. He skipped under the police crime scene tape, let himself in.

Stood there.

A knock at the door brought him out of his reverie.

'We're closed,' he shouted.

A muffled voice replied to him. He recognized it.

'Come in, then. It's open.'

Footsteps in the hall. Then Turnbull appeared in the office. He looked around the place, took in the destruction, eyes fell on Donovan standing in the middle of it.

'Christ, they did a number on it all right,' he said.

Donovan nodded.

'Here.' Turnbull extended his arm. In his hand was a carrier bag. 'For you.'

Donovan took it, opened it. A bottle of Laphroaig, still in its tin. Donovan looked at him.

'Said I'd replace it,' said Turnbull.

Donovan almost broke into a smile. 'And it's not cheap shit, either.'

'Get the glasses out, then.'

Donovan went into the kitchen. Thankfully, damage there was minimal. He brought back two glasses, swung an office chair round, sat on it. Turnbull did likewise. Donovan unsealed the bottle, poured.

'Cheers.'

'Cheers.'

They drank. Sat in silence.

'So,' said Donovan eventually, 'you here to run me in?'

'I don't think so,' said Turnbull. 'You'll have to make a statement, you'll be questioned, but I doubt it'll go any further. I'll get you out of it. I owe you one.'

'Thanks.'

'You too.'

Talk turned to Nattrass and her double collar. 'Should have seen it sooner,' said Turnbull. 'Used a stun gun he must have bought off the internet. Should have known from the unidentified bruises. We were checking where Nell's studio was. Pity we didn't find it quicker.'

'Easy to be wise in hindsight,' said Donovan.

'Yeah. And the cellar. Full of freezers. And the freezers full of body parts.' Turnbull shook his head. 'We'll be trying to put those together for months.'

'Doubt you'll have much luck,' said Donovan. 'Think how many girls just disappear every month. Girls who no one even knows are here.'

Turnbull nodded his head sadly, sipped his whisky. 'Yeah. But we got the result. Good work all round, I suppose.'

'Nearly,' said Donovan. 'Should have been a simple job for my team. Put in the hours and go home. Now look what's happened to Amar. Look what Peta went through.'

'And you.'

Donovan nodded.

They talked some more, the conversation getting looser and more inconsequential as the whisky kicked in. Eventually Turnbull stood up.

'Better go,' he said.

'Back to the office?'

'Given the rest of the day off. Thought I'd go home. See what's there. Start salvaging.'

'Good idea. Will you still have a job to go back to?'

Turnbull shrugged. 'Hope so. What about you?'

Donovan shrugged. 'Stick around here for a bit. Go over to Peta's later. Visit the hospital. Start picking up the pieces.'

'Rebuild Albion?'

'Yeah. I hope so.'

The two men shook hands. Turnbull left.

Donovan stood alone in the room again, the whisky

swirling around his head. He took another shot, finding his thoughts calmer, his way forward clearer. Then another to capitalize on that feeling. Then another just to be sure.

He sighed. Wondered what to do next. How to start rebuilding.

Further thought was cut short. His mobile was ringing. He answered it.

Sharkey.

'What?' said Donovan, preparing a verbal volley. But Sharkey's tone, his words, silenced him.

'What?' asked Donovan again, his tone more serious this time.

Sharkey paused. 'It's David,' he said.

Donovan swallowed hard. Waited.

'Your son. We've found him.'